HONORÉ DE BALZAC

Born at Tours, 20th May 1799. Educated at the Collège de Vendôme. Attended the law schools at the Sorbonne and spent three years in the offices of a notary and a solicitor. In 1820 he abandoned law for literature and lived in poverty for two years at Paris. After a long and difficult relationship of seventeen years he married a Polish countess, Madame Hanska, 14th March 1850. Died on 17th August in the same year at Paris. Buried in Père-Lachaise.

HONORÉ DE BALZAC

The Country Doctor

TRANSLATED BY
ELLEN MARRIAGE

INTRODUCTION BY
MARCEL GIRARD

DENT: LONDON
EVERYMAN'S LIBRARY
DUTTON: NEW YORK

© Introduction, J. M. Dent & Sons Ltd, 1961
All rights reserved
Made in Great Britain
at the
Aldine Press · Letchworth · Herts
for
J. M. DENT & SONS LTD
Aldine House · Bedford Street · London
First included in Everyman's Library 1911
Last reprinted 1968

NO. 530

SBN: 460 00530 8

TO

MY MOTHER

'For a wounded heart—shadow and silence.'

INTRODUCTION

READERS of *The Country Doctor* are unlikely to experience the same emotions as are inspired by other works of Balzac. It is hardly a novel. With no regular plot and no dramatic action properly so called, this book is made up of a series of episodes, interlaced with political and moral dissertations that will perhaps seem clumsy, ridiculous and disconnected. Only one character holds our attention from the first: that of the doctor; the rest are a colourless lot, merging into the landscape, where they go about their business like so many ants. This time Balzac leaves nothing to our imagination: he wished above all to touch and convince us.

The Country Doctor was written more than a year before the general idea of the *Comédie humaine* was conceived. Nevertheless Balzac subsequently brought it into his concerted scheme without the slightest difficulty, and the volume takes its place quite naturally among the *Scènes de la vie de campagne*, alongside *Les Paysans* and *The Curé de village*. A provincial himself, Balzac always remained very close to the village folk of Touraine, near whom, each summer, he returned to live. He had watched them carefully, and had made several drafts of 'scenes from village life'. Foreseeing the wealth of material to be derived from a field hitherto unexploited by French literature, he wrote in 1831: 'Rural and peasant life awaits its historian.' The year 1832 provided him with the opportunity to assume that role.

To be more exact, the present work was born of a shock which the author sustained at the sight of nature's beauties in the Alps. The Marquise de Castries, to whom Balzac had for some months been paying assiduous court, happened to be staying at Aix-les-Bains in Savoy, and our young novelist joined her there at the end of August 1832. His letters inform us that about 20th September he and his friend made a trip into the massif and visited the abbey of the Grande Chartreuse, north of Grenoble. No doubt the sight of those hospitable mountains and those delightful wooded valleys of Dauphiné awoke in him the love of country things, and, helped by love, aroused in him an inspiration that would not be gainsaid. Setting aside all other work upon which he was engaged, he threw himself heart and soul into *The Country Doctor*. On 23rd September he informed his mother that he had written this book 'in three days and three nights', and promised before long to send her a 'fine fat manuscript' which she could exchange for 1,000 francs with the publisher Mame-Delaunay. This was exactly the sum he required in order to be able to accompany his beautiful marquise to Italy.

As things turned out, Balzac did not follow Madame de Castries to Naples, and the work did not appear until September 1833. The publisher brought an action because the time limit had not been observed, and the printer's evidence in this case is irrefutable: the manuscript was not completed until July 1833. It must therefore be admitted that the work was not written, in the form in which we know it, 'in three days and three nights', or at least that the author subsequently revised and thoroughly remodelled it. Monsieur Bernard Guyon's examination of the drafts preserved at the Château de Chantilly confirms that the task of creation lasted for ten months, with interruptions, fresh starts and changes of direction. In this space of time Balzac underwent various trials, conceived new sentiments and new ideas, until the final content of his book proved to be manifestly different from the project he had suddenly formed during the feverish days of August 1832.

Some have maintained that *The Country Doctor* was written chiefly under literary influences. This is not true. No doubt, finding himself in places already celebrated by Jean-Jacques Rousseau, Balzac called to mind the *Nouvelle*

Héloïse, which he had read and re-read enthusiastically throughout his youth. The opposition between 'death in the valley and death on the mountain' had long since been used by Rousseau. He also remembered Oliver Goldsmith, who had created the eternal prototype of all 'village romances' based upon close observation. Did he not confide in a letter to his friend Zulina Carraud that he had determined 'to surpass *The Vicar of Wakefield*'? While it is natural that he should have had his predecessors in mind, he was in no way indebted to them for essentials, least of all in the depicting of landscape. All the places he describes belong to reality. It has been possible to recognize (under the name of Voreppe) the village to which Dr Benassis retired, and even the house which he occupied. Without being able to guarantee the perfect truth of this assimilation, we must agree that Balzac did not produce the elements of his romance from his own imagination—those valleys, those woods, those fields, that road, those houses, which we visit in company with the good doctor and his guest, Commandant Genestas. He had actually seen the people and the things which he describes, and this is true in the case of all his novels. In the preface to *La Fille aux yeux d'or* he defined his method in these startling words: 'Writers never invent anything.' By utilizing and combining the observations which he himself had made in course of his trip to the Grande Chartreuse, he managed to fashion a small romantic world, whose exact situation we may hesitate to identify, but which presents in all its detail a remarkable appearance of authenticity. Reality, once again, has fertilized the genius of the story-teller.

Does this mean that the interest of *The Country Doctor* is restricted to the information it provides upon rural life in France about 1830? This book, though an historical record, is equally a profession of faith. We must, therefore, say a word about Balzac's political and social convictions at this period of his life.

First, they were liberal opinions. After the revolution of 1830 Balzac ranged himself among the legitimist royalists, i.e. among the reactionaries who were unwilling to accept the establishment of a constitutional monarchy. *The Country Doctor* is fully representative of these ideas. We can say of it, more than of any other work, that it was written, as Balzac later declared in his foreword to the *Comédie humaine*, in the light of those 'two eternal manifestations which are monarchy and religion'.

Balzac had definitely moved from abstract to active politics about 1831, under the influence of his extremist friends. The Duc de Fitzjames, uncle of the beautiful Marquise de Castries, urged him to offer himself as a Deputy, and it was impossible to refuse. After all, was not this the means of attaining at one stroke both love and glory? During the course of 1831 and 1832 he contributed several articles to the legitimist journals. The heads of the party soon gave him their official backing, and he stood for election on 13th June 1832, in the little city of Chinon in Touraine, where he had friends. He received only a few derisory votes; but he would not renounce political activity, still less political preaching, of which his later novels are full.

In a way then *The Country Doctor* may seem to be a kind of electoral manifesto. The ideas expressed by Benassis are exactly equivalent to those of Balzac. This is proved by the fact that one of the doctor's discourses is taken directly from an article by our author 'on modern government'. He attacks universal suffrage, denounces the dangers of election, exalts the role of the aristocracy, upholds the necessity of social hierarchies. Here we recognize the commonplaces of that reactionary propaganda which was nourished in France by Joseph de Maistre and above all by the writings of the Vicomte de Bonald. Of the latter, as to some extent of Balzac himself, we can say with Lamartine that 'he was the honest and eloquent apostle of a kind of sublime and hazy theocracy, which would be the poetry of politics if God deigned to appoint His own viceroys and earthly ministers'. But let us not attribute too much importance to Balzac in this capacity. His political ideas count for little more than do his taste for fashionable circles, his pretentions to elegance, his sudden passions for duchesses and marchionesses, his mania for collecting walking-sticks and for adding 'de' to the plebeian name 'Balzac'.

Much more serious are his economic views. In this respect also Balzac was indubitably a child of his age. The lyrical and sentimental romanticism of the 1820's was succeeded by a romanticism which has been described as 'utilitarian' or 'social'. Most writers of that age were influenced by the social reformers, particularly by Saint-Simon. The problems of the production and distribution of wealth engaged the attention successively of Lamartine, Hugo, Vigny, George Sand, Sainte-Beuve, Lamennais, Michelet and many other Utopian or idealist thinkers. It must be admitted that Balzac approached these questions with an infinitely more realistic mind. 'Oh, I am under no illusions,' exclaims Benassis; 'I have fashioned no idyll on the subject of my people. I have accepted them for what they are, poor peasants neither wholly good nor wholly bad. . . .' Here we are concerned with basket-making and pottery, of rearing cattle, with the leather industry and the hat industry; with how to create new goods by intelligence and labour; with how civilization expands indefinitely through dialectic: 'need engenders industry, industry commerce, commerce gain, gain prosperity, and prosperity useful ideas'. Karl Marx admired Balzac, placing him in the front rank of novelists whose testimony confirmed his own opinions. But Keynes likewise found in him food for thought. With poetic fervour Balzac describes the multiplication of riches! His words are a hymn to production and human activity: abundant harvests, new houses, wide roads lined with trees, humming factories, industries, schools, large families; the whole village is carried away by a sort of epic movement towards progress and raising the standard of life. But there is nothing supernatural here: Benassis is content to employ the simple laws of nature.

This passion for creation and life in all its forms explains why Balzac made his hero a doctor—a doctor and not a priest. Balzac, like Benassis himself after the death of his son, certainly hesitated as to which of these two forms of apostolate he should assign him; that much is clear from his drafts. Ten years later he wrote *Le Curé de village*, with limited success; but in 1832 he was not yet ready for this great subject. Besides, the character of the priest was much less suited to the defence of a purely economic and material activity, such as that which Benassis undertakes. Here the priest appears only at intervals in the guise of Fr Janvier, a pale conventional figure who serves as a pendant to the no less banal image of the 'judge'. For the rest, Balzac had only to dip into his memory to find the model of his leading character. At the age of twenty he had known and admired an old friend of his family, Dr Bossion, who had devoted himself to the regeneration of a small market-town in the neighbourhood of Paris. His sister Laura tells us that Bossion was the original of Benassis, and in fact this good man's tomb [1] in the cemetery at L'Isle-Adam still bears an inscription very much like that of Dr Benassis. It has also been suggested that Balzac may have drawn his inspiration from a certain Dr Rome of Voreppe, near the Grande Chartreuse, who enjoyed a great reputation for intelligence and kindness. What is more certain is that he had read— since he himself had printed it on the press which he owned at this period—a work by Madame Guizot on Jean-Frédéric Oberlin, Protestant pastor of a small village in Alsace. He also knew Stoeber's biography of Oberlin, which had been published at Strasbourg in 1881, for he made use of it while

[1] He died in 1821.

writing *Louis Lambert*. The famous pastor is represented there as a 'religious philanthropist'; his programme of economic development derives from the same principles as those of Benassis; and the account of his funeral recalls another in *The Country Doctor*, with the peasants, all in tears, flocking to show their gratitude. Comparative study of the two texts affords convincing evidence that Balzac found in the biography of Jean-Frédéric Oberlin much of the technical matter of which the first two chapters of his book are largely composed and which makes them what he intended them to be—a veritable 'treatise on practical civilization'.

The purely romantic element appears mainly in the fourth chapter, into which Balzac has infused even more of himself. The aged Dr Benassis, monarch of the village where he carries on a regular social apostolate, is Balzac's imaginary picture of his own humanitarian endeavours, such as he would have undertaken if he had had the power to do so. The young Benassis, devoured by passion, committing many faults, wounded by sorrow and remorse, is a reflection of Balzac's actual life. The 'Country Doctor's Confession' is his own confession with very little alteration.

There exist two versions of Benassis's 'Confession'. The first, published in 1914 by Spoelberch de Lovenjoul and carefully edited by Bernard Guyon in 1951, sprang spontaneously from his heart after the break with Madame de Castries in October 1832. This woman's life is itself a complete romance. Beautiful, and married to one of the greatest names in France, she had experienced the scandal of her liaison with an Austrian diplomat, young Prince Metternich, to whom she had borne a son; and she had encountered misfortune when her consumptive lover died in her arms during a visit to Italy in 1829. When Balzac made her acquaintance in Paris, in the spring of 1832, she was thirty-four years old, and led a secluded life near the home of her uncle, the Duc de Fitzjames. The young writer, who had just published *La Femme de trente ans* at the age of thirty-three, became interested in her, fell in love with her and became her devoted servant, while the uncle sought to make use of his budding fame with a view to strengthening the ranks of the legitimist party. In August he rejoined her at Aix-les-Bains, hoping to make a conquest, which seemed to him to be justified by her somewhat imprudent coquetry and some tokens which she had already been delighted to give him. The journey to the Grande Chartreuse was intended, it seems, to bring the affair to a happy issue. Alas! things turned out quite differently. At the end of a painful scene, which took place at Geneva on 9th or 10th October, Balzac received a final, categorical refusal, and that was the end. 'The previous day', he wrote, 'I was everything to her; next day I was nothing.' After this 'day of mourning' he cancelled the Italian journey which was to have been paid for with the 1,000 francs earned by *The Country Doctor*. He took refuge with his faithful friend Madame Carraud near Angoulême, then at Nemours, where he was received by the ever-compassionate Madame de Berny, now aged fifty-five, who, like a mother, once more consoled her young prodigal lover. The first version of the 'Country Doctor's Confession' tells of the great lady's cruel sport, the grief of her victim, his desire for vengeance and his ultimate withdrawal to a life of retirement and solitude. It was then that there leaped from his pen the well-known phrase which occurs twice on the doctor's lips: 'For a wounded heart—shadow and silence.' Balzac inscribed this phrase at the head of his book as if to emphasize the personal note.

Thus the principal elements of *The Country Doctor* had been assembled by October 1832. Balzac, however, did not release it, and thereby caused serious loss to his publisher. He set about writing another work, which was originally intended to bear the significant title *Ne touchez pas à la hache!* but which finally appeared in 1834 as *La Duchesse de*

Langeais, and in which he once again depicted the 'heartless woman'. Now one cannot fail to recognize this portrait as Madame de Castries, and indeed it moved the lady herself to profound indignation. Balzac, who had disguised himself as General de Montriveau, devised a fearful vengeance—the entry into religion and the death of this too beautiful, imprudent and coquettish woman. In order to avoid drawing yet another picture of the same interplay of love and pride, he had to modify Benassis's past. Besides, he may have thought that a mere lover's grudge was not in keeping with the hero's character and hardly justified his irrevocable retirement from the world. Accordingly he wrote a second 'Country Doctor's Confession', more dramatic and more moral. But Balzac once more extracted the whole episode from his own flesh! In this new version we still see reflections from his sentimental life, which was particularly unsettled during the two years 1832 and 1833.

The final account of Benassis's unhappy experiences includes two episodes: (1) his liaison with a girl who dies leaving him a child; (2) his new love and his engagement to Evelina, and their ultimate separation when his earlier sin comes to light. Now consider the dates. The printer's remarks at the trial make it quite clear that the second confession was not written before the end of June 1833. Between October 1832 and the completion of the novel two events had convulsed Balzac's life and forced the affair of Madame le Castries into the background.

The first is his liaison with a sublime young woman whose identity was not discovered until 1956: Marie Dufrisnoy, whose features reappear in *Eugénie Grandet*, the 'Maria' of the dedication. 'Love me for a year,' he had told her; 'I will love you all my life.' On 12th October 1833 he confided to his sister that he was 'a father'. In June he was already viewing this prospect of fatherhood with all the feelings of guilt that were destined to follow. And so Benassis, like Balzac, is not a victim, but a culprit; he retires into solitude in order to expiate his crime. His son dies, but he retains a strong sense of paternity. He treats La Fosseuse as his daughter; he adopts Genestas's son; he decides, in his own words, 'to educate this country as a tutor educates a child'; and on his tomb the villagers inscribe: 'The Father of Us All'. In Balzac's case too the paternal feeling overflows into his work. In 1834 he wrote *Père Goriot*, the tragedy of fatherhood.

The second episode of these stormy years is his amorous correspondence with Madame Hanska, a Polish aristocrat whose first letter is dated 28th February 1832, and whose identity Balzac did not learn until January 1833. As we know, after eighteen years of epistolary relations, Balzac went and married her in Russia five months before his death. Madame Hanska's christian name was Evelina, which Balzac conferred upon his heroine. There is of course a great difference between the chaste maiden of the novel and the noble wife of Count Hanski (*née* Rzewuska), owner of vast estates in the Ukraine; nevertheless their respective states of mind are very much akin. In her letters, only two of which escaped destruction (notably that of 7th November 1832), Madame Hanska expresses lofty religious and moral sentiments exactly like those we find in Evelina's last letter. 'She will tremble with joy', wrote Balzac, speaking of his Polish friend, 'when she sees that her name inhabited my mind, that it was present to my thought, and that I gave her name to all that seemed to me best and most noble in young womanhood.'

Thus Madame de Castries is no longer present in the definitive version of *The Country Doctor*. Madame Hanska has replaced her in the novel as in life. The gay marquise who had refused herself to him remains only in *La Duchesse de Langeais*, where she is pilloried. And as if to proclaim his revenge, when he decides to publish *La Duchesse de Langeais* he post-dates it by nearly a year and has it printed 'Geneva, 26 January 1834'. That was the date upon which and the place where Countess Hanska, who had travelled purposely from the Ukraine, gave herself to him for the first time. What more striking way of declaring that his pride, wounded by one great lady, had found its compensation in another?

In June 1833, however, the balance had not been restored, and the sentiments which dominate *The Country Doctor* are those of frustration and guilt. This state of mind led him not only to philanthropy, but also to religion. Balzac would never write a more truly Christian book. True he did not approve of the purely contemplative life of certain religious orders, and one passage of the book harshly condemns monasteries of men. But it is not unreasonable to think that his visit to the Grande Chartreuse, together with the impression caused by some magnificent scenery, helped to reawaken the religious spirit of his childhood. Read again the description put into the mouth of Benassis: it is a perfect echo of the letters which he wrote at that time to his family and friends. He read this motto on the door of a cell: '*Fuge, late, tace*' ('Flee the world, live hidden, be silent'). Benassis was tempted to bury himself alive according to the Rule of St Bruno. Finally he chose action, 'active prayer'. His life is never again sullied: this good man became at the same time a saint. This novel then, as Balzac wrote to Madame Hanska, a devout Catholic, is 'altogether evangelical'; it is 'a poetic rendering of *The Imitation of Jesus Christ*'. It presents Christianity as a 'complete system of opposition to the depraved tendencies of man'. 'It is a salutary work,' he used also to say, 'worthy of the Prix Montyon', the prize for virtue awarded each year by the Académie Française. From this standpoint he was quite right in believing that he had surpassed *The Vicar of Wakefield*!

An exhaustive study of the book would require analysis of many other aspects. In particular we should have to pass in review the various characters who come marching

by 'from the side of the valley and the side of the mountain':
the usurer Taboureau, the farmers who watch their sons die,
those who have lost the head of the family, old Moreau and
his wife, Madame Vigneau awaiting the birth of her child,
Butifer the poacher, the judge, the mayor, Janvier the parish
priest, and above all La Fosseuse, a wild creature, one of
life's misfits standing midway between a tragic past and an
enigmatic future. They come suddenly upon the scene, then
quickly depart, as in a picaresque novel, by the simple
expedient of a 'cross-country' ride. They are merely
sketched, but they impress themselves upon the memory, so
real they are in physical features and in feelings. Let us say
just a word about the old soldiers (Genestas, Goguelot,
Gondrin) who at one point occupy the centre of the stage,
and in a more general way about the problems raised by the
third chapter, which is entitled 'The Napoleon of the
People'.

This popular account of the Napoleonic campaigns is so
different from the rest of the work that it was published
separately in *Europe Littéraire*, 19th June 1833, and ensures
by itself the author's lasting fame. Even today these pages,
remarkable for their strength, their rhythm, their style and
colour, are the most successful part of the book. In a film
devoted to Napoleon, Goguelat's narrative provides the
entire scenario and commentary.

The presence of this episode in *The Country Doctor* is
easily explained by that in 1832 Balzac had given advance
notice of a great romance inspired by military history and
entitled *La Bataille*. He had formally promised it to Mame,
the publisher, but he worked for several months at the
subject without being able to write more than the beginning
of the first sentence: 'On 16th May 1809, about noon . . .'
He had so many other projects in his head that the work
was never produced, although several episodes of the
Scènes de la vie militaire are probably derived from this
initial source. Finally he decided to incorporate in his

Country Doctor a chapter on Napoleon, which he would be able, first of all, to publish separately.

At that time the theme of Napoleon's achievement was extraordinarily popular. Until the middle of the century most writers did homage to this vogue, which became for some a veritable cult. The greatest, among them Hugo and Byron, yielded to the romantic prestige of that amazing individual, who, starting from nothing, raised himself by his own ability to the summit of power and glory, and suddenly collapsed with the vast empire he had built. What of the rank and file of his campaigns? They forgot the grief and suffering, and were content to recall the prodigious achievements of the Superman. Many, refusing to believe that he was dead, listened greedily to exaggerated tales of his exploits told at evening gatherings by old soldiers who had survived the battles. Such men were still to be found in the villages; covered with wounds and decorations, provided with a meagre pension or no pension at all after twenty years of fighting in all parts of the world, they lived partly by public charity and partly by tilling the land. The character of the 'soldier husbandman' was one of the most popular; the magic surrounding his name was kept alive by the poems of Béranger, Raffet's views and Épinal's figures, which were distributed by pedlars.

Balzac in turn depicted these veterans of the Old Guard, but with even greater effect thanks to his astonishing instinct for the spoken word. Here again scholars claim to have discovered the origin of Goguelat's narrative. They refer to a kind of 'sketch' which the famous caricaturist and man of letters Henri Monnier (the originator of 'Joseph Prudhomme') liked to recite and mime. It appears that his 'History of Napoleon told at an Evening Gathering' was a little masterpiece. Balzac had on several occasiona persuaded him to give a recital. But a fragment of Henri Monnier's text has come to light, and a comparison with Balzac is most revealing: it was our novelist who provided him with that style and that extraordinary sense of movement which reproduces, so to speak, the very march of the emperor's battalions across Europe, from Madrid to Moscow. It was he who added these 'marvellous' elements, such as the Red Man, and endowed the humble sapper Goguelat with all the grandeurs of the bards of Greece.

Must we regard the chapter on 'The Napoleon of the People' as a mere digression and pass stern judgment on the composition of the novel, despite the precautions taken by Balzac to prepare the reader and to 'knit' this episode into the whole? I think not. Goguelat's narrative has its function in the profound signification of *The Country Doctor*: Napoleon enables us to make the exact assessment of Benassis. By means of a bold counterpoint, Balzac calls up two forms of genius side by side: the one vainglorious and resplendent, crushing men like some pitiless god, the greatest of all in the order of power; the other modest, unfortunate and resigned, the little doctor of a remote mountain village, but great in the order of charity. Nor indeed are the villagers mistaken when, in their own way, they pay equal homage to the hero and the saint.

But what is Balzac? He is the creator of Benassis, he is Benassis himself, half real and half imaginary. And Balzac judges himself great also, great as Benassis, greater perhaps than Napoleon! Did he not, on 2nd September 1832, write to his friend Zulma Carraud: 'I really believe I am going to die in peace. I have done something great for my country. *This book, in my opinion, is worth more than laws and battles won. It is the Gospel in action*'?

Marcel Girard.

1961.

NOTE

The present volume is a reprint of the translation made by Miss Ellen Marriage for the edition of the *Comédie Humaine*, in forty uniform volumes, edited by George Saintsbury.

BIBLIOGRAPHY

SCÈNES DE LA VIE PRIVÉE

At the Sign of the Cat and Racket, etc. (*La Maison du Chat-qui-pelote. Le Bal de Sceaux. La Bourse. La Vendetta. Mme Firmiani*).

La Grande Bretêche, etc. (*La Grande Bretêche. La Paix du ménage. La Fausse Maîtresse. Étude de femme. Autre étude de femme. Albert Savarus*). Translated by Mrs Clara Bell.

A Daughter of Eve (*Une Fille d'Ève. Mémoires de deux jeunes mariées*). Translated by Mrs R. S. Scott.

A Woman of Thirty, etc. (*La Femme de trente ans. La Femme abandonnée. La Grenadière. Le Message. Gobseck*). Translated by Miss Ellen Marriage.

A Marriage Settlement (*Le Contrat de mariage. Un Début dans la vie. Une Double Famille*).

Modeste Mignon (*Modeste Mignon*). Translated by Mrs Clara Bell.

Béatrix (*Béatrix*). Translated by James Waring.

The Atheist's Mass, etc. (*La Messe de l'athée. Honorine. Le Colonel Chabert. L'Interdiction. Pierre Grassou*). Translated by Mrs Clara Bell.

SCÈNES DE LA VIE DE PROVINCE

Ursule Mirouët (*Ursule Mirouët*). Translated by Mrs Clara Bell.

Eugénie Grandet (*Eugénie Grandet*). Translated by Miss Ellen Marriage.

Pierrette and The Abbé Birotteau (*Les Célibataires—I. Pierrette. Le Curé de Tours*). Translated by Mrs Clara Bell.

A Bachelor's Establishment (*Les Célibataires—II. Un Ménage de garçon*). Translated by Mrs Clara Bell.

Parisians in the Country (*Les Parisiens en province. L'Illustre Gaudissart. La Muse du département*).

The Jealousies of a Country Town (*Les Rivalités. La Vieille Fille. Le Cabinet des antiques*).

The Lily of the Valley (*Le Lys dans la vallée*). Translated by James Waring.

Lost Illusions (*Illusions perdues—I. Les Deux Poètes. Ève et David*). Translated by Miss Ellen Marriage.

A Distinguished Provincial at Paris (*Illusions perdues—II. Un Grand Homme de province à Paris.* 1 and 2). Translated by Miss Ellen Marriage.

SCÈNES DE LA VIE PARISIENNE

A Harlot's Progress. 2 vols. (*Splendeurs et misères des courtisanes*). Translated by James Waring.

The Unconscious Mummers, etc. (*Les Comédiens sans le savoir. Un Prince de la Bohème. Un Homme d'affaires. Gaudissart II. La Maison Nucingen. Facino Cane*). Translated by Miss Ellen Marriage.

The Thirteen (*Histoire des treize. Ferragus. La Duchesse de Langeais*).

Old Goriot (*Le Père Goriot*). Translated by Miss Ellen Marriage.

The Rise and Fall of César Birotteau (*Grandeur et décadence de César Birotteau*). Translated by Miss Ellen Marriage.

A Princess's Secrets (*Les Secrets de la Princesse de Cadignan. Les Employés*).

Cousin Betty (*Les Parents pauvres—I. La Cousine Bette*). Translated by James Waring.

Cousin Pons (*Les Parents pauvres—II. Le Cousin Pons*). Translated by Miss Ellen Marriage.

SCÈNES DE LA VIE POLITIQUE

A Gondreville Mystery (*Une Ténébreuse Affaire. Un Épisode sous la Terreur*).

The Seamy Side of History (*L'Envers de l'histoire contemporaine. Z. Marcas*). Translated by Mrs Clara Bell.

The Member for Arcis (*Le Député d'Arcis*).

SCÈNES DE LA VIE MILITAIRE

The Chouans (*Les Chouans*). Translated by Miss Ellen Marriage.

SCÈNES DE LA VIE DE CAMPAGNE

The Country Doctor (*Le Médecin de campagne*). Translated by Miss Ellen Marriage.

The Country Parson (*Le Curé de village*). Translated by Miss Ellen Marriage.

The Peasantry (*Les Paysans*). Translated by Miss Ellen Marriage.

ÉTUDES PHILOSOPHIQUES

The Wild Ass's Skin (*La Peau de chagrin*). Translated by Miss Ellen Marriage.

The Quest of the Absolute (*La Recherche de l'absolu*). Translated by Miss Ellen Marriage.

A Father's Curse, etc. (*L'Enfant maudit. Gambara. Massimilla Doni. Maître Cornélius*).

The Unknown Masterpiece, etc. (*Le Chef-d'œuvre inconnu, Jésus-Christ en Flandre. Melmoth réconcilié. Les Marana. Adieu. Le Réquisitionnaire. El Verdugo. Un Drame au bord de la mer. L'Auberge rouge. L'Elixir de longue vie*). Translated by Miss Ellen Marriage.

About Catherine de' Medici (*Sur Catherine de Médicis*). Translated by Mrs Clara Bell.

Seraphita (*Séraphita, Louis Lambert. Les Proscrits*). Translated by Mrs Clara Bell.

The Middle Classes (*Les Petits Bourgeois*).

BIOGRAPHY AND CRITICISM

C. L. Kenney: *Balzac: his Life and Letters,* 1878; J. M. Burton: *Honoré de Balzac and his Figures of Speech,* 1921; W. H. Royce: *A Balzac Bibliography,* 1929. *Lives* by Sir F. Wedmore, 1887; F. Lawton, 1910; F. Gribble, 1930; S. Zweig, 1947; H. J. Hunt, *Balzac's Comédie Humaine,* 1964; A. Maurois, *Prometheus; The Life of Balzac,* 1965; E. James Oliver, *Honoré de Balzac,* 1966; F. Marceau, *Balzac and his World* (trans.), 1967.

CONTENTS

THE COUNTRYSIDE AND THE MAN

ON a lovely spring morning in the year 1829, a man of fifty or thereabouts was wending his way on horseback along the mountain road that leads to a large village near the Grande Chartreuse. This village is the market town of a populous canton that lies within the limits of a valley of some considerable length. The melting of the snows had filled the boulder-strewn bed of the torrent (often dry) that flows through this valley, which is closely shut in between two parallel mountain barriers, above which the peaks of Savoy and of Dauphiné tower on every side.

All the scenery of the country that lies between the chain of the two Mauriennes is very much alike; yet here in the district through which the stranger was travelling there are soft undulations of the land, and varying effects of light which might be sought for elsewhere in vain. Sometimes the valley, suddenly widening, spreads out a soft irregularly shaped carpet of grass before the eyes; a meadow constantly watered by the mountain streams that keep it fresh and green at all seasons of the year. Sometimes a roughly built saw-mill appears in a picturesque position, with its stacks of long pine trunks with the bark peeled off, and its mill stream, brought from the bed of the torrent in great square wooden pipes, with masses of dripping filament issuing from every crack. Little cottages, scattered here and there, with their gardens full of blossoming fruit trees, call up the ideas that are aroused by the sight of industrious poverty; while the thought of ease, secured after long years of toil, is suggested by some larger houses farther on, with their red roofs of flat round tiles, shaped

like the scales of a fish.   There is no door, moreover, that
does not duly exhibit a basket in which the cheeses are
hung up to dry.   Every roadside and every croft is adorned
with vines; which here, as in Italy, they train to grow about
dwarf elm-trees, whose leaves are stripped off to feed the
cattle.

Nature, in her caprice, has brought the sloping hills on
either side so near together in some places, that there is no
room for fields, or buildings, or peasants' huts.   Nothing
lies between them but the torrent, roaring over its water-
falls between two lofty walls of granite that rise above it,
their sides covered with the leafage of tall beeches and dark
fir-trees to the height of a hundred feet.   The trees, with
their different kinds of foliage, rise up straight and tall,
fantastically coloured by patches of lichen, forming
magnificent colonnades, with a line of straggling hedgerow
of guelder rose, brier rose, box, and arbutus above and
below the roadway at their feet.   The subtle perfume of
this undergrowth was mingled just then with scents from
the wild mountain region and with the aromatic fragrance
of young larch shoots, budding poplars, and resinous pines.

Here and there a wreath of mist about the heights
sometimes hid and sometimes gave glimpses of the grey
crags, that seemed as dim and vague as the soft flecks of
cloud dispersed among them.   The whole face of the
country changed every moment with the changing light
in the sky; the hues of the mountains, the soft shades of
their lower slopes, the very shape of the valleys seemed to
vary continually.   A ray of sunlight through the tree-
stems, a clear space made by nature in the woods, or a
landslip here and there, coming as a surprise to make a
contrast in the foreground, made up an endless series of
pictures delightful to see amid the silence, at the time of
year when all things grow young, and when the sun fills
a cloudless heaven with a blaze of light.   In short, it
was a fair land—it was the land of France!

The traveller was a tall man, dressed from head to foot in a suit of blue cloth, which must have been brushed just as carefully every morning as the glossy coat of his horse. He held himself firm and erect in the saddle like an old cavalry officer. Even if his black cravat and doe-skin gloves, the pistols that filled his holsters, and the valise securely fastened to the crupper behind him had not combined to mark him out as a soldier, the air of unconcern that sat on his face, his regular features (scarred though they were with the smallpox), his determined manner, self-reliant expression, and the way he held his head, all revealed the habits acquired through military discipline, of which a soldier can never quite divest him-self, even after he has retired from service into private life.

Any other traveller would have been filled with wonder at the loveliness of this Alpine region, which grows so bright and smiling as it becomes merged in the great valley systems of southern France; but the officer, who no doubt had previously traversed a country across which the French armies had been drafted in the course of Napoleon's wars, enjoyed the view before him without appearing to be surprised by the many changes that swept across it. It would seem that Napoleon has extinguished in his soldiers the sensation of wonder; for an impassive face is a sure token by which you may know the men who served ere-while under the short-lived yet deathless Eagles of the great emperor. The traveller was, in fact, one of those soldiers (seldom met with nowadays) whom shot and shell have respected, although they have borne their part on every battle-field where Napoleon commanded.

There had been nothing unusual in his life. He had fought valiantly in the ranks as a simple and loyal soldier, doing his duty as faithfully by night as by day, and whether in or out of his officer's sight. He had never dealt a sabre stroke in vain, and was incapable of giving one too many. If he wore at his buttonhole the rosette of an officer of the Legion of Honour, it was because the unanimous voice of his regiment had singled him out as the man who best deserved to receive it after the battle of Borodino.

He belonged to that small minority of undemonstrative retiring natures, who are always at peace with themselves, and who are conscious of a feeling of humiliation at the mere thought of making a request, no matter what its nature may be. So promotion had come to him tardily, and by virtue of the slowly working laws of seniority. He had been made a sub-lieutenant in 1802, but it was not until 1829 that he became a major, in spite of the greyness of his moustaches. His life had been so blameless that no man in the army, not even the general himself, could approach him without an involuntary feeling of respect. It is possible that he was not forgiven for this indisputable superiority by those who ranked above him; but, on the other hand, there was not one of his men that did not feel for him something of the affection of children for a good mother. For them he knew how to be at once indulgent and severe. He himself had also once served in the ranks, and knew the sorry joys and gaily endured hardships of the soldier's lot. He knew the errors that may be passed over and the faults that must be punished in his men, 'his children,' as he always called them—and when on campaign he readily gave them leave to forage for provision for man and horse among the wealthier classes.

His own personal history lay buried beneath the deepest reserve. Like almost every military man in Europe, he had only seen the world through cannon smoke, or in the brief intervals of peace that occurred so seldom during the emperor's continual wars with the rest of Europe. Had he or had he not thought of marriage? The question remained unsettled. Although no one doubted that Commandant Genestas had made conquests during his sojourn in town after town and country after country where he had taken part in the festivities given and received by the officers, yet no one knew this for a certainty. There was no prudery about him; he would not decline to join a pleasure party; he in no way offended against military standards; but when questioned as to his affairs of the heart, he either kept silence or answered with a jest. To the words, 'How about you, commandant?' addressed to him by an officer over the wine, his reply was: 'Pass the bottle, gentlemen.'

M. Pierre Joseph Genestas was an unostentatious kind of Bayard. There was nothing romantic nor picturesque about him—he was too thoroughly commonplace. His ways of living were those of a well-to-do man. Although he had nothing beside his pay, and his pension was all that he had to look to in the future, the major always kept two years' pay untouched, and never spent his allowances, like some shrewd old men of business with whom cautious prudence has almost become a mania. He was so little of a gambler that if, when in company, someone was wanted to cut in or to take a bet of écarté, he usually fixed his eyes on his boots; but though he did not allow himself any extravagances, he conformed in every way to custom.

His uniforms lasted longer than those of any other officer in his regiment, as a consequence of the sedulously careful habits that somewhat straitened means had so instilled into him, that they had come to be like a second nature. Perhaps he might have been suspected of meanness if it had not been for the fact that with wonderful disinterestedness and all a comrade's readiness, his purse would be opened for some hare-brained boy who had ruined himself at cards or by some other folly. He did a service of this kind with such thoughtful tact, that it seemed as though he himself had at one time lost heavy sums at play; he never considered that he had any right to control the actions of his debtor; he never made mention of the loan. He was the child of his company; he was alone in the world, so he had adopted the army for his fatherland, and the regiment for his family. Very rarely, therefore, did anyone seek the motives underlying his praiseworthy turn for thrift; for it pleased others, for the most part, to set it down to a not unnatural wish to increase the amount of the savings that were to render his old age comfortable. Till the eve of his promotion to the rank of lieutenant-colonel of cavalry it was fair to suppose that it was his ambition to retire in the course of some campaign with a colonel's epaulettes and pension.

If Genestas's name came up when the officers gossiped after drill, they were wont to classify him among the men who begin with taking the good-conduct prize at school, and who, throughout the term of their natural lives, continue to be punctilious, conscientious, and passionless—as good as white bread, and just as insipid. Thoughtful minds, however, regarded him very differently. Not seldom it would happen that a glance, or an expression as full of significance as the utterance of a savage, would drop from him and bear witness to past storms in his soul; and a careful study of his placid brow revealed a power of stifling down and repressing his passions into inner depths, that had been dearly bought by a lengthy acquaintance with the perils and disastrous hazards of war. An officer who had only just joined the regiment, the son of a peer of France, had said one day of Genestas, that he would have made one of the most conscientious of priests, or the most upright of tradesmen.

'Add, the least of a courtier among marquises,' put in Genestas, scanning the young puppy, who did not know that his commandant could overhear him.

There was a burst of laughter at the words, for the lieutenant's father cringed to all the powers that be; he was a man of supple intellect, accustomed to jump with every change of government, and his son took after him.

Men like Genestas are met with now and again in the

French army; natures that show themselves to be wholly great at need, and relapse into their ordinary simplicity when the action is over; men that are little mindful of fame and reputation, and utterly forgetful of danger. Perhaps there are many more of them than the short-comings of our own characters will allow us to imagine. Yet, for all that, anyone who believed that Genestas was perfect would be strangely deceiving himself. The major was suspicious, given to violent outbursts of anger, and apt to be tiresome in argument; he was full of national prejudices, and above all things, would insist that he was in the right, when he was, as a matter of fact, in the wrong. He retained the liking for good wine that he had acquired in the ranks. If he rose from a banquet with all the gravity befitting his position, he seemed serious and pensive, and had no mind at such times to admit anyone into his confidence.

Finally, although he was sufficiently acquainted with the customs of society and with the laws of politeness, to which he conformed as rigidly as if they had been military regulations; though he had real mental power, both natural and acquired; and although he had mastered the art of handling men, the science of tactics, the theory of sabre play, and the mysteries of the farrier's craft, his learning had been prodigiously neglected. He knew in a hazy kind of way that Caesar was a Roman Consul, or an Emperor, and that Alexander was either a Greek or a Macedonian; he would have conceded either quality or origin in both cases without discussion. If the conversation turned on science or history, he was wont to become thoughtful, and to confine his share in it to little approving nods, like a man who by dint of profound thought has arrived at scepticism.

When, at Schönbrunn, on 13th May 1809 Napoleon wrote the bulletin addressed to the Grand Army, then the masters of Vienna, in which he said that *like Medea, the*

Austrian princes had slain their children with their own hands; Genestas, who had been recently made a captain, did not wish to compromise his newly conferred dignity by asking who Medea was; he relied upon Napoleon's character, and felt quite sure that the emperor was incapable of making any announcement not in proper form to the Grand Army and the House of Austria. So he thought that Medea was some archduchess whose conduct laid her open to criticism. Still, as the matter might have some bearing on the art of war, he felt uneasy about the Medea of the bulletin until a day arrived, when Mlle Raucourt revived the tragedy of *Medea*. The captain saw the placard, and did not fail to repair to the Théâtre Français that evening, to see the celebrated actress in her mythological role, concerning which he gained some information from his neighbours.

A man, however, who as a private soldier had possessed sufficient force of character to learn to read, write, and cipher, could clearly understand that as a captain he ought to continue his education. So from this time forth he read new books and romances with avidity, in this way gaining a half-knowledge, of which he made a very fair use. He went so far in his gratitude to his teachers as to undertake the defence of Pigault-Lebrun, remarking that in his opinion, he was instructive and not seldom profound.

This officer, whose acquired practical wisdom did not allow him to make any journey in vain, had just come from Grenoble, and was on his way to the Grande Chartreuse, after obtaining on the previous evening a week's leave of absence from his colonel. He had not expected that the journey would be a long one; but when, league after league, he had been misled as to the distance by the lying statements of the peasants, he thought it would be prudent not to venture any farther without fortifying the inner man. Small as were his chances of finding any housewife in her dwelling at a time when everyone was hard at work in the fields, he stopped before a little cluster of cottages that stood about a piece of land common to all of them, more or less describing a square, which was open to all comers.

The surface of the soil thus held in conjoint ownership was hard and carefully swept, but intersected by open drains. Roses, ivy, and tall grasses grew over the cracked and disjointed walls. Some rags were drying on a miserable currant bush that stood at the entrance of the square. A pig wallowing in a heap of straw was the first inhabitant encountered by Genestas. At the sound of horse hoofs the creature grunted, raised its head, and put a great black cat to flight. A young peasant girl, who was carrying a bundle of grass on her head, suddenly appeared, followed at a distance by four little brats, clad in rags, it is true, but vigorous, sunburned, picturesque, bold-eyed, and riotous; thorough little imps, looking like angels. The sun shone down with an indescribable purifying influence upon the air, the wretched cottages, the heaps of refuse, and the unkempt little crew.

The soldier asked whether it was possible to obtain a cup of milk. All the answer the girl made him was a hoarse cry. An old woman suddenly appeared on the threshold of one of the cabins, and the young peasant girl passed on into a cowshed, with a gesture that pointed out the aforesaid old woman, towards whom Genestas went; taking care at the same time to keep a tight hold on his horse, lest the children who already were running about under his hoofs should be hurt. He repeated his request, with which the housewife flatly refused to comply. She would not, she said, disturb the cream on the pans full of milk from which butter was to be made. The officer overcame this objection by undertaking to repay her amply for the wasted cream, and then tied up his horse at the door, and went inside the cottage.

The four children belonging to the woman all appeared to be of the same age—an odd circumstance which struck the commandant. A fifth clung about her skirts; a weak, pale, sickly looking child, who doubtless needed more care than the others, and who on that account was the best beloved, the Benjamin of the family.

Genestas seated himself in a corner by the fireless hearth. A sublime symbol met his eyes on the high mantel-shelf above him—a coloured plaster cast of the Virgin with the Child Jesus in her arms. Bare earth made the flooring of the cottage. It had been beaten level in the first instance, but in course of time it had grown rough and uneven, so that though it was clean, its ruggedness was not unlike that of the magnified rind of an orange. A sabot filled with salt, a frying-pan, and a large kettle hung inside the chimney. The farther end of the room was completely filled by a four-post bed-stead, with a scalloped valance for decoration. The walls were black; there was an opening to admit the light above the worm-eaten door; and here and there were a few stools consisting of rough blocks of beech-wood, each set upon three wooden legs; a hutch for bread, a large wooden dipper, a bucket and some earthen milk-pans, a spinning-wheel on the top of the bread-hutch, and a few wicker mats for draining cheeses. Such were the ornaments and household furniture of the wretched dwelling.

The officer, who had been absorbed in flicking his riding-whip against the floor, presently became a witness to a piece of by-play, all unsuspicious though he was that any drama was about to unfold itself. No sooner had the old woman, followed by her scald-headed Benjamin, disappeared through a door that led into her dairy, than the four children, after having stared at the soldier as long as they wished, drove away the pig by way of a beginning. This animal, their accustomed playmate, having come as far as the threshold, the little brats made such an energetic attack upon him, that he was forced to beat a hasty retreat. When the enemy had been driven without, the children besieged the latch of a door that gave way before their united efforts, and slipped out of the worn staple that held it; and finally they bolted into a kind of fruit-loft, where they very soon fell to munching the dried plums, to the amusement of the commandant, who watched this spectacle. The old woman, with the face like parchment and the dirty ragged clothing, came back at this moment, with a jug of milk for her visitor in her hand.

'Oh! you good-for-nothings!' cried she.

She ran to the children, clutched an arm of each child, bundled them into the room, and carefully closed the door of her storehouse of plenty. But she did not take their prunes away from them.

'Now, then, be good, my pets! If one did not look after them,' she went on, looking at Genestas, 'they would eat up the whole lot of prunes, the madcaps!'

Then she seated herself on a three-legged stool, drew the little weakling between her knees, and began to comb and wash his head with a woman's skill and with motherly assiduity. The four small thieves hung about. Some of them stood, others leant against the bed or the bread-hutch. They gnawed their prunes without saying a word, but they kept their sly and mischievous eyes fixed upon the stranger. In spite of grimy countenances and noses that stood in need of wiping, they all looked strong and healthy.

'Are they your children?' the soldier asked the old woman.

'Asking your pardon, sir, they are charity-children. They give me three francs a month and a pound's weight of soap for each of them.'

'But it must cost you twice as much as that to keep them, good woman?'

'That is just what M. Benassis tells me, sir; but if

other folk will board the children for the same money, one has to make it do. Nobody wants the children, but for all that there is a good deal of performance to go through before they will let us have them. When the milk we give them comes to nothing, they cost us scarcely anything. Besides that, three francs is a great deal, sir; there are fifteen francs coming in, to say nothing of the five pounds' weight of soap. In our part of the world you would simply have to wear your life out before you would make ten sous a day.'

'Then you have some land of your own?' asked the commandant.

'No, sir. I had some land once when my husband was alive; since he died I have done so badly that I had to sell it.'

'Why, how do you reach the year's end without debts,' Genestas went on, 'when you bring up children for a livelihood and wash and feed them on two sous a day?'

'Well, we never get to St Sylvester's Day without debt, sir.' She went on without ceasing to comb the child's hair. 'But so it is—Providence helps us out. I have a couple of cows. Then my daughter and I do some gleaning at harvest-time, and in winter we pick up firewood. Then at night we spin. Ah! we never want to see another winter like this last one, that is certain! I owe the miller seventy-five francs for flour. Luckily he is M. Benassis's miller. M. Benassis, ah! he is a friend to poor people. He has never asked for his due from anybody, and he will not begin with us. Besides, our cow has a calf, and that will set us a bit straighter.'

The four orphans for whom the old woman's affection represented all human guardianship had come to an end of their prunes. As their foster-mother's attention was taken up by the officer with whom she was chatting, they seized the opportunity, and banded themselves together in a compact file, so as to make yet another assault upon the

latch of the door that stood between them and the tempting
heap of dried plums. They advanced to the attack, not like
French soldiers, but as stealthily as Germans, impelled
by frank animal greediness.

'Oh! you little rogues! Do you want to finish them
up?'

The old woman rose, caught the strongest of the four,
administered a gentle slap on the back, and flung him out
of the house. Not a tear did he shed, but the others
remained breathless with astonishment.

'They give you a lot of trouble——'

'Oh! no, sir, but they can smell the prunes, the little
dears. If I were to leave them alone here for a moment,
they would stuff themselves with them.'

'You are very fond of them?'

The old woman raised her head at this, and looked at
him with gentle malice in her eyes.

'Fond of them!' she said. 'I have had to part with
three of them already. I only have the care of them until
they are six years old,' she went on with a sigh.

'But where are your own children?'

'I have lost them.'

'How old are you?' Genestas asked, to efface the
impression left by his last question.

'I am thirty-eight years old, sir. It will be two years
come next St John's Day since my husband died.'

She finished dressing the poor sickly mite, who seemed
to thank her by a loving look in his faded eyes.

'What a life of toil and self-denial!' thought the cavalry
officer.

Beneath a roof worthy of the stable wherein Jesus
Christ was born, the hardest duties of motherhood were
fulfilled cheerfully and without consciousness of merit.
What hearts were these that lay so deeply buried in neg-
lect and obscurity! What wealth, and what poverty!
Soldiers, better than other men, can appreciate the element

of grandeur to be found in heroism in sabots, in the Evangel clad in rags. The Book may be found elsewhere, adorned, embellished, tricked out in silk and satin and brocade, but here, of a surety, dwelt the spirit of the Book. It was impossible to doubt that Heaven had some holy purpose underlying it all, at the sight of the woman who had taken a mother's lot upon herself, as Jesus Christ had taken the form of a man, who gleaned and suffered and ran into debt for her little waifs; a woman who defrauded herself in her reckonings, and would not own that she was ruining herself that she might be a mother. One was constrained to admit, at the sight of her, that the good upon earth have something in common with the angels in heaven; Commandant Genestas shook his head as he looked at her.

'Is M. Benassis a clever doctor?' he asked at last.

'I do not know, sir, but he cures poor people for nothing.'

'It seems to me that this is a man and no mistake!' he went on, speaking to himself.

'Oh! yes, sir, and a good man too! There is scarcely anyone hereabouts that does not put his name in their prayers, morning and night!'

'That is for you, mother,' said the soldier, as he gave her several coins, 'and that is for the children,' he went on, as he added another crown. 'Is M. Benassis's house still a long way off?' he asked, when he had mounted his horse.

'Oh! no, sir, a bare league at most.'

The commandant set out, fully persuaded that two leagues remained ahead of him. Yet after all he soon caught a glimpse through the trees of the little town's first cluster of houses, and then of all the roofs that crowded about a conical steeple, whose slates were secured to the angles of the wooden framework by sheets of tin that glittered in the sun. This sort of roof, which has a peculiar appearance, denotes the nearness of the borders of Savoy, where it is very common. The valley is wide at this particular point, and a fair number of houses pleasantly situated, either in the little plain or along the side of the mountain stream, lend human interest to the well-tilled spot, a stronghold with no apparent outlet among the mountains that surround it.

It was noon when Genestas reined in his horse beneath an avenue of elm-trees half-way up the hill-side, and only a few paces from the town, to ask the group of children who stood before him for M. Benassis's house. At first the children looked at each other, then they scrutinized the stranger with the expression that they usually wear when they set eyes upon anything for the first time; a different curiosity and a different thought in every little face. Then the boldest and merriest of the band, a little bright-eyed urchin, with bare, muddy feet, repeated his words over again, in child fashion.

'M. Benassis's house, sir?' adding, 'I will show you the way there.'

He walked along in front of the horse, prompted quite as much by a wish to gain a kind of importance by being in the stranger's company, as by a child's love of being useful, or the imperative craving to be doing something, that possesses mind and body at his age. The officer followed him for the entire length of the principal street of the country town. The way was paved with cobble-stones, and wound in and out among the houses, which their owners had erected along its course in the most arbitrary fashion. In one place a bakehouse had been built out into the middle of the roadway; in another a gable protruded, partially obstructing the passage, and yet farther on a mountain stream flowed across it in a runnel. Genestas noticed a fair number of roofs of tarred shingle, but yet more of them were thatched; a few were tiled, and some seven or eight (belonging no doubt to the curé, the justice of the peace, and some of the wealthier townsmen) were covered with slates. There was a total absence of regard for appearances befitting a village at the end of the world, which had nothing beyond it, and no connection with any other place. The people who lived in it seemed to belong to one family that dwell beyond the limits of the bustling world, with which the collector of taxes and a few ties of the very slenderest alone served to connect them.

When Genestas had gone a step or two farther, he saw on the mountain-side a broad road that rose above the village. Clearly there must be an old town and a new town; and, indeed, when the commandant reached a spot where he could slacken the pace of his horse, he could easily see between the houses some well-built dwellings whose new roofs brightened the old-fashioned village. An avenue of trees rose above these new houses, and from among them came the confused sounds of several industries. He heard the songs peculiar to busy toilers, a murmur of many workshops, the rasping of files, and the sound of falling hammers. He saw the thin lines of smoke from the chimneys of each household, and the more copious outpouring from the forges of the van-builder, the blacksmith, and the farrier. At length, at the very end of the village towards which his guide was taking him, Genestas beheld scattered farms and well-tilled fields and plantations of trees in thorough order. It might have been a little corner of Brie, so hidden away in a great fold of the land, that at first sight its existence would not be suspected between the little town and the mountains that closed the country round.

Presently the child stopped.

'There is the door of *his* house,' he remarked.

The officer dismounted and passed his arm through the bridle. Then, thinking that the labourer is worthy of his hire, he drew a few sous from his waistcoat pocket, and held them out to the child, who looked astonished at this, opened his eyes very wide, and stayed on, without thanking him, to watch what the stranger would do next.

'Civilization has not made much headway hereabouts,' thought Genestas; 'the religion of work is in full force, and begging has not yet come thus far.'

His guide, more from curiosity than from any interested motive, propped himself against the wall that rose to the height of a man's elbow. Upon this wall, which enclosed the yard belonging to the house, there ran a black wooden railing on either side of the square pillars of the gates. The lower part of the gates themselves was of solid wood that had been painted grey at some period in the past; the upper part consisted of a grating of yellowish spear-shaped bars. These decorations, which had lost all their colour, gradually rose on either half of the gates till they reached the centre where they met; their spikes forming, when both leaves were shut, an outline similar to that of a pine-cone. The worm-eaten gates themselves, with their patches of velvet lichen, were almost destroyed by the alternate action of sun and rain. A few aloe plants and some chance-sown pellitory grew on the tops of the square pillars of the gates, which all but concealed the stems of a couple of thornless acacias that raised their tufted spikes, like a pair of green powder-puffs, in the yard.

The condition of the gateway revealed a certain care-lessness in its owner which did not seem to suit the officer's turn of mind. He knitted his brows like a man who is obliged to relinquish some illusion. We usually judge others by our own standard; and although we indulgently forgive our own shortcomings in them, we condemn them harshly for the lack of our special virtues. If the commandant had expected M. Benassis to be a methodical or practical man, there were unmistakable indications of absolute indifference as to his material concerns in the state of the gates of his house. A soldier possessed by

Genestas's passion for domestic economy could not help at once drawing inferences as to the life and character of its owner from the gateway before him; and this, in spite of his habits of circumspection, he in no wise failed to do. The gates were left ajar, moreover—another piece of carelessness!

Encouraged by this countrified trust in all comers, the officer entered the yard without ceremony, and tethered his horse to the bars of the gate. While he was knotting the bridle, a neighing sound from the stable caused both horse and rider to turn their eyes involuntarily in that direction. The door opened, and an old servant put out his head. He wore a red woollen bonnet, exactly like the Phrygian cap in which Liberty is tricked out, a piece of headgear in common use in this country.

As there was room for several horses, this worthy individual, after inquiring whether Genestas had come to see M. Benassis, offered the hospitality of the stable to the newly arrived steed, a very fine animal, at which he looked with an expression of admiring affection. The commandant followed his horse to see how things were to go with it. The stable was clean, there was plenty of litter, and there was the same peculiar air of sleek content about M. Benassis's pair of horses that distinguishes the curé's horse from all the rest of his tribe. A maidservant from within the house came out upon the flight of steps and waited. She appeared to be the proper authority to whom the stranger's inquiries were to be addressed, although the stableman had already told him that M. Benassis was not at home.

'The master has gone to the flour-mill,' said he. 'If you like to overtake him, you have only to go along the path that leads to the meadow; and the mill is at the end of it.'

Genestas preferred seeing the country to waiting about indefinitely for Benassis's return, so he set out along the way that led to the flour-mill. When he had gone beyond the irregular line traced by the town upon the hill-side, he came in sight of the mill and the valley, and of one of the loveliest landscapes that he had ever seen.

The mountains bar the course of the river, which forms a little lake at their feet, and raise their crests above it, tier on tier. Their many valleys are revealed by the changing hues of the light, or by the more or less clear outlines of the mountain ridges fledged with their dark forests of pines. The mill had not long been built. It stood just where the mountain stream fell into the little lake. There was all the charm about it peculiar to a lonely house surrounded by water and hidden away behind the heads of a few trees that love to grow by the water-side. On the farther bank of the river, at the foot of a mountain with a faint red glow of sunset upon its highest crest, Genestas caught a glimpse of a dozen deserted cottages. All the windows and doors had been taken away, and sufficiently large holes were conspicuous in the dilapidated roofs, but the surrounding land was laid out in fields that were highly cultivated, and the old garden spaces had been turned into meadows, watered by a system of irrigation as artfully contrived as that in use in Limousin. Unconsciously the commandant paused to look at the ruins of the village before him.

How is it that men can never behold any ruins, even of the humblest kind, without feeling deeply stirred? Doubtless it is because they seem to be a typical representation of evil fortune whose weight is felt so differently by different natures. The thought of death is called up by a churchyard, but a deserted village puts us in mind of the sorrows of life; death is but one misfortune always foreseen, but the sorrows of life are infinite. Does not the thought of the infinite underlie all great melancholy?

The officer reached the stony path by the mill-pond before he could hit upon an explanation of this deserted village. The miller's lad was sitting on some sacks of corn near the door of the house. Genestas asked for M. Benassis.

'M. Benassis went over there,' said the miller, pointing out one of the ruined cottages.

'Has the village been burnt down?' asked the commandant.

'No, sir.'

'Then how did it come to be in this state?' inquired Genestas.

'Ah! how?' the miller answered, as he shrugged his shoulders and went indoors; 'M. Benassis will tell you that.'

The officer went over a rough sort of bridge built up of boulders taken from the torrent bed, and soon reached the house that had been pointed out to him. The thatched roof of the dwelling was still entire; it was covered with moss indeed, but there were no holes in it, and the door and its fastenings seemed to be in good repair. Genestas saw a fire on the hearth as he entered, an old woman kneeling in the chimney-corner before a sick man seated in a chair, and another man, who was standing with his face turned toward the fire-place. The house consisted of a single room, which was lighted by a wretched window covered with linen cloth. The floor was of beaten earth; the chair, a table, and a truckle-bed comprised the whole of the furniture. The commandant had never seen anything so poor and bare, not even in Russia, where the moujiks' huts are like the dens of wild beasts. Nothing within it spoke of ordinary life; there were not even the simplest appliances for cooking food of the commonest description. It might have been a dog kennel without a drinking-pan. But for the truckle-bed, a smock-frock hanging from a nail, and some sabots filled with straw, which composed the invalid's entire wardrobe, this cottage would have looked as empty as the others. The aged peasant woman upon her knees was devoting all her attention to keeping the sufferer's feet in a tub filled with a brown liquid. Hearing a footstep and the clank of spurs, which sounded strangely in ears accustomed to the plodding pace of country folk, the man turned towards Genestas. A sort of surprise, in which the old woman shared, was visible in his face.

'There is no need to ask if you are M. Benassis,' said the soldier. 'You will pardon me, sir, if, as a stranger impatient to see you, I have come to seek you on your field of battle, instead of awaiting you at your house. Pray do not disturb yourself; go on with what you are doing. When it is over, I will tell you the purpose of my visit.'

Genestas half seated himself upon the edge of the table, and remained silent. The firelight shone more brightly in the room than the faint rays of the sun, for the mountain crests intercepted them, so that they seldom reached this corner of the valley. A few branches of resinous pinewood made a bright blaze, and it was by the light of this fire that the soldier saw the face of the man towards whom he was drawn by a secret motive, by a wish to seek him out, to study and to know him thoroughly well. M. Benassis, the local doctor, heard Genestas with indifference, and with folded arms he returned his bow, and went back to his patient, quite unaware that he was being subjected to a scrutiny as earnest as that which the the soldier turned upon him.

Benassis was a man of ordinary height, broad-shouldered and deep-chested. A capacious green overcoat, buttoned up to the chin, prevented the officer from observing any characteristic details of his personal appearance; but his dark and motionless figure served as a strong relief to his face, which caught the bright light of the blazing fire. The face was not unlike that of a satyr; there was the same slightly protruding forehead, full, in this case, of prominences, all more or less denoting character; the same turned-up nose, with a sprightly cleavage at the tip; the same high cheek-bones. The lines of the mouth were crooked; the lips, thick and red. The chin turned sharply upwards. There was an alert, animated look in the brown eyes, to which their pearly whites gave great brightness, and which expressed passions now subdued. His iron-grey hair, the deep wrinkles in his face, the bushy eyebrows that had grown white already, the veins on his protuberant nose, the tanned face covered with red blotches, everything about him, in short, indicated a man of fifty and the hard work of his profession. The officer could come to no conclusion as to the capacity of the head, which was covered by a close cap; but hidden though it was, it seemed to him to be one of the square-shaped kind that gave rise to the expression 'square-headed.' Genestas was accustomed to read the indications that mark the features of men destined to do great things, since he had been brought into close relations with the energetic natures sought out by Napoleon; so he suspected that there must be some mystery in this life of obscurity, and said to himself as he looked at the remarkable face before him:

'How comes it that he is still a country doctor?'

When he had made a careful study of this countenance, that, in spite of its resemblance to other human faces, revealed an inner life nowise in harmony with a commonplace exterior, he could not help sharing the doctor's interest in his patient; and the sight of that patient completely changed the current of his thoughts.

Much as the old cavalry officer had seen in the course of his soldier's career, he felt a thrill of surprise and horror at the sight of a human face which could never have been lighted up with thought—a livid face in which a look of dumb suffering showed so plainly—the same look that is sometimes worn by a child too young to speak, and too weak to cry any longer; in short, it was the wholly animal face of an old dying cretin. The cretin was the one variety of the human species with which the commandant had not yet come in contact. At the sight of the deep, circular folds of skin on the forehead, the sodden, fish-like eyes, and the head, with its short, coarse, scantily growing hair—a head utterly divested of all the faculties of the senses—who would not have experienced, as Genestas did, an instinctive feeling of repulsion for a being that had neither the physical beauty of an animal nor the mental endowments of man, who was possessed of neither instinct nor reason, and who had never heard nor spoken any kind of articulate speech? It seemed difficult to expend any regrets over the poor wretch now visibly drawing towards the very end of an existence which had not been life in any sense of the word; yet the old woman watched him with touching anxiety, and was rubbing his legs where the hot water did not reach them with as much tenderness as if he had been her husband. Benassis himself, after a close scrutiny of the dull eyes and corpse-like face, gently took the cretin's hand and felt his pulse.

'The bath is doing no good,' he said, shaking his head; 'let us put him to bed again.'

He lifted the inert mass himself, and carried him across to the truckle-bed, from whence, no doubt, he had just taken him. Carefully he laid him at full length, and straightened the limbs that were growing cold already, putting the head and hands in position, with all the heed that a mother could bestow upon her child.

'It is all over, death is very near,' added Benassis, who remained standing by the bedside.

The old woman gazed at the dying form, with her hands on her hips. A few tears stole down her cheeks. Genestas remained silent. He was unable to explain to himself how it was that the death of a being that concerned him so little should affect him so much. Unconsciously he shared the feelings of boundless pity that these hapless creatures excite among the dwellers in the sunless valleys wherein nature has placed them. This sentiment has degenerated into a kind of religious superstition in families to which cretins belong; but does it not spring from the most beautiful of Christian virtues— from charity, and from a belief in a reward hereafter, that most effectual support of our social system, and the one thought that enables us to endure our miseries? The hope of inheriting eternal bliss helps the relations of these unhappy creatures and all others round about them to exert on a large scale, and with sublime devotion, a mother's ceaseless protecting care over an apathetic creature who does not understand it in the first instance, and who in a little while forgets it all. Wonderful power of religion! that has brought a blind beneficence to the aid of an equally blind misery. Wherever cretins exist, there is a popular belief that the presence of one of these creatures brings luck to a family—a superstition that serves to sweeten lives which, in the midst of a town population, would be condemned by a mistaken philanthropy to submit to the harsh discipline of an asylum. In the higher end of the valley of the Isère, where cretins are very numerous, they lead an out-of-door life with the cattle which they are taught to herd. There, at any rate, they are at large, and receive the reverence due to misfortune.

A moment later the village bell clinked at slow regular intervals, to acquaint the flock with the death of one of their number. In the sound that reached the cottage but faintly across the intervening space, there was a thought of religion which seemed to fill it with a melancholy peace. The tread of many feet echoed up the road, giving notice of an approaching crowd of people—a crowd that uttered not a word. Then suddenly the chanting of the Church broke the stillness, calling up the confused thoughts that take possession of the most sceptical minds, and compel them to yield to the influence of the touching harmonies of the human voice. The Church was coming to the aid of a creature that knew her not. The curé appeared, preceded by a choir-boy, who bore the crucifix, and followed by the sacristan carrying the vase of holy water, and by some fifty women, old men, and children, who had all come to add their prayers to those of the Church. The doctor and the soldier looked at each other, and silently withdrew to a corner to make room for the kneeling crowd within and without the cottage. During the consoling ceremony of the Viaticum, celebrated for one who had never sinned, but to whom the Church on earth was bidding a last farewell, there were signs of real sorrow on most of the rough faces of the gathering, and tears flowed over rugged cheeks that sun and wind and labour in the fields had tanned and wrinkled. The sentiment of voluntary kinship was easy to explain. There was not one in the place who had not pitied the unhappy creature, not one who would not have given him his daily bread. Had he not met with a father's care from every child, and found a mother in the merriest little girl?

'He is dead,' said the curé.

The words struck his hearers with the most unfeigned dismay. The tall candles were lighted, and several people undertook to watch with the dead that night. Benassis and the soldier went out. A group of peasants in the doorway stopped the doctor to say:

'Ah! if you have not saved his life, sir, it was doubtless because God wished to take him to Himself.'

'I did my best, children,' the doctor answered.

When they had come a few paces from the deserted village, whose last inhabitant had just died, the doctor spoke to Genestas.

'You would not believe, sir, what real solace is contained for me in what those peasants have just said. Ten years ago I was very nearly stoned to death in this village. It is empty to-day, but thirty families lived in it then.'

Genestas's face and gesture so plainly expressed an

inquiry, that, as they went along, the doctor told him the story promised by this beginning.

'When I first settled here, sir, I found a dozen cretins in this part of the canton,' and the doctor turned round to point out the ruined cottages for the officer's benefit. 'All the favourable conditions for spreading the hideous disease are there; the air is stagnant, the hamlet lies in the valley bottom, close beside a torrent supplied with water by the melted snows, and the sunlight only falls on the mountain-top, so that the valley itself gets no good of the sun. Marriages among these unfortunate creatures are not forbidden by law, and in this district they are protected by superstitious notions, of whose power I had no conception—superstitions which I blamed at first, and afterwards came to admire. So cretinism was in a fair way to spread all over the valley from this spot. Was it not doing the country a great service to put a stop to this mental and physical contagion? But imperatively as the salutary changes were required, they might cost the life of any man who endeavoured to bring them about. Here, as in other social spheres, if any good is to be done, we come into collision not merely with vested interests, but with something far more dangerous to meddle with—religious ideas crystallized into superstitions, the most permanent form taken by human thought. I feared nothing.

'In the first place, I sought for the position of mayor in the canton, and in this I succeeded. Then, after obtaining a verbal sanction from the prefect, and by paying down the money, I had several of these unfortunate creatures transported over to Aiguebelle, in Savoy, by night. There are a great many of them there, and they were certain to be very kindly treated. When this act of humanity came to be known, the whole countryside looked upon me as a monster. The curé preached against me. In spite of all the pains I took to explain to all the shrewder heads of the little place the immense importance of being rid of the idiots, and in spite of the fact that I gave my services gratuitously to the sick people of the district, a shot was fired at me from the corner of a wood.

'I went to the Bishop of Grenoble and asked him to change the curé. Monseigneur was good enough to allow me to choose a priest who would share in my labours, and it was my happy fortune to meet with one of those rare natures that seem to have dropped down from heaven. Then I went on with my enterprise. After preparing people's minds, I made another transportation by night, and six more cretins were taken away. In this second attempt I had the support of several people to whom I had rendered some service, and I was backed by the members of the Communal Council, for I had appealed to their parsimonious instincts, showing them how much it cost to support the poor wretches, and pointing out how largely they might gain by converting their plots of ground (to which the idiots had no proper title) into allotments which were needed in the township.

'All the rich were on my side; but the poor, the old women, the children, and a few pig-headed people were violently opposed to me. Unluckily it so fell out that my last removal had not been completely carried out. The cretin whom you have just seen, not having returned to his house, had not been taken away, so that the next morning he was the sole remaining example of his species in the village. There were several families still living there; but though they were little better than idiots, they were, at any rate, freed from the taint of cretinism. I determined to go through with my work, and came officially in open day to take the luckless creature from his dwelling. I had no sooner left my house than my intention got abroad. The cretin's friends were there before me, and in front of his hovel I found a crowd of women and children and old people, who hailed my arrival with insults accompanied by a shower of stones.

'In the midst of the uproar I should perhaps have fallen a victim to the frenzy that possesses a crowd excited by its own outcries and stirred up by one common feeling, but the cretin saved my life! The poor creature came out of his hut, and raised the clucking sound of his voice. He seemed to be an absolute ruler over the fanatical mob, for the sight of him put a sudden stop to the clamour. It occurred to me that I might arrange a compromise, and thanks to the quiet so opportunely restored, I was able to propose and explain it. Of course, those who approved of my schemes would not dare to second me in this emergency, their support was sure to be of a purely passive kind, while these superstitious folk would exert the most active vigilance to keep their last idol among them; it was impossible, it seemed to me, to take him away from them. So I promised to leave the cretin in peace in his dwelling, with the understanding that he should live quite by himself, and that the remaining families in the village should cross the stream and come to live in the town, in some new houses which I myself undertook to build, adding to each house a piece of ground for which the commune was to repay me later on.

'Well, my dear sir, it took me fully six months to overcome their objection to this bargain, however much it may have been to the advantage of the village families. The affection which they have for their wretched hovels in country districts is something quite unexplainable. No matter how unwholesome his hovel may be, a peasant clings far more to it than a banker does to his mansion. The reason of it? That I do not know. Perhaps thoughts and feelings are strongest in those who have but few of them, simply because they have but few. Perhaps material things count for much in the lives of those who live so little in thought; certain it is that the less they have, the dearer their possessions are to them. Perhaps, too, it is with the peasant as with the prisoner—he does not squander the powers of his soul, he centres them all upon a single idea, and this is how his feelings come to be so exceedingly strong. Pardon these reflections on the part of a man who seldom exchanges ideas with anyone. But, indeed, you must not suppose, sir, that I am much taken up with these far-fetched considerations. We all have to be active and practical here.

'Alas! the fewer ideas these poor folk have in their heads, the harder it is to make them see where their real interests lie. There was nothing for it but to give my whole attention to every trifling detail of my enterprise. One and all made me the same answer, one of those sayings, filled with homely sense, to which there is no possible reply: "But your houses are not yet built, sir!" they used to say. "Very good," said I, "promise me that as soon as they are finished you will come and live in them."

'Luckily, sir, I obtained a decision to the effect that the whole of the mountain-side above the now deserted village was the property of the township. The sum of money brought in by the woods on the higher slopes paid for the building of the new houses and for the land on which they stood. They were built forthwith; and when once one of my refractory families was fairly settled in, the rest of them were not slow to follow. The benefits of the change were so evident that even the most bigoted believer in the village, which you might call soulless as well as sunless, could not but appreciate them. The final decision in this matter, which gave some property to the commune, in the possession of which we were confirmed by the Council of State, made me a person of great importance in the canton. But what a lot of worry there was over it!' the doctor remarked, stopping short, and raising a hand which he let fall again—a gesture that spoke volumes. 'No one knows, as I do, the distance between the town and the Prefecture—whence nothing comes out—and from the Prefecture to the Council of State—where nothing can be got in.

'Well, after all,' he resumed, 'peace be to the powers of this world! They yielded to my importunities, and that is saying a great deal. If you only knew the good that came of a carelessly scrawled signature! Why, sir, two years after I had taken these momentous trifles in hand, and had carried the matter through to the end, every poor family in the commune had two cows at least, which they pastured on the mountain-side, where (without waiting this time for an authorization from the Council of State) I had established a system of irrigation by means of cross trenches, like those in Switzerland, Auvergne, and Limousin. Much to their astonishment, the townspeople saw some capital meadows springing up under their eyes, and thanks to the improvement in the pasturage, the yield of milk was very much larger. The results of this triumph were great indeed. Everyone followed the example set by my system of irrigation; cattle were multiplied; the area of meadow land and every kind of out-turn increased. I had nothing to fear after that. I could continue my efforts to improve this, as yet, untilled corner of the earth; and to civilize those who dwelt in it, whose minds had hitherto lain dormant.

'Well, sir, folk like us, who live out of the world, are very talkative. If you ask us a question, there is no knowing where the answer will come to an end; but to cut it short—there were about seven hundred souls in the valley when I came to it, and now the population numbers some two thousand. I had gained the good opinion of everyone in that matter of the last cretin; and when I had constantly shown that I could rule both mildly and firmly, I became a local oracle. I did everything that I could to win their confidence; I did not ask for it, nor did I appear to seek it; but I tried to inspire everyone with the deepest respect for my character, by the scrupulous way in which

I always fulfilled my engagements, even when they were of the most trifling kind. When I had pledged myself to the care of the poor creature whose death you have just witnessed, I looked after him much more effectually than any of his previous guardians had done. He has been fed and cared for as the adopted child of the commune. After a time the dwellers in the valley ended by understanding the service which I had done them in spite of themselves, but for all that, they still cherish some traces of that old superstition of theirs. Far be it from me to blame them for it; has not their cult of the cretin often furnished me with an argument when I have tried to induce those who had possession of their faculties to help the unfortunate? But here we are,' said Benassis, when after a moment's pause he saw the roof of his own house.

Far from expecting the slightest expression of praise or of thanks from his listener, it appeared from his way of telling the story of this episode in his administrative career, that he had been moved by an unconscious desire to pour out the thoughts that filled his mind, after the manner of folk that live very retired lives.

'I have taken the liberty of putting my horse in your stable, sir,' said the commandant, 'for which in your goodness you will perhaps pardon me when you learn the object of my journey hither.'

'Ah! yes, what is it?' asked Benassis, appearing to shake off his preoccupied mood, and to recollect that his companion was a stranger to him. The frankness and unreserve of his nature had led him to accept Genestas as an acquaintance.

'I have heard of the almost miraculous recovery of M. Gravier of Grenoble, whom you received into your house,' was the soldier's answer. 'I have come to you, hoping that you will give a like attention to my case, although I have not a similar claim to your benevolence; and yet, I am possibly not undeserving of it. I am an old soldier, and wounds of long standing give me no peace. It will take you at least a week to study my condition, for the pain only comes back at intervals, and——'

'Very good, sir,' Benassis broke in; 'M. Gravier's room is in readiness. Come in.'

They went into the house, the doctor flinging open the door with an eagerness that Genestas attributed to his pleasure at receiving a boarder.

'Jacquotte!' Benassis called out. 'This gentleman will dine with us.'

'But would it not be as well for us to settle about the payment?'

'Payment for what?' inquired the doctor.

'For my board. You cannot keep me and my horse as well, without——'

'If you are wealthy, you will repay me amply,' Benassis replied; 'and if you are not, I will take nothing whatever.'

'Nothing whatever seems to me to be too dear,' said Genestas. 'But, rich or poor, will ten francs a day (not including your professional services) be acceptable to you?'

'Nothing could be less acceptable to me than payment for the pleasure of entertaining a visitor,' the doctor answered, knitting his brows; 'and as to my advice, you shall have it if I like you, and not unless. Rich people shall not have my time by paying for it; it belongs exclusively to the folk here in the valley. I do not care about fame or fortune, and I look for neither praise nor gratitude from my patients. Any money which you may pay me will go to the druggists in Grenoble, to pay for the medicine required by the poor of the neighbourhood.'

Anyone who had heard the words flung out, abruptly, it is true, but without a trace of bitterness in them, would have said to himself with Genestas: 'Here is a man made of good human clay.'

'Well, then, I will pay you ten francs a day, sir,' the soldier answered, returning to the charge with wonted pertinacity, 'and you will do as you choose after that. We shall understand each other better, now that the question is settled,' he added, grasping the doctor's hand with eager cordiality. 'In spite of my ten francs, you shall see that I am by no means a Tartar.'

After this passage of arms, in which Benassis showed not the slightest sign of a wish to appear generous or to pose as a philanthropist, the supposed invalid entered his doctor's house. Everything within it was in keeping with the ruinous state of the gateway, and with the clothing worn by its owner. There was an utter disregard for everything not essentially useful, which was visible even in the smallest trifles. Benassis took Genestas through the kitchen, that being the shortest way to the dining-room.

Had the said kitchen belonged to an inn, it could not have been more smoke-begrimed; and if there was a sufficiency of cooking-pots within its precincts, this lavish supply was Jacquotte's doing—Jacquotte who had formerly been the curé's housekeeper—Jacquotte who always said 'we,' and who ruled supreme over the doctor's household. If, for instance, there was a brightly polished warming-pan above the mantel-shelf, it probably hung there because Jacquotte liked to sleep warm of a winter night, which led her incidentally to warm her master's sheets. He never took a thought about anything; so she was wont to say.

It was on account of a defect, which anyone else would have found intolerable, that Benassis had taken her into his service. Jacquotte had a mind to rule the house, and a woman who would rule his house was the very person that the doctor wanted. So Jacquotte bought and sold, made alterations about the place, set up and took down, arranged and disarranged everything at her own sweet will; her master had never raised a murmur. Over the yard, the stable, the manservant, and the kitchen, in fact, over the whole house and garden and its master, Jacquotte's sway was absolute. She looked out fresh linen, saw to the washing, and laid in provisions without consulting anybody. She decided everything that went on in the house, and the date when the pigs were to be killed. She scolded the gardener, decreed the menu at breakfast and dinner, and went from cellar to garret, and from garret to cellar, setting everything to rights according to her notions, without a word of opposition of any sort or description. Benassis had made but two stipulations—he wished to dine at six o'clock, and that the household expenses should not exceed a certain fixed sum every month.

A woman whom everyone obeys in this way is always singing, so Jacquotte laughed and warbled on the staircase; she was always humming something when she was not singing, and singing when she was not humming. Jacquotte had a natural liking for cleanliness, so she kept the house neat and clean. If her tastes had been different, it would have been a sad thing for M. Benassis (so she was wont to say), for the poor man was so little particular that you might feed him on cabbage for partridges, and he would not find it out; and if it were not for her, he would very often wear the same shirt for a week on end. Jacquotte, however, was an indefatigable folder of linen, a born rubber and polisher of furniture, and a passionate lover of a perfectly religious and ceremonial cleanliness of the most scrupulous, the most radiant, and most fragrant kind. A sworn foe to dust, she swept and scoured and washed without ceasing.

The condition of the gateway caused her acute distress. On the first day of every month for the past ten years, she had extorted from her master a promise that he would replace the gate with a new one, that the walls of the house should be lime-washed, and that everything should be made quite straight and proper about the place; but so far, the master had not kept his word. So it happened that whenever she fell to lamenting over

Benassis's deeply rooted carelessness about things, she nearly always ended solemnly in these words, with which all her praises of her master usually terminated:

'You cannot say that he is a fool, because he works such miracles, as you may say, in the place; but, all the same, he is a fool at times, such a fool that you have to do everything for him as if he were a child.'

Jacquotte loved the house as if it had belonged to her; and when she had lived in it for twenty-two years, had she not some grounds for deluding herself on that head? After the curé's death the house had been for sale; and Benassis, who had only just come into the country, had bought it as it stood, with the walls about it and the ground belonging to it, together with the plate, wine, and furniture, the old sundial, the poultry, the horse, and the woman-servant. Jacquotte was the very pattern of a working housekeeper, with her clumsy figure, and her bodice, always of the same dark brown print with large red spots on it, which fitted her so tightly that it looked as if the material must give way if she moved at all. Her colourless face, with its double chin, looked out from under a round plaited cap, which made her look paler than she really was. She talked incessantly, and always in a loud voice—this short, active woman, with the plump, busy hands. Indeed, if Jacquotte was silent for a moment, and took a corner of her apron so as to turn it up in a triangle, it meant that a lengthy expostulation was about to be delivered for the benefit of master or man. Jacquotte was beyond all doubt the happiest cook in the kingdom; for, that nothing might be lacking in a measure of felicity as great as may be known in this world below, her vanity was continually gratified— the townspeople regarded her as an authority of an indefinite kind, and ranked her somewhere between the mayor and the park-keeper.

The master of the house found nobody in the kitchen when he entered it.

'Where the devil are they all gone?' he asked. 'Pardon me for bringing you in this way,' he went on, turning to Genestas. 'The front entrance opens into the garden, but I am so little accustomed to receive visitors that— Jacquotte!' he called in rather peremptory tones.

A woman's voice answered to the name from the interior of the house. A moment later Jacquotte, assuming the offensive, called in her turn to Benassis, who forthwith went into the dining-room.

'Just like you, sir!' she exclaimed; 'you never do like anybody else. You always ask people to dinner without telling me beforehand, and you think that everything is settled as soon as you have called for Jacquotte! You are not going to have the gentleman sit in the kitchen, are you? Is not the *salon* to be unlocked and a fire to be lighted? Nicolle is there, and will see after everything. Now take the gentleman into the garden for a minute; that will amuse him; if he likes to look at pretty things, show him the arbour of hornbeam-trees that the poor dear old gentleman made. I shall have time then to lay the cloth, and to get everything ready, the dinner and the *salon* too.'

'Yes. But, Jacquotte,' Benassis went on, 'the gentleman is going to stay with us. Do not forget to give a look round M. Gravier's room, and see about the sheets and things, and——'

'Now you are not going to interfere about the sheets, are you?' asked Jacquotte. 'If he is to sleep here, I know what must be done for him perfectly well. You have not so much as set foot in M. Gravier's room these ten months past. There is nothing to see there, the place is as clean as a new pin. Then will the gentleman make some stay here?' she continued in a milder tone.

'Yes.'

'How long will he stay?'

'Faith, I do not know. What does it matter to you?'

'What does it matter to me, sir? Oh! very well, what does it matter to me? Did anyone ever hear the like! And the provisions and all that, and——'

At any other time she would have overwhelmed her master with reproaches for his breach of trust, but now she followed him into the kitchen before the torrent of words had come to an end. She had guessed that there was a prospect of a boarder, and was eager to see Genestas, to whom she made a very deferential curtsy, while she scanned him from head to foot. A thoughtful and dejected expression gave a harsh look to the soldier's face. In the dialogue between master and servant the former had appeared to him in the light of a nonentity; and although he regretted the fact, this revelation had lessened the high opinion that he had formed of the man whose persistent efforts to save the district from the horrors of cretinism had won his admiration.

'I do not like the looks of that fellow at all!' said Jacquotte to herself.

'If you are not tired, sir,' said the doctor to his supposed patient, 'we will take a turn round the garden before dinner.'

'Willingly,' answered the commandant.

They went through the dining-room, and reached the garden by way of a sort of vestibule at the foot of the staircase between the *salon* and the dining-room. Beyond a great glass door at the farther end of the vestibule lay a flight of stone steps which adorned the garden side of the house. The garden itself was divided into four large squares of equal size by two paths that intersected each other in the form of a cross, a box edging along their sides. At the farther end there was a thick, green alley of hornbeam-trees, which had been the joy and pride of the late owner. The soldier seated himself on a worm-eaten bench, and saw neither the trellis-work nor the espaliers, nor the vegetables of which Jacquotte took such great care. She followed the traditions of the epicurean churchman to whom this valuable garden owed its origin; but Benassis himself regarded it with sufficient indifference.

The commandant turned their talk from the trivial matters which had occupied them by saying to the doctor:

'How comes it, sir, that the population of the valley has been trebled in ten years? There were seven hundred souls in it when you came, and to-day you say that they number more than two thousand.'

'You are the first person who has put that question to me,' the doctor answered. 'Though it has been my aim to develop the capabilities of this little corner of the earth to the utmost, the constant pressure of a busy life has not left me time to think over the way in which (like the mendicant brother) I have made "broth from a flint" on a large scale. M. Gravier himself, who is one of several who have done a great deal for us, and to whom I was able to render a service by re-establishing his health, has never given a thought to the theory, though he has been everywhere over our mountain-sides with me, to see its practical results.'

There was a moment's silence, during which Benassis followed his own thoughts, careless of the keen glance by which his guest tried to fathom him.

'You ask how it came about, my dear sir?' the doctor resumed. 'It came about quite naturally through the working of the social law by which the need and means of supplying it are correlated. Herein lies the whole story. Races who have no wants are always poor. When I first came to live here in this township, there were about a hundred and thirty peasant families in it, and some two hundred hearths in the valley. The local authorities were such as might be expected in the prevailing wretchedness of the population. The mayor himself could not write, and the deputy-mayor was a small farmer, who lived beyond the limits of the commune. The justice of the peace was a poor devil who had nothing but his salary, and who was forced to relinquish the registration of births, marriages, and deaths to his clerk, another hapless wretch was was scarcely able to understand his duties. The old curé had died at the age of seventy, and his curate, a quite uneducated man, had just succeeded to his position. These people comprised all the intelligence of the district over which they ruled.

'Those who dwelt amidst these lovely natural surroundings grovelled in squalor and lived upon potatoes, milk, butter, and cheese. The only produce that brought in any money was the cheese, which most of them carried in small baskets to Grenoble or its outskirts. The richer or the more energetic among them sowed buckwheat for home consumption; sometimes they raised a crop of barley or oats, but wheat was unknown. The only trader in the place was the mayor, who owned a saw-mill and bought up timber at a low price to sell again. In the absence of roads, his tree trunks had to be transported during the summer season; each log was dragged along one at a time, and with no small difficulty, by means of a chain attached to a halter about his horse's neck, and an iron hook at the farther end of the chain, which was driven into the wood. Anyone who went to Grenoble, whether on horseback or afoot, was obliged to follow a track high up on the mountain-side, for the valley was quite impassable. The pretty road between this place and the first village that you reach as you come into the canton (the way along which you must have come) was nothing but a slough at all seasons of the year.

'Political events and revolutions had never reached this inaccessible country—it lay completely beyond the limits of social stir and change. Napoleon's name, and his alone, had penetrated hither; he is held in great veneration, thanks to one or two old soldiers who have returned to their native homes, and who of evenings tell marvellous tales about his adventures and his armies for the benefit of these simple folk. Their coming back is, moreover, a puzzle that no one can explain. Before I came here, the young men who went into the army all stayed in it for good. This fact in itself is a sufficient revelation of the wretched condition of the country. I need not give you a detailed description of it.

'This, then, was the state of things when I first came to the canton, which has several contented, well-tilled, and fairly prosperous communes belonging to it upon the other side of the mountains. I will say nothing about the hovels in the town; they were neither more nor less than stables, in which men and animals were indiscriminately huddled together. As there was no inn in the place, I was obliged to ask the curate for a bed, he being in possession, for the time being, of this house, then offered for sale. Putting to him question after question, I came to have some slight knowledge of the lamentable condition of the country with the pleasant climate, the fertile soil, and the natural productiveness that had impressed me so much.

'At that time, sir, I was seeking to shape a future for myself that should be as little as possible like the troubled life that had left me weary; and one of those thoughts came into my mind that God gives to us at times, to enable us to take up our burdens and bear them. I resolved to develop all the resources of this country, just as a tutor develops the capacities of a child. Do not think too much of my benevolence; the pressing need that I felt for turning my thoughts into fresh channels entered too much into my motives. I had determined to give up the remainder of my life to some difficult task. A lifetime would be required to bring about the needful changes in a canton that nature had made so wealthy, and man so poor; and I was tempted by the practical difficulties that stood in the way. As soon as I found, that I could secure the curé's house and plenty of waste land at a small cost, I solemnly devoted myself to the calling of a country surgeon—the very last position that a man aspires to take. I determined to become the friend of the poor, and to expect no reward of any kind from them. Oh! I did not indulge in any illusions as to the nature of the country people, nor as to the hindrances that lie in the way of every attempt to bring about a better state of things among men or their surroundings. I have never made idyllic pictures of my people; I have taken them at their just worth—as poor peasants, neither wholly good nor wholly bad, whose constant toil never allows them to indulge in emotion, though they can feel acutely at times. Above all things, in fact, I clearly understood that I should do nothing with them except through an appeal to their selfish interests, and by schemes for their immediate well-being. The peasants are one and all the sons of St Thomas, the doubting apostle— they always like words to be supported by visible facts.

'Perhaps you will laugh at my first start, sir,' the doctor went on after a pause. 'I began my difficult enterprise by introducing the manufacture of baskets. The poor folk used to buy the wicker mats on which they drain their cheeses, and all the baskets needed for the insignificant trade of the district. I suggested to an intelligent young fellow that he might take on lease a good-sized piece of land by the side of the torrent. Every year the floods deposited a rich alluvial soil on this spot, where there should be no difficulty in growing osiers. I reckoned out the quantity of wicker-work of various kinds required from time to time by the canton, and went over to Grenoble, where I found out a young craftsman, a clever worker, but without any capital. When I had discovered him, I soon made up my mind to set him up in business here. I undertook to advance the money for the osiers required for his work until my osier-farmer should be in a position to supply him. I induced him to sell his baskets at rather lower prices than they asked for them in Grenoble, while, at the same time, they were better made. He entered into my views completely. The osier-beds and the basket-making were two business speculations whose results were only appreciated after the lapse of four years. Of course, you know that osiers must be three years old before they are fit to cut.

'At the commencement of operations, the basket-maker was boarded and lodged gratuitously. Before very long he married a woman from Saint Laurent du Pont, who had a little money. Then he had a house built, in a healthy and very airy situation which I chose, and my advice was followed as to the internal arrangements. Here was a triumph! I had created a new industry, and had brought a producer and several workers into the town. I wonder if you will regard my elation as childish?

'For the first few days after my basket-maker had set up his business, I never went past his shop but my heart beat somewhat faster. And when I saw the newly built house, with the green-painted shutters, the vine beside the doorway, and the bench and bundles of osiers before it; when I saw a tidy, neatly dressed woman within it, nursing a plump, pink and white baby among the workmen, who were singing merrily and busily plaiting their wicker-work under the superintendence of a man who but lately had looked so pinched and pale, but now had an atmosphere of prosperity about him; when I saw all this, I confess that I could not forgo the pleasure of turning basket-maker for a moment, of going into the shop to hear how things went with them, and of giving myself up to a feeling of content that I cannot express in words, for I had all their happiness as well as my own to make me glad. All my hopes became centred on this house, where the man dwelt who had been the first to put a steady faith in me. Like the basket-maker's wife, clasping her first nursling to her breast, did not I already fondly cherish the hopes of the future of this poor district?

'I had to do so many things at once,' he went on, 'I came into collision with other people's notions, and met with violent opposition, fomented by the ignorant mayor to whose office I had succeeded, and whose influence had dwindled away as mine increased. I determined to make him my deputy, and a confederate in my schemes of benevolence. Yes, in the first place, I endeavoured to instil enlightened ideas into the densest of all heads. Through his self-love and cupidity I gained a hold upon my man. During six months, as we dined together, I took him deeply into my confidence about my projected improvements. Many people would think this intimacy one of the most painful inflictions in the course of my task; but was he not a tool of the most valuable kind? Woe to him who despises his axe, or flings it carelessly aside! Would it not have been very inconsistent, moreover, if I, who wished to improve a district, had shrunk back at the thought of improving one man in it?

'A road was our first and most pressing need in bringing about a better state of things. If we could obtain permission from the municipal council to make a hard road, so as to put us in communication with the highway to Grenoble, the deputy mayor would be the first gainer by it; for instead of dragging his timber over rough tracks at a great expense, a good road through the canton would enable him to transport it more easily, and to engage in a traffic on a large scale, in all kinds of wood, that would bring in money—not a miserable six hundred francs a year, but handsome sums which would mean a certain fortune for him some day. Convinced at last, he became my proselytizer.

'Through the whole of one winter the ex-mayor got into the way of explaining to our citizens that a good road for wheeled traffic would be a source of wealth to the whole country round, for it would enable everyone to do a trade with Grenoble; he held forth on this head at the tavern while drinking with his intimates. When the municipal council had authorized the making of the road, I went to the prefect and obtained some money from the charitable funds at the disposal of the department, in order to pay for the hire of carts, for the commune was unable to undertake the transport of road metal for lack of wheeled conveyances. The ignorant began to murmur against me, and to say that I wanted to bring the days of the *corvée* back again; this made me anxious to finish this important work, that they might speedily appreciate its benefits. With this end in view, every Sunday during my first year of office I drew the whole population of the township, willing or unwilling, up on to the mountain, where I myself had traced out on a hard bottom the road between our village and the highway to Grenoble. Materials for making it were fortunately to be had in plenty all along the site.

'The tedious enterprise called for a great deal of patience on my part. Some who were ignorant of the law would refuse at times to give their contribution of labour; others, again, who had not bread to eat, really could not afford to lose a day. Corn had to be distributed among these last, and the others must be soothed with friendly words. Yet by the time we had finished two-thirds of the road, which in all is about two leagues in length, the people had so thoroughly recognized its advantages, that the remaining third was accomplished with a spirit that surprised me. I added to the future wealth of the commune by planting a double row of poplars along the ditch on either side of the way. The trees are already almost worth a fortune, and they make our road look like a king's highway. It is almost always dry, by reason of its position, and it was so well made that the annual cost of maintaining it is a bare two hundred francs. I must show it to you, for you cannot have seen it; you must have come by the picturesque way along the valley bottom, a road which the people decided to make for themselves three years later, so as to connect the various farms that were made there at that time. In three years ideas had rooted themselves in the common sense of this township, hitherto so lacking in intelligence that a passing traveller would perhaps have thought it hopeless to attempt to instil them. But to continue.

'The establishment of the basket-maker was an example set before these poverty-stricken folk that they might profit by it. And if the road was to be a direct cause of the future wealth of the canton, all the primary forms of industry must be stimulated, or these two germs of a better state of things would come to nothing. My own work went forward by slow degrees, as I helped my osier farmer and wicker-worker and saw to the making of the road.

'I had two horses, and the timber merchant, the deputy mayor, had three. He could only have them shod whenever he went over to Grenoble, so I induced a farrier to take up his abode here, and undertook to find him plenty of work. On the same day I met with a discharged soldier, who had nothing but his pension of a hundred francs, and was sufficiently perplexed about his future. He could read and write, so I engaged him as secretary to the mayor; as it happened, I was lucky enough to find a wife for him, and his dreams of happiness were fulfilled.

'Both of these new families needed houses, as well as the basket-maker and twenty-two others from the cretin village; soon afterwards twelve more households were established in the place. The workers in each of these families were at once producers and consumers. They were masons, carpenters, joiners, slaters, blacksmiths, and glaziers; and there was work enough to last them for a long time, for had they not their own houses to build when they had finished those for other people? Seventy, in fact, were built in the commune during my second year of office. One form of production demands another. The additions to the population of the township had created fresh wants, hitherto unknown among these dwellers in poverty. The wants gave rise to industries, and industries to trade, and the gains of trade raised the standard of comfort, which in its turn gave them practical ideas.

'The various workmen wished to buy their bread ready baked, so we came to have a baker. Buckwheat could no longer be the food of a population which, awakened from its lethargy, had become essentially active. They lived on buckwheat when I first came among them, and I wished to effect a change to rye, or a mixture of rye and wheat in the first instance, and finally to see a loaf of white bread even in the poorest household. Intellectual progress to my thinking was entirely dependent on a general improvement in the conditions of life. The presence of a butcher in a district says as much for its intelligence as for its wealth. The worker feeds himself, and a man who feeds himself thinks. I had made a very careful study of the soil, for I foresaw a time when it would be necessary to grow wheat. I was sure of launching the place in a very prosperous agricultural career, and of doubling the population, when once it had begun to work. And now the time had come.

'M. Gravier, of Grenoble, owned a great deal of land in the commune, which brought him in no rent, but which might be turned into corn-growing land. He is the head of a department in the Prefecture, as you know. It was a kindness for his own countryside quite as much as my earnest entreaties that won him over. He had very benevolently yielded to my importunities on former occasions, and I succeeded in making it clear to him that in so doing he had wrought unconsciously for his own benefit. After several days spent in pleadings, consultation, and talk, the matter was thrashed out. I undertook to guarantee him against all risks in the undertaking, from which his wife, a woman of no imagination, sought to frighten him. He agreed to build four farmhouses with a hundred acres of land attached to each, and promised to advance the sums required to pay for clearing the ground, for seeds, ploughing gear, and cattle, and for making occupation roads.

'I myself also started two farms, quite as much for the sake of bringing my waste land into cultivation as with a view to giving an object-lesson in the use of modern methods in agriculture. In six weeks' time the population of the town increased to three hundred people. Homes for several families must be built on the six farms; there was a vast quantity of land to be broken up; the work called for labourers. Wheelwrights, drainmakers, journeymen, and labourers of all kinds flocked in. The road to Grenoble was covered with carts that came and went. All the countryside was astir. The circulation of money had made everyone anxious to earn it, apathy had ceased, the place had awakened.

'The story of M. Gravier, one of those who did so much for this canton, can be concluded in a few words. In spite of cautious misgivings, not unnatural in a man occupying an official position in a provincial town, he advanced more than forty thousand francs, on the faith of my promises, without knowing whether he should ever see them back again. To-day every one of his farms is let for a thousand francs. His tenants have thriven so well that each of them owns at least a hundred acres, three hundred sheep, twenty cows, ten oxen, and five horses, and employs more than twenty persons.

'But to resume. Our farms were ready by the end of the fourth year. Our wheat harvest seemed miraculous to the people in the district, heavy as the first crop off the land ought to be. How often during that year I trembled for the success of my work! Rain or drought might spoil everything by diminishing the belief in me that was already felt. When we began to grow wheat, it necessitated the mill that you have seen, which brings me in about five hundred francs a year. So the peasants say that "there is luck about me" (that is the way they put it), and believe in me as they believe in their relics. These new undertakings—the farms, the mill, the plantations, and the roads—have given employment to all the various kinds of workers whom I had called in. Although the buildings fully represent the value of the sixty thousand francs of capital, which we sunk in the district, the outlay was more than returned to us by the profits on the sales which the consumers occasioned. I never ceased my efforts to put vigour into this industrial life which was just beginning. A nurseryman took my advice and came to settle in the place, and I preached wholesome doctrine to the poor concerning the planting of fruit trees, in order that some day they should obtain a monopoly of the sale of fruit in Grenoble.

"'You take your cheeses there as it is," I used to tell them, "why not take poultry, eggs, vegetables, game, hay and straw, and so forth?" All my counsels were a source of fortune; it was a question of who should follow them first. A number of little businesses were started; they went on at first but slowly, but from day to day their progress became more rapid; and now sixty carts full of the various products of the district set out every Monday for Grenoble, and there is more buckwheat grown for poultry food than they used to sow for human consumption. The trade in timber grew to be so considerable that it was subdivided, and since the fourth year of our industrial era, we have had dealers in firewood, squared timber, planks, bark, and later on, in charcoal. In the end four new saw-mills were set up, to turn out the planks and beams of timber.

'When the ex-mayor had acquired a few business notions, he felt the necessity of learning to read and write. He compared the prices that were asked for wood in various neighbourhoods, and found such differences in his favour, that he secured new customers in one place after another, and now a third of the trade in the department passes through his hands. There has been such a sudden increase in our traffic that we find constant work for three wagon-builders and two harness-makers, each of them employing three hands at least. Lastly, the quantity of ironware that we use is so large that an agricultural implement and tool maker has removed into the town, and is very well satisfied with the result.

'The desire of gain develops a spirit of ambition, which has ever since impelled our workers to extend their field from the township to the canton, and from the canton to the department, so as to increase their profits by increasing their sales. I had only to say a word to point out new openings to them, and their own sense did the rest. Four years had been sufficient to change the face of the township. When I had come through it first, I did not catch the slightest sound; but in less than five years from that time, there was life and bustle everywhere. The gay songs, the shrill or murmuring sounds made by the tools in the workshops rang pleasantly in my ears. I watched the comings and goings of a busy population congregated in the clean and wholesome new town, where plenty of trees had been planted. Every one of them seemed conscious of a happy lot, every face shone with the content that comes through a life of useful toil.

'I look upon these five years as the first epoch of prosperity in the history of our town,' the doctor went on after a pause. 'During that time I had prepared the ground and sowed the seed in men's minds as well as in the land. Henceforward industrial progress could not be stayed, the population was bound to go forward. A second epoch was about to begin. This little world very soon desired to be better clad. A shoemaker came, and with him a haberdasher, a tailor, and a hatter. This dawn of luxury brought us a butcher and a grocer and a midwife, who became very necessary to me, for I lost a great deal of time over maternity cases. The stubbed wastes yielded excellent harvests, and the superior quality of our agricultural produce was maintained through the increased supply of manure. My enterprise could now develop itself; everything followed on quite naturally.

'When the houses had been rendered wholesome, and their inmates gradually persuaded to feed and clothe themselves better, I wanted the dumb animals to feel the benefit of these beginnings of civilization. All the excellence of cattle, whether as a race or as individuals, and, in consequence, the quality of the milk and meat, depends upon the care that is expended upon them. I took the sanitation of cowsheds for the text of my sermons. I showed them how an animal that is properly housed and well cared for is more profitable than a lean neglected beast, and the comparison wrought a gradual change for the better in the lot of the cattle in the commune. Not one of them was ill treated. The cows and oxen were rubbed down as in Switzerland and Auvergne. Sheepfolds, stables, byres, dairies, and barns were rebuilt after the pattern of the roomy, well-ventilated, and consequently healthy steadings that M. Gravier and I had constructed. Our tenants became my apostles. They made rapid converts of unbelievers, demonstrating the soundness of my doctrines by their prompt results. I lent money to those who needed it, giving the preference to hardworking poor people, because they served as an example. Any unsound or sickly cattle or beasts of poor quality were quickly disposed of by my advice, and replaced by fine specimens. In this way our dairy produce came, in time, to command higher prices in the market than that sent by other communes. We had splendid herds, and as a consequence, capital leather.

'This step forward was of great importance, and in this wise. In rural economy nothing can be regarded as trifling. Our hides used to fetch scarcely anything, and the leather we made was of little value, but when once our leather and hides were improved, tanneries were easily established along the waterside. We became tanners, and business rapidly increased.

'Wine, properly speaking, had been hitherto unknown; a thin, sour beverage like verjuice had been their only drink, but now wineshops were established to supply a natural demand. The oldest tavern was enlarged and transformed into an inn, which furnished mules to pilgrims to the Grande Chartreuse who began to come our way, and after two years there was enough business for two innkeepers.

'The justice of the peace died just as our second prosperous epoch began, and luckily for us, his successor had formerly been a notary in Grenoble who had lost most of his fortune by a bad speculation, though enough of it yet remained to cause him to be looked upon in the village as a wealthy man. It was M. Gravier who induced him to settle among us. He built himself a comfortable house and helped me by uniting his efforts to mine. He also laid out a farm, and broke up and cleaned some of the waste land, and at this moment he has three chalets up above on the mountain-side. He has a large family. He dismissed the old registrar and the clerk, and in their place installed better-educated men, who worked far harder, moreover, than their predecessors had done. One of the heads of these two new households started a distillery of potato-spirit, and the other was a woolwasher; each combined these occupations with their official work, and in this way two valuable industries were created among us.

'Now that the commune had some revenues of its own, no opposition was raised in any quarter when they were spent on building a town hall, with a free school for elementary education in the building and accommodation for a teacher. For this important post I had selected a poor priest who had taken the oath, and had therefore been cast out by the department, and who at last found a refuge among us for his old age. The schoolmistress is a very worthy woman who had lost all that she had, and was in great distress. We made up a nice little sum for her, and she has just opened a boarding-school for girls to which the wealthy farmers hereabouts are beginning to send their daughters.

'If so far, sir, I have been entitled to tell you the story of my own doings as the chronicle of this little spot of earth, I have reached the point when M. Janvier, the new parson, began to divide the work of regeneration with me. He has been a second Fénelon, unknown beyond the narrow limits of a country parish, and by some secret of his own has infused a spirit of brotherliness and of charity among these folk that has made them almost like one large family. M. Dufau, the justice of the peace, was a later comer, but he in an equal degree deserves the gratitude of the people here.

'I will put the whole position before you in figures that will make it clearer than any words of mine. At this moment the commune owns two hundred acres of woodland, and a hundred and sixty acres of meadow. Without running up the rates, we give a hundred crowns to supplement the curé's stipend, we pay two hundred francs to the rural policeman, and as much again to the schoolmaster and schoolmistress. The maintenance of the roads costs us five hundred francs, while necessary repairs to the town hall, the parsonage, and the church, with some few other expenses, also amount to a similar sum. In fifteen years' time there will be a thousand francs' worth of wood to fell for every hundred francs' worth cut now, and the taxes will not cost the inhabitants a penny. This commune is bound to become one of the richest in France. But perhaps I am taxing your patience, sir?' said Benassis, suddenly discovering that his companion wore such a pensive expression that it seemed as though his attention was wandering.

'No! no!' answered the commandant.

'Our trade, handicrafts, and agriculture so far only supplied the needs of the district,' the doctor went on. 'At a certain point our prosperity came to a standstill. I wanted a post office, and sellers of tobacco, stationery, powder and shot. The receiver of taxes had hitherto preferred to live elsewhere, but now I succeeded in persuading him to take up his abode in the town, holding out as inducements the pleasantness of the place and of the new society. As time and place permitted I had succeeded in producing a supply of everything for which I had first created a need, in attracting families of hardworking people into the district, and in implanting a desire to own land in them all. So by degrees, as they saved a little money, the waste land began to be broken up; spade husbandry and small holdings increased; so did the value of property on the mountain.

'Those struggling folk who, when I knew them first, used to walk over to Grenoble carrying their few cheeses for sale, now made the journey comfortably in a cart, and took fruit, eggs, chickens, and turkeys, and before they were aware of it, everyone was a little richer. Even those who came off worst had a garden at any rate, and grew early vegetables and fruit. It became the children's work to watch the cattle in the fields, and at last it was found to be a waste of time to bake bread at home. Here were signs of prosperity!

'But if this place was to be a permanent forge of industry, fuel must be constantly added to the fire. The town had not as yet a renascent industry which could maintain this commercial process, an industry which should make great transactions, a warehouse, and a market necessary. It is not enough that a country should lose none of the money that forms its capital; you will not increase its prosperity by more or less ingenious devices for causing this amount to circulate, by means of production and consumption, through the greatest possible number of hands. That is not where your problem lies. When a country is fully developed and its production keeps pace with its consumption, if private wealth is to increase as well as the wealth of the community at large, there must be exchanges with other communities, which will keep a balance on the right side of the balance sheet. This thought has led states with a limited territorial basis like Tyre, Carthage, Venice, Holland, and England, for instance, to secure the carrying trade. I cast about for some such notion as this to apply to our little world, so as to inaugurate a third commercial epoch. Our town is so much like any other, that our prosperity was scarcely visible to a passing stranger; it was only for me that it was astonishing. The folk had come together by degrees; they themselves were a part of the change, and could not judge of its effects as a whole.

'Seven years had gone by when I met with two strangers, the real benefactors of the place, which perhaps some day they will transform into a large town. One of them is a Tyrolese, an exceedingly clever fellow, who makes rough shoes for country people's wear, and boots for people of fashion in Grenoble as no one can make them, not even in Paris itself. He was a poor strolling musician, who, singing and working, had made his way through Italy; one of those busy Germans who fashion the tools for their own work, and make the instrument that they play upon. When he came to the town he asked if anyone wanted a pair of shoes. They sent him to me, and I gave him an order for two pairs of boots, for which he made his own lasts. The foreigner's skill surprised me. He gave accurate and consistent answers to the questions I put, and his face and manner confirmed the good opinion I had formed of him. I suggested that he should settle in the place, undertaking to assist him in business in every way that I could; in fact, I put a fairly large sum of money at his disposal. He accepted my offer. I had my own ideas in this. The quality of our leather had improved; and why should we not use it ourselves, and before very long make our own shoes at moderate prices?

'It was the basket-maker's business over again on a larger scale. Chance had put an exceedingly clever hard-working man in my way, and he must be retained so that a steady and profitable trade might be given to the place. There is a constant demand for footgear, and a very slight difference in price is felt at once by the purchaser.

'This was my reasoning, sir, and fortunately events have justified it. At this time we have five tanyards, each of which has its bark-mill. They take all the hides produced in the department itself, and even draw part of their supply from Provence; and yet the Tyrolese uses more leather than they can produce, and has forty work-people in his employ!

'I happened on the other man after a fashion no whit less strange, but you might find the story tedious. He is just an ordinary peasant, who discovered a cheaper way of making the great broad-brimmed hats that are worn in this part of the world. He sells them in other cantons, and even sends them into Switzerland and Savoy. So long as the quality and the low prices can be maintained, here are two inexhaustible sources of wealth for the canton, which suggested to my mind the idea of establishing three fairs in the year. The prefect, amazed at our industrial progress, lent his aid in obtaining the royal ordinance which authorized them, and last year we held our three fairs. They are known as far as Savoy as the Shoe Fair and the Hat Fair.

'The head clerk of a notary in Grenoble heard of these changes. He was poor, but he is a well-educated, hard-working young fellow, and Mlle Gravier was engaged to be married to him. He went to Paris to ask for an authorization to establish himself here as a notary, and his request was granted. As he had not had to pay for his appointment, he could afford to build a house in the market square of the new town, opposite the house of the justice of the peace. We have a market once a week, and a considerable amount of business is transacted in corn and cattle.

'Next year a druggist surely ought to come among us, and next we want a clockmaker, a furniture dealer, and a bookseller; and so, by degrees, we shall have all the desirable luxuries of life. Who knows but that at last we shall have a number of substantial houses, and give ourselves all the airs of a small city? Education has made such strides that there has never been any opposition made at the council-board when I proposed that we should restore our church and build a parsonage; nor when I brought forward a plan for laying out a fine open space, planted with trees, where the fairs could be held, and a further scheme for a survey of the township, so that its future streets should be wholesome, spacious, and wisely planned.

'This is how we came to have nineteen hundred hearths in the place of a hundred and thirty-seven; three thousand head of cattle instead of eight hundred; and for a population of seven hundred, no less than two thousand persons are living in the township, or three thousand, if the people down the valley are included. There are twelve houses belonging to wealthy people in the commune, there are a hundred well-to-do families, and two hundred more which are thriving. The rest have their own exertions to look to.

Everyone knows how to read and write, and we subscribe to seventeen different newspapers.

'We have poor people still among us—there are far too many of them, in fact; but we have no beggars, and there is work enough for all. I have so many patients that my daily round taxes the powers of two horses. I can go anywhere for five miles round at any hour without fear; for if anyone was minded to fire a shot at me, his life would not be worth ten minutes' purchase. The undemonstrative affection of the people is my sole gain from all these changes, except the radiant "Good day, M. Benassis," that everyone gives me as I pass. You will understand, of course, that the wealth incidentally acquired through my model farms has only been a means and not an end.'

'If everyone followed your example in other places, sir, France would be great indeed, and might laugh at the rest of Europe!' cried Genestas enthusiastically.

'But I have kept you out here for half an hour,' said Benassis; 'it is growing dark, let us go in to dinner.'

The doctor's house, on the side facing the garden, consists of a ground floor and a single storey, with a row of five windows in each; dormer windows also project from the tiled mansard-roof. The green-painted shutters are in startling contrast with the grey tones of the walls. A vine wanders along the whole side of the house, a pleasant strip of green like a frieze, between the two storeys. A few struggling Bengal roses make shift to live as best they may, half drowned at times by the drippings from the gutterless eaves.

As you enter the large vestibule, the *salon* lies to your right; it contains four windows, two of which look into the yard, and two into the garden. Ceiling and wainscot are panelled, and the walls are hung with seventeenth-century tapestry—pathetic evidence that the room had

been the object of the late owner's aspiration, and that
he had lavished all that he could spare upon it. The
great roomy arm-chairs, covered with brocaded damask;
the old-fashioned, gilded candle-sconces above the chimney
piece, and the window curtains with their heavy tassels,
showed that the curé had been a wealthy man. Benassis
had made some additions to this furniture, which was not
without a character of its own. He had placed two
smaller tables, decorated with carved wooden garlands,
between the windows on opposite sides of the room, and
had put a clock, in a case of tortoise-shell, inlaid with
copper, upon the mantel-shelf. The doctor seldom
occupied the *salon*; its atmosphere was damp and close,
like that of a room that is always kept shut. Memories
of the dead curé still lingered about it; the peculiar scent
of his tobacco seemed to pervade the corner by the hearth
where he had been wont to sit. The two great easy-
chairs were symmetrically arranged on either side of the
fire, which had not been lighted since the time of M.
Gravier's visit; the bright flames from the pine logs lighted
the room.

'The evenings are chilly even now,' said Benassis; 'it
is pleasant to see a fire.'

Genestas was meditating. He was beginning to understand the doctor's indifference to his everyday surroundings.

'It is surprising to me, sir, that you, who possess real
public spirit, should have made no effort to enlighten the
government, after accomplishing so much.'

Benassis began to laugh, but without bitterness; he
said, rather sadly:

'You mean that I should draw up some sort of memorial
on various ways of civilizing France? You are not the
first to suggest it, sir; M. Gravier has forestalled you.
Unluckily, governments cannot be enlightened, and a
government which regards itself as a diffuser of light is the

least open to enlightenment. What we have done for our canton, every mayor ought, of course, to do for his; the magistrate should work for his town, the sub-prefect for his district, the prefect for the department, and the minister for France, each acting in his own sphere of interest. For the few miles of country road that I persuaded our people to make, another would succeed in constructing a canal or a highway; and for my encouragement of the peasants' trade in hats, a minister would emancipate France from the industrial yoke of the foreigner by encouraging the manufacture of clocks in different places, by helping to bring to perfection our iron and steel, our tools and appliances, or by bringing silk or dyer's woad into cultivation.

'In commerce, "encouragement" does not mean protection. A really wise policy should aim at making a country independent of foreign supply, but this should be effected without resorting to the pitiful shifts of customs duties and prohibitions. Industries must work out their own salvation, competition is the life of trade. A protected industry goes to sleep, and monopoly, like the protective tariff, kills it outright. The country upon which all others depend for their supplies will be the land which will promulgate free trade, for it will be conscious of its power to produce its manufactures at prices lower than those of any of its competitors. France is in a better position to attain this end than England, for France alone possesses an amount of territory sufficiently extensive to maintain a supply of agricultural produce at prices that will enable the worker to live on low wages; the Administration should keep this end in view, for therein lies the whole modern question. I have not devoted my life to this study, dear sir; I found my work by accident, and late in the day. Such simple things as these are too slight, moreover, to build into a system; there is nothing wonderful about them, they do not lend themselves to theories; it is their misfortune to be merely practically useful. And then work cannot be done quickly. The man who means to succeed in these ways must daily look to find within himself the stock of courage needed for the day, a courage in reality of the rarest kind, though it does not seem hard to practise, and meets with little recognition—the courage of the schoolmaster, who must say the same things over and over again. We all honour the man who has shed his blood on the battle-field, as you have done; but we ridicule this other whose life-fire is slowly consumed in repeating the same words to children of the same age. There is no attraction for any of us in obscure well-doing. We know nothing of the civic virtue that led the great men of ancient times to serve their country in the lowest rank whenever they did not command. Our age is afflicted with a disease that makes each of us seek to rise above his fellows, and there are more saints than shrines among us.

'This is how it has come to pass. The monarchy fell, and we lost Honour, Christian Virtue faded with the religion of our forefathers, and our own ineffectual attempts at government have destroyed patriotism. Ideas can never utterly perish, so these beliefs linger on in our midst, but they do not influence the great mass of the people, and Society has no support but Egoism. Every individual believes in himself. For us the future means egoism; further than that we cannot see. The great man who shall save us from the shipwreck which is imminent will no doubt avail himself of individualism when he makes a nation of us once more; but until this regeneration comes, we bide our time in a materialistic and utilitarian age. Utilitarianism—to this conclusion have we come. We are all rated, not at our just worth, but according to our social importance. People will scarcely look at an energetic man if he is in shirt sleeves. The Government itself is pervaded by this idea. A minister sends a paltry medal to a sailor who has saved a dozen lives at the risk of his own, while the deputy who sells his vote to those in power receives the Cross of the Legion of Honour.

'Woe to a people made up of such men as these! For nations, like men, owe all the strength and vitality that is in them to noble thoughts and aspirations, and men's feelings shape their faith. But when self-interest has taken the place of faith, and each one of us thinks only of himself, and believes in himself alone, how can you expect to find among us much of that civil courage whose very essence consists in self-renunciation? The same principle underlies both military and civil courage, although you soldiers are called upon to yield your lives up once and for all, while ours are given slowly drop by drop, and the battle is the same for both, although it takes different forms.

'The man who would fain civilize the lowliest spot on earth needs something besides wealth for the task. Knowledge is still more necessary; and knowledge, and patriotism, and integrity are worthless unless they are accompanied by a firm determination on his part to set his own personal interests completely aside, and to devote himself to a social idea. France, no doubt, possesses more than one well-educated man and more than one patriot in every commune; but I am fully persuaded that not every canton can produce a man who to these valuable qualifications unites the unflagging will and pertinacity with which a blacksmith hammers out iron.

'The Destroyer and the Builder are two manifestations of Will: the one prepares the way, and the other accomplishes the work; the first appears in the guise of a spirit of evil, and the second seems like the spirit of good. Glory falls to the Destroyer, while the Builder is forgotten; for evil makes a noise in the world that rouses little souls to admiration, while good deeds are slow to make themselves heard. Self-love leads us to prefer the more conspicuous part. If it should happen that any public work is undertaken without an interested motive it will only be by accident, until the day when education has changed our ways of regarding things in France.

'Yet suppose that this change had come to pass, and that all of us were public-spirited citizens; in spite of our comfortable lives among trivialities, should we not be in a fair way to become the most wearied, wearisome, and unfortunate race of philistines under the sun?

'I am not at the helm of State, the decision of great questions of this kind is not within my province; but, setting these considerations aside, there are other difficulties in the way of laying down hard and fast rules as to government. In the matter of civilization, everything is relative. Ideas that suit one country admirably are fatal in another—men's minds are as various as the soils of the globe. If we have so often been ill governed, it is because a faculty for government, like taste, is the outcome of a very rare and lofty attitude of mind. The qualifications for the work are found in a natural bent of the soul rather than in the possession of scientific formulae. No one need fear, however, to call himself a statesman, for his actions and motives cannot be justly estimated; his real judges are far away, and the results of his deeds are even more remote. We have a great respect here in France for men of ideas—a keen intellect exerts a great attraction for us; but ideas are of little value where a resolute will is the one thing needful. Administration, as a matter of fact, does not consist in forcing more or less wise methods and ideas upon the great mass of the nation, but in giving to the ideas, good or bad, that they already possess a practical turn which will make them conduce to the general welfare of the State. If old-established prejudices and customs bring a country into a bad way, the people will renounce their errors of their own accord. Are not losses the result of economical errors of every kind? And is it not, therefore, to everyone's interest to rectify them in the long run?

'Luckily I found a *tabula rasa* in this district. They have followed my advice, and the land is well cultivated; but there had been no previous errors in agriculture, and the soil was good to begin with, so that it has been easy to introduce the five-ply shift, artificial grasses, and potatoes. My methods did not clash with people's prejudices. The faultily constructed ploughshares in use in some parts of France were unknown here, the hoe sufficed for the little field work that they did. Our wheelwright extolled my wheeled ploughs because he wished to increase his own business, so I secured an ally in him; but in this matter, as in all others, I sought to make the good of one conduce to the good of all.

'Then I turned my attention to another kind of production, that should increase the welfare rather than the wealth of these poor folk. I have brought nothing from without into this district; I have simply encouraged the people to seek beyond its limits for a market for their produce, a measure that could not but increase their prosperity in a way that they felt immediately. They had no idea of the fact, but they themselves were my apostles, and their works preached my doctrines. Something else must also be borne in mind. We are barely five leagues from Grenoble. There is plenty of demand in a large city for produce of all kinds, but not every commune is situated at the gates of a city. In every similar undertaking the nature, situation, and resources of the country must be taken into consideration, and a careful study must be made of the soil, of the people themselves, and of many other things; and no one should expect to have vines grow in Normandy. So no tasks can be more various than those of government, and its general principles must be few in number. The law is uniform, but not so the land and the minds and customs

of those who dwell in it; and the administration of the law
is the art of carrying it out in such a manner that no
injury is done to people's interests. Every place must
be considered separately.

'On the other side of the mountain at the foot of which
our deserted village lies, they find it impossible to use
wheeled ploughs, because the soil is not deep enough.
Now if the mayor of the commune were to take it into
his head to follow in our footsteps, he would be the ruin
of his neighbourhood. I advised him to plant vineyards;
they had a capital vintage last year in the little district,
and their wine is exchanged for our corn.

'Then, lastly, it must be remembered that my words
carried a certain weight with the people to whom I preached
and that we were continually brought into close contact.
I cured my peasants' complaints; an easy task, for a nourish-
ing diet is, as a rule, all that is needed to restore them to
health and strength. Either through thrift, or through
sheer poverty, the country people starve themselves; any
illness among them is caused in this way, and as a rule
they enjoy very fair health.

'When I first decided to devote myself to this life of
obscure renunciation, I was in doubt for a long while
whether to become a curé, a country doctor, or a justice
of the peace. It is not without reason that people speak
collectively of the priest, the lawyer, and the doctor as
"men of the black robe"—so the saying goes. The first
heals the wounds of the soul, the second those of the purse,
and the third those of the body. They represent the
three principal elements necessary to the existence of
society—conscience, property, and health. At one time
the first, and at a later period the second was all-impor-
tant in the State. Our predecessors on this earth thought,
perhaps not without reason, that the priest, who prescribed what men should think, ought to be paramount;
so the priest was king, pontiff, and judge in one, for in

those days belief and faith were everything. All this has been changed in our day; and we must even take our epoch as we find it. But I, for one, believe that the progress of civilization and the welfare of the people depend on these three men. They are the three powers who bring home to the people's minds the ways in which facts, interests, and principles affect them. They themselves are three great results produced in the midst of the nation by the operation of events, by the ownership of property, and by the growth of ideas. Time goes on and brings changes to pass, property increases or diminishes in men's hands, all the various readjustments have to be duly regulated, and in this way principles of social order are established. If civilization is to spread itself, and production is to be increased, the people must be made to understand the way in which the interests of the individual harmonize with national interests which resolve themselves into facts, interests, and principles. As these three professions are bound to deal with these issues of human life, it seemed to me that they must be the most powerful civilizing agencies of our time. They alone afford to a man of wealth the opportunity of mitigating the fate of the poor, with whom they daily bring him in contact.

'The peasant is always more willing to listen to the man who lays down rules for saving him from bodily ills than to the priest who exhorts him to save his soul. The first speaker can talk of this earth, the scene of the peasant's labours, while the priest is bound to talk to him of heaven, with which, unfortunately, the peasant nowadays concerns himself very little indeed; I say unfortunately, because the doctrine of a future life is not only a consolation, but a means by which men may be governed. Is not religion the one power that sanctions social laws? We have but lately vindicated the existence of God. In the absence of a religion, the Government was driven to invent the

Terror, in order to carry its laws into effect; but the terror was the fear of man, and it has passed away.

'When a peasant is ill, when he is forced to lie on his pallet, and while he is recovering, he cannot help himself, he is forced to listen to logical reasoning, which he can understand quite well if it is put clearly before him. This thought made a doctor of me. My calculations for the peasants were made along with them. I never gave advice unless I was quite sure of the results, and in this way compelled them to admit the wisdom of my views. The people require infallibility. Infallibility was the making of Napoleon; he would have been a god if he had not filled the world with the sound of his fall at Waterloo. If Mahomet founded a permanent religion after conquering the third part of the globe, it was by dint of concealing his deathbed from the crowd. The same rules hold good for the great conqueror and for the provincial mayor, and a nation or a commune is much the same sort of crowd; indeed, the great multitude of mankind is the same everywhere.

'I have been exceedingly firm with those whom I have helped with money; if I had not been inflexible on this point they all would have laughed at me. Peasants, no less than worldlings, end by despising the man that they can deceive. He has been cheated? Clearly, then, he must have been weak; and it is might alone that governs the world. I have never charged a penny for my professional advice, except to those who were evidently rich people; but I have not allowed the value of my services to be overlooked at all, and I always make them pay for medicine unless the patient is exceedingly poor. If my peasants do not pay me in money, they are quite aware that they are in my debt; sometimes they satisfy their consciences by bringing oats for my horses, or corn, when it is cheap. But if the miller were to send me some eels as a return for my advice, I should tell him that he is too generous for such a small matter. My politeness bears fruit. In the winter I shall have some sacks of flour for the poor. Ah! sir, they have kind hearts, these people, if one does not slight them, and to-day I think more good and less evil of them than I did formerly.'

'What a deal of trouble you have taken!' said Genestas.

'Not at all,' answered Benassis. 'It was no more trouble to say something useful than to chatter about trifles; and whether I chatted or joked, the talk always turned on them and their concerns wherever I went. They would not listen to me at first. I had to overcome their dislikes; I belonged to the middle classes—that is to say, I was a natural enemy. I found the struggle amusing. An easy or an uneasy conscience—that is all the difference that lies between doing well or ill; the trouble is the same in either case. If scoundrels would but behave themselves properly, they might be million-aires instead of being hanged. That is all.'

'The dinner is growing cold, sir!' cried Jacquotte, in the doorway.

Genestas caught the doctor's arm.

'I have only one comment to offer on what I have just heard,' he remarked. 'I am not acquainted with any account of the wars of Mahomet, so that I can form no opinions as to his military talents; but if you had only watched the emperor's tactics during the campaign in France, you might well have taken him for a god; and if he was beaten on the field of Waterloo, it was because he was more than mortal, it was because the earth found his weight too heavy to bear, and sprang from under his feet! On every other subject I entirely agree with you; no question about it, whoever hatched you did a good day's work.'

'Come,' exclaimed Benassis with a smile, 'let us sit down to dinner.'

The walls of the dining-room were panelled from floor

to ceiling, and painted grey. The furniture consisted of a few straw-bottomed chairs, a sideboard, some cupboards, a stove, and the late owner's celebrated clock; there were white curtains in the window, and a white cloth on the table, about which there was no sign of luxury. The dinner service was of plain white earthenware; the soup, made after the traditions of the late curé, was the most concentrated kind of broth that was ever set to simmer by any mortal cook. The doctor and his guest had scarcely finished it when a man rushed into the kitchen, and in spite of Jacquotte, suddenly invaded the dining-room.

'Well, what is it?' asked the doctor.

'It is this, sir. The mistress, our Mme Vigneau, has turned as white as white can be, so that we are frightened about her.'

'Oh, well, then,' Benassis said cheerfully, 'I must leave the table,' and he rose to go.

In spite of the doctor's entreaties, Genestas flung down his table-napkin, and swore in soldierly fashion that he would not finish his dinner without his host. He returned indeed to the *salon*; and as he warmed himself by the fire, he thought over the troubles that no man may escape, the troubles that are found in every lot that it falls to man to endure here upon earth.

Benassis soon came back, and the two future friends sat down again.

'Taboureau has just come up to speak to you,' said Jacquotte to her master, as she brought in the dishes that she had kept hot for them.

'Who can be ill at his place?' asked the doctor.

'No one is ill, sir. I think from what he said that it is some matter of his own that he wants to ask you about; he is coming back again.'

'Very good. This Taboureau,' Benassis went on, addressing Genestas, 'is for me a whole philosophical treatise; take a good look at him when he comes, he is sure to amuse you. He was a labourer, a thrifty hard-working man, eating little and getting through a great deal of work. As soon as the rogue came to have a few crowns of his own, his intelligence began to develop; he watched the progress which I had originated in this little district with an eye to his own profit. He has made quite a fortune in eight years' time, that is to say, a fortune for our part of the world. Very likely he may have a couple of score thousand francs by now. But if I were to give you a thousand guesses you would never find out how he made the money. He is a usurer, and his scheme of usury is so profoundly and so cleverly based upon the requirements of the whole canton, that I should merely waste my time if I were to take it upon myself to undeceive them as to the benefits which they reap, in their own opinion, from their dealings with Taboureau. When this devil of a fellow saw everyone cultivating his own plot of ground, he hurried about buying grain so as to supply the poor with the requisite seed. Here, as everywhere else, the peasants and even some of the farmers had no ready money with which to pay for seed. To some, Master Taboureau would lend a sack of barley, for which he was to receive a sack of rye at harvest time, and to others a measure of wheat for a sack of flour. At the present day the man has extended this curious business of his all over the department; and unless something happens to prevent him, he will go on and very likely make a million. Well, my dear sir, Taboureau the labourer, an obliging, hard-working, good-natured fellow, used to lend a helping hand to any-one who asked him; but as his gains have increased *Monsieur* Taboureau has become litigious, arrogant, and somewhat given to sharp practice. The more money he makes, the worse he grows. The moment that the peasant forsakes his life of toil pure and simple for the leisured existence of the landowning classes, he becomes intolerable. There is a certain kind of character, partly virtuous, partly vicious, half educated, half ignorant, which will always be the despair of governments. You will see an example of it in Taboureau. He looks simple, and even doltish; but when his interests are in question, he is certainly profoundly clever.'

A heavy footstep announced the approach of the grain lender.

'Come in, Taboureau!' cried Benassis.

Thus forewarned by the doctor, the commandant scrutinized the peasant in the doorway. Taboureau was decidedly thin, and stooped a little. He had a bulging forehead covered with wrinkles, and a cavernous face in which two small grey eyes with a dark spot in either of them seemed to be pierced rather than set. The lines of the miser's mouth were close and firm, and his narrow chin turned up to meet an exaggeratedly hooked nose. His hair was turning grey already, and deep furrows which converged above the prominent cheek-bones spoke of the wily shrewdness of a horse-dealer and of a life spent in journeying about. He wore a blue coat in fairly clean condition, the square side-pocket flaps stuck out above his hips, and the skirts of the coat hung loose in front, so that a white-flowered waistcoat was visible. There he stood firmly planted on both feet, leaning upon a thick stick with a knob at the end of it. A little spaniel had followed the grain-dealer, in spite of Jacquotte's efforts, and was crouching beside him.

'Well, what is it?' Benassis asked as he turned to this being.

Taboureau gave a suspicious glance at the stranger seated at the doctor's table, and said:

'It is not a case of illness, Mr Mayor, but you understand how to doctor the ailments of the purse just as well as those of the body. We have had a little difficulty with a man over at Saint-Laurent, and I have come to ask your advice about it.'

'Why not see the justice of the peace or his clerk?'

'Oh, because you are so much cleverer, sir, and I shall feel more sure about my case if I can have your countenance.'

'My good Taboureau, I am willing to give medical advice to the poor without charging for it; but I cannot look into the lawsuits of a man who is as wealthy as you are for nothing. It costs a good deal to acquire that kind of knowledge.'

Taboureau began to twist his hat about.

'If you want my advice, in order to save the hard coin you would have to pay to the lawyer folk over in Grenoble, you must send a bag of rye to the widow Martin, the woman who is bringing up the charity children.'

Why, yes, I will do it with all my heart, sir, if you think it necessary. Can I talk about this business of mine without troubling the gentleman there?' he added, with a look at Genestas.

The doctor nodded, so Taboureau went on.

'Well, then, sir, two months ago a man from Saint-Laurent came over here to find me. "Taboureau," said he to me, "could you sell me a hundred and thirty-seven measures of barley?" "Why not?" says I, "that is my trade. Do you want it immediately?" "No," he says, "I want it for the beginning of spring, in March." So far, so good. Well, we drive our bargain, and we drink a glass, and we agree that he is to pay me the price that barley fetched at Grenoble last market day, and I am to deliver it in March. I am to warehouse it at owner's risk, and no allowance for shrinkage of course. But barley goes up and up, my dear sir; the barley rises like boiling milk. Then I am hard up for money, and I sell my barley. Quite natural, sir, was it not?'

'No,' said Benassis, 'the barley had passed out of

your ownership, you were only warehousing it. And suppose the barley had gone down in value, would you not have compelled your buyer to take it at the price you agreed upon?'

'But very likely he would not have paid me, sir. One must look out for oneself! The seller ought to make a profit when the chance comes in his way; and, after all, the goods are not yours until you have paid for them. That is so, Captain, is it not? For you can see that the gentleman has been in the army.'

'Taboureau,' Benassis said sternly, 'ill luck will come to you. Sooner or later God punishes ill deeds. How can you, knowing as much as you do, a capable man moreover, and a man who conducts his business honourably, set examples of dishonesty to the canton? If you allow such proceedings as this to be taken against you, how can you expect that the poor will remain honest people and will not rob you? Your labourers will cheat you out of part of their working hours, and everyone here will be demoralized. You are in the wrong. Your barley was as good as delivered. If the man from Saint-Laurent had fetched it himself, you would not have gone there to take it away from him; you have sold something that was no longer yours to sell, for your barley had already been turned into money which was to be paid down at the stipulated time. But go on.'

Genestas gave the doctor a significant glance, to call his attention to Taboureau's impassive countenance. Not a muscle had stirred in the usurer's face during this reprimand; there was no flush on his forehead, and no sign of emotion in his little eyes.

'Well, sir, I am called upon to supply the barley at last winter's price. Now *I* consider that I am not bound to do so.'

'Look here, Taboureau, deliver that barley and be very quick about it, or make up your mind to be respected by nobody in future. Even if you gained the day in a case like this, you would be looked upon as an unscrupulous man who does not keep to his word, and is not bound by promises, or by honour, or——'

'Go on, there is nothing to be afraid of; tell me that I am a scamp, a scoundrel, a thief outright. You can say things like that in business without insulting anybody, M. le Maire. 'Tis each for himself in business, you know.'

'Well, then, why deliberately put yourself in a position in which you deserve to be called by such names?'

'But if the law is on my side, sir?'

'But the law will certainly *not* be on your side.'

'Are you quite sure about it, sir? Certain sure? For you see it is an important matter.'

'Certainly I am. Quite sure. If I were not at dinner I would have down the Code, and you should see for yourself. If the case comes on, you will lose it, and you will never set foot in my house again, for I do not wish to receive people whom I do not respect. Do you understand? You will lose your case.'

'Oh! no, not at all, I shall not lose it, sir,' said Taboureau. 'You see, sir, it is this way; it is the man from Saint-Laurent who owes *me* the barley; I bought it of him, and now he refuses to deliver it. I just wanted to make quite certain that I should gain my case before going to any expense at the court about it.'

Genestas and the doctor exchanged glances; each concealed his amazement at the ingenious device by which the man had sought to learn the truth about this point of law.

'Very well, Taboureau, your man is a swindler; you should not make bargains with such people.'

'Ah! sir, they understand business, those people do.'

'Good-bye, Taboureau.'

'Your servant, gentlemen.'

'Well, now,' remarked Benassis, when the usurer had gone, 'if that fellow were in Paris, do you not think that he would be a millionaire before very long?'

After dinner, the doctor and his visitor went back to the *salon*, and all the rest of the evening until bedtime they talked about war and politics; Genestas evincing a most violent dislike of the English in the course of conversation.

'May I know whom I have the honour of entertaining as a guest?' asked the doctor.

'My name is Pierre Bluteau,' answered Genestas; 'I am a captain stationed at Grenoble.'

'Very well, sir. Do you care to adopt M. Gravier's plan? In the morning after breakfast he liked to go on my rounds with me. I am not at all sure that you will find anything to interest you in the things that occupy me—they are so very commonplace. For, after all, you own no land about here, nor are you the mayor of the place, and you will see nothing in the canton that you cannot see elsewhere; one thatched cottage is just like another. Still you will be in the open air, and you will have something to take you out of doors.'

'No proposal could give me more pleasure. I did not venture to make it myself, lest I should thrust myself upon you.'

Commandant Genestas (who shall keep his own name in spite of the fictitious appellation which he had thought fit to give himself) followed his host to a room on the first floor above the *salon*.

'That is right,' said Benassis, 'Jacquotte has lighted a fire for you. If you want anything, there is a bell-pull, close to the head of the bed.'

'I am not likely to want anything, however small, it seems to me,' exclaimed Genestas. 'There is even a boot-jack. Only an old trooper knows what a boot-jack is worth! There are times, when one is out on a campaign,

sir, when one is ready to burn down a house to come
by a knave of a boot-jack. After a few marches, one
on the top of another, or above all, after an engagement, there are times when a swollen foot and the soaked
leather will not part company, pull as you will; I have
had to lie down in my boots more than once. One can
put up with the annoyance so long as one is by oneself.'

The commandant's wink gave a kind of profound
slyness to his last utterance; then he began to make a
survey. Not without surprise, he saw that the room was
neatly kept, comfortable, and almost luxurious.

'What splendour!' was his comment. 'Your own
room must be something wonderful.'

'Come and see,' said the doctor; 'I am your neighbour,
there is nothing but the staircase between us.'

Genestas was again surprised when he entered the
doctor's room, a bare-looking apartment with no adornment on the walls save an old-fashioned wall-paper of a
yellowish tint with a pattern of brown roses over it; the
colour had gone in patches here and there. There was a
roughly painted iron bedstead, two grey cotton curtains
were suspended from a wooden bracket above it, and a
threadbare strip of carpet lay at the foot; it was like a
bed in a hospital. By the bed-head stood a rickety cup-
board on four feet with a door that continually rattled
with a sound like castanets. Three chairs and a couple
of straw-bottomed arm-chairs stood about the room, and
on a low chest of drawers in walnut wood stood a basin,
and a ewer of obsolete pattern with a lid, which was kept in
place by a leaden rim round the top of the vessel. This
completed the list of the furniture.

The grate was empty. All the apparatus required for
shaving lay about in front of an old mirror suspended
above the painted stone chimney-piece by a bit of string.
The floor was clean and carefully swept, but it was worn
and splintered in various places, and there were hollows

in it here and there. Grey cotton curtains bordered with a green fringe adorned the two windows. The scrupulous cleanliness maintained by Jacquotte gave a certain air of distinction to this picture of simplicity, but everything in it, down to the round table littered with stray papers, and the very pens on the writing-desk, gave the idea of an almost monastic life—a life so wholly filled with thought and feeling of a wider kind that outward surroundings had come to be matters of no moment. An open door allowed the commandant to see a smaller room, which doubtless the doctor seldom occupied. It was scarcely kept in the same condition as the adjoining apartment; a few dusty books lay strewn about over the no less dusty shelves, and from the rows of labelled bottles it was easy to guess that the place was devoted rather to the dispensing of drugs than to scientific studies.

'Why this difference between your room and mine, you will ask?' said Benassis. 'Listen a moment. I have always blushed for those who put their guests in the attics, who furnish them with mirrors that distort everything to such a degree that anyone beholding himself might think that he was smaller or larger than nature made him, or suffering from an apoplectic stroke or some other bad complaint. Ought we not to do our utmost to make a room as pleasant as possible during the time that our friend can be with us? Hospitality, to my thinking, is a virtue, a pleasure, and a luxury; but in whatever light it is considered, nay, even if you regard it as a speculation, ought not our guest or our friend to be made much of? Ought not every refinement of luxury to be reserved for him?'

'So the best furniture is put into your room, where a thick carpet is laid down; there are hangings on the walls, and a clock and wax candles; and for you Jacquotte will do her best; she has no doubt brought a night-light, and a pair of new slippers and some milk, and her warming-pan

too for your benefit. I hope that you will find that
luxurious arm-chair the most comfortable seat you have
ever sat in, it was a discovery of the late curé's; I do not
know where he found it, but it is a fact that if you wish to
meet with the perfection of comfort, beauty, or convenience,
you must ask counsel of the Church. Well, I hope that
you will find everything in your room to your liking. You
will find some good razors and excellent soap, and all the
trifling details that make one's own home so pleasant.
And if my views on the subject of hospitality should not
at once explain the difference between your room and
mine, to-morrow, M. Bluteau, you will arrive at a wonderfully clear comprehension of the bareness of my room and
the untidy condition of my study, when you see all the
continual comings and goings here. Mine is not an
indoor life, to begin with. I am almost always out of
the house, and if I stay at home, peasants come in at
every moment to speak to me. My body and soul and
house are all theirs. Why should I worry about social
conventions in these matters, or trouble myself over the
damage unintentionally done to floors and furniture by
these worthy folk? Such things cannot be helped.
Luxury properly belongs to the boudoir and the guest-
chamber, to great houses and châteaux. In short, as
I scarcely do more than sleep here, what do I want with
the superfluities of wealth? You do not know, moreover, how little I care for anything in this world.'

They wished each other a friendly good night with a
warm shake of the hand, and went to bed. But before
the commandant slept, he came to more than one conclusion as to the man who hour by hour grew greater in
his eyes.

A DOCTOR'S ROUND

THE first thing next morning Genestas went to the stable, drawn thither by the affection that every man feels for the horse that he rides. Nicolle's method of rubbing down the animal was quite satisfactory.

'Up already, Commandant Bluteau?' cried Benassis, as he came upon his guest. 'You hear the drum beat in the morning wherever you go, even in the country! You are a regular soldier!'

'Are you all right?' replied Genestas, holding out his hand with a friendly gesture.

'I am never really all right,' answered Benassis, half merrily, half sadly.

'Did you sleep well, sir?' inquired Jacquotte.

'Faith, yes, my beauty; the bed as you made it was fit for a queen.'

Jacquotte's face beamed as she followed her master and his guest, and when she had seen them seat themselves at table, she remarked to Nicolle:

'He is not a bad sort, after all, that officer gentleman.'

'I am sure he is not, he has given me two francs already.'

'We will begin to-day by calling at two places where there have been deaths,' Benassis said to his visitor as they left the dining-room. 'Although doctors seldom deign to confront their supposed victims, I will take you round to the two houses, where you will be able to make some interesting observations of human nature; and the scenes to which you will be a witness will show you that in the expression of their feelings our folk among the hills differ greatly from the dwellers in the lowlands. Up among the mountain peaks in our canton they cling to customs that bear the impress of an older time, and that vaguely recall scenes in the Bible. Nature has traced out a line over our mountain ranges; the whole appearance of the country is different on either side of it. You find strength of character up above, flexibility and quickness of perception below; they have larger ways of regarding things among the hills, while the bent of the lowlands is always towards the material interests of existence. I have never seen a difference so strongly marked, unless it has been in the Val d'Ajou, where the northern side is peopled by a tribe of idiots, and the southern by an intelligent race. There is nothing but a stream in the valley bottom to separate these two populations, which are utterly dissimilar in every respect, as different in face and stature as in manners, customs, and occupation. A fact of this kind should compel those who govern a country to make very extensive studies of local differences before passing laws that are to affect the great mass of the people. But the horses are ready, let us start!'

In a short time the two horsemen reached a house in a part of the township that was overlooked by the mountains of the Grande Chartreuse. Before the door of the dwelling, which was fairly clean and tidy, they saw a coffin, set upon two chairs, and covered with a black pall. Four tall candles stood about it, and on a stool near by there was a shallow brass dish full of holy water, in which a branch of green boxwood was steeping. Every passer-by went into the yard, knelt by the side of the dead, said a paternoster, and sprinkled a few drops of holy water on the bier. Above the black cloth that covered the coffin rose the green sprays of a jessamine that grew beside the doorway, and a twisted vine-shoot, already in leaf, overran the lintel. Even the saddest ceremonies demand that things shall appear to the best advantage, and in obedience to this vaguely felt requirement a young girl had been sweeping the front of the house. The dead man's eldest son, a young peasant about twenty-two years of age, stood motionless, leaning against the door-post. The tears in his eyes came and went without falling, or perhaps he furtively brushed them away. Benassis and Genestas saw all the details of this scene as they stood beyond the low wall; they fastened their horses to one of the row of poplar trees that grew along it, and entered the yard just as the widow came out of the byre. A woman carrying a jug of milk was with her, and spoke.

'Try to bear up bravely, my poor Pelletier,' she said.

'Ah! my dear, after twenty-five years of life together, it is very hard to lose your man,' and her eyes brimmed over with tears. 'Will you pay the two sous?' she added, after a moment, as she held out her hand to her neighbour.

'There, now! I had forgotten about it,' said the other woman, giving her the coin. 'Come, neighbour, don't take on so. Ah! there is M. Benassis!'

'Well, poor mother, how are you going on? A little better?' asked the doctor.

'Well,' she said, as the tears fell fast, 'we must go on, all the same, that is certain. I tell myself that my man is out of pain now. He suffered so terribly! But come inside, sir. Jacques, set some chairs for these gentlemen. Come, stir yourself a bit. Lord bless you! if you were to stop there for a century, it would not bring your poor father back again. And now, you will have to do the work of two.'

'No, no, good woman, leave your son alone, we will not sit down. You have a boy there who will take care of you, and who is quite fit to take his father's place.'

'Go and change your clothes, Jacques,' cried the widow; 'you will be wanted directly.'

'Well, good-bye, mother,' said Benassis.

'Your servant, gentlemen.'

'Here, you see, death is looked upon as an event for which everyone is prepared,' said the doctor, 'it brings no interruption to the course of family life, and they will not even wear mourning of any kind. No one cares to be at the expense of it; they are all either too poor or too parsimonious in the villages hereabouts, so that mourning is unknown in country districts. Yet the custom of wearing mourning is something better than a law or a usage, it is an institution somewhat akin to all moral obligations. But in spite of our endeavours, neither M. Janvier nor I have succeeded in making our peasants understand the great importance of public demonstrations of feeling for the maintenance of social order. These good folk who have only just begun to think and act for themselves are slow as yet to grasp the changed conditions which should attach them to these theories. They have only reached those ideas which conduce to economy and to physical welfare; in the future, if someone else carries on this work of mine, they will come to understand the principles that serve to uphold and preserve public order and justice. As a matter of fact, it is not sufficient to be an honest man, you must appear to be honest in the eyes of others. Society does not live by moral ideas alone; its existence depends upon actions in harmony with those ideas.

'In most country communes, out of a hundred families deprived by death of their head, there are only a few individuals capable of feeling more keenly than the others, who will remember the death for very long; in a year's time the rest will have forgotten all about it. Is not this forgetfulness a sore evil? A religion is the very heart of a nation; it expresses their feelings and their thoughts, and exalts them by giving them an object; but unless outward and visible honour is paid to a God, religion cannot exist; and, as a consequence, human ordinances lose all their force. If the conscience belongs to God and to Him only, the body is amenable to social law. Is it not, therefore, a first step towards atheism to efface every sign of pious sorrow in this way, to neglect to impress on children who are not yet old enough to reflect, and on all other people who stand in need of example, the necessity of obedience to human law, by openly manifested resignation to the will of Providence, who chastens and consoles, who bestows and takes away worldly wealth? I confess that, after passing through a period of sneering incredulity, I have come during my life here to recognize the value of the rites of religion and of religious observances in the family, and to discern the importance of household customs and domestic festivals. The family will always be the basis of human society. Law and authority are first felt there; there, at any rate, the habit of obedience should be learned. Viewed in the light of all their consequences, the spirit of the family and paternal authority are two elements but little developed as yet in our new legislative system. Yet in the family, the commune, the department, lies the whole of our country. The laws ought therefore to be based on these three great divisions.

'In my opinion marriages, the birth of infants, and the deaths of heads of households cannot be surrounded with too much circumstance. The secret of the strength of Catholicism, and of the deep root that it has taken in the ordinary life of man, lies precisely in this—that it steps in to invest every important event in his existence with a pomp that is so naïvely touching, and so grand, whenever the priest rises to the height of his mission and brings his office into harmony with the sublimity of Christian doctrine.

'Once I looked upon the Catholic religion as a cleverly exploited mass of prejudices and superstitions, which an intelligent civilization ought to deal with according to its deserts. Here I have discovered its political necessity and its usefulness as a moral agent; here, moreover, I have come to understand its power, through a knowledge of the actual thing which the word expresses. Religion means a bond or tie, and certainly a cult—or, in other words, the outward and visible form of religion is the only force that can bind the various elements of society together and mould them into a permanent form. Lastly, it is also here that I have felt the soothing influence that religion sheds over the wounds of humanity, and (without going further into the subject) I have seen how admirably it is suited to the fervid temperaments of southern races.

'Let us take the road up the hill-side,' said the doctor, interrupting himself; 'we must reach the plateau up there. Thence we shall look down upon both valleys, and you will see a magnificent view. The plateau lies three thousand feet above the level of the Mediterranean; we shall see over Savoy and Dauphiné, and the mountain ranges of the Lyonnais and Rhône. We shall be in another commune, a hill commune, and on a farm belonging to M. Gravier you will see the kind of scene of which I have spoken. There the great events of life are invested with a solemnity which comes up to my ideas. Mourning for the dead is rigorously prescribed. Poor people will beg in order to purchase black clothing, and no one refuses to give in such a case. There are few days in which the widow does not mention her loss; she always speaks of it with tears, and her grief is as deep after ten days of sorrow as on the morning after her bereavement. Manners are patriarchal: the father's authority is unlimited, his word is law. He takes his meals sitting by himself at the head of the table; his wife and children wait upon him, and those about him never address him without using certain respectful forms of speech, while everyone remains standing and uncovered in his presence. Men brought up in this atmosphere are conscious of their dignity; to my way of thinking, it is a noble education to be brought up among these customs. And, for the most part, they are upright, thrifty, and hard-working people in this commune. The father of every family, when he is old and past work, divides his property equally among his children, and they support him; that is the usual way here. An old man of ninety, in the last century, who had divided everything he had among his four children, went to live with each one in turn for three months in the year. As he left the oldest to go to the home of a younger brother, one of his friends asked him: "Well, are you satisfied with the arrangement?" "Faith! yes," the old man answered: "they have treated me as if I had been their own child." That answer of his seemed so remarkable to an officer then stationed at Grenoble, that he repeated it in more than one Parisian *salon*. That officer was the celebrated moralist Vauvenargues, and in this way the beautiful saying came to the knowledge of another writer named Chamfort. Ah! still more forcible phrases are often struck out among us, but they lack a historian worthy of them.

'I have come across Moravians and Lollards in Bohemia and Hungary,' said Genestas. 'They are a kind of people something like your mountaineers, good folk who endure the sufferings of war with angelic patience.'

'Men living under simple and natural conditions are bound to be almost alike in all countries. Sincerity of life takes but one form. It is true that a country life often extinguishes thought of a wider kind; but evil propensities are weakened and good qualities are developed by it. In fact, the fewer the numbers of the human beings collected together in a place, the less crime, evil thinking, and general bad behaviour will be found in it. A pure atmosphere counts for a good deal in purity of morals.'

The two horsemen, who had been climbing the stony

road at a foot pace, now reached the level space of which
Benassis had spoken. It is a strip of land lying round
about the base of a lofty mountain peak, a bare surface
of rock with no growth of any kind upon it; deep clefts
are riven in its sheer inaccessible sides. The grey crest
of the summit towers above the ledge of fertile soil which
lies around it, a domain sometimes narrower, sometimes
wider, and altogether about a hundred acres in extent.
Here, through a vast break in the line of the hills to the
south, the eye sees French Maureinne, Dauphiné, the
crags of Savoy, and the far-off mountains of the Lyonnais. Genestas was gazing from this point, over a land
that lay far and wide in the spring sunlight, when there
arose the sound of a wailing cry.

'Let us go on,' said Benassis; 'the wail for the dead
has begun, that is the name they give to this part of the
funeral rites.'

On the western slope of the mountain peak, the commandant saw the buildings belonging to a farm of some
size. The whole place formed a perfect square. The
gateway consisted of a granite arch, impressive in its
solidity, which added to the old-world appearance of
the buildings with the ancient trees that stood about
them, and the growth of plant life on the roofs. The
house itself lay at the farther end of the yard. Barns,
sheepfolds, stables, cowsheds, and other buildings lay on
either side, and in the midst was the great pool where the
manure had been laid to rot. On a thriving farm such a
yard as this is usually full of life and movement, but
to-day it was silent and deserted. The poultry were
shut up, the cattle were all in the byres, there was scarcely
a sound of animal life. Both stables and cowsheds had
been carefully locked, and a clean path to the house had
been swept across the yard. The perfect neatness which
reigned in a place where everything as a rule was in dis-
order, the absence of stirring life, the stillness in so noisy

a spot, the calm serenity of the hills, the deep shadow cast by the towering peak—everything combined to make a strong impression on the mind.

Genestas was accustomed to painful scenes, yet he could not help shuddering as he saw a dozen men and women standing weeping outside the door of the great hall. '*The master is dead!*' they wailed; the unison of voices gave appalling effect to the words which they repeated twice during the time required to cross the space between the gateway and the farmhouse door. To this wailing lament succeeded moans from within the house; the sound of a woman's voice came through the casements.

'I dare not intrude upon such grief as this,' said Genestas to Benassis.

'I always go to visit a bereaved family,' the doctor answered, 'either to certify the death, or to see that no mischance caused by grief has befallen the living. You need not hesitate to come with me. The scene is impressive, and there will be such a great many people that no one will notice your presence.'

As Genestas followed the doctor, he found, in fact, that the first room was full of relations of the dead. They passed through the crowd and stationed themselves at the door of a bedroom that opened out of the great hall which served the whole family for a kitchen and a sitting-room; the whole colony, it should rather be called, for the great length of the table showed that some forty people lived in the house. Benassis's arrival interrupted the discourse of a tall, simply dressed woman, with thin locks of hair, who held the dead man's hand in hers in a way that spoke eloquently.

The dead master of the house had been arrayed in his best clothes, and now lay stretched out cold and stiff upon the bed. They had drawn the curtains aside; the thought of heaven seemed to brood over the quiet face and the white hair—it was like the closing scene of a drama. On either side of the bed stood the children and the nearest relations of the husband and wife. These last stood in a line on either side; the wife's kin upon the left, and those of her husband on the right. Both men and women were kneeling in prayer, and almost all of of them in tears. Tall candles stood about the bed. The curé of the parish and his assistants had taken their places in the middle of the room, beside the bier. There was something tragical about the scene, with the head of the family lying before the coffin, which was waiting to be closed down upon him for ever.

'Ah!' cried the widow, turning as she saw Benassis, 'if the skill of the best of men could not save you, my dear lord, it was because it was ordained in heaven that you should precede me to the tomb! Yes, this hand of yours, that used to press mine so kindly, is cold! I have lost my dear helpmate for ever, and our household has lost its beloved head, for truly you were the guide of us all! Alas! there is not one of those who are weeping with me who has not known all the worth of your nature, and felt the light of your soul, but I alone knew all the patience and the kindness of your heart. Oh! my husband, my husband! must I bid you farewell for ever? Farewell to you, our stay and support! Farewell to you, my dear master! And we, your children, for to each of us you gave the same fatherly love, all we, your children, have lost our father!'

The widow flung herself upon the dead body and clasped it in a tight embrace, as if her kisses and the tears with which she covered it could give it warmth again; during the pause came the wail of the servants:

'*The master is dead!*'

'Yes,' the widow went on, 'he is dead! Our beloved who gave us our bread, who sowed and reaped for us, who watched over our happiness, who guided us through life, who ruled so kindly among us. *Now* I may speak in his praise, and say that he never caused me the slightest sorrow; he was good and strong and patient. Even while we were torturing him for the sake of his health, so precious to us, "Let it be, children, it is all no use," the dear lamb said, just in the same tone of voice with which he had said: "Everything is all right, friends," only a few days before. Ah! good God! a few days ago! A few days have been enough to take away the gladness from our house and to darken our lives, to close the eyes of the best, most upright, most revered of men. No one could plough as he could. Night or day he would go about over the mountains, he feared nothing, and when he came back he had always a smile for his wife and children. Ah! he was our best beloved! It was dull here by the fireside when *he* was away, and our food lost all its relish. Oh! how will it be now, when our guardian angel will be laid away under the earth, and we shall never see him any more? Never any more, dear kinsfolk and friends; never any more, my children! Yes, my children have lost their kind father, our relations and friends have lost their good kinsman and their trusty friend, the household has lost its master, and I have lost everything!'

She took the hand of the dead again, and knelt, so that she might press her face close to his as she kissed it. The servants' cry: '*The master is dead!*' was again repeated three times.

Just then the eldest son came to his mother to say, 'The people from Saint Laurent have just come, mother; we want some wine for them.'

'Take the keys,' she said in a low tone, and in a different voice from that in which she had just expressed her grief; 'you are the master of the house, my son; see that they receive the welcome that your father would have given them; do not let them find any change.

'Let me have one more long look,' she went on. 'But,

alas! my good husband, you do not feel my presence now, I cannot bring back warmth to you! I only wish that I could comfort you still, could let you know that so long as I live you will dwell in the heart that you made glad, could tell you that I shall be happy in the memory of my happiness—that the dear thought of you will live on in this room. Yes, so long as God spares me, this room shall be filled with memories of you. Hear my vow, dear husband! Your couch shall always remain as it is now. I will sleep in it no more, since you are dead; henceforward, while I live, it shall be cold and empty. With you, I have lost all that makes a woman; her master, husband, father, friend, companion, and helpmate; I have lost all!'

'*The master is dead!*' the servants wailed. Others raised the cry, and the lament became general. The widow took a pair of scissors that hung at her waist, cut off her hair, and laid the locks in her husband's hand. Deep silence fell on them all.

'That act means that she will not marry again,' said Benassis; 'this determination was expected by many of the relatives.'

'Take it, dear lord!' she said; her emotion brought a tremor to her voice that went to the hearts of all who heard her. 'I have sworn to be faithful; I give this pledge to you to keep in the grave. We shall thus be united for ever, and through love of your children I will live on among the family in whom you used to feel yourself young again. Oh, that you could hear me, my husband! the pride and joy of my heart! Oh, that you could know that all my power to live, now you are dead, will yet come from you; for I shall live to carry out your sacred wishes and to honour your memory.'

Benassis pressed Genestas's hand as an invitation to follow him, and they went out. By this time the first room was full of people who had come from another mountain commune; all of them waited in meditative silence, as if the sorrow and grief that brooded over the house had already taken possession of them. As Benassis and the commandant crossed the threshold, they overheard a few words that passed between one of the newcomers and the eldest son of the late owner.

'Then when did he die?'

'Oh!' exclaimed the eldest son, a man of five-and-twenty years of age, 'I did not see him die. He asked for me, and I was not there!' His voice was broken with sobs, but he went on: 'He said to me the night before: "You must go over to the town, my boy, and pay our taxes; my funeral will put that out of your minds, and we shall be behindhand, a thing that has never happened before." It seemed the best thing to do, so I went; and while I was gone, he died, and I never received his last embrace. I have always been at his side, but he did not see me near him at the last in my place where I had always been.'

'*The master is dead!*'

'Alas! he is dead, and I was not there to receive his last words and his latest sigh. And what did the taxes matter? Would it not have been better to lose all our money than to leave home just then? Could all that we have make up to me for the loss of his last farewell. No. Indeed no! If *your* father falls ill, Jean, do not go away and leave him, or you will lay up a lifelong regret for yourself.'

'My friend,' said Genestas, 'I have seen thousands of men die on the battle-field; death did not wait to let their children bid them farewell; take comfort, you are not the only one.'

'But a father who was such a good man!' he replied, bursting into fresh tears.

Benassis took Genestas in the direction of the farm buildings.

'The funeral oration will only cease when the body

has been laid in its coffin,' said the doctor, 'and the weeping woman's language will grow more vivid and impassioned all the while. But a woman only acquires the right to speak in such a strain before so imposing an audience by a blameless life. If the widow could reproach herself with the smallest of shortcomings, she would not dare to utter a word; for if she did, she would pronounce her own condemnation, she would be at the same time her own accuser and judge. Is there not something sublime in this custom which thus judges the living and the dead? They only begin to wear mourning after a week has elapsed, when it is publicly worn at a meeting of all the family. Their near relations spend the week with the widow and children, to help them to set their affairs in order and to console them. A family gathering at such a time produces a great effect on the minds of the mourners; the consideration for others which possesses men when they are brought into close contact acts as a restraint on violent grief. On the last day, when the mourning garb has been assumed, a solemn banquet is given, and their relations take leave of them. All this is taken very seriously. Anyone who was slack in fulfilling his duties after the death of the head of a family would have no one at his own funeral.'

The doctor had reached the cowhouse as he spoke; he opened the door and made the commandant enter, that he might show it to him.

'All our cowhouses have been rebuilt after this pattern, captain. Look! Is it not magnificent?'

Genestas could not help admiring the huge place. The cows and oxen stood in two rows, with their tails towards the side walls, and their heads in the middle of the shed. Access to the stalls was afforded by a fairly wide space between them and the wall; you could see their horned heads and shining eyes through the lattice work, so that it was easy for the master to run his eyes over the cattle. The fodder was placed on some staging erected above the stalls, so that it fell into the racks below without waste of labour or material. There was a wide-paved space down the centre, which was kept clean, and ventilated by a thorough draught of air.

'In the winter time,' Benassis said, as he walked with Genestas down the middle of the cowhouse, 'both men and women do their work here together in the evenings. The tables are set out here, and in this way the people keep themselves warm without going to any expense. The sheep are housed in the same way. You would not believe how quickly the beasts fall into orderly ways. I have often wondered to see them come in; each knows her proper place, and allows those who take precedence to pass in before her. Look! there is just room enough in each stall to do the milking and to rub the cattle down; and the floor slopes a little to facilitate drainage.'

'One can judge of everything else from the sight of this cowhouse,' said Genestas; 'without flattery, these are great results indeed!'

'We have had some trouble to bring them about,' Benassis answered; 'but then, see what fine cattle they are!'

'They are splendid beasts certainly; you had good reason to praise them to me,' answered Genestas.

'Now,' said the doctor, when he had mounted his horse and passed under the gateway, 'we are going over some of the newly cleared waste, and through the corn land. I have christened this little corner of our commune "La Beauce."'

For about an hour they rode at a foot pace across fields in a state of high cultivation, on which the soldier complimented the doctor; then they came down the mountain-side into the township again, talking whenever the pace of their horses allowed them to do so. At last they reached a narrow glen, down which they rode into the main valley.

'I promised yesterday,' Benassis said to Genestas,

'to show you one of the two soldiers who left the army and came back to us after the fall of Napoleon. We shall find him somewhere hereabouts, if I am not mistaken. The mountain streams flow into a sort of natural reservoir or tarn up here; the earth they bring down has silted it up, and he is engaged in clearing it out. But if you are to take any interest in the man, I must tell you his history. His name is Gondrin. He was only eighteen years old when he was drawn in the great conscription of 1792, and drafted into a corps of gunners. He served as a private soldier in Napoleon's campaigns in Italy, followed him to Egypt, and came back from the East after the Peace of Amiens. In the time of the Empire he was incorporated in the Pontoon Troop of the Guard, and was constantly on active service in Germany; lastly the poor fellow made the Russian campaign.'

'We are brothers-in-arms then, to some extent,' said Genestas; 'I have made the same campaigns. Only an iron frame could stand the tricks played by so many different climates. My word for it, those who are still standing on their stumps after marching over Italy, Egypt, Germany, Portugal, and Russia must have applied to Providence and taken out a patent for living.'

'Just so, you will see a solid fragment of a man,' answered Benassis. 'You know all about the Retreat from Moscow; it is useless to tell you about it. This man I have told you of is one of the pontooners of the Beresina; he helped to construct the bridge by which the army made the passage, and stood waist-deep in water to drive in the first piles. General Eblé, who was in command of the pontooners, could only find forty-two men who were plucky enough, in Gondrin's phrase, to tackle that business. The general himself came down to the stream to hearten and cheer the men, promising each of them a pension of a thousand francs and the Cross of the Legion of Honour. The first who went down into the Beresina had his leg taken off by a block of ice, and the man himself was washed away; but you will better understand the difficulty of the task when you hear the end of the story. Of the forty-two volunteers, Gondrin is the only one alive to-day. Thirty-nine of them lost their lives in the Beresina, and the two others died miserably in a Polish hospital.

'The poor fellow himself only returned from Wilna in 1814, to find the Bourbons restored to power. General Eblé (of whom Gondrin cannot speak without tears in his eyes) was dead. The pontooner was deaf, and his health was shattered; and as he could neither read nor write, he found no one left to help him or to plead his cause. He begged his way to Paris, and while there made application at the War Office, not for the thousand francs of extra pension which had been promised to him, nor yet for the Cross of the Legion of Honour, but only for the bare pension due to him after twenty-two years of service, and I do not know how many campaigns. He did not obtain his pension or his travelling expenses; he did not even receive his arrears of pay. He spent a year in making fruitless solicitations, holding out his hands in vain to those whom he had saved; and at the end of it he came back here, sorely disheartened but resigned to his fate. This hero unknown to fame does draining work on the land, for which he is paid ten sous the fathom. He is accustomed to working in a marshy soil, and so, as he says, he gets jobs which no one else cares to take. He can make about three francs a day by clearing out ponds, or draining meadows that lie under water. His deafness makes him seem surly, and he is not naturally inclined to say very much, but there is a good deal in him.

'We are very good friends. He dines with me on the day of Austerlitz, on the emperor's birthday, and on the anniversary of the disaster at Waterloo, and during the dessert he always receives a napoleon to pay for his wine every quarter. Everyone in the commune shares in my feeling of respect for him; if he would allow them to support him, nothing would please them better. At every house to which he goes the people follow my example, and show their esteem by asking him to dine with them. It is a feeling of pride that leads him to work, and it is only as a portrait of the emperor that he can be induced to take my twenty-franc piece. He has been deeply wounded by the injustice that has been done him; but I think regret for the Cross is greater than the desire for his pension.

'He has one great consolation. After the bridges had been constructed across the Beresina, General Eblé presented such of the pontooners as were not disabled to the emperor, and Napoleon embraced poor Gondrin—perhaps but for that accolade he would have died ere now. This memory and the hope that some day Napoleon will return are all that Gondrin lives by. Nothing will ever persuade him that Napoleon is dead, and so convinced is he that the emperor's captivity is wholly and solely due to the English, that I believe he would be ready on the slightest pretext to take the life of the best-natured alderman that ever travelled for pleasure in foreign parts.'

'Let us go on as fast as possible!' cried Genestas. He had listened to the doctor's story with rapt attention, and now seemed to recover consciousness of his surroundings. 'Let us hurry! I long to see that man!'

Both of them put their horses to a gallop.

'The other soldier that I spoke of,' Benassis went on, 'is another of those men of iron who had knocked about everywhere with our armies. His life, like that of all French soldiers, has been made up of bullets, sabre strokes, and victories; he has had a very rough time of it, and has only worn the woollen epaulettes. He has a fanatical affection for Napoleon, who conferred the Cross upon him on the field of Valontina. He is of a jovial turn of mind, and like a genuine Dauphinois, has always looked after his own interests, has his pension, and the honours of the Legion. Goguelat is his name. He was an infantry man, who exchanged into the Guard in 1812. He is Gondrin's better half, so to speak, for the two have taken up house together. They both lodge with a pedlar's widow, and make over their money to her. She is a kind soul, who boards them and looks after them and their clothes as if they were her children.

'In his quality of local postman, Goguelat carries all the news of the countryside, and a good deal of practice acquired in this way has made him an orator in great request at up-sittings, and the champion teller of stories in this district. Gondrin looks upon him as a very knowing fellow, and something of a wit; and whenever Goguelat talks about Napoleon, his comrade seems to understand what he is saying from the movement of his lips. There will be an up-sitting (as they call it) in one of my barns to-night. If these two come over to it, and we can manage to see without being seen, I shall treat you to a view of the spectacle. But here we are, close to the ditch, and I do not see my friend the pontooner.'

The doctor and the commandant looked everywhere about them; Gondrin's soldier's coat lay there beside a heap of black mud, and his wheelbarrow, spade, and pick-axe were visible, but there was no sign of the man himself along the various pebbly watercourses, for the wayward mountain streams had hollowed out channels that were almost overgrown with low bushes.

'He cannot be so very far away. Gondrin! Where are you?' shouted Benassis.

Genestas first saw the curling smoke from a tobacco pipe rise among the brushwood on a bank of rubbish not far away. He pointed it out to the doctor, who shouted again. The old pontooner raised his head at this, recognized the mayor, and came towards them down a little pathway.

'Well, old friend,' said Benassis, making a sort of speaking-trumpet with his hand. 'Here is a comrade of yours, who was out in Egypt, come to see you.'

Gondrin raised his face at once and gave Genestas a swift, keen, and searching look, one of those glances by which old soldiers are wont at once to take the measure of any impending danger. He saw the red ribbon that the commandant wore, and made a silent and respectful military salute.

'If the Little Corporal were alive,' the officer cried, 'you would have the Cross of the Legion of Honour and a handsome pension besides, for every man who wore epaulettes on the other side of the river owed his life to you on the 1st of October 1812. But I am not the Minister of War, my friend,' the commandant added as he dismounted, and with a sudden rush of feeling he grasped the labourer's hand.

The old pontooner drew himself up at the words, he knocked the ashes from his pipe, and put it in his pocket.

'I only did my duty, sir,' he said, with his head bent down; 'but others have not done their duty by me. They asked for my papers! Why, the Twenty-ninth Bulletin, I told them, must do instead of my papers!'

'But you must make another application, comrade. You are bound to have justice done you in these days, if influence is brought to bear in the right quarter.'

'Justice!' cried the veteran. The doctor and the commandant shuddered at the tone in which he spoke.

In the brief pause that followed, both the horsemen looked at the man before them, who seemed like a fragment of the wreck of great armies which Napoleon had filled with men of bronze sought out from among three generations. Gondrin was certainly a splendid specimen of that seemingly indestructible mass of men which might be cut to pieces but never gave way. The old man was scarcely five feet high, wide across the shoulders, and broad-chested; his face was sunburned, furrowed with deep wrinkles, but the outlines were still firm in spite of the hollows in it, and one could see even now that it was the face of a soldier. It was a rough-hewn countenance, his forehead seemed like a block of granite; but there was a weary expression about his face, and the grey hairs hung scantily about his head, as if life were waning there already. Everything about him indicated unusual strength; his arms were covered thickly with hair, and so was the chest, which was visible through the opening of his coarse shirt. In spite of his almost crooked legs, he held himself firm and erect, as if nothing could shake him.

'Justice,' he said once more; 'there never will be justice for the like of us. We cannot send bailiffs to the Government to demand our dues for us; and as the wallet must be filled somehow,' he said, striking his stomach, 'we cannot afford to wait. Moreover, these gentry who lead snug lives in government offices may talk and talk, but their words are not good to eat, so I have come back again here to draw my pay out of the commonalty,' he said, striking the mud with his spade.

'Things must not be left in that way, old comrade,' said Genestas. 'I owe my life to you, and it would be ungrateful of me if I did not lend you a hand. I have not forgotten the passage over the bridges in the Beresina, and it is fresh in the memories of some brave fellows of my acquaintance; they will back me up, and the nation shall give you the recognition you deserve.'

'You will be called a Bonapartist! Please do not meddle in the matter, sir. I have gone to the rear now, and I have dropped into my hole here like a spent bullet. But after riding on camels through the desert, and drinking my glass by the fireside in Moscow, I never thought that I should come back to die here beneath the trees that my father planted,' and he began to work again.

'Poor old man!' said Genestas, as they turned to go.

'I should do the same if I were in his place; we have lost our father. Everything seems dark to me now that I have seen that man's hopelessness,' he went on, addressing Benassis; 'he does not know how much I am interested in him, and he will think that I am one of those gilded rascals who cannot feel for a soldier's sufferings.'

He turned quickly and went back, grasped the veteran's hand, and spoke loudly in his ear:

'I swear by the Cross I wear—the Cross of Honour it used to be—that I will do all that man can do to obtain your pension for you; even if I have to swallow a dozen refusals from the minister, and to petition the king and the dauphin and the whole shop!'

Old Gondrin quivered as he heard the words. He looked hard at Genestas and said: 'Haven't you served in the ranks?' The commandant nodded. The pontooner wiped his hand and took that of Genestas, which he grasped warmly and said:

'I made the army a present of my life, general, when I waded out into the river yonder, and if I am still alive, it is all so much to the good. One moment! Do you care to see to the bottom of it? Well, then, ever since *somebody* was pulled down from his place, I have ceased to care about anything. And, after all,' he went on more cheerfully, as he pointed to the land, 'they have made over twenty thousand francs to me here, and I am taking it out in detail, as *he* used to say!'

'Well, then, comrade,' said Genestas, touched by the grandeur of this forgiveness, 'at least you shall have the only thing that you cannot prevent me from giving to you, here below.' The commandant tapped his heart, looked once more at the old pontooner, mounted his horse again, and went his way side by side with Benassis.

'Such cruelty as this on the part of a government foments the strife between rich and poor,' said the doctor. 'People who exercise a little brief authority have never given a serious thought to the consequences that must follow an act of injustice done to a man of the people. It is true that a poor man who needs must work for his daily bread cannot long keep up the struggle; but he can talk, and his words find an echo in every sufferer's heart, so that one bad case of this kind is multiplied, for everyone who hears of it feels it as a personal wrong, and the leaven works. Even this is not so serious, but something far worse comes of it. Among the people, these cases of injustice bring about a chronic state of smothered hatred for their social superiors. The middle class become the poor man's enemy; they lie without the bounds of his moral code, he tells lies to them and robs them without scruple; indeed, theft ceases to be a crime or a misdemeanour, and is looked upon as an act of vengeance.

'When an official, who ought to see that the poor have justice done them, uses them ill and cheats them of their due, how can we expect the poor starving wretches to bear their troubles meekly and to respect the rights of property? It makes me shudder to think that some under-strapper whose business it is to dust papers in a government office, has pocketed Gondrin's promised thousand francs of pension. And yet there are folk who, never having measured the excess of the people's sufferings, accuse the people of excess in the day of their vengeance! When a government has done more harm than good to individuals, its further existence depends on the merest accident, the masses square the account after their fashion by upsetting it. A statesman ought always to imagine Justice with the poor at her feet, for justice was only invented for the poor.'

When they had come within the compass of the township, Benassis saw two people walking along the road in front of them, and turned to his companion, who had been absorbed for some time in thought.

'You have seen a veteran soldier resigned to his life of wretchedness, and now you are about to see an old agricultural labourer who is submitting to the same lot. The man there ahead of us has dug and sown and toiled for others all his life.'

Genestas looked and saw an old labourer making his way along the road, in company with an aged woman. He seemed to be afflicted with some form of sciatica, and limped painfully along. His feet were encased in a wretched pair of sabots, and a sort of wallet hung over his shoulder. Several tools lay in the bottom of the bag; their handles, blackened with long use and the sweat of toil, rattled audibly together; while the other end of the wallet behind his shoulder held bread, some walnuts, and a few fresh onions. His legs seemed to be warped, as it were, his back was bent by continual toil; he stooped so much as he walked that he leant on a long stick to steady himself. His snow-white hair escaped from under a battered hat, grown rusty by exposure to all sorts of weather, and mended here and there with visible stitches of white thread. His clothes, made of a kind of rough canvas, were a mass of patches of con- trasting colours. This piece of humanity in ruins lacked none of the characteristics that appeal to our hearts when we see ruins of other kinds.

His wife held herself somewhat more erect. Her clothing was likewise a mass of rags, and the cap that she wore was of the coarsest materials. On her back she carried a rough earthen jar by means of a thong passed through the handles of the great pitcher, which was round in shape and flattened at the sides. They both looked up when they heard the horses approaching, saw that it was Benassis, and stopped.

The man had worked till he was almost past work, and his faithful helpmate was no less broken with toil. It was painful to see how the summer sun and the winter's cold had blackened their faces, and covered them with such deep wrinkles that their features were hardly discernible. It was not their life history that had been engraven on their faces; but it might be gathered from their attitude and bearing. Incessant toil had been the lot of both; they had worked and suffered together; they had had many troubles and few joys to share; and now, like captives grown accustomed to their prison, they seemed to be too familiar with wretchedness to heed it, and to take everything as it came. Yet a certain frank light-heartedness was not lacking in their faces; and on a closer view, their monotonous life, the lot of so many a poor creature, wellnigh seemed an enviable one. Trouble had set its unmistakable mark upon them, but petty cares had left no traces there.

'Well, my good Father Moreau, I suppose there is no help for it, and you must always be working?'

'Yes, M. Benassis, there are one or two more bits of waste that I mean to clear for you before I knock off work,' the old man answered cheerfully, and a light shone in his little black eyes.

'Is that wine that your wife there is carrying? If you will not take a rest now, you ought at any rate to take wine.'

'I take a rest? I should not know what to do with myself. The sun and the fresh air put life into me when I am out of doors and busy grubbing up the land. As to the wine, sir, yes, that is wine sure enough, and it is all through your contriving I know that the mayor at Courteil lets us have it for next to nothing. Ah, you managed it very cleverly, but all the same, I know you had a hand in it.'

'Oh! come, come! Good-day, mother. You are going to work on that bit of land of Champferlu's to-day of course?'

'Yes, sir; I made a beginning there yesterday evening.'

'Capital!' said Benassis. 'It must be a satisfaction to you, at times, to see this hill-side. You two have broken up almost the whole of the land on it yourselves.'

'Lord! yes, sir,' answered the old woman, 'it has been our doing! We have fairly earned our bread.'

'Work, you see, and land to cultivate are the poor man's consols. That good man would think himself disgraced if he went into the poorhouse or begged for his bread; he would choose to die pickaxe in hand, out in the open, in the sunlight. Faith, he bears a proud heart in him. He has worked until work has become his very life; and yet death has no terrors for him! He is a profound philosopher, little as he suspects it. Old Moreau's case suggested the idea to me of founding an almshouse for the country people of the district; a refuge for those who, after working hard all their lives, have reached an honourable old age of poverty.

'I had by no means expected to make the fortune which I have acquired here; indeed, I myself have no use for it, for a man who has fallen from the pinnacle of his hopes needs very little. It costs but little to live, the idler's life alone is a costly one, and I am not sure that the unproductive consumer is not robbing the community at large. There was some discussion about Napoleon's pension after his fall; it came to his ears, and he said that five francs a day and a horse to ride was all that he needed. I meant to have no more to do with money when I came here; but after a time I saw that money means power, and that it is in fact a necessity, if any good is to be done. So I have made arrangements in my will for turning my house into an almshouse, in which old people who have not Moreau's fierce independence can end their days. Part of the income of nine thousand francs brought in by the mill and the rest of my property will be devoted to giving outdoor relief in hard winters to those who really stand in need of it.

'This foundation will be under the control of the Municipal Council, with the addition of the curé, who is to be president; and in this way the money made in the district will be returned to it. In my will I have laid down the lines on which this institution is to be conducted; it would be tedious to go over them, it is enough to say that I have thought it all out very carefully. I have also created a trust fund, which will some day enable the commune to award several scholarships for children who show signs of promise in art or science. So, even after I am gone, my work of civilization will continue. When you have set yourself to do anything, Captain Bluteau, something within you urges you on, you see, and you cannot bear to leave it unfinished. This craving within us for order and for perfection is one of the signs that point most surely to a future existence. Now, let us quicken our pace, I have my round to finish, and there are five or six more patients still to be visited.'

They cantered on for some time in silence, till Benassis said laughingly to his companion: 'Come now, Captain Bluteau, you have drawn me out and made me chatter like a magpie, and you have not said a syllable about your own history, which must be an interesting one. When a soldier has come to your time of life, he has seen so much that he must have more than one adventure to tell about.'

'Why, my history has been simply the history of the army,' answered Genestas. 'Soldiers are all after one pattern. Never in command, always giving and taking sabre-cuts in my place, I have lived just like everybody else. I have been wherever Napoleon led us, and have borne a part in every battle in which the Imperial Guard has struck a blow; but everybody knows all about these events. A soldier has to look after his horse, to endure hunger and thirst at times, to fight whenever there is fighting to be done, and there you have the whole history of his life. As simple as saying good-bye, is it not? Then there are battles in which your horse casts a shoe at the outset, and lands you in a quandary; and as far as you are concerned, that is the whole of it. In short, I have seen so many countries, that seeing them has come to be a matter of course; and I have seen so many men die, that I have come to value my own life at nothing.'

'But you yourself must have been in danger at times, and it would be interesting to hear you tell of your personal adventures.'

'Perhaps,' answered the commandant.

'Well, then, tell me about the adventure that made the deepest impression upon you. Come! do not hesitate. I shall not think that you are wanting in modesty even if you should tell me of some piece of heroism on your part; and when a man is quite sure that he will not be misunderstood, ought he not to find a kind of pleasure in saying: "I did thus"?'

'Very well, then, I will tell you about something that gives me a pang of remorse from time to time. During fifteen years of warfare it never once happened that I killed a man, save in legitimate defence of self. We are drawn up in line, and we charge; and if we do not strike down those before us, they will begin to draw blood without asking leave, so you have to kill if you do not mean to be killed, and your conscience is quite easy. But once I broke a comrade's back; it happened in a singular way, and it has been a painful thing to me to think of afterwards—the man's dying grimace haunts me at times. But you shall judge for yourself.

'It was during the retreat from Moscow,' the commandant went on. 'The Grand Army had ceased to be itself; we were more like a herd of over-driven cattle. Good-bye to discipline! The regiments had lost sight of their colours, everyone was his own master, and the emperor (one need not scruple to say it) knew that it was useless to attempt to exert his authority when things had gone so far. When we reached Studzianka, a little place on the other side of the Beresina, we came upon human dwellings for the first time after several days.

There were barns and peasants' cabins to destroy, and pits full of potatoes and beetroot; the army had been without victual, and now it fairly ran riot, the first comers, as you might expect, making a clean sweep of everything.

'I was one of the last to come up. Luckily for me, sleep was the one thing that I longed for just then. I caught sight of a barn and went into it. I looked round and saw a score of generals and officers of high rank, all of them men who, without flattery, might be called great. Junot was there, and Narbonne, the emperor's aide-de-camp, and all the chiefs of the army. There were common soldiers there as well, not one of whom would have given up his bed of straw to a marshal of France. Some who were leaning their backs against the wall had dropped off to sleep where they stood, because there was no room to lie down; others lay stretched out on the floor—it was a mass of men packed together so closely for the sake of warmth, that I looked about in vain for a nook to lie down in. I walked over this flooring of human bodies; some of the men growled, the others said nothing, but no one budged. They would not have moved out of the way of a cannon ball just then; but under the circumstances, one was not obliged to practise the maxims laid down by the *Child's Guide to Manners*. Groping about, I saw at the end of the barn a sort of ledge up above in the roof; no one had thought of scrambling up to it, possibly no one had felt equal to the effort. I clambered up and ensconced myself upon it; and as I lay there at full length, I looked down at the men huddled together like sheep below. It was a pitiful sight, yet it almost made me laugh. A man here and there was gnawing a frozen carrot, with a kind of animal satisfaction expressed in his face; and thunderous snores came from generals who lay muffled up in ragged cloaks. The whole barn was lighted by a blazing pine log; it might have set the place on fire, and no one would have troubled to get up and put it out.

'I lay down on my back, and, naturally, just before I dropped off, my eyes travelled to the roof above me, and then I saw that the main beam which bore the weight of the joists was being slightly shaken from east to west. The blessed thing danced about in fine style. "Gentlemen," said I, "one of our friends outside has a mind to warm himself at our expense." A few moments more and the beam was sure to come down. "Gentlemen! gentlemen!" I shouted, "we shall all be killed in a minute! Look at the beam there!" and I made such a noise that my bed-fellows awoke at last. Well, sir, they all stared up at the beam, and then those who had been sleeping turned round and went off to sleep again, while those who were eating did not even stop to answer me.

'Seeing how things were, there was nothing for it but to get up and leave my place, and run the risk of finding it taken by somebody else, for all the lives of this heap of heroes were at stake. So out I go. I turn the corner of the barn and come upon a great devil of a Würtemberger, who was tugging at the beam with a certain enthusiasm. "Aho! aho!" I shouted, trying to make him understand that he must desist from his toil. "*Gehe mir aus dem Gesicht, oder ich schlag dich todt!*—Get out of my sight, or I will kill you," he cried. "Ah! yes, just so, *Gué mire aous dem guesit*," I answered; "but that is not the point." I picked up his gun that he had left on the ground, and broke his back with it; then I turned in again, and went off to sleep. Now you know the whole business.'

'But that was a case of self-defence, in which one man suffered for the good of many, so you have nothing to reproach yourself with,' said Benassis.

'The rest of them thought that it had only been my fancy; but fancy or no, a good many of them are living comfortably in fine houses to-day, without feeling their hearts oppressed by gratitude.'

'Then would you only do people a good turn in order

to receive that exorbitant interest called gratitude?' said Benassis, laughing. 'That would be asking a great deal for your outlay.'

'Oh, I know quite well that all the merit of a good deed evaporates at once if it benefits the doer in the slightest degree,' said Genestas. 'If he tells the story of it, the toll brought in to his vanity is a sufficient substitute for gratitude. But if every doer of kindly actions always held his tongue about them, those who reaped the benefits would hardly say very much either. Now the people, according to your system, stand in need of examples, and how are they to hear of them amid this general reticence? Again, there is this poor pontooner of ours, who saved the whole French army, and who was never able to tell his tale to any purpose; suppose that he had lost the use of his limbs, would the consciousness of what he had done have found him in bread? Answer me that, philosopher!'

'Perhaps the rules of morality cannot be absolute,' Benassis answered; 'though this is a dangerous idea, for it leaves the egotist free to settle cases of conscience in his own favour. Listen, captain; is not the man who never swerves from the principles of morality greater than he who transgresses them, even through necessity? Would not our veteran, dying of hunger, and unable to help himself, be worthy to rank with Homer? Human life is doubtless a final trial of virtue as of genius, for both of which a better world is waiting. Virtue and genius seem to me to be the fairest forms of that complete and constant surrender of self that Jesus Christ came among men to teach. Genius sheds its light in the world and lives in poverty all its days, and virtue sacrifices itself in silence for the general good.'

'I quite agree with you, sir,' said Genestas; 'but those who dwell on earth are men after all, and not angels; we are not perfect.'

'That is quite true,' Benassis answered. 'And as for errors, I myself have abused the indulgence. But ought we not to aim, at any rate, at perfection? Is not virtue a fair ideal which the soul must always keep before it, a standard set up by Heaven?'

'Amen,' said the soldier. 'An upright man is a magnificent thing, I grant you; but, on the other hand, you must admit that virtue is a divinity who may indulge in a scrap of gossip now and then in the strictest propriety.'

The doctor smiled, but there was a melancholy bitterness in his tone as he said: 'Ah! sir, you regard things with the lenience natural to those who live at peace with themselves; and I with all the severity of one who sees much that he would fain obliterate in the story of his life.'

The two horsemen reached a cottage beside the bed of the torrent, the doctor dismounted and went into the house. Genestas, on the threshold, looked over the bright spring landscape that lay without, and then at the dark interior of the cottage, where a man was lying in bed. Benassis examined his patient, and suddenly exclaimed: 'My good woman, it is no use my coming here unless you carry out my instructions! You have been giving him bread; you want to kill your husband, I suppose? Botheration! If after this you give him anything besides tisane of couch-grass, I will never set foot in here again, and you can look where you like for another doctor.'

'But, dear M. Benassis, my old man was starving, and when he had eaten nothing for a whole fortnight——'

'Oh, yes, yes. Now will you listen to me? If you let your husband eat a single mouthful of bread before I give him leave to take solid food, you will kill him, do you hear?'

'He shall not have anything, sir. Is he any better?' she asked, following the doctor to the door.

'Why, no. You have made him worse by feeding

him. Shall I never get it into your stupid heads that you must not stuff people who are being dieted?

'The peasants are incorrigible,' Benassis went on, speaking to Genestas. 'If a patient has eaten nothing for two or three days, they think he is at death's door, and they cram him with soup or wine or something. Here is a wretched woman for you that has all but killed her husband.'

'Kill my husband with a little mite of a sop in wine!'

'Certainly, my good woman. It amazes me that he is still alive after that mess you cooked for him. Mind that you do exactly as I have told you.'

'Yes, dear sir, I would far rather die myself than lose him.'

'Oh! as to that I shall soon see. I shall come again to-morrow evening to bleed him.

'Let us walk along the side of the stream,' Benassis said to Genestas; 'there is only a footpath between this cottage and the next house where I must pay a call. That man's little boy will hold our horses.'

'You must admire this lovely valley of ours a little,' he went on; 'it is like an English garden, is it not? The labourer who lives in the cottage which we are going to visit has never got over the death of one of his children. The eldest boy, he was only a lad, would try to do a man's work last harvest-tide; it was beyond his strength, and before the autumn was out he died of a decline. This is the first case of really strong fatherly love that has come under my notice. As a rule, when their children die, the peasant's regret is for the loss of a useful chattel, and a part of their stock-in-trade, and the older the child, the heavier their sense of loss. A grown-up son or daughter is so much capital to the parents. But this poor fellow really loved that boy of his. "Nothing can comfort me for my loss," he said one day when I came across him out in the fields. He had forgotten all about his work, and was standing there motionless, leaning on his scythe; he had picked up his hone, it lay in his hand, and he had forgotten to use it. He has never spoken since of his grief to me, but he has grown sad and silent. Just now it is one of his little girls who is ill.'

Benassis and his guest reached the little house as they talked. It stood beside a pathway that led to a bark-mill. They saw a man about forty years of age, standing under a willow-tree, eating bread that had been rubbed with a clove of garlic.

'Well, Gasnier, is the little one doing better?'

'I do not know, sir,' he said dejectedly, 'you will see; my wife is sitting with her. In spite of all your care, I am very much afraid that death will come to empty my home for me.'

'Do not lose heart, Gasnier. Death is too busy to take up his abode in any dwelling.'

Benassis went into the house, followed by the father. Half an hour later he came out again. The mother was with him this time, and he spoke to her: 'You need have no anxiety about her now; follow out my instructions; she is out of danger.'

'If you are growing tired of this sort of thing,' the doctor said to the officer, as he mounted his horse, 'I can put you on the way to the town, and you can return.'

'No, I am not tired of it, I give you my word.'

'But you will only see cottages everywhere, and they are all alike; nothing, to outward seeming, is more mono-tonous than the country.'

'Let us go on,' said the officer.

They rode on in this way for several hours, and after going from one side of the canton to the other, they re-turned towards evening to the precincts of the town.

'I must just go over there,' the doctor said to Genestas, as he pointed out a place where a cluster of elm-trees grew. 'Those trees may possibly be two hundred years old,' he went on, 'and that is where the woman lives, on whose account the lad came to fetch me last night at dinner, with a message that she had turned quite white.'

'Was it anything serious?'

'No,' said Benassis, 'an effect of pregnancy. It is the last month with her, a time at which some women suffer from spasms. But by way of precaution, I must go in any case to make sure that there are no further alarming symptoms; I shall see her through her confinement myself. And, moreover, I should like to show you one of our new industries; there is a brickfield here. It is a good road; shall we gallop?'

'Will your animal keep up with mine?' asked Genestas. 'Heigh! Neptune!' he called to his horse, and in a moment the officer had been carried far ahead, and was lost to sight in a cloud of dust, but in spite of the paces of his horse he still heard the doctor beside him. At a word from Benassis his own horse left the commandant so far behind that the latter only came up with him at the gate of the brickfield, where the doctor was quietly fastening the bridle to the gate-post.

'The devil take it!' cried Genestas, after a look at the horse, that was neither sweated nor blown. 'What kind of animal have you there?'

'Ah!' said the doctor, 'you took him for a screw! The history of this fine fellow would take up too much time just now; let it suffice to say that Roustan is a thoroughbred barb from the Atlas Mountains, and a barbary horse is as good as an Arab. This one of mine will gallop up the mountain roads without turning a hair, and will never miss his footing in a canter along the brink of a precipice. He was a present to me, and I think that I deserved it, for in this way a father sought to repay me for his daughter's life. She is one of the wealthiest heiresses in Europe, and she was at the brink of death when I found her on the road to Savoy. If I were to tell you how I cured that young lady, you would take me for a quack. Aha! that is the sound of the bells on the horses and the rumbling of a wagon; it is coming along this way; let us see, perhaps that is Vigneau himself; and if so, take a good look at him!'

In another moment the officer saw a team of four huge horses, like those which are owned by prosperous farmers in Brie. The harness, the little bells, and the knots of braid in their manes, were clean and smart. The great wagon itself was painted bright blue, and perched aloft in it sat a stalwart, sunburnt youth, who shouldered his whip like a gun and whistled a tune.

'No,' said Benassis, 'that is only the wagoner. But see how the master's prosperity in business is reflected by all his belongings, even by the carter's wagon! Is it not a sign of a capacity for business not very often met with in remote country places?'

'Yes, yes, it all looks very smart, indeed,' the officer answered.

'Well, Vigneau has two more wagons and teams like that one, and he has a small pony besides for business purposes, for he does a trade over a wide area. And only four years ago he had nothing in the world! Stay, that is a mistake—he had some debts. But let us go in.'

'Is Mme Vigneau in the house?' Benassis asked of the young wagoner.

'She is out in the garden, sir; I saw her just now by the hedge down yonder; I will go and tell her that you are here.'

Genestas followed Benassis across a wide open space with a hedge about it. In one corner various heaps of clay had been piled up, destined for tiles and pantiles, and a stack of brushwood and logs (fuel for the kiln no doubt) lay in another part of the enclosure. Farther away some workmen were pounding chalk stones and tempering the clay in a space enclosed by hurdles. The tiles, both round and square, were made under the great elms opposite the gateway, in a vast green arbour bounded by the roofs of the drying-shed, and near this last the yawning mouth of the kiln was visible. Some long-handled shovels lay about the worn cinder path. A second row of buildings had been erected parallel with these. There was a sufficiently wretched dwelling which housed the family, and some outbuildings—sheds and stables and a barn. The cleanliness that predominated throughout, and the thorough repair in which everything was kept, spoke well for the vigilance of the master's eyes. Some poultry and pigs wandered at large over the field.

'Vigneau's predecessor,' said Benassis, 'was a good-for-nothing, a lazy rascal who cared about nothing but drink. He had been a workman himself; he could keep a fire in his kiln and could put a price on his work, and that was about all he knew; he had no energy, and no idea of business. If no one came to buy his wares of him, they simply stayed on hand and were spoiled, and so he lost the value of them. So he died of want at last. He had ill-treated his wife till she was almost idiotic, and she lived in a state of abject wretchedness. It was so painful to see this laziness and incurable stupidity, and I so much disliked the sight of the tile-works, that I never came this way if I could help it. Luckily, both the man and his wife were old people. One fine day the tile-maker had a paralytic stroke, and I had him removed to the hospital at Grenoble at once. The owner of the tile-works agreed to take it over without disputing about its condition, and I looked round for new tenants who would take their part in improving the industries of the canton.

'Mme Gravier's waiting-maid had married a poor workman, who was earning so little with the potter who employed him that he could not support his household. He listened to my advice, and actually had sufficient courage to take a lease of our tile-works, when he had not so much as a penny. He came and took up his abode here, taught his wife, her aged mother, and his own mother how to make tiles, and made workmen of them. How they managed, I do not know, upon my honour! Vigneau probably borrowed fuel to heat his kiln, he certainly worked by day, and fetched in his materials in basket-loads by night; in short, no one knew what boundless energy he brought to bear upon his enterprise; and the two old mothers, clad in rags, worked like negroes. In this way Vigneau contrived to fire several batches, and lived for the first year on bread that was hardly won by the toil of his household.

'Still, he made a living. His courage, patience, and sterling worth interested many people in him, and he began to be known. He was indefatigable. He would hurry over to Grenoble in the morning, and sell his bricks and tiles there; then he would return home about the middle of the day, and go back again to the town at night. He seemed to be in several places at once. Towards the end of the first year he took two little lads to help him. Seeing how things were, I lent him some money, and since then from year to year the fortunes of the family have steadily improved. After the second year was over the two old mothers no longer moulded bricks nor pounded stones; they looked after the little gardens, made the soup, mended the clothes, they did spinning in the evenings, and gathered firewood in the daytime; while the young wife, who can read and write, kept the accounts. Vigneau had a small horse, and rode on his business errands about the neighbourhood; next he thoroughly studied the art of brick- and tile-making, discovered how to make excellent square white paving-tiles, and sold them for less than the usual prices. In the third year he had a cart and a pair of horses, and at the same time his wife's appearance became almost elegant. Everything about his household improved with the improvement in his business, and everywhere there was the same neatness, method, and thrift that had been the making of his little fortune.

'At last he had work enough for six men, to whom he pays good wages; he employs a wagoner, and everything about him wears an air of prosperity. Little by little, in short, by dint of taking pains and extending his business, his income has increased. He bought the tile-works last year, and next year he will rebuild his house. To-day all the worthy folk there are well clothed and in good health. His wife, who used to be so thin and pale when the burden of her husband's cares and anxieties used to press so hardly upon her, has recovered her good looks, and has grown quite young and pretty again. The two old mothers are thoroughly happy, and take the deepest interest in every detail of the housekeeping or of the business. Work has brought money, and the money that brought freedom from care brought health and plenty and happiness. The story of this household is a living history in miniature of the commune since I have known it, and of all young industrial states. The tile factory that used to look so empty, melancholy, ill-kept, and useless, is now in full work, astir with life, and well stocked with everything required. There is a good stock of wood here, and all the raw material for the season's work: for, as you know, tiles can only be made during a few months in the year, between June and September. Is it not a pleasure to see all this activity? My tile-maker has done his share of the work in every building in the place. He is always wide awake, always coming and going, always busy—"the devourer," they call him in these parts.'

Benassis had scarcely finished speaking when the wicket gate which gave entrance to the garden opened, and a nicely dressed young woman appeared. She came forward as quickly as her condition allowed, though the

two horsemen hastened towards her. Her attire somewhat recalled her former quality of lady's-maid, for she
wore a pretty cap, a pink dress, a silk apron, and white
stockings. Mme Vigneau, in short, was a nice-looking
woman, sufficiently plump, and if she was somewhat
sunburned, her natural complexion must have been very
fair. There were a few lines still left in her forehead,
traced there by the troubles of past days, but she had a
bright and winsome face. She spoke in a persuasive
voice, as she saw that the doctor came no farther: 'Will
you not do me the honour of coming inside and resting
for a moment, M. Benassis?'

'Certainly we will. Come this way, captain.'

'The gentlemen must be very hot! Will you take a
little milk or some wine? M. Benassis, please try a little
of the wine that my husband has been so kind as to buy
for my confinement. You will tell me if it is good.'

'You have a good man for your husband.'

'Yes, sir,' she turned and spoke in quiet tones, 'I am
very well off.'

'We will not take anything, Mme Vigneau; I only
came round this way to see that nothing troublesome had
happened.'

'Nothing,' she said. 'I was busy out in the garden,
as you saw, turning the soil over for the sake of something
to do.'

Then the two old mothers came out to speak to Benassis,
and the young wagoner planted himself in the middle of
the yard, in a spot from whence he could have a good
view of the doctor.

'Let us see, let me have your hand,' said Benassis,
addressing Mme Vigneau; and as he carefully felt her
pulse, he stood in silence, absorbed in thought. The
three women, meanwhile, scrutinized the commandant
with the undisguised curiosity that country people do
not scruple to express.

'Nothing could be better!' cried the doctor cheerily.

'Will she be confined soon?' both the mothers asked together.

'This week beyond a doubt. Is Vigneau away from home?' he asked, after a pause.

'Yes, sir,' the young wife answered; 'he is hurrying about settling his business affairs, so as to be able to stay at home during my confinement, the dear man!'

'Well, my children, go on and prosper; continue to increase your wealth and to add to your family.'

The cleanliness of the almost ruinous dwelling filled Genestas with admiration.

Benassis saw the officer's astonishment, and said: 'There is no one like Mme Vigneau for keeping a house clean and tidy like this. I wish that several people in the town would come here to take a lesson.'

The tile-maker's wife blushed and turned her head away; but the faces of the two old mothers beamed with pleasure at the doctor's words, and the three women walked with them to the spot where the horses were waiting.

'Well, now,' the doctor said to the two old women, 'here is happiness for you both! Were you not longing to be grandmothers?'

'Oh, do not talk about it,' said the young wife; 'they will drive me crazy among them. My two mothers wish for a boy, and my husband would like to have a little girl. It will be very difficult to please them all, I think.'

'But you yourself,' asked Benassis; 'what is your wish?'

'Ah, sir, I wish for a child of my own.'

'There! She is a mother already, you see,' said the doctor to the officer, as he laid his hand on the bridle of his horse.

'Good-bye, M. Benassis; my husband will be sadly disappointed to learn that you have been here when he was not at home to see you.'

'He has not forgotten to send the thousand tiles to the Grange-aux-Belles for me?'

'You know quite well, sir, that he would keep all the orders in the canton waiting to serve you. Why, taking your money is the thing that troubles him most; but I always tell him that your crowns bring luck with them, and so they do.'

'Good-bye,' said Benassis.

A little group gathered about the bars across the entrance to the tile-works. The three women, the young wagoner, and two workmen who had left off work to greet the doctor, lingered there to have the pleasure of being with him until the last moment, as we are wont to linger with those we love. The promptings of men's hearts must everywhere be the same, and in every land friendship expresses itself in the same gracious ways.

Benassis looked at the height of the sun and spoke to his companion:

'There are still two hours of daylight left; and if you are not too hungry, we will go to see someone with whom I nearly always spend the interval between the last of my visits and the hour for dinner. She is a charming girl whom everyone here calls my "good friend." That is the name that they usually give to an affianced bride; but you must not imagine that there is the slightest imputation of any kind implied or intended by the use of the word in this case. Poor child, the care that I have taken of her has, as may be imagined, made her an object of jealousy, but the general opinion entertained as to my character has prevented any spiteful gossip. If no one understands the apparent caprice that has led me to make an allowance to La Fosseuse, so that she can live without being compelled to work, nobody has any doubts as to her character. I have watched over her with friendly care, and everyone knows that I should never hesitate to marry her if my affection for her exceeded the limits of friendship. But no woman exists for me here in the canton or anywhere else,' said the doctor, forcing a smile. 'Some natures feel a tyrannous need to attach themselves to some one thing or being which they single out from among the beings and things around them; this need is felt most keenly by a man of quick sympathies, and all the more pressingly if his life has been made desolate. So, trust me, it is a favourable sign if a man is strongly attached to his dog or his horse! Among the suffering flock which chance has given into my care, this poor little sufferer has come to be for me like the pet lamb that the shepherd lasses deck with ribbons in my own sunny land of Languedoc; they talk to it and allow it to find pasture by the side of the cornfields, and its leisurely pace is never hurried by the shepherd's dog.'

Benassis stood with his hand on his horse's mane as he spoke, ready to spring into the saddle, but making no effort to do so, as though the thought that stirred in him were but little in keeping with rapid movements.

'Let us go,' he said at last; 'come with me and pay her a visit. I am taking you to see her; does not that tell you that I treat her as a sister?'

As they rode on their way again, Genestas said to the doctor: 'Will you regard it as inquisitiveness on my part if I ask to hear more of La Fosseuse? I have come to know the story of many lives through you, and hers cannot be less interesting than some of these.'

Benassis stopped his horse as he answered. 'Perhaps you will not share in the feelings of interest awakened in me by La Fosseuse. Her fate is like my own; we have both alike missed our vocation; it is the similarity of our lots that occasions my sympathy for her and the feelings that I experience at the sight of her. You either followed your natural bent when you entered upon a military career, or you took a liking for your calling after you had adopted it, otherwise you would not have borne the heavy yoke of military discipline till now; you, therefore, cannot understand the sorrows of a soul that must always feel renewed within it the stir of longings that can never be realized; nor the pining existence of a creature forced to live in an alien sphere. Such sufferings as these are known only to these natures and to God who sends their afflictions, for they alone can know how deeply the events of life affect them. You yourself have seen the miseries produced by long wars, till they have almost ceased to impress you, but have you never detected a trace of sadness in your mind at the sight of a tree bearing sere leaves in the midst of spring, some tree that is pining and dying because it has been planted in soil in which it could not find the sustenance required for its full development? Ever since my twentieth year, there has been something painful and melancholy for me about the drooping of a stunted plant, and now I cannot bear the sight and turn my head away. My youthful sorrow was a vague presentiment of the sorrows of my later life; it was a kind of sympathy between my present and a future dimly foreshadowed by the life of the tree that before its time was going the way of all trees and men.'

'I thought that you had suffered when I saw how kind you were.'

'You see, sir,' the doctor went on without any reply to the remark made by Genestas, 'that to speak of La Fosseuse is to speak of myself. La Fosseuse is a plant in an alien soil; a human plant moreover, consumed by sad thoughts that have their source in the depths of her nature, and that never cease to multiply. The poor girl is never well and strong. The soul within her kills the body. This fragile creature was suffering from the sorest of all troubles, a trouble which receives the least possible sympathy from our selfish world, and how could I look on with indifferent eyes? for I, a man, strong to wrestle with pain, was nightly tempted to refuse to bear the burden of a sorrow like hers. Perhaps I might actually have refused to bear it but for a thought of religion which soothes my impatience and fills my heart with sweet illusions. Even if we were not children of the same Father in heaven, La Fosseuse would still be my sister in suffering!'

Benassis pressed his knees against his horse's sides, and swept ahead of Commandant Genestas, as if he shrank from continuing this conversation any further. When their horses were once more cantering abreast of each other, he spoke again: 'Nature has created this poor girl for sorrow,' he said, 'as she has created other women for joy. It is impossible to do otherwise than believe in a future life at the sight of natures thus predestined to suffer. La Fosseuse is sensitive and highly strung. If the weather is dark and cloudy, she is depressed; she "weeps when the sky is weeping," a phrase of her own; she sings with the birds; she grows happy and serene under a cloudless sky; the loveliness of a bright day passes into her face; a soft sweet perfume is an inexhaustible pleasure to her; I have seen her take delight the whole day long in the scent breathed forth by some mignonette; and, after one of those rainy mornings that bring out all the soul of the flowers and give indescribable freshness and brightness to the day, she seems to overflow with gladness like the green world around her. If it is close and hot, and there is thunder in the air, La Fosseuse feels a vague trouble that nothing can soothe. She lies on her bed, complains of numberless different ills, and does not know what ails her. In answer to my questions, she tells me that her bones are melting, that she is dissolving into water; her "heart has left her," to quote another of her sayings.

'I have sometimes come upon the poor child suddenly and found her in tears, as she gazed at the sunset effects we sometimes see here among our mountains, when bright masses of cloud gather and crowd together and pile themselves above the golden peaks of the hills. "Why are you crying, little one?" I have asked her. "I do not know, sir," has been the answer; "I have grown so stupid with looking up there; I have looked and looked, till I hardly know where I am." "But what do you see there?" "I cannot tell you, sir," and you might question her in this way all the evening, yet you would never draw a word from her; but she would look at you, and every glance would seem full of thoughts, or she would sit with tears in her eyes, scarcely saying a word, apparently rapt in musing. Those musings of hers are so profound that you fall under the spell of them; on me, at least, she has the effect of a cloud overcharged with electricity. One day I plied her with questions; I tried with all my might to make her talk; at last I let fall a few rather hasty words; and, well—she burst into tears.

'At other times La Fosseuse is bright and winning, active, merry, and sprightly; she enjoys talking, and the ideas which she expresses are fresh and original. She is however quite unable to apply herself steadily to any kind of work. When she was out in the fields she used to spend whole hours in looking at a flower, in watching the water flow, in gazing at the wonders in the depths of the clear, still river pools, at the picturesque mosaic made up of pebbles and earth and sand, of water plants and green moss, and the brown soil washed down by the stream, a deposit full of soft shades of colour, and of hues that contrast strangely with each other.

'When I first came to the district the poor girl was starving. It hurt her pride to accept the bread of others; and it was only when driven to the last extremity of want and suffering that she could bring herself to ask for charity. The feeling that this was a disgrace would often give her energy, and for several days she worked in the fields; but her strength was soon exhausted, and illness obliged her to leave the work that she had begun. She had scarcely recovered when she went to a farm on the outskirts of the town and asked to be taken on to look after the cattle; she did her work well and intelligently, but after a while she left without giving any reason for so doing. The constant toil, day after day, was no doubt too heavy a yoke for one who is all independence and caprice. Then she set herself to look for mushrooms or for truffles, going over to Grenoble to sell them. But the gaudy trifles in the town were very tempting, the few small coins in her hand seemed to be great riches; she would forget her poverty and buy ribbons and finery, without a thought for to-morrow's bread. But if some other girl here in the town took a fancy to her brass crucifix, her agate heart, or her velvet ribbon, she would make them over to her at once, glad to give happiness, for she lives by generous impulses. So La Fosseuse was loved and pitied and despised by turns. Everything in her nature was a cause of suffering to her—her indolence, her kindness of heart, her coquetry; for she is coquettish, dainty, and inquisitive, in short, she is a woman; she is as simple as a child, and, like a child, she is carried away by her tastes and her impressions. If you tell her about some noble deed, she trembles, her colour rises, her heart throbs fast, and she sheds tears of joy; if you begin a story about robbers, she turns pale with terror. You could not find a more sincere, open-hearted, and scrupulously loyal nature anywhere; if you were to give a hundred gold pieces into her keeping, she would bury them in some out-of-the-way nook and beg her bread as before.'

There was a change in Benassis's tone as he uttered these last words.

'I once determined to put her to the proof,' he said, 'and I repented of it. It is like espionage to bring a test to bear upon another, is it not? It means that we suspect them at any rate.'

Here the doctor paused, as though some inward reflection engrossed him; he was quite unconscious of the
embarrassment that his last remark had caused to his
companion, who busied himself with disentangling the
reins in order to hide his confusion. Benassis soon
resumed his talk.

'I should like to find a husband for my Fosseuse. I
should be glad to make over one of my farms to some
good fellow who would make her happy. And she would
be happy. The poor girl would love her children to
distraction; for motherhood, which develops the whole
of a woman's nature, would give full scope to her over-
flowing sentiments. She has never cared for anyone,
however. Yet her impressionable nature is a danger to
her. She knows this herself, and when she saw that I
recognized it, she admitted the excitability of her temperament to me. She belongs to the small minority of
women whom the slightest contact with others causes
to vibrate perilously; so that she must be made to value
herself on her discretion and her womanly pride. She is
as wild and shy as a swallow! Ah! what a wealth of
kindness there is in her! Nature meant her to be a rich
woman; she would be so beneficent: for a well-loved
woman; she would be so faithful and true. She is only
twenty-two years old, and is sinking already beneath
the weight of her soul; a victim to highly strung nerves,
to an organization either too delicate or too full of power.
A passionate love for a faithless lover would drive her
mad, my poor Fosseuse! I have made a study of her
temperament, recognized the reality of her prolonged
nervous attacks, and of the swift mysterious recurrence
of her uplifted moods. I found that they were immediately dependent on atmospheric changes and on the
variations of the moon, a fact which I have carefully
verified; and since then I have cared for her, as a creature
unlike all others, for she is a being whose ailing existence

I alone can understand. As I have told you, she is the pet lamb. But you shall see her; this is her cottage.'

They had come about one-third of the way up the mountain-side. Low bushes grew on either hand along the steep paths which they were ascending at a foot pace. At last, at a turn in one of the paths, Genestas saw La Fosseuse's dwelling, which stood on one of the largest knolls on the mountain. Around it was a green sloping space of lawn about three acres in extent, planted with trees, and surrounded by a wall high enough to serve as a fence, but not so high as to shut out the view of the landscape. Several rivulets that had their source in this garden formed little cascades among the trees. The brick-built cottage with a low roof that projected several feet was a charming detail in the landscape. It consisted of a ground floor and a single storey, and stood facing the south. All the windows were in the front of the house, for its small size and lack of depth from back to front made other openings unnecessary. The doors and shutters were painted green, and the underside of the penthouses had been lined with deal boards in the German fashion, and painted white. The rustic charm of the whole little dwelling lay in its spotless cleanliness.

Climbing plants and brier roses grew about the house; a great walnut-tree had been allowed to remain among the flowering acacias and trees that bore sweet-scented blossoms, and a few weeping willows had been set by the little streams in the garden space. A thick belt of pines and beeches grew behind the house, so that the picturesque little dwelling was brought out into strong relief by the sombre width of background. At that hour of the day, the air was fragrant with the scents from the hill-sides and the perfume from La Fosseuse's garden. The sky overhead was clear and serene, but low clouds hung on the horizon, and the far-off peaks had begun to take the deep rose hues that the sunset often brings. At the height which they had reached the whole valley lay before their eyes, from distant Grenoble to the little lake at the foot of the circle of crags by which Genestas had passed on the previous day. Some little distance above the house a line of poplars on the hill indicated the highway that led to Grenoble. Rays of sunlight fell slantwise across the little town which glittered like a diamond, for the soft red light which poured over it like a flood was reflected by all its window-panes. Genestas reined in his horse at the sight, and pointed to the dwellings in the valley, to the new town, and to La Fosseuse's house.

'Since the victory of Wagram, and Napoleon's return to the Tuileries in 1815,' he said, with a sigh, 'nothing has so stirred me as the sight of all this. I owe this pleasure to you, sir, for you have taught me to see beauty in a landscape.'

'Yes,' said the doctor, smiling as he spoke, 'it is better to build towns than to storm them.'

'Oh, sir, how about the taking of Moscow and the surrender of Mantua! Why, you do not really know what that means! Is it not a glory for all of us? You are a good man, but Napoleon also was a good man. If it had not been for England, you both would have understood each other, and our emperor would never have fallen. There are no spies here,' said the officer, looking around him, 'and I can say openly that I love him, now that he is dead! What a ruler! He knew every man when he saw him! He would have made you a Councillor of State, for he was a great administrator himself; even to the point of knowing how many cartridges were left in the men's boxes after an action. Poor man! While you were talking about La Fosseuse, I thought of him, and how he was lying dead in St Helena! Was that the kind of climate and country to suit *him*, whose seat had been a throne, and who had lived with his feet in the

stirrups; what? They say that he used to work in the
garden. The deuce! He was not made to plant cab-
bages. . . . And now we must serve the Bourbons, and
loyally, sir; for, after all, France is France, as you were
saying yesterday.'

Genestas dismounted as he uttered these last words,
and mechanically followed the example set by Benassis,
who fastened his horse's bridle to a tree.

'Can she be away?' said the doctor, when he didn't see
La Fosseuse on the threshold. They went into the house,
but there was no one in the sitting-room on the ground
floor.

'She must have heard the sound of a second horse,'
said Benassis, with a smile, 'and has gone upstairs to put
on her cap, or her sash, or some piece of finery.'

He left Genestas alone, and went upstairs in search of
La Fosseuse. The commandant made a survey of the
room. He noticed the pattern of the paper that covered
the walls—roses scattered over a grey background—and
the straw matting that did duty for a carpet on the floor.
The arm-chair, the table, and the smaller chairs were
made of wood from which the bark had not been removed.
The room was not without ornament; some flower-stands,
as they might be called, made of osiers and wooden hoops,
had been filled with moss and flowers, and the windows
were draped by white dimity curtains bordered with a
scarlet fringe. There was a mirror above the chimney-
piece, where a plain china jar stood between two candle-
sticks. Some calico lay on the table; shirts, apparently,
had been cut out and begun, several pairs of gussets were
finished, and a work-basket, scissors, needles, and thread,
and all a needlewoman's requirements lay beside them.
Everything was as fresh and clean as a shell that the sea
has tossed up on the beach. Genestas saw that a kitchen
lay on the other side of the passage, and that the staircase was at the farther end of it. The upper storey, like

the ground floor, evidently consisted of two rooms only. 'Come, do not be frightened,' Benassis was saying to La Fosseuse; 'come downstairs!'

Genestas promptly retreated into the sitting-room when he heard these words, and in another moment a slender girl, well and gracefully made, appeared in the doorway. She wore a gown of cambric, covered with narrow pink stripes, and cut low at the throat, so as to display a muslin chemisette. Shyness and timidity had brought the colour to a face which had nothing very remarkable about it save a certain flatness of feature which called to mind the Cossack and Russian countenances that since the disasters of 1814 have unfortunately come to be so widely known in France. La Fosseuse was, in fact, very like these men of the North. Her nose turned up at the end, and was sunk in her face, her mouth was wide and her chin small, her hands and arms were red and, like her feet, were of the peasant type, large and strong. Although she had been used to an outdoor life, to exposure to the sun and the scorching summer winds, her complexion had the bleached look of withered grass; but after the first glance this made her face more interesting, and there was such a sweet expression in her blue eyes, so much grace about her movements, and such music in her voice, that little as her features seemed to harmonize with the disposition which Benassis had praised to the commandant, the officer recognized in her the capricious and ailing creature, condemned to suffering by a nature that had been thwarted in its growth.

La Fosseuse deftly stirred the fire of dry branches and turfs of peat, then sat down in an arm-chair and took up one of the shirts that she had begun. She sat there under the officer's eyes, half bashful, afraid to look up, and calm to all appearance; but her bodice rose and fell with the rapid breathing that betrayed her nervousness, and it struck Genestas that her figure was very graceful.

'Well, my poor child, is your work going on nicely?'
said Benassis, taking up the material intended for the
shirts, and passing it through his fingers.

La Fosseuse gave the doctor a timid and beseeching
glance.

'Do not scold me, sir,' she entreated; 'I have not
touched them to-day, although they were ordered by you,
and for people who need them very badly. But the
weather has been so fine! I wandered out and picked a
quantity of mushrooms and white truffles, and took them
over to Jacquotte; she was very much pleased, for some
people are coming to dinner. I was so glad that I thought
of it; something seemed to tell me to go to look for
them.'

She began to ply her needle again.

'You have a very pretty house here, mademoiselle,'
said Genestas, addressing her.

'It is not mine at all, sir,' she said, looking at the
stranger, and her eyes seemed to grow red and tearful;
'it belongs to M. Benassis,' and she turned towards the
doctor with a gentle expression on her face.

'You know quite well, my child, that you will never
have to leave it,' he said, as he took her hand in his.

La Fosseuse suddenly rose and left the room.

'Well,' said the doctor, addressing the officer, 'what
do you think of her?'

'There is something strangely touching about her,'
Genestas answered. 'How very nicely you have fitted
up this little nest of hers!'

'Bah! a wallpaper at fifteen or twenty sous; it was
carefully chosen, but that was all. The furniture is
nothing very much either, my basket-maker made it for
me; he wanted to show his gratitude; and La Fosseuse
made the curtains herself out of a few yards of calico.
This little house of hers, and her simple furniture, seem
pretty to you, because you come upon them up here on

a hill-side in a forlorn part of the world where you did not expect to find things clean and tidy. The reason of the prettiness is a kind of harmony between the little house and its surroundings. Nature has set picturesque groups of trees and running streams about it, and has scattered her fairest flowers among the grass, her sweet-scented wild strawberry blossoms, and her lovely violets. . . . Well, what is the matter?' asked Benassis, as La Fosseuse came back to them.

'Oh! nothing, nothing,' she answered. 'I fancied that one of my chickens was missing, and had not been shut up.'

Her remark was disingenuous, but this was only noticed by the doctor, who said in her ear: 'You have been crying!'

'Why do you say things like that to me before some-one else?' she asked in reply.

'Mademoiselle,' said Genestas, 'it is a great pity that you live here all by yourself; you ought to have a mate in such a charming cage as this.'

'That is true,' she said, 'but what would you have? I am poor, and I am hard to please. I feel that it would not suit me at all to carry the soup out into the fields, nor to push a hand-cart; to feel the misery of those whom I should love, and have no power to put an end to it; to carry my children in my arms all day, and patch and re-patch a man's rags. The curé tells me that such thoughts as these are not very Christian; I know that myself, but how can I help it? There are days when I would rather eat a morsel of dry bread than cook anything for my dinner. Why would you have me worry some man's life out with my failings? He would perhaps work himself to death to satisfy my whims, and that would not be right. Pshaw! an unlucky lot has fallen to me, and I ought to bear it by myself.'

'And besides, she is a born do-nothing,' said Benassis. 'We must take my poor Fosseuse as we find her. But all that she has been saying to you simply means that she has never loved as yet,' he added, smiling. Then he rose and went out on to the lawn for a moment.

'You must be very fond of M. Benassis?' asked Genestas.

'Oh! yes, sir; and there are plenty of people hereabouts who feel as I do—that they would be glad to do anything in the world for him. And yet he who cures other people has some trouble of his own that nothing can cure. You are his friend, perhaps you know what it is? Who could have given pain to such a man, who is the very image of God on earth? I know a great many here who think that the corn grows faster if he has passed by their field in the morning.'

'And what do you think yourself?'

'I, sir? When I have seen him,' she seemed to hesitate, then she went on, 'I am happy all the rest of the day.'

She bent her head over her work, and plied her needle with unwonted swiftness.

'Well, has the captain been telling you something about Napoleon?' said the doctor, as he came in again.

'Have you seen the emperor, sir?' cried La Fosseuse, gazing at the officer's face with eager curiosity.

'*Parbleu!*' said Genestas, 'hundreds of times!'

'Oh! how I should like to know something about the army!'

'Perhaps we will come to take a cup of coffee with you to-morrow, and you shall hear "something about the army," dear child,' said Benassis, who laid his hand on her shoulder and kissed her brow. 'She is my daughter, you see!' he added, turning to the commandant; 'there is something wanting in the day, somehow, when I have not kissed her forehead.'

La Fosseuse held Benassis's hand in a tight clasp as she murmured: 'Oh! you are very kind!'

They left the house; but she came after them to see them mount. She waited till Genestas was in the saddle, and then whispered in Benassis's ear: 'Tell me who that gentleman is.'

'Aha!' said the doctor, putting a foot in the stirrup, 'a husband for you, perhaps.'

She stood on the spot where they left her, absorbed in watching their progress down the steep path; and when they came past the end of the garden, they saw her already perched on a little heap of stones, so that she might still keep them in view and give them a last nod of farewell.

'There is something very unusual about that girl, sir,' Genestas said to the doctor when they had left the house far behind.

'There is, is there not?' he answered. 'Many a time I have said to myself that she will make a charming wife, but I can only love her as a sister or a daughter, and in no other way; my heart is dead.'

'Has she any relations?' asked Genestas. 'What did her father and mother do?'

'Oh, it is quite a long story,' answered Benassis. 'Neither her father nor mother nor any of her relations are living. Everything about her down to her name interested me. La Fosseuse was born here in the town. Her father, a labourer from Saint Laurent du Pont, was nicknamed *Le Fosseur*, which is no doubt a contraction of *fossoyeur*, for the office of sexton had been in his family time out of mind. All the sad associations of the grave-yard hang about the name. Here, as in some other parts of France, there is an old custom, dating from the times of the Latin civilization, in virtue of which a woman takes her husband's name, with the addition of a feminine termination, and this girl has been called La Fosseuse, after her father.

'The labourer had married the waiting-woman of some countess or other who owns an estate at a distance of a few leagues. It was a love-match. Here, as in all country districts, love is a very small element in a marriage.

The peasant, as a rule, wants a wife who will bear him
children, a housewife who will make good soup and take
it out to him in the fields, who will spin and make his
shirts and mend his clothes. Such a thing had not happened for a long while in a district where a young man
not unfrequently leaves his betrothed for another girl
who is richer by three or four acres of land. The fate of
Le Fosseur and his wife was scarcely happy enough to
induce our Dauphinois to forsake their calculating habits
and practical way of regarding things. La Fosseuse,
who was a very pretty woman, died when her daughter
was born, and her husband's grief for his loss was so great
that he followed her within the year, leaving nothing in
the world to his little one except an existence whose
continuance was very doubtful—a mere feeble flicker of a
life. A charitable neighbour took the care of the baby
upon herself, and brought her up till she was nine years
old. Then the burden of supporting La Fosseuse became too heavy for the good woman; so at the time of
year when travellers are passing along the roads, she sent
her charge to beg for her living upon the highways.

'One day the little orphan asked for bread at the
countess's château, and they kept the child for her mother's
sake. She was to be waiting-maid some day to the
daughter of the house, and was brought up to this end.
Her young mistress was married five years later; but
meanwhile the poor little thing was the victim of all the
caprices of wealthy people, whose beneficence for the
most part is not to be depended upon even while it lasts.
They are generous by fits and starts; sometimes patrons,
sometimes friends, sometimes masters, in this way they
falsify the already false position of the poor children in
whom they interest themselves, and trifle with the hearts,
the lives, and futures of their protégées, whom they regard very lightly. From the first La Fosseuse became
almost a companion to the young heiress; she was taught

to read and write, and her future mistress sometimes amused herself by giving her music lessons. She was treated sometimes as a lady's companion, sometimes as a waiting-maid, and in this way they made an incomplete being of her. She acquired a taste for luxury and for dress, together with manners ill-suited to her real position. She has been roughly schooled by misfortune since then, but the vague feeling that she is destined for a higher lot has not been effaced in her.

'A day came at last, however, a fateful day for the poor girl, when the young countess (who was married by this time) discovered La Fosseuse arrayed in one of her ball dresses, and dancing before a mirror. La Fosseuse was no longer anything but a waiting-maid, and the orphan girl, then sixteen years of age, was dismissed without pity. Her idle ways plunged her once more into poverty; she wandered about begging by the road-side, and working at times as I have told you. Sometimes she thought of drowning herself, sometimes also of giving herself to the first comer; she spent most of her time thinking dark thoughts, lying by the side of a wall in the sun, with her face buried in the grass, and passersby would sometimes throw a few halfpence to her, simply because she asked them for nothing. One whole year she spent in a hospital at Annecy after heavy toil in the harvest field; she had only undertaken the work in the hope that it would kill her, and that so she might die. You should hear her herself when she speaks of her feelings and ideas during this time of her life; her simple confidences are often very curious.

'She came back to the little town at last, just about the time when I decided to take up my abode in it. I wanted to understand the minds of the people beneath my rule; her character struck me, and I made a study of it; then when I became aware of her physical infirmities, I determined to watch over her. Perhaps in time she may grow accustomed to work with her needle, but, whatever happens, I have secured her future.'

'She is quite alone up there?' said Genestas.

'No. One of my herdswomen sleeps in the house,' the doctor answered. 'You did not see my farm buildings which lie behind the house. They are hidden by the pine-trees. Oh! she is quite safe. Moreover, there are no libertines here in the valley; if any come among us by any chance, I send them into the army, where they make excellent soldiers.'

'Poor girl!' said Genestas.

'Oh! the folk round about do not pity her at all,' said Benassis; 'on the other hand, they think her very lucky; but there is this difference between her and the other women, God has given strength to them and weakness to her, and they do not see that.'

The moment that the two horsemen came out upon the road to Grenoble, Benassis stopped with an air of satisfaction; a different view had suddenly opened out before them; he foresaw its effect upon Genestas, and wished to enjoy his surprise. As far as the eye could see, two green walls sixty feet high rose above a road which was rounded like a garden path. The trees had not been cut or trimmed, each one preserved the magnificent palm-branch shape that makes the Lombard poplar one of the grandest of trees; there they stood, a natural monument which a man might well be proud of having reared. The shadow had already reached one side of the road, transforming it into a vast wall of black leaves, but the setting sun shone full upon the other side, which stood out in contrast, for the young leaves at the tips of every branch had been dyed a bright golden hue, and, as the breeze stirred through the waving curtain, it gleamed in the light.

'You must be very happy here!' cried Genestas. 'The sight of this must be all pleasure to you.'

'The love of Nature is the only love that does not
deceive human hopes. There is no disappointment here,'
said the doctor. 'Those poplars are ten years old; have you
ever seen any that are better grown than these of mine?'

'God is great!' said the soldier, coming to a stand in
the middle of the road, of which he saw neither beginning
nor end.

'You do me good,' cried Benassis. 'It was a pleasure
to hear you say over again what I have so often said in
the midst of this avenue. There is something holy about
this place. Here, we are like two mere specks; and the
feeling of our own littleness always brings us into the
presence of God.'

They rode on slowly and in silence, listening to their
horses' hoof-beats; the sound echoed along the green
corridor as it might have done beneath the vaulted roof
of a cathedral.

'How many things have a power to stir us which town-
dwellers do not suspect,' said the doctor. 'Do you
notice the sweet scent given off by the gum of the poplar
buds, and the resin of the larches? How delightful it is!'

'Listen!' exclaimed Genestas. 'Let us wait a moment.'

A distant sound of singing came to their ears.

'Is it a woman or a man, or is it a bird?' asked the
commandant in a low voice. 'Is it the voice of this
wonderful landscape!'

'It is something of all these things,' the doctor answered,
as he dismounted and fastened his horse to a branch of a
poplar-tree.

He made a sign to the officer to follow his example
and to come with him. They went slowly along a footpath between two hedges of blossoming hawthorn which
filled the damp evening air with its delicate fragrance.
The sun shone full into the pathway; the light and warmth
were very perceptible after the shade thrown by the long
wall of poplar-trees; the still powerful rays poured a

flood of red light over a cottage at the end of the stony track. The ridge of the cottage roof was usually a bright green with its overgrowth of mosses and house-leeks, and the thatch was brown as a chestnut shell, but just now it seemed to be powdered with a golden dust. The cottage itself was scarcely visible through the haze of light; the ruinous wall, the doorway, and everything about it was radiant with a fleeting glory and a beauty due to chance, such as is sometimes seen for an instant in a human face, beneath the influence of a strong emotion that brings warmth and colour into it. In a life under the open sky and among the fields, the transient and tender grace of such moments as these draws from us the wish of the apostle who said to Jesus Christ upon the mountain: 'Let us build a tabernacle and dwell here.'

The wide landscape seemed at that moment to have found a voice whose purity and sweetness equalled its own sweetness and purity, a voice as mournful as the dying light in the west—for a vague reminder of Death is divinely set in the heavens, and the sun above gives the same warning that is given here on earth by the flowers and the bright insects of a day. There is a tinge of sadness about the radiance of sunset, and the melody was sad. It was a song widely known in days of yore, a ballad of love and sorrow that once had served to stir the national hatred of France for England. Beaumarchais, in a later day, had given it back its true poetry by adapting it for the French theatre and putting it into the mouth of a page, who pours out his heart to his stepmother. Just now it was simply the air that rose and fell. There were no words; the plaintive voice of the singer touched and thrilled the soul.

'It is the swan's song,' said Benassis. 'That voice does not sound twice in a century for human ears. Let us hurry; we must put a stop to the singing! The child is killing himself; it would be cruel to listen to him any

longer. Be quiet, Jacques! Come, come, be quiet!'
cried the doctor.

The music ceased. Genestas stood motionless and
overcome with astonishment. A cloud had drifted
across the sun, the landscape and the voice were both
mute. Shadow, chillness, and silence had taken the
place of the soft glory of the light, the warm breath of
the breeze, and the child's singing.

'What makes you disobey me?' asked Benassis. 'I
shall not bring you any more rice pudding nor snail
broth! No more fresh dates and white bread for you!
So you want to die and break your poor mother's heart,
do you?'

Genestas came into a little yard, which was sufficiently
clean and tidily kept, and saw before him a lad of fifteen,
who looked as delicate as a woman. His hair was fair
but scanty, and the colour in his face was so bright that
it seemed hardly natural. He rose up slowly from the
bench where he was sitting, beneath a thick bush of
jessamine and some blossoming lilacs that were running
riot, so that he was almost hidden among the leaves.

'You know very well,' said the doctor, 'that I told
you not to talk, not to expose yourself to the chilly evening
air, and to go to bed as soon as the sun was set. What
put it into your head to sing?'

'Well, M. Benassis, it was so very warm out here,
and it is so nice to feel warm! I am always cold. I
felt so happy that without thinking I began to try over
Malbrouk s'en va-t-en guerre, just for fun, and then I
began to listen to myself because my voice was something like the sound of the flute your shepherd plays.'

'Well, my poor Jacques, this must not happen again;
do you hear? Let me have your hand,' and the doctor
felt his pulse.

The boy's eyes had their usual sweet expression, but
just now they shone with a feverish light.

'It is just as I thought, you are covered with perspiration,' said Benassis. 'Your mother has not come in yet?'

'No, sir.'

'Come! go indoors and get into bed.'

The young invalid went back into the cottage, followed by Benassis and the officer.

'Just light a candle, Captain Bluteau,' said the doctor, who was helping Jacques to take off his rough, tattered clothing.

When Genestas had struck a light, and the interior of the room was visible, he was surprised by the extreme thinness of the child, who seemed to be little more than skin and bone. When the little peasant had been put to bed, Benassis tapped the lad's chest, and listened to the ominous sounds made in this way by his fingers; then, after some deliberation, he drew back the coverlet over Jacques, stepped back a few paces, folded his arms across his chest, and closely scrutinized his patient.

'How do you feel, my little man?'

'Quite comfortable, sir.'

A table, with four spindle legs, stood in the room; the doctor drew it up to the bed, found a tumbler and a phial on the mantel-shelf, and composed a draught, by carefully measuring a few drops of brown liquid from the phial into some water, Genestas holding the light the while.

'Your mother is very late.'

'She is coming, sir,' said the child; 'I can hear her footsteps on the path.'

The doctor and the officer looked around them while they waited. At the foot of the bed there was a sort of mattress made of moss, on which, doubtless, the mother was wont to sleep in her clothes, for there were neither sheets nor coverlet. Genestas pointed out this bed to Benassis, who nodded slightly to show that he likewise had already admired this motherly devotion. There was a clatter of sabots in the yard, and the doctor went out.

'You will have to sit up with Jacques to-night, Mother Colas. If he tells you that his breathing is bad, you must let him drink some of the draught that I have poured into the tumbler on the table. Take care not to let him have more than two or three sips at a time; there ought to be enough in the tumbler to last him all through the night. Above all things, do not touch the phial, and change the child's clothing at once. He is perspiring heavily.'

'I could not manage to wash his shirts to-day, sir; I had to take the hemp over to Grenoble, as we wanted the money.'

'Very well, then, I will send you some shirts.'

'Then is he worse, my poor lad?' asked the woman.

'He has been so imprudent as to sing, Mother Colas; and it is not to be expected that any good can come of it; but do not be hard upon him nor scold him. Do not be downhearted about it; and if Jacques complains overmuch, send a neighbour to fetch me. Good-bye.'

The doctor called to his friend, and they went back along the footpath.

'Is that little peasant consumptive?' asked Genestas.

'He certainly is,' replied Benassis. 'Science cannot save him, unless Nature works a miracle. Our professors at the École de Médecine in Paris often used to speak to us of the phenomenon which you have just witnessed. Some maladies of this kind bring about changes in the voice-producing organs that give the sufferer a short-lived power of song that no trained voice can surpass. I have made you spend a melancholy day, sir,' said the doctor when he was once more in the saddle. 'Suffering and death everywhere, but everywhere also resignation. All these peasant folk take death philosophically; they fall ill, say nothing about it, and take to their beds like dumb animals. But let us say no more about death, and let us quicken our horses' pace a little; we ought to reach the town before nightfall, so that you may see the new quarter.'

'Eh! some place is on fire over there,' said Genestas, pointing to a spot on the mountain, where a sheaf of flames was rising.

'It is not a dangerous fire. Our lime-burner is heating his kiln, no doubt. It is a newly started industry, which turns our heather to account.'

There was a sudden report of a gun, followed by an involuntary exclamation from Benassis, who said, with an impatient gesture, 'If that is Butifer, we shall see which of us two is the stronger.'

'The shot came from that quarter,' said Genestas, indicating a beech-wood up above them on the mountain-side. 'Yes, up there; you may trust an old soldier's ear.

'Let us go there at once!' cried Benassis, and he made straight for the little wood, urging his horse at a furious speed across the ditches and fields, as if he were riding a steeplechase, in his anxiety to catch the sportsman red-handed.

'The man you are after has made off,' shouted Genestas, who could scarcely keep up with him.

Benassis wheeled his horse round sharply, and came back again. The man of whom he was in search soon appeared on the top of a perpendicular crag, a hundred feet above the level of the two horsemen.

'Butifer!' shouted Benassis when he saw that this figure carried a fowling-piece; 'come down!'

Butifer recognized the doctor, and replied by a respectful and friendly sign which showed that he had every intention of obeying.

'I can imagine that if a man were driven to it by fear or by some overmastering impulse he might possibly contrive to scramble up to that point among the rocks,' said Genestas; 'but how will he manage to come down again?'

'I have no anxiety on that score,' answered Benassis; 'the wild goats must feel envious of that fellow yonder! You will see.'

The emergencies of warfare had accustomed the commandant to gauge the real worth of men; he admired the wonderful quickness of Butifer's movements, the sure-footed grace with which the hunter swung himself down the rugged sides of the crag, to the top of which he had so boldly climbed. The strong, slender form of the mountaineer was gracefully poised in every attitude which the precipitous nature of the path compelled him to assume; and so certain did he seem of his power to hold on at need, that if the pinnacle of rock on which he took his stand had been a level floor, he could not have set his foot down upon it more calmly. He carried his fowling-piece as if it had been a light walking cane. Butifer was a young man of middle height, thin, muscular, and in good training; his beauty was of a masculine order, which impressed Genestas on a closer view.

Evidently he belonged to the class of smugglers who ply their trade without resorting to violent courses, and who only exert patience and craft to defraud the Government. His face was manly and sunburnt. His eyes, which were bright as an eagle's, were of a clear yellow colour, and his sharply cut nose with its slight curve at the tip was very much like an eagle's beak. His cheeks were covered with down, his red lips were half open, giving a glimpse of a set of teeth of dazzling whiteness. His beard, moustache, and the reddish whiskers, which he allowed to grow, and which curled naturally, still further heightened the masculine and forbidding expression of his face. Everything about him spoke of strength. He was broad-chested; constant activity had made the muscles of his hands curiously firm and prominent. There was the quick intelligence of a savage about his glances; he looked resolute, fearless, and imperturbable, like a man accustomed to put his life in peril, and whose physical and mental strength had been so often tried by dangers of every kind, that he no longer felt any doubts about himself. He wore a blouse that had suffered a good deal from thorns and briers, and he had a pair of leather soles bound to his feet by eel-skin thongs, and a pair of torn and tattered blue linen breeches through which his legs were visible, red, wiry, hard, and muscular as those of a stag.

'There you see the man who once fired a shot at me,' Benassis remarked to the commandant in a low voice. 'If at this moment I were to signify to him my desire to be rid of anyone, he would kill them without scruple.— Butifer!' he went on, addressing the poacher, 'I fully believed you to be a man of your word; I pledged mine for you because I had your promise. My promise to the public prosecutor at Grenoble was based upon your vow never to go poaching again, and to turn over a new leaf and become a steady, industrious worker. You fired that shot just now, and here you are, on the Comte de Labranchoir's estate! Eh! you miscreant? Suppose his keeper had happened to hear you? It is a lucky thing for you that I shall take no formal cognizance of this offence; if I did, you would come up as an old offender, and of course you have no gun licence! I let you keep that gun of yours out of tenderness for your attachment to the weapon.'

'It is a beauty,' said the commandant, who recognized a duck gun from Saint Étienne.

The smuggler raised his head and looked at Genestas by way of acknowledging the compliment.

'Butifer,' continued Benassis, 'if your conscience does not reproach you, it ought to do so. If you are going to begin your old tricks again, you will find yourself once more in a park enclosed by four stone walls, and no power on earth will save you from the hulks; you will be a marked man, and your character will be ruined. Bring your gun to me to-night, I will take care of it for you.'

Butifer gripped the barrel of his weapon in a convulsive clutch.

'You are quite right, sir,' he said; 'I have done wrong, I have broken bounds, I am a cur. My gun ought to go to you, but when you take it away from me, you take all that I have in the world. The last shot which my mother's son will fire shall be through my own head. . . . What would you have? I did as you wanted me. I kept quiet all the winter; but the spring came, and the sap rose. I am not used to day labour. It is not in my nature to spend my life in fattening fowls; I cannot stoop about turning over the soil for vegetables, nor flourish a whip and drive a cart, nor scrub down a horse in a stable all my life, so I must die of starvation, I suppose? I am only happy when I am up there,' he went on after a pause, pointing to the mountains. 'And I have been about among the hills for the past week; I got a sight of a chamois, and I have the chamois there,' he said, pointing to the top of the crag; 'it is at your service! Dear M. Benassis, leave me my gun. Listen! I will leave the commune —faith I will! I will go to the Alps; the chamois-hunters will not say a word; on the contrary, they will receive me with open arms. I shall come to grief at the bottom of some glacier; but, if I am to speak my mind, I would rather live for a couple of years among the heights, where there are no governments, nor excisemen, nor game-keepers, nor public prosecutors, than grovel in a marsh for a century. You are the only one that I shall be sorry to leave behind; all the rest of them bore me! When you are in the right, at any rate you don't worry one's life out——'

'And how about Louise?' asked Benassis. Butifer paused and turned thoughtful.

'Eh! learn to read and write, my lad,' said Genestas; 'come and enlist in my regiment, have a horse to ride, and turn carabineer. If they once sound "to horse" for something like a war, you will find out that Providence made you to live in the midst of cannon, bullets, and battalions, and they will make a general of you.'

'Ye-es, if Napoleon was back again,' answered Butifer.

'You know our agreement,' said the doctor. 'At the second infraction of it, you undertook to go for a soldier. I give you six months in which to learn to read and write, and then I will find up some young gentleman who wants a substitute.'

Butifer looked at the mountains.

'Oh! you shall not go to the Alps,' cried Benassis. 'A man like you, a man of his word, with plenty of good stuff in him, ought to serve his country and command a brigade, and not come to his end trailing after a chamois. The life that you are leading will take you straight to the convicts' prison. After over-fatiguing yourself, you are obliged to take a long rest; and, in the end, you will fall into idle ways that will be the ruin of any notions of orderly existence that you have; you will get into the habit of putting your strength to bad uses, and you will take the law into your own hands. I want to put you, in spite of yourself, into the right path.'

'So I am to pine and fret myself to death? I feel suffocated whenever I am in a town. I cannot hold out for more than a day, in Grenoble, when I take Louise there——'

'We all have our whims, which we must manage to control, or turn them to account for our neighbour's benefit. But it is late, and I am in a hurry. Come to see me to-morrow, and bring your gun along with you. We will talk this over, my my boy. Good-bye. Go and sell your chamois in Grenoble.'

The two horsemen went on their way.

'That is what I call a man,' said Genestas.

'A man in a bad way,' answered Benassis. 'But what help is there for it? You heard what he said. Is it not

lamentable to see such fine qualities running to waste?
If France were invaded by a foreign foe, Butifer at the
head of a hundred young fellows would keep a whole
division busy in Maurienne for a month; but in a time
of peace the only outlets for his energy are those which
set the law at defiance. He must wrestle with something;
whenever he is not risking his neck he is at odds with
society, he lends a helping hand to smugglers. The
rogue will cross the Rhône, all by himself, in a little boat,
to take shoes over into Savoy; he makes good his retreat,
heavy laden as he is, to some inaccessible place high up
among the hills, where he stays for two days at a time,
living on dry crusts. In short, danger is as welcome to
him as sleep would be to anybody else, and by dint of
experience he has acquired a relish for extreme sensations
that has totally unfitted him for ordinary life. It vexes
me that a man like that should take a wrong turn and
gradually go to the bad, become a bandit, and die on the
gallows. But, see, captain, how our village looks from
here!'

Genestas obtained a distant view of a wide circular
space, planted with trees; a fountain surrounded by
poplars stood in the middle of it. Round the enclosures
were high banks on which a triple line of trees of different
kinds were growing; the first row consisted of acacias,
the second of Japanese varnish trees, and some young
elms grew on the highest row of all.

'That is where we hold our fair,' said Benassis. 'That
is the beginning of the High Street, by those two handsome houses that I told you about; one belongs to the
notary, and the other to the justice of the peace.'

They came at that moment into a broad road, fairly
evenly paved with large cobble-stones. There were
altogether about a hundred new houses on either side of
it, and almost every house stood in a garden.

The view of the church with its doorway made a pretty

termination to this road. Two more roads had been
recently planned out half-way down the course of the
first, and many new houses had already been built along
them. The town hall stood opposite the parsonage, in
the square by the church. As Benassis went down the
road, women and children and men who had just finished
their day's work promptly appeared in their doorways
to wish him good evening, the men took off their caps,
and the little children danced and shouted about his horse,
as if the animal's good nature were as well known as the
kindness of its master. The gladness was undemonstrative; there was the instinctive delicacy of all deep
feeling about it, and it had the same pervasive power.
At the sight of this welcome it seemed to Genestas that
the doctor had been too modest in his description of the
affection with which he was regarded by the people of the
district. His truly was a sovereignty of the sweetest
kind; a right royal sovereignty moreover, for its title was
engraven in the hearts of its subjects. However dazzling
the rays of glory that surround a man, however great the
power that he enjoys, in his inmost soul he soon comes
to a just estimate of the sentiments that all external action
causes for him. He very soon sees that no change has
been wrought in him, that there is nothing new and
nothing greater in the exercise of his physical faculties,
and discovers his own real nothingness. Kings, even
should they rule over the whole world, are condemned
to live in a narrow circle like other men. They must
even submit to the conditions of their lot, and their happiness depends upon the personal impressions that they
receive. But Benassis met with nothing but goodwill and
loyalty throughout the district.

III

THE NAPOLEON OF THE PEOPLE

'PRAY, come in, sir!' cried Jacquotte. 'A pretty time the gentlemen have been waiting for you! It is always the way! You always manage to spoil the dinner for me whenever it ought to be particularly good. Everything is cooked to death by this time——'

'Oh! well, here we are,' answered Benassis with a smile.

The two horsemen dismounted, and went off to the *salon*, where the guests invited by the doctor were assembled.

'Gentlemen,' he said, taking Genestas by the hand, 'I have the honour of introducing to you M. Bluteau, captain of a regiment of cavalry stationed at Grenoble—an old soldier, who has promised me that he will stay among us for a little while.'

Then, turning to Genestas, he presented to him a tall, thin, grey-haired man, dressed in black.

'This gentleman,' said Benassis, 'is M. Dufau, the justice of the peace of whom I have already spoken to you, and who has so largely contributed to the prosperity of the commune.' Then he led his guest up to a pale, slight young man of middle height, who wore spectacles, and was also dressed in black. 'And this is M. Tonnelet,' he went on, 'M. Gravier's son-in-law, and the first notary who came to live in the village.'

The doctor next turned to a stout man, who seemed to belong half to the peasant, half to the middle class, the owner of a rough-pimpled but good-humoured countenance.

'This is my worthy colleague M. Cambon,' he went

on, 'the timber-merchant, to whom I owe the confidence and goodwill of the people here. He was one of the promoters of the road which you have admired. I have no need to tell you the profession of this gentleman,' Benassis added, turning to the curé. 'Here is a man whom no one can help loving.'

There was an irresistible attraction in the moral beauty expressed by the curé's countenance, which engrossed Genestas's attention. Yet a certain harshness and austerity of outline might make M. Janvier's face seem unpleasing at a first glance. His attitude, and his slight, emaciated frame, showed that he was far from strong physically, but the unchanging serenity of his face bore witness to the profound inward peace of the Christian and to the strength that comes from purity of heart. Heaven seemed to be reflected in his eyes, and the inextinguishable fervour of charity which glowed in his heart appeared to shine from them. The gestures that he made but rarely were simple and natural; his appeared to be a quiet and retiring nature, and there was a modesty and simplicity like that of a young girl about his actions. At first sight he inspired respect and a vague desire to be admitted to his friendship.

'Ah! Mr Mayor,' he said, bending as though to escape from Benassis's eulogium.

Something in the curé's tones brought a thrill to Genestas's heart, and the two insignificant words uttered by this stranger priest plunged him into musings that were almost devout.

'Gentlemen,' said Jacquotte, who came into the middle of the room, and there took her stand, with her hands on her hips, 'the soup is on the table.'

Invited by Benassis, who summoned each in turn so as to avoid questions of precedence, the doctor's five guests went into the dining-room; and after the curé, in low and quiet tones, had repeated a *Benedicite*, they took their places at table. The cloth that covered the table was of that peculiar kind of damask linen invented in the time of Henry IV by the brothers Graindorge, the skilful weavers who gave their name to the heavy fabric so well known to housekeepers. The linen was of dazzling whiteness, and fragrant with the scent of the thyme that Jacquotte always put into her wash-tubs. The dinner service was of white porcelain, edged with blue, and was in perfect order. The decanters were of the old-fashioned octagonal kind still in use in the provinces, though they have disappeared elsewhere. Grotesque figures had been carved on the horn handles of the knives. These relics of ancient splendour, which, nevertheless, looked almost new, seemed to those who scrutinized them to be in keeping with the kindly and open-hearted nature of the master of the house.

The lid of the soup-tureen drew a momentary glance from Genestas; he noticed that it was surmounted by a group of vegetables in high relief, skilfully coloured after the manner of Bernard Palissy, the celebrated sixteenth-century craftsman.

There was no lack of character about the group of men thus assembled. The powerful heads of Genestas and Benassis contrasted admirably with M. Janvier's apostolic countenance; and in the same fashion the elderly faces of the justice of the peace and the deputy-mayor brought out the youthfulness of the notary. Society seemed to be represented by these various types. The expression of each one indicated contentment with himself and with the present, and a faith in the future. M. Tonnelet and M. Janvier, who were still young, loved to make forecasts of coming events, for they felt that the future was theirs; while the other guests were fain rather to turn their talk upon the past. All of them faced the things of life seriously, and their opinions seemed to reflect a double tinge of soberness, on the one hand, from the twilight hues of wellnigh forgotten joys that could never more be revived for them; and, on the other, from the grey dawn which gave promise of a glorious day.

'You must have had a very tiring day, sir?' said M. Cambon, addressing the curé.

'Yes, sir,' answered M. Janvier, 'the poor cretin and old Pelletier were buried at different hours.'

'Now we can pull down all the hovels of the old village,' Benassis remarked to his deputy. 'When the space on which the houses stand has been grubbed up, it will mean at least another acre of meadow land for us; and furthermore, there will be a clear saving to the commune of the hundred francs that it used to cost to keep Chautard the cretin.'

'For the next three years we ought to lay out the hundred francs in making a single-span bridge to carry the lower road over the main stream,' said M. Cambon. 'The townsfolk and the people down the valley have fallen into the way of taking a short cut across that patch of land of Jean-François Pastoureau's; before they have done they will cut it up in a way that will do a lot of harm to that poor fellow.'

'I am sure that the money could not be put to a better use,' said the justice of the peace. 'In my opinion the abuse of the right of way is one of the worst nuisances in a country district. One-tenth of the cases that come before the court are caused by unfair easements. The rights of property are infringed in this way almost with impunity in many and many a commune. A respect for law and a respect for property are ideas too often disregarded in France, and it is most important that they should be inculcated. Many people think that there is something dishonourable in assisting the law to take its course. "Go and be hanged somewhere else," is a saying which seems to be dictated by an unpraiseworthy generosity of feeling; but at bottom it is nothing but a hypocritical formula—a sort of veil which we throw over our own selfishness. Let us own to it, we lack patriotism! The true patriot is the citizen who is so deeply impressed with a sense of the importance of the laws that he will see them carried out even at his own cost and inconvenience. If you let the criminal go in peace, are you not making yourself answerable for the crimes he will commit?'

'It is all of a piece,' said Benassis. 'If the mayors kept their roads in better order, there would not be so many footpaths. And if the members of municipal councils knew a little better, they would uphold the small landowner and the mayor when the two combine to oppose the establishment of unfair easements. The fact that château, cottage, field, and tree are all equally sacred would then be brought home in every way to the ignorant; they would be made to understand that Right is just the same in all cases, whether the value of the property in question be large or small. But such salutary changes cannot be brought about all at once. They depend almost entirely on the moral condition of the population, which we can never completely reform without the potent aid of the curés. This remark does not apply to you in any way, M. Janvier.'

'Nor do I take it to myself,' laughed the curé. 'Is not my heart set on bringing the teaching of the Catholic religion to co-operate with your plans of administration? For instance, I have often tried, in my pulpit discourses on theft, to imbue the folk of this parish with the very ideas of Right to which you have just given utterance. For truly, God does not estimate theft by the value of the thing stolen, He looks at the thief. That has been the gist of the parables which I have tried to adapt to the comprehension of my parishioners.'

'You have succeeded, sir,' said Cambon. 'I know the change you have brought about in people's ways of looking at things, for I can compare the commune as it is now with the commune as it used to be. There are

certainly very few places where the labourers are as careful as ours are about keeping to time in their working
hours. The cattle are well looked after; any damage
that they do is done by accident. There is no pilfering
in the woods, and finally you have made our peasants
clearly understand that the leisure of the rich is the reward
of a thrifty and hard-working life.'

'Well, then,' said Genestas, 'you ought to be pretty
well pleased with your infantry, M. le Curé.'

'We cannot expect to find angels anywhere here below,
captain,' answered the priest. 'Wherever there is poverty,
there is suffering too; and suffering and poverty are
strong compelling forces which have their abuses, just as
power has. When the peasants have a couple of leagues
to walk to their work, and have to tramp back wearily
in the evening, they perhaps see sportsmen taking short
cuts over ploughed land and pasture so as to be back to
dinner a little sooner, and is it to be supposed that they
will hesitate to follow the example? And of those who in
this way beat out a footpath such as these gentlemen have
just been complaining about, which are the real offenders,
the workers or the people who are simply amusing themselves? Both the rich and the poor give us a great deal of
trouble in these days. Faith, like power, ought always to
descend from the heights above us, in heaven or on earth;
and certainly in our times the upper classes have less
faith in them than the mass of the people, who have
God's promise of heaven hereafter as a reward for evils
patiently endured. With due submission to ecclesi-
astical discipline, and deference to the views of my
superiors, I think that for some time to come we should
be less exacting as to questions of doctrine, and rather
endeavour to revive the sentiment of religion in the hearts
of the intermediary classes, who debate over the maxims
of Christianity instead of putting them in practice. The
philosophism of the rich has set a fatal example to the poor,

and has brought about intervals of too long duration when men have faltered in their allegiance to God. Such ascendency as we have over our flocks to-day depends entirely on our personal influence with them; is it not deplorable that the existence of religious belief in a commune should be dependent on the esteem in which a single man is held? When the preservative force of Christianity permeating all classes of society shall have put life into the new order of things, there will be an end of sterile disputes about doctrine. The cult of a religion is its form; societies only exist by forms. You have your standard, we have the cross——'

'I should very much like to know, sir,' said Genestas, breaking in upon M. Janvier, 'why you forbid these poor folk to dance on Sunday.'

'We do not quarrel with dancing in itself, captain; it is forbidden because it leads to immorality, which troubles the peace of the countryside and corrupts its manners. Does not the attempt to purify the spirit of the family and to maintain the sanctity of family ties strike at the root of the evil?'

'Some irregularities are always to be found in every district I know,' said M. Tonnelet, 'but they very seldom occur among us. Perhaps there are peasants who remove their neighbour's landmark without much scruple; or they may cut a few osiers that belong to someone else, if they happen to want some; but these are mere peccadilloes compared with the wrongdoing that goes on among a town population. Moreover, the people in this valley seem to me to be devoutly religious.'

'Devout?' queried the curé with a smile; 'there is no fear of fanaticism here.'

'But,' objected Cambon, 'if the people all went to mass every morning, sir, and to confession every week, how would the fields be cultivated? And three priests would hardly be enough.'

'Work is prayer,' said the curé. 'Doing one's duty brings a knowledge of the religious principles which are a vital necessity to society.'

'How about patriotism?' asked Genestas.

'Patriotism can only inspire a short-lived enthusiasm,' the curé answered gravely; 'religion gives it permanence. Patriotism consists in a brief impulse of forgetfulness of self and self-interest, while Christianity is a complete system of opposition to the depraved tendencies of mankind.'

'And yet, during the wars undertaken by the Revolution, patriotism——'

'Yes, we worked wonders at the time of the Revolution,' said Benassis, interrupting Genestas; 'but only twenty years later, in 1814, our patriotism was extinct; while, in former times, a religious impulse moved France and Europe to fling themselves upon Asia a dozen times in the course of a century.'

'Maybe it is easier for two nations to come to terms when the strife has arisen out of some question of material interests,' said the justice of the peace; 'while wars undertaken with the idea of supporting dogmas are bound to be interminable, because the object can never be clearly defined.'

'Well, sir, you are not helping anyone to fish!' put in Jacquotte, who had removed the soup with Nicolle's assistance. Faithful to her custom, Jacquotte herself always brought in every dish one after another, a plan which had its drawbacks, for it compelled gluttonous folk to overeat themselves, and the more abstemious, having satisfied their hunger at an early stage, were obliged to leave the best part of the dinner untouched.

'Gentlemen,' said the curé, with a glance at the justice of the peace, 'how can you allege that religious wars have had no definite aim? Religion in olden times was such a powerful binding force, that material interests and religious questions were inseparable. Every soldier, therefore, knew quite well what he was fighting for.'

'If there has been so much fighting about religion,' said Genestas, 'God must have built up the system very perfunctorily. Should not a divine institution impress men at once by the truth that is in it?'

All the guests looked at the curé.

'Gentlemen,' said M. Janvier, 'religion is something that is felt and that cannot be defined. We cannot know the purpose of the Almighty; we are no judges of the means He employs.'

'Then, according to you, we are to believe in all your rigmaroles,' said Genestas, with the easy good humour of a soldier who has never given a thought to these things.

'The Catholic religion, better than any other, resolves men's doubts and fears; but even were it otherwise, I might ask you if you run any risks by believing in its truths.'

'None worth speaking of,' answered Genestas.

'Good! and what risks do you not run by not believing? But let us talk of the worldly aspect of the matter, which most appeals to you. The finger of God is visible in human affairs; see how He directs them by the hand of His vicar on earth. How much men have lost by leaving the path traced out for them by Christianity! So few think of reading Church history, that erroneous notions deliberately sown among the people lead them to condemn the Church; yet the Church has been a pattern of perfect government such as men seek to establish to-day. The principle of election made it for a long while a great political power. Except the Catholic Church, there was no single religious institution which was founded upon liberty and equality. Everything was ordered to this end. The father-superior, the abbot, the bishop, the general of an order, and the pope were then chosen conscientiously for their fitness for the requirements of the Church. They were the expression of its intelligence, of the thinking-power of the Church, and blind obedience was therefore their due. I will say nothing of the ways in which society has benefited by that power which has created modern nations and has inspired so many poems, so much music, so many cathedrals, statues, and pictures. I will simply call your attention to the fact that your modern systems of popular election, of two chambers, and of juries all had their origin in provincial and oecumenical councils, and in the episcopate and college of cardinals; but there is this difference—the views of civilization held by our present-day philosophy seem to me to fade away before the sublime and divine conception of Catholic communion, the type of a universal social communion brought about by the word and the fact that are combined in religious dogma. It would be very difficult for any modern political system, however perfect people may think it, to work once more such miracles as were wrought in those ages when the Church was the stay and support of the human intellect.'

'Why?' asked Genestas.

'Because, in the first place, if the principle of election is to be the basis of a system, absolute equality among the electors is a first requirement; they ought to be "equal quantities," to make use of a mathematical term, and that is a state of things which modern politics will never bring about. Then, great social changes can only be effected by means of some common sentiment so powerful that it brings men into concerted action, while latter-day philosophism has discovered that law is based upon personal interest, which keeps men apart. Men full of the generous spirit that watches with tender care over the trampled rights of the suffering poor, were more often found among the nations of past ages than in our generation. The priesthood, also, which sprang from the middle classes, resisted material forces and stood between the people and their enemies. But the territorial possessions of the

Church and her temporal power, which seemingly made her position yet stronger, ended by crippling and weakening her action. As a matter of fact, if the priest has possessions and privileges, he at once appears in the light of an oppressor. He is paid by the State, therefore he is an official: if he gives his time, his life, his whole heart, this is a matter of course, and nothing more than he ought to do; the citizens expect and demand his devotion; and the spontaneous kindliness of his nature is dried up. But, let the priest be vowed to poverty, let him turn to his calling of his own free will, let him stay himself on God alone, and have no resource on earth but the hearts of the faithful, and he becomes once more the missionary of America, he takes the rank of an apostle, he has all things under his feet. Indeed, the burden of wealth drags him down, and it is only by renouncing everything that he gains dominion over all men's hearts.'

M. Janvier had compelled the attention of everyone present. No one spoke; for all the guests were thoughtful. It was something new to hear such words as these in the mouth of a simple curé.

'There is one serious error, M. Janvier, among the truths to which you have given expression,' said Benassis. 'As you know, I do not like to raise discussions on points of general interest which modern authorities and modern writers have called in question. In my opinion, a man who has thought out a political system, and who is conscious that he has within him the power of applying it in practical politics, should keep his mind to himself, seize his opportunity and act; but if he dwells in peaceful obscurity as a simple citizen, is it not sheer lunacy to think to bring the great mass over to his opinion by means of individual discussions? For all that, I am about to argue with you, my dear pastor, for I am speaking before sensible men, each of whom is accustomed always to bring his individual light to a common search for the truth. My ideas may seem strange to you, but they are the outcome of much thought caused by the calamities of the last forty years. Universal suffrage, which finds such favour in the sight of those persons who belong to the constitutional opposition, as it is called, was a capital institution in the Church, because (as you yourself have just pointed out, dear pastor) the individuals of whom the Church was composed were all well educated, disciplined by religious feeling, thoroughly imbued with the spirit of the same system, well aware of what they wanted and whither they were going. But modern Liberalism rashly made war upon the prosperous government of the Bourbons, by means of ideas which, should they triumph, would be the ruin of France and of the Liberals themselves. This is well known to the leaders of the Left, who are merely endeavouring to get the power into their own hands. If (which Heaven forbid) the middle classes ranged under the banner of the opposition should succeed in over-throwing those social superiorities which are so repugnant to their vanity, another struggle would follow hard upon their victory. It would not be very long before the middle classes in their turn would be looked upon by the people as a sort of *noblesse*; they would be a sorry kind of *noblesse*, it is true, but their wealth and privileges would seem so much the more hateful in the eyes of the people because they would have a closer vision of these things. I do not say that the nation would come to grief in this struggle, but society would perish anew; for the day of triumph of a suffering people is always brief, and involves disorders of the worst kind. There would be no truce in a desperate strife arising out of an inherent or acquired difference of opinion among the electors. The less enlightened and more numerous portion would sweep away social inequalities, thanks to a system in which votes are reckoned by count and not by weight. Hence it follows that a government is never more strongly organized, and as a consequence is never more perfect, than when it has been established for the protection of Privilege of the most restricted kind. By Privilege I do not at this moment mean the old abuses by which certain rights were conceded to a few, to the prejudice of the many; no, I am using it to express the social circle of the governing class. The governing class is in some sort the heart of the State. But throughout creation Nature has confined the vital principle within a narrow space, in order to concentrate its power; and so it is with the body politic. I will illustrate this thought of mine by examples. Let us suppose that there are a hundred peers in France, there are only one hundred causes of offence. Abolish the peerage, and all wealthy people will constitute the privileged class; instead of a hundred, you will have ten thousand, instead of removing class distinctions, you have merely widened the mischief. In fact, from the people's point of view, the right to live without working is in itself a privilege. The unproductive consumer is a robber in their eyes. The only work that they understand has palpable results; they set no value on intellectual labour—the kind of labour which is the principal source of wealth to them. So by multiplying causes of offence in this way, you extend the field of battle; the social war would be waged at all points instead of being confined within a limited circle; and when attack and resistance become general, the ruin of a country is imminent. Because the rich will always be fewer in number, the victory will be to the poor as soon as it comes to actual fighting. I will throw the burden of proof on history.

'The institution of Senatorial Privilege enabled the Roman Republic to conquer the world. The Senate preserved the tradition of authority. But when the *equites* and the *novi homines* had extended the governing class by adding to the numbers of the Patricians, the State came to ruin. In spite of Sylla, and after the time of Julius Caesar, Tiberius raised it into the Roman Empire; the system was embodied in one man, and all authority was centred in him, a measure which prolonged the magnificent sway of the Roman for several centuries. The emperor had ceased to dwell in Rome when the Eternal City fell into the hands of barbarians. When the conqueror invaded our country, the Franks who divided the land among themselves invented feudal privilege as a safeguard for property. The hundred or the thousand chiefs who owned the country, established their institutions with a view to defending the rights gained by conquest. The duration of the feudal system was co-existent with the restriction of Privilege. But when the *leudes* (an exact translation of the word *gentlemen*) from five hundred became fifty thousand, there came a revolution. The governing power was too widely diffused; it lacked force and concentration; and they had not reckoned with the two powers, Money and Thought, that had set those free who had been beneath their rule. So the victory over the monarchical system, obtained by the middle classes with a view to extending the number of the privileged class, will produce its natural effect— the people will triumph in turn over the middle classes. If this trouble comes to pass, the indiscriminate right of suffrage bestowed upon the masses will be a dangerous weapon in their hands. The man who votes, criticizes. An authority that is called in question is no longer an authority. Can you imagine a society without a governing authority? No, you cannot. Therefore, authority means force, and a basis of just judgment should underlie force. Such are the reasons which have led me to think that the principle of popular election is a most fatal one for modern governments. I think that my attachment to the poor and suffering classes has been sufficiently proved, and that no one will accuse me of bearing any ill will towards them; but though I admire the sublime patience and resignation with which they tread the path of toil, I must pronounce them to be unfit to take part in the government. The proletariat seem to me to be the minors of a nation, and ought to remain in a condition of tutelage. Therefore, gentlemen, the word *election*, to my thinking, is in a fair way to cause as much mischief as the words *conscience* and *liberty*, which, ill defined and ill understood, were flung broadcast among the people, to serve as watchwords of revolt and incitements to destruction. It seems to me to be a right and necessary thing that the masses should be kept in tutelage for the good of society.'

'This system of yours runs so clean contrary to everybody's notions nowadays, that we have some right to ask your reasons for it,' said Genestas, interrupting the doctor.

'By all means, captain.'

'What is this the master is saying?' cried Jacquotte, as she went back to her kitchen. 'There he is, the poor dear man, and what is he doing but advising them to crush the people! And they are listening to him——'

'I would never have believed it of M. Benassis,' answered Nicolle.

'If I require that the ignorant masses should be governed by a strong hand,' the doctor resumed, after a brief pause, 'I should desire at the same time that the framework of the social system should be sufficiently yielding and elastic to allow those who have the will and are conscious of their ability to emerge from the crowd, to rise and take their place among the privileged classes. The aim of power of every kind is its own preservation. In order to live, a government, to-day as in the past, must press the strong men of the nation into its service, taking them from every quarter, so as to make them its defenders, and to remove from among the people the men of energy who incite the masses to insurrection. By opening out in this way to the public ambition paths that are at once difficult and easy, easy for strong wills, difficult for weak or imperfect ones, a State averts the perils of the revolutions caused by the struggles of men of superior powers to rise to their proper level. Our long agony of forty years should have made it clear to any man who has brains that social superiorities are a natural outcome of the order of things. They are of three kinds that cannot be questioned—the superiority of the thinker, the superiority of the politician, the superiority of wealth. Is not that as much as to say, genius, power, and money, or, in yet other words, the cause, the means, and the effect? But suppose a kind of social *tabula rasa*, every social unit perfectly equal, an increase of population everywhere in the same ratio, and give the same amount of land to each family; it would not be long before you would again have all the existing inequalities of fortune; it is glaringly evident, therefore, that there are such things as superiority of fortune, of thinking capacity, and of power, and we must make up our minds to this fact; but the masses will always regard rights that have been most honestly acquired as privileges, and as a wrong done to themselves.

'The social contract founded upon this basis will be a perpetual pact between those who have and those who have not. And acting on these principles, those who benefit by the laws will be the law-makers, for they necessarily have the instinct of self-preservation, and foresee their dangers. It is even more to their interest than to the interest of the masses themselves that the latter should be quiet and contented. The happiness of the people should be ready made for the people. If you look at society as a whole from this point of view, you will soon see, as I do, that the privilege of election ought only to be exercised by men who possess wealth, power, or intelligence, and you will likewise see that the action of the deputies they may choose to represent them should be considerably restricted.

'The maker of laws, gentlemen, should be in advance of his age. It is his business to ascertain the tendency of erroneous notions popularly held, to see the exact direction in which the ideas of a nation are tending; he labours for the future rather than for the present, and for the rising generation rather than for the one that is passing away. But if you call in the masses to make the laws, can they rise above their own level? Nay. The more faithfully an assembly represents the opinions held by the crowd, the less it will know about government, the less lofty its ideas will be, and the more vague and vacillating its policy, for the crowd is and always will be simply a crowd, and this especially with us in France. Law involves submission to regulations; man is naturally opposed to rules and regulations of all kinds, especially if they interfere with his interests; so is it likely that the masses will enact laws that are contrary to their own inclinations? No.

'Very often legislation ought to run counter to the prevailing tendencies of the time. If the law is to be shaped by the prevailing habits of thought and tendencies of a nation, would not that mean that in Spain a direct encouragement would be given to idleness and religious intolerance; in England, to the commercial spirit; in Italy, to the love of the arts that may be the expression of a society, but by which no society can entirely exist; in Germany, feudal, class distinctions would be fostered; and here, in France, popular legislation would promote the spirit of frivolity, the sudden craze for an idea, and the readiness to split into factions which has always been our bane.

'What has happened in the forty years since the electors took it upon themselves to make laws for France? We have something like forty thousand laws! A people with forty thousand laws might as well have none at all. Is it likely that five hundred mediocrities (for there are never more than a hundred great minds to do the work of any one century), is it likely that five hundred mediocrities will have the wit to rise to the level of these considerations? Not they! Here is a constant stream of men poured forth from five hundred different places; they will interpret the spirit of the law in divers manners, and there should be a unity of conception in the law.

'But I will go yet further. Sooner or later an assembly of this kind comes to be swayed by one man, and instead of a dynasty of kings, you have a constantly changing and costly succession of prime ministers. There comes a Mirabeau, or a Danton, a Robespierre, or a Napoleon, or proconsuls, or an emperor, and there is an end of deliberations and debates. In fact, it takes a determinate amount of force to raise a given weight; the force may be distributed, and you may have a less or greater number of levers, but it comes to the same thing in the end, the force must be in proportion to the weight. The weight in this case is the ignorant and suffering mass of people who form the lowest stratum of society. The attitude of authority is bound to be repressive, and great concentration of the governing power is needed to neutralize the force of a popular movement. This is the application of the principle that I unfolded when I spoke just now of the way in which the class privileged to govern should be restricted. If this class is composed of men of ability, they will obey this natural law, and compel the country to obey. If you collect a crowd of mediocrities together, sooner or later they will fall under the dominion of a stronger head. A deputy of talent understands the reasons for which a government exists; the mediocre deputy simply comes to terms with force. An assembly either obeys an idea, like the Convention in the time of the Terror; a powerful personality, like the Corps Législatif

under the rule of Napoleon; or falls under the domi-
nation of a system or of wealth, as it has done in our own
day. The Republican Assembly, that dream of some
innocent souls, is an impossibility. Those who would
fain bring it to pass are either grossly deluded dupes or
would-be tyrants. Do you not think that there is something ludicrous about an Assembly which gravely sits in
debate upon the perils of a nation which ought to be
roused into immediate action? It is only right of course
that the people should elect a body of representatives
who will decide questions of supplies and of taxation;
this institution has always existed, under the sway of the
most tyrannous ruler no less than under the sceptre of the
mildest of princes. Money is not to be taken by force;
there are natural limits to taxation, and if they are over-
stepped, a nation either rises up in revolt, or lays itself
down to die. Again, if this elective body, changing
from time to time according to the needs and ideas of
those whom it represents, should refuse obedience to a
bad law in the name of the people, well and good. But
to imagine that five hundred men, drawn from every
corner of the kingdom, will make a good law! Is it not
a dreary joke, for which the people will sooner or later
have to pay? They have a change of masters, that is all.

'Authority ought to be given to one man, he alone
should have the task of making the laws; and he should
be a man who, by force of circumstances, is continually
obliged to submit his actions to general approbation.
But the only restraints that can be brought to bear upon
the exercise of power, be it the power of the one, of the
many, or of the multitude, are to be found in the religious
institutions of a country. Religion forms the only ade-
quate safeguard against the abuse of supreme power. When
a nation ceases to believe in religion, it becomes ungovern-
able in consequence, and its prince perforce becomes a
tyrant. The Chambers that occupy an intermediate

place between rulers and their subjects are powerless to prevent these results, and can only mitigate them to a very slight extent; Assemblies, as I have said before, are bound to become the accomplices of tyranny on the one hand, or of insurrection on the other. My own leanings are towards a government by one man; but though it is good, it cannot be absolutely good, for the results of every policy will always depend upon the condition and the beliefs of the nation. If a nation is in its dotage, if it has been corrupted to the core by philosophism and the spirit of discussion, it is on the high road to despotism, from which no form of free government will save it. And, at the same time, a righteous people will nearly always find liberty even under a despotic rule. All this goes to show the necessity for restricting the right of election within very narrow limits, the necessity for a strong government, the necessity for a powerful religion which makes the rich man the friend of the poor, and enjoins upon the poor an absolute submission to their lot. It is, in fact, really imperative that the Assemblies should be deprived of all direct legislative power, and should confine themselves to the registration of laws and to questions of taxation.

'I know that different ideas from these exist in many minds. To-day, as in past ages, there are enthusiasts who seek for perfection, and who would like to have society better ordered than it is at present. But innovations which tend to bring about a kind of social topsy-turvydom, ought only to be undertaken by general consent. Let the innovators have patience. When I remember how long it has taken Christianity to establish itself; how many centuries it has taken to bring about a purely moral revolution which surely ought to have been accomplished peacefully, the thought of the horrors of a revolution, in which material interests are concerned, makes me shudder, and I am for maintaining existing institutions. "Each shall have his own thought," is the dictum of Christianity; "Each man shall have his own field," says modern law; and in this, modern law is in harmony with Christianity. Each shall have his own thought; that is a consecration of the rights of intelligence; and each shall have his own field, is a consecration of the right to property that has been acquired by toil. Hence our society. Nature has based human life upon the instinct of self-preservation, and social life is founded upon personal interest. Such ideas as these are, to my thinking, the very rudiments of politics. Religion keeps these two selfish sentiments in subordination by the thought of a future life; and in this way the harshness of the conflict of interests has been somewhat softened. God has mitigated the sufferings that arise from social friction by a religious sentiment which raises self-forgetfulness into a virtue; just as He has moderated the friction of the mechanism of the universe by laws which we do not know. Christianity bids the poor bear patiently with the rich, and commands the rich to lighten the burdens of the poor; these few words, to my mind, contain the essence of all laws, human and divine!'

'I am no statesman,' said the notary; 'I see in a ruler a liquidator of society which should always remain in liquidation; he should hand over to his successor the exact value of the assets which he received.'

'I am no statesman, either,' said Benassis, hastily interrupting the notary. 'It takes nothing but a little common sense to better the lot of a commune, of a canton, or of an even wider district; a department calls for some administrative talent, but all these four spheres of action are comparatively limited, the outlook is not too wide for ordinary powers of vision, and there is a visible connection between their interests and the general progress made by the State.

'But in yet higher regions, everything is on a larger

scale, the horizon widens, and from the standpoint where he is placed, the statesman ought to grasp the whole situation. It is only necessary to consider liabilities due ten years hence, in order to bring about a great deal of good in the case of the department, the district, the canton, or the commune; but when it is a question of the destinies of a nation, a statesman must forsee a more distant future and the course that events are likely to take for the next hundred years. The genius of a Colbert or of a Sully avails nothing, unless it is supported by the energetic will that makes a Napoleon or a Cromwell. A great minister, gentlemen, is a great thought written at large over all the years of a century of prosperity and splendour for which he has prepared the way. Steadfast perseverance is the virtue of which he stands most in need; and in all human affairs does not steadfast perseverance indicate a power of the very highest order? We have had for some time past too many men who think only of the ministry instead of the nation, so that we cannot but admire the real statesman as the vastest human Poetry. Ever to look beyond the present moment, to foresee the ways of Destiny, to care so little for power that he only retains it because he is conscious of his usefulness, while he does not overestimate his strength; ever to lay aside all personal feeling and low ambitions, so that he may always be master of his faculties, and foresee, will, and act without ceasing; to compel himself to be just and impartial, to keep order on a large scale, to silence his heart that he may be guided by his intellect alone, to be neither apprehensive nor sanguine, neither suspicious nor confiding, neither grateful nor ungrateful, never to be unprepared for an event, nor taken at unawares by an idea; to live, in fact, with the requirements of the masses ever in his mind, to spread the protecting wings of his thought above them, to sway them by the thunder of his voice and the keenness of his glance; seeing all the while not the details of affairs, but the great issues at stake, is not that to be something more than a mere man? Therefore the names of the great and noble fathers of nations cannot but be household words for ever.'

There was silence for a moment, during which the guests looked at one another.

'Gentlemen, you have not said a word about the army!' cried Genestas. 'A military organization seems to me to be the real type on which all good civil society should be modelled; the Sword is the guardian of a nation.'

The justice of the peace laughed softly.

'Captain,' he said, 'an old lawyer once said that empires began with the sword and ended with the desk; we have reached the desk stage by this time.'

'And now that we have settled the fate of the world, gentlemen, let us change the subject. Come, captain, a glass of Hermitage,' cried the doctor, laughing.

'Two, rather than one,' said Genestas, holding out his glass. 'I mean to drink them both to your health—to a man who does honour to the species.'

'And who is dear to all of us,' said the curé in gentle tones.

'Do you mean to force me into the sin of pride, M. Janvier?'

'M. le curé has only said in a low voice what all the canton says aloud,' said Cambon.

'Gentlemen, I propose that we take a walk to the parsonage by moonlight, and see M. Janvier home.'

'Let us start,' said the guests, and they prepared to accompany the curé.

'Shall we go to the barn?' said the doctor, laying a hand on Genestas's arm. They had taken leave of the curé and the other guests. 'You will hear them talking about Napoleon, Captain Bluteau. Goguelat, the postman, is there, and there are several of his cronies who are sure to draw him out on the subject of the idol of the

people. Nicolle, my stableman, has set a ladder so that
we can climb up on to the hay; there is a place from
which we can look down on the whole scene. Come along,
an up-sitting is something worth seeing, believe me. It
will not be the first time that I have hidden in the hay
to overhear a soldier's tales or the stories that peasants
tell among themselves. We must be careful to keep out
of sight though, as these good folk turn shy and put
on company manners as soon as they see a stranger.'

'Eh! my dear sir,' said Genestas, 'have I not often
pretended to be asleep so as to hear my troopers talking
out on bivouac? My word, I once heard a droll yarn
reeled off by an old quartermaster for some conscripts
who were afraid of war; I never laughed so heartily in
any theatre in Paris. He was telling them about the
Retreat from Moscow, he told them that the army had
nothing but the clothes they stood up in, that their wine
was iced, that the dead stood stock-still in the road just
where they were, that they had seen White Russia, and
that they currycombed the horses there with their teeth,
that those who were fond of skating had fine times of it,
and people who had a fancy for savoury ices had as much
as they could put away, that the women were generally
poor company, but that the only thing they could really
complain of was the want of hot water for shaving. In
fact, he told them such a pack of absurdities, that even
an old quartermaster who had lost his nose with a frost-
bite, so that they had dubbed him *Nezrestant*, was fain
to laugh.'

'Hush!' said Benassis, 'here we are. I will go first;
follow after me.'

Both of them scaled the ladder and hid themselves in
the hay, in a place from whence they could have a good
view of the party below, who had not heard a sound
overhead. Little groups of women were clustered about
three or four candles. Some of them sewed, others were

spinning, a good few of them were doing nothing, and sat with their heads strained forward, and their eyes fixed on an old peasant who was telling a story. The men were standing about for the most part, or lying at full length on the trusses of hay. Every group was absolutely silent. Their faces were barely visible by the flickering gleams of the candles by which the women were working, although each candle was surrounded by a glass globe filled with water, in order to concentrate the light. The thick darkness and shadow that filled the roof and all the upper part of the barn seemed still further to diminish the light that fell here and there upon the workers' heads with such picturesque effects of light and shade. Here, it shone full upon the bright wondering eyes and brown forehead of a little peasant maiden; and there the straggling beams brought out the outlines of the rugged brows of some of the older men, throwing up their figures in sharp relief against the dark background, and giving a fantastic appearance to their worn and weather-stained garb. The attentive attitude of all these people and the expression on all their faces showed that they had given themselves up entirely to the pleasure of listening, and that the narrator's sway was absolute. It was a curious scene. The immense influence that poetry exerts over every mind was plainly to be seen. For is not the peasant who demands that the tale of wonder should be simple, and that the impossible should be wellnigh credible, a lover of poetry of the purest kind?

'She did not like the look of the house at all,' the peasant was saying as the two newcomers took their places where they could overhear him; 'but the poor little hunchback was so tired out with carrying her bundle of hemp to market, that she went in; besides, the night had come, and she could go no further. She only asked to be allowed to sleep there, and ate nothing but a crust of bread that she took from her wallet. And inasmuch as the woman who kept house for the brigands knew nothing about what they had planned to do that night, she let the old woman into the house, and sent her upstairs without a light. Our hunchback throws herself down on a rickety truckle bed, says her prayers, thinks about her hemp, and is dropping off to sleep. But before she is fairly asleep, she hears a noise, and in walk two men carrying a lantern, and each man had a knife in his hand. Then fear came upon her; for in those times, look you, they used to make *pâtés* of human flesh for the seigneurs, who were very fond of them. But the old woman plucked up heart again, for she was so thoroughly shrivelled and wrinkled that she thought they would think her a poorish sort of diet. The two men went past the hunchback and walked up to a bed that there was in the great room, and in which they had put the gentleman with the big portmanteau, the one that passed for a *negromancer*. The taller man holds up the lantern and takes the gentleman by the feet, and the short one, that had pretended to be drunk, clutches hold of his head and cuts his throat, clean, with one stroke, swish! Then they leave the head and body lying in its own blood up there, steal the portmanteau, and go downstairs with it. Here is our woman in a nice fix! First of all she thinks of slipping out, before anyone can suspect it, not knowing that Providence had brought her there to glorify God and to bring down punishment on the murderers. She was in a great fright, and when one is frightened one thinks of nothing else. But the woman of the house had asked the two brigands about the hunchback, and that had alarmed them. So back they come, creeping softly up the wooden staircase. The poor hunchback curls up in a ball with fright, and she hears them talking about her in whispers.

"'Kill her, I tell you.'"

"'No need to kill her.'"

"'Kill her!'"

"'No!'"

'Then they come in. The woman, who was no fool, shuts her eyes and pretends to be asleep. She sets to work to sleep like a child, with her hand on her heart, and takes to breathing like a cherub. The man opens the lantern and shines the light straight into the eyes of the sleeping old woman—she does not move an eyelash, she is in such a terror for her neck.

"'She is sleeping like a log; you can see that quite well,' so says the tall one.

"'Old women are so cunning!' answers the short man. "I will kill her. We shall feel easier in our minds. Besides, we will salt her down to feed the pigs."

'The old woman hears all this talk, but she does not stir.

"'Oh! it is all right, she is asleep,' says the short ruffian, when he saw that the hunchback had not stirred.

'That is how the old woman saved her life. And she may be fairly called courageous; for it is a fact that there are not many girls here who could have breathed like cherubs while they heard that talk going on about the pigs. Well, the two brigands set to work to lift up the dead man; they wrap him round in the sheets and chuck him out into the little yard; and the old woman hears the pigs scampering up to eat him, and grunting, *Hon! hon!*

'So when morning comes,' the narrator resumed after a pause, 'the woman gets up and goes down, paying a couple of sous for her bed. She takes up her wallet, goes on just as if nothing had happened, asks for the news of the countryside, and gets away in peace. She wants to run. Running is quite out of the question, her legs fail her for fright; and lucky it was for her that she could not run, for this reason. She had barely gone half a quarter of a league before she sees one of the brigands

coming after her, just out of craftiness to make quite
sure that she had seen nothing. She guesses this, and
sits herself down on a boulder.

'"What is the matter, good woman?" asks the short
one, for it was the shorter one and the wickeder of the
two who was dogging her.

'"Oh! master," says she, "my wallet is so heavy, and
I am so tired, that I badly want some good man to give
me his arm" (sly thing, only listen to her!) "if I am to
get back to my poor home."

'Thereupon the brigand offers to go along with her,
and she accepts his offer. The fellow takes hold of her
arm to see if she is afraid. Not she! She does not
tremble a bit, and walks quietly along. So there they
are, chatting away as nicely as possible, all about farming,
and the way to grow hemp, till they come to the outskirts of the town where the hunchback lived, and the
brigand made off for fear of meeting some of the sheriff's
people. The woman reached her house at midday, and
waited there till her husband came home; she thought
and thought over all that had happened on her journey
and during the night. The hemp-grower came home in
the evening. He was hungry; something must be got
ready for him to eat. So while she greases her frying-
pan, and gets ready to fry something for him, she tells
him how she sold her hemp, and gabbles away as females
do, but not a word does she say about the pigs, nor about
the gentleman who was murdered and robbed and eaten.
She holds her frying-pan in the flames so as to clean it,
draws it out again to give it a wipe, and finds it full of
blood.

'"What have you been putting into it?" says she to
her man.

'"Nothing," says he.

'She thinks it must have been a nonsensical piece of
woman's fancy, and puts her frying-pan into the fire

again. . . . *Pouf!* A head comes tumbling down the chimney!

'"Oh! look! It is nothing more nor less than the dead man's head," says the old woman. "How he stares at me! What does he want!"

'" *You must avenge me!* " says a voice.

'"What an idiot you are!" said the hemp-grower. "Always seeing something or other that has no sort of sense about it! Just you all over."

'He takes up the head, which snaps at his finger, and pitches it out into the yard.

'"Get on with my omelette," he says, "and do not bother yourself about that. 'Tis a cat."

'"A cat!" says she; "it was as round as a ball."

'She puts back her frying-pan on the fire. . . . *Pouf!* Down comes a leg this time, and they go through the whole story again. The man was no more astonished at the foot than he had been at the head, he snatched up the leg and threw it out at the door. Before they had finished, the other leg, both arms, the body, the whole murdered traveller, in fact, came down piecemeal. No omelette all this time! The old hemp-seller grew very hungry indeed.

'"By my salvation!" said he, "when once my omelette is made we will see about satisfying that man yonder."

'"So you admit, now, that it was a man?" said the hunchback wife. "What made you say that it was not a head a minute ago, you great worry?"

'The woman breaks the eggs, fries the omelette, and dishes it up without any more grumbling; somehow this squabble began to make her feel very uncomfortable. Her husband sits down and begins to eat. The hunchback was frightened, and said that she was not hungry.

'"Tap! tap!" There was a stranger rapping at the door.

'"Who is there?"

'"The man that died yesterday!"

'"Come in," answers the hemp-grower.

'So the traveller comes in, sits himself down on a three-legged stool, and says: "Are you mindful of God, who gives eternal peace to those who confess His Name? Woman! You saw me done to death, and you have said nothing! I have been eaten by the pigs! The pigs do not enter Paradise, and therefore I, a Christian man, shall go down into hell, all because a woman forsooth will not speak, a thing that has never been known before. You must deliver me," and so on, and so on.

'The woman, who was more and more frightened every minute, cleaned her frying-pan, put on her Sunday clothes, went to the justice, and told him about the crime, which was brought to light, and the robbers were broken on the wheel in proper style on the market-place. This good work accomplished, the woman and her husband always had the finest hemp you ever set eyes on. Then, which pleased them still better, they had something that they had wished for for a long time, to wit, a man-child, who in course of time became a great lord of the king's.

'That is the true story of *The Courageous Hunchback Woman.*'

'I do not like stories of that sort; they make me dream at night,' said La Fosseuse. 'Napoleon's adventures are much nicer, I think.'

'Quite true,' said the keeper. 'Come now, M. Goguelat, tell us about the emperor.'

'The evening is too far gone,' said the postman, 'and I do not care about cutting short the story of a victory.'

'Never mind, let us hear about it all the same! We know the stories, for we have heard you tell them many a time; but it is always a pleasure to hear them.'

'Tell us about the emperor!' cried several voices at once.

'You will have it?' answered Goguelat. 'Very good,

but you will see that there is no sense in the story when it is gone through at a gallop. I would rather tell you all about a single battle. Shall it be Champ-Aubert, where we ran out of cartridges, and furbished them just the same with the bayonet?'

'No, the emperor! the emperor!'

The old infantryman got up from his truss of hay and glanced round about on those assembled, with the peculiar sombre expression in which may be read all the miseries, adventures, and hardships of an old soldier's career. He took his coat by the two skirts in front, and raised them, as if it were a question of once more packing up the knapsack in which his kit, his shoes, and all he had in the world used to be stowed; for a moment he stood leaning all his weight on his left foot, then he swung the right foot forward, and yielded with a good grace to the wishes of his audience. He swept his grey hair to one side, so as to leave his forehead bare, and flung back his head and gazed upwards, as if to raise himself to the lofty height of the gigantic story that he was about to tell.

'Napoleon, you see, my friends, was born in Corsica, which is a French island warmed by the Italian sun; it is like a furnace there, everything is scorched up, and they keep on killing each other from father to son for generations all about nothing at all—'tis a notion they have. To begin at the beginning, there was something extraordinary about the thing from the first; it occurred to his mother, who was the handsomest woman of her time, and a shrewd soul, to dedicate him to God, so that he should escape all the dangers of infancy and of his after life; for she had dreamed that the world was on fire on the day he was born. It was a prophecy! So she asked God to protect him, on condition that Napoleon should re-establish His holy religion, which had been thrown to the ground just then. That was the agreement; we shall see what came of it.

'Now, do you follow me carefully, and tell me whether what you are about to hear is natural.

'It is certain sure that only a man who had had imagination enough to make a mysterious compact would be capable of going farther than anybody else, and of passing through volleys of grape-shot and showers of bullets which carried us off like flies, but which had a respect for his head. I myself had particular proof of that at Eylau. I see him yet; he climbs a hillock, takes his field-glass, looks along our lines, and says: "That is going on all right." One of your deep fellows, with a bunch of feathers in his cap, used to plague him a good deal from all accounts, following him about everywhere, even when he was getting his meals. This fellow wants to do something clever, so as soon as the emperor goes away he takes his place. Oh! swept away in a moment! And that is the last of the bunch of feathers! You understand quite clearly that Napoleon had undertaken to keep his secret to himself. That is why those who accompanied him, and even his especial friends, used to drop like nuts: Duroc, Bessières, Lannes—men as strong as bars of steel, which he cast into shape for his own ends. And here is a final proof that he was the child of God, created to be the soldier's father; for no one ever saw him as a lieutenant or a captain. He is a commandant straight off! Ah! yes, indeed! He did not look more than four-and-twenty, but he was an old general ever since the taking of Toulon, when he made a beginning by showing the rest that they knew nothing about handling cannon. Next thing he does, he tumbles upon us. A little slip of a general-in-chief of the army of Italy, which had neither bread nor ammunition nor shoes nor clothes—a wretched army as naked as a worm.

'"Friends," he said, "here we all are together. Now, get it well into your pates that in a fortnight's time from now you will be the victors, and dressed in new clothes;

you shall all have greatcoats, strong gaiters, and famous pairs of shoes; but, my children, you will have to march on Milan to take them, where all these things are."

'So they marched. The French, crushed as flat as a pancake, held up their heads again. There were thirty thousand of us tatterdemalions against eighty thousand swaggerers of Germans—fine tall men and well equipped; I can see them yet. Then Napoleon, who was only Bonaparte in those days, breathed goodness knows what into us, and on we marched night and day. We rap their knuckles at Montenotte; we hurry on to thrash them at Rivoli, Lodi, Arcola, and Millesimo, and we never let them go. The army came to have a liking for winning battles. Then Napoleon hems them in on all sides, these German generals did not know where to hide themselves so as to have a little peace and comfort; he drubs them soundly, cribs ten thousand of their men at a time by surrounding them with fifteen hundred Frenchmen, whom he makes to spring up after his fashion, and at last he takes their cannon, victuals, money, ammunition, and everything they have that is worth taking; he pitches them into the water, beats them on the mountains, snaps at them in the air, gobbles them up on the earth, and thrashes them everywhere.

'There are the troops in full feather again! For, look you, the emperor (who, for that matter, was a wit) soon sent for the inhabitant, and told him that he had come there to deliver him. Whereupon the civilian finds us free quarters and makes much of us, so do the women, who showed great discernment. To come to a final end; in Ventose '96, which was at that time what the month of March is now, we had been driven up into a corner of the *Pays des Marmottes*; but after the campaign, lo and behold! we were the masters of Italy, just as Napoleon had prophesied. And in the month of March following, in one year and in two campaigns, he

brings us within sight of Vienna; we had made a clean
sweep of them. We had gobbled down three armies one
after another, and taken the conceit out of four Austrian
generals; one of them, an old man who had white hair,
had been roasted like a rat in the straw before Mantua.
The kings were suing for mercy on their knees. Peace
had been won. Could a mere mortal have done that?
No. God helped him, that is certain. He distributed
himself about like the five loaves in the Gospel, commanded on the battle-field all day, and drew up his plans
at night. The sentries always saw him coming and
going; he neither ate nor slept. Therefore, recognizing
these prodigies, the soldier adopts him for his father.
But, forward!

'The other folk there in Paris, seeing all this, say among
themselves:

'"Here is a pilgrim who appears to take his instructions from Heaven above; he is uncommonly likely to lay
a hand on France. We must let him loose on Asia or
America, and that, perhaps, will keep him quiet."

'The same thing was decreed for him as for Jesus
Christ; for, as a matter of fact, they give him orders to go
on duty down in Egypt. See his resemblance to the Son
of God! That is not all, though. He calls all his fire-
eaters about him, all those into whom he had more particularly put the devil, and talks to them in this way:

'"My friends, for the time being they are giving us
Egypt to stop our mouths. But we will swallow down
Egypt in a brace of shakes, just as we swallowed Italy,
and private soldiers shall be princes, and shall have broad
lands of their own. Forward!"

'"Forward, lads!" cry the sergeants.

'So we come to Toulon on the way to Egypt. Whereupon the English put to sea with all their fleet. But
when we are on board, Napoleon says to us:

'"They will not see us; and it is right and proper

that you should know henceforward that your general has a star in the sky that guides us and watches over us!"

'So said, so done. As we sailed over the sea we took Malta, by way of an orange to quench his thirst for victory, for he was a man who must always be doing something. There we are in Egypt. Well and good. Different orders. The Egyptians, look you, are men who, ever since the world has been the world, have been in the habit of having giants to reign over them, and armies like swarms of ants; because it is a country full of genii and crocodiles, where they have built up pyramids as big as our mountains, the fancy took them to stow their kings under the pyramids, so as to keep them fresh, a thing which mightily pleases them all round out there. Whereupon, as we landed, the Little Corporal said to us:

'"My children, the country which you are about to conquer worships a lot of idols which you must respect, because the Frenchman ought to be on good terms with all the world, and fight people without giving annoyance. Get it well into your heads to let everything alone at first; for we shall have it all by and by! And forward!"

'So far so good. But all those people had heard a prophecy of Napoleon, under the name of *Kebir Bonaberdis*, a word which in their lingo means, "The Sultan fires a shot," and they feared him like the devil. So the Grand Turk, Asia, and Africa have recourse to magic, and they send a demon against us, named the Mahdi, who it was thought had come down from heaven on a white charger which, like its master, was bullet-proof, and the pair of them lived on the air of that part of the world. There are people who have seen them, but for my part I cannot give you any certain information about them. They were the divinities of Arabia and of the Mamelukes who wished their troopers to believe that the Mahdi had the power of preventing them from dying in battle. They gave out that he was an angel sent down to wage war on Napoleon, and to get back Solomon's Seal, part of their paraphernalia which they pretended our general had stolen. You will readily understand that we made them cry *peccavi* all the same.

'Ah, just tell me how they came to know about that compact of Napoleon's? Was that natural?

'They took it into their heads for certain that he commanded the genii, and that he went from place to place like a bird in the twinkling of an eye; and it is a fact that he was everywhere. At length it came about that he carried off a queen of theirs. She was the private property of a Mameluke, who, although he had several more of them, flatly refused to strike a bargain, though "the other" offered all his treasures for her and diamonds as big as pigeon's eggs. When things had come to that pass, they could not well be settled without a good deal of fighting; and there was fighting enough for everybody and no mistake about it.

'Then we are drawn up before Alexandria, and again at Gizeh, and before the Pyramids. We had to march over the sands and in the sun; people whose eyes dazzled used to see water that they could not drink and shade that made them fume. But we made short work of the Mamelukes as usual, and everything goes down before the voice of Napoleon, who seizes Upper and Lower Egypt and Arabia, far and wide, till we came to the capitals of kingdoms which no longer existed, where there were thousands and thousands of statues of all the devils in creation, all done to the life, and another curious thing too, any quantity of lizards. A confounded country where anyone could have as many acres of land as he wished for as little as he pleased.

'While he was busy inland, where he meant to carry out some wonderful ideas of his, the English burn his fleet for him in Aboukir Bay, for they never could do enough to annoy us. But Napoleon, who was respected east and west, and called "My son" by the Pope, and "My dear father" by Mahomet's cousin, makes up his mind to have his revenge on England, and to take India in exchange for his fleet. He set out to lead us into Asia, by way of the Red Sea, through a country where there were palaces for halting-places, and nothing but gold and diamonds to pay the troops with, when the Mahdi comes to an understanding with the Plague, and sends it among us to make a break in our victories. Halt! Then every man files off to that parade from which no one comes back on his two feet. The dying soldier cannot take Acre, into which he forces an entrance three times with a warrior's impetuous enthusiasm; the Plague was too strong for us; there was not even time to say: "Your servant, sir!" to the Plague. Every man was down with it. Napoleon alone was as fresh as a rose; the whole army saw him drinking in the Plague without its doing him any harm whatever.

'There now, my friends, was that natural, do you think?

'The Mamelukes, knowing that we were all on the sick-list, want to stop our road; but it was no use trying that nonsense with Napoleon. So he spoke to his familiars, who had tougher skins than the rest:

'"Go and clear the road for me."

'Junot, who was his devoted friend, and a first-class fighter, only takes a thousand men, and makes a clean sweep of the Pasha's army, which had the impudence to bar our way. Thereupon back we come to Cairo, our headquarters, and now for another story.

'Napoleon being out of the country, France allowed the people in Paris to worry the life out of her. They kept back the soldiers' pay and all their linen and clothing, left them to starve, and expected them to lay down law to the universe, without taking any further trouble in the matter. They were idiots of the kind that amuse themselves with chattering instead of setting themselves to knead the dough. So our armies were defeated, France could not keep her frontiers; The Man was not there. I say The Man, look you, because that was how they called him; but it was stuff and nonsense, for he had a star of his own and all his other peculiarities, it was the rest of us that were mere men. He hears this history of France after his famous battle of Aboukir, where with a single division he routed the grand army of the Turks, twenty-five thousand strong, and jostled more than half of them into the sea, rrrah! without losing more than three hundred of his own men. That was his last thunder-clap in Egypt. He said to himself, seeing that all was lost down there: "I know that I am the saviour of France, and to France I must go."

'But you must clearly understand that the army did not know of his departure; for if they had, they would have kept him there by force to make him Emperor of the East. So there we all are without him, and in low spirits, for he was the life of us. He leaves Kléber in command, a great watch-dog who passed in his checks at Cairo, murdered by an Egyptian whom they put to death by spiking him with a bayonet, which is their way of guillotining people out there; but he suffered so much, that a soldier took pity on the scoundrel and handed his flask to him; and the Egyptian turned up his eyes then and there with all the pleasure in life. But there is not much fun for us about this little affair. Napoleon steps aboard of a little cockle-shell, a mere nothing of a skiff, called the *Fortune*, and in the twinkling of an eye, and in the teeth of the English, who were blockading the place with vessels of the line and cruisers and everything that carries canvas, he lands in France, for he always had the faculty of taking the sea at a stride. Was that natural? Bah! as soon as he is landed at Fréjus, it is as good as saying that he has set foot in Paris. Everybody there worships him; but he calls the Government together.

'"What have you done to my children, the soldiers?" he says to the lawyers. "You are a set of good-for-nothings who make fools of other people, and feather your own nests at the expense of France. It will not do. I speak in the name of everyone who is discontented."

'Thereupon they want to put him off and to get rid of him; but not a bit of it! He locks them up in the barracks where they used to argufy and makes them jump out of the windows. Then he makes them follow in his train, and they all become as mute as fishes and supple as tobacco pouches. So he becomes Consul at a blow. He was not the man to doubt the existence of the Supreme Being; he kept his word with Providence, who had kept His promise in earnest; he sets up religion again, and gives back the churches, and they ring the bells for God and Napoleon. So everyone is satisfied: *primo*, the priests with whom he allows no one to meddle; *segondo*, the merchant folk who carry on their trades without fear of the *rapiamus* of the law that had pressed too heavily on them; *tertio*, the nobles; for people had fallen into an unfortunate habit of putting them to death, and he puts a stop to this.

'But there were enemies to be cleared out of the way, and he was not the one to go to sleep after mess; and his eyes, look you, travelled all over the world as if it had been a man's face. The next thing he did was to turn up in Italy; it was just as if he had put his head out of the window and the sight of him was enough; they gulp down the Austrians at Marengo like a whale swallowing gudgeons! *Haouf!* The French Victories blew their trumpets so loud that the whole world could hear the noise, and there was an end of it.

'"We will not keep on at this game any longer!" say the Germans.

'"That is enough of this sort of thing," say the others.

'Here is the upshot. Europe shows the white feather, England knuckles under, general peace all round, and kings and peoples pretending to embrace each other. While then and there the emperor hits on the idea of the Legion of Honour, there's a fine thing if you like!

'He spoke to the whole army at Boulogne. "In France," so he said, "every man is brave. So the civilian who does gloriously shall be the soldier's sister, the soldier shall be his brother, and both shall stand together beneath the flag of honour."

'By the time that the rest of us who were away down there in Egypt had come back again, everything was changed. We had seen him last as a general, and in no time we find that he is emperor! And when this was settled (and it may safely be said that everyone was satisfied) there was a holy ceremony such as never was seen under the canopy of heaven. Faith, France gave herself to him, like a handsome girl to a lancer, and the Pope and all his cardinals in robes of red and gold come across the Alps on purpose to anoint him before the army and the people, who clap their hands.

'There is one thing that it would be very wrong to keep back from you. While he was in Egypt, in the desert not far away from Syria, *the Red Man* had appeared to him on the mountain of Moses, in order to say: "Everything is going on well." Then again, on the eve of the victory at Marengo, the Red Man springs to his feet in front of the emperor for the second time, and says to him:

'"You shall see the world at your feet; you shall be Emperor of the French, King of Italy, master of Holland, ruler of Spain, Portugal, and the Illyrian Provinces, protector of Germany, saviour of Poland, first Eagle of the Legion of Honour," and all the rest of it.

'That Red Man, look you, was a notion of his own,

who ran on errands and carried messages, so many people say, between him and his star. I myself have never believed that; but the Red Man is, undoubtedly, a fact. Napoleon himself spoke of the Red Man who lived up in the roof of the Tuileries, and who used to come to him, he said, in moments of trouble and difficulty. So on the night after his coronation Napoleon saw him for the third time, and they talked over a lot of things together.

'Then the emperor goes straight to Milan to have himself crowned King of Italy, and then came the real triumph of the soldier. For everyone who could write became an officer forthwith, and pensions and gifts of duchies poured down in showers. There were fortunes for the staff that never cost France a penny, and the Legion of Honour was as good as an annuity for the rank and file; I still draw my pension on the strength of it. In short, here were armies provided for in a way that had never been seen before! But the emperor, who knew that he was to be emperor over everybody, and not only over the army, bethinks himself of the bourgeois, and sets them to build fairy monuments in places that had been as bare as the back of my hand till then. Suppose, now, that you are coming out of Spain and on the way to Berlin; well, you would see triumphal arches, and in the sculpture upon them the common soldiers are done every bit as beautifully as the generals!

'In two or three years Napoleon fills his cellars with gold; makes bridges, palaces, roads, scholars, festivals, laws, fleets, and harbours; he spends millions on millions, ever so much, and ever so much more to it, so that I have heard it said that he could have paved the whole of France with five-franc pieces if the fancy had taken him; and all this without putting any taxes on you people here. So when he was comfortably seated on his throne, and so thoroughly the master of the situation, that all Europe was waiting for leave to do anything for him that he might happen to want; as he had four brothers and three sisters, he said to us, just as it might be by way of conversation, in the order of the day:

"'Children, is it fitting that your emperor's relations should beg their bread? No; I want them all to be luminaries, like me in fact! Therefore, it is urgently necessary to conquer a kingdom for each one of them, so that the French nation may be masters everywhere, so that the Guard may make the whole earth tremble, and France may spit wherever she likes, and every nation shall say to her, as it is written on my coins: 'God protects you!'"

"'All right!" answers the army; "we will fish up kingdoms for you with the bayonet."

'Ah! there was no backing out of it, look you! If he had taken it into his head to conquer the moon, we should have had to put everything in train, pack our knapsacks, and scramble up; luckily, he had no wish for that excursion. The kings who were used to the comforts of a throne, of course, objected to be lugged off, so we had marching orders. We march, we get there, and the earth begins to shake to its centre again. What times they were for wearing out men and shoe-leather! And the hard knocks that they gave us! Only Frenchmen could have stood it. But you are not ignorant that a Frenchman is a born philosopher; he knows that he must die a little sooner or a little later. So we used to die without a word, because we had the pleasure of watching the emperor do *this* on the maps.'

Here the soldier swung quickly round on one foot, so as to trace a circle on the barn floor with the other.

"'There, that shall be a kingdom," he used to say, and it was a kingdom. What fine times they were! Colonels became generals whilst you were looking at them, generals became marshals of France, and marshals

became kings. There is one of them still left on his
feet to keep Europe in mind of those days, Gascon though
he may be, and a traitor to France that he might keep his
crown; and he did not blush for his shame, for, after all,
a crown, look you, is made of gold. The very sappers
and miners who knew how to read became great nobles
in the same way. And I who am telling you all this have
seen in Paris eleven kings and a crowd of princes all round
about Napoleon, like rays about the sun! Keep this well
in your minds, that as every soldier stood a chance of
having a throne of his own (provided he showed himself
worthy of it), a corporal of the Guard was by way of being
a sight to see, and they gaped at him as he went by; for
everyone came by his share after a victory, it was made
perfectly clear in the bulletin. And what battles they
were! Austerlitz, where the army was manœuvred as if
it had been a review; Eylau, where the Russians were
drowned in a lake, just as if Napoleon had breathed on
them and blown them in; Wagram, where the fighting
was kept up for three whole days without flinching. In
short, there were as many battles as there are saints in the
calendar.

'Then it was made clear beyond a doubt that Napoleon
bore the Sword of God in his scabbard. He had a regard
for the soldier. He took the soldier for his child. He
was anxious that you should have shoes, shirts, greatcoats, bread, and cartridges; but he kept up his majesty,
too, for reigning was his own particular occupation.
But, all the same, a sergeant, or even a common soldier,
could go up to him and call him "Emperor," just as you
might say "My good friend" to me at times. And he
would give an answer to anything you put before him.
He used to sleep on the snow just like the rest of us—in
short, he looked almost like an ordinary man; but I who
am telling you all these things have seen him myself with
grape-shot whizzing about his ears, no more put out by it

than you are at this moment; never moving a limb, watching through his field-glass, always looking after his business; so we stood our ground likewise, as cool and calm as John the Baptist. I do not know how he did it; but whenever he spoke, a something in his words made our hearts burn within us; and just to let him see that we were his children, and that it was not in us to shirk or flinch, we used to walk just as usual right up to the sluts of cannon that were belching smoke and vomiting battalions of balls, and never a man would so much as say: "Look out!" It was a something that made dying men raise their heads to salute him and cry: "Long live the Emperor!"

'Was that natural? Would you have done this for a mere man?

'Thereupon, having fitted up all his family, and things having so turned out that the Empress Josephine (a good woman for all that) had no children, he was obliged to part company with her, although he loved her not a little. But he must have children, for reasons of State. All the crowned heads of Europe, when they heard of his difficulty, squabbled among themselves as to who should find him a wife. He married an Austrian princess, so they say, who was the daughter of the Caesar, a man of antiquity whom everybody talks about, not only in our country, where it is said that most things were his doing, but also all over Europe. And so certain sure is that, that I who am talking to you have been myself across the Danube, where I saw the ruins of a bridge built by that man; and it appeared that he was some connection of Napoleon's at Rome, for the emperor claimed succession there for his son.

'So, after his wedding, which was a holiday for the whole world, and when they let the people off their taxes for ten years to come (though they had to pay them just the same, after all, because the excisemen took no notice of the proclamation)—after his wedding, I say, his wife

had a child who was King of Rome; a child was born a
king while his father was alive, a thing that had never
been seen in the world before! That day a balloon set
out from Paris to carry the news to Rome, and went all
the way in one day. There, now! Is there one of you
who will stand me out that there was nothing supernatural in that? No, it was decreed on high. And the
mischief take those who will not allow that it was wafted
over by God Himself, so as to add to the honour and
glory of France!

'But there was the Emperor of Russia, a friend of our
emperor's, who was put out because he had not married
a Russian lady. So the Russian backs up our enemies
the English; for there had always been something to
prevent Napoleon from putting a spoke in their wheel.
Clearly an end must be made of fowl of that feather.
Napoleon is vexed, and he says to us:

'"Soldiers! You have been the masters of every
capital in Europe, except Moscow, which is allied to
England. So, in order to conquer London and India,
which belongs to them in London, I find it absolutely
necessary that we go to Moscow."

'Thereupon the greatest army that ever wore gaiters,
and left its footprints all over the globe, is brought together, and drawn up with such peculiar cleverness, that
the emperor passed a million of men in review, all in a
single day.

'"*Hourra!*" cry the Russians, and there is all Russia
assembled, a lot of brutes of Cossacks that you never
can come up with! It was country against country, a
general stramash; we had to look out for ourselves. "It
was all Asia against Europe," as the Red Man had said
to Napoleon. "All right," Napoleon had answered, "I
shall be ready for them."

'And there, in fact, were all the kings who came to
lick Napoleon's hand. Austria, Prussia, Bavaria, Saxony,

Poland, and Italy, all speaking us fair and going along
with us; it was a fine thing! The Eagles had never cooed
before as they did on parade in those days, when they
were reared above all the flags of all the nations of Europe.
The Poles could not contain their joy because the emperor
had a notion of setting up their kingdom again; and ever
since Poland and France have always been like brothers.
In short, the army shouts: "Russia shall be ours!"

'We cross the frontiers, all the lot of us. We march
and countermarch, but never a Russian do we see. At
last all our watch-dogs are encamped at Borodino. That
was where I received the Cross, and there is no denying
that it was a cursed battle. The emperor was not easy
in his mind; he had seen the Red Man, who said to him:
"My child, you are going a little too fast for your feet;
you will run short of men, and your friends will play you
false."

'Thereupon the emperor proposes a treaty. But
before he signs it, he says to us:

'"Let us give these Russians a drubbing!"

'"All right!" cried the army.

'"Forward!" say the sergeants.

'My clothes were all falling to pieces, my shoes were
worn out with trapesing over those roads out there, which
are not good going at all. But it is all one. "Since here
is the last of the row," said I to myself, "I mean to get
all I can out of it."

'We were posted before the great ravine; we had seats
in the front row. The signal is given, and seven hundred
guns begin a conversation fit to make the blood spurt
from your ears. One should give the devil his due, and
the Russians let themselves be cut in pieces just like
Frenchmen; they did not give way, and we made no
advance.'

'"Forward!" is the cry; "here is the emperor!"

'So it was. He rides past us at a gallop, and makes

a sign to us that a great deal depends on our carrying the redoubt. He puts fresh heart into us; we rush forward, I am the first man to reach the gorge. Ah! good God! how they fell, colonels, lieutenants, and common soldiers, all alike! There were shoes to fit up those who had none, and epaulettes for the knowing fellows that knew how to write. . . . Victory is the cry all along the line! And, upon my word, there were twenty-five thousand Frenchmen lying on the field. No more, I assure you! Such a thing was never seen before; it was just like a field when the corn is cut, with a man lying there for every ear of wheat. That sobered the rest of us. The Man comes, and we make a circle round about him, and he coaxes us round (for he could be very nice when he chose), and persuades us to dine with Duke Humphrey, when we were as hungry as hunters. Then our consoler distributes the Crosses of the Legion of Honour himself, salutes the dead, and says to us: "On to Moscow!"

'"To Moscow, so be it!" says the army.

'We take Moscow. What do the Russians do but set fire to their city! There was a blaze, two leagues of bonfire that burned for two days! The buildings fell about our ears like slates, and molten lead and iron came down in showers; it was really horrible; it was a light to see our sorrows by, I can tell you! The emperor said: "There, that is enough of this sort of thing; all my men shall stay here."

'We amuse ourselves for a bit by recruiting and re-pairing our frames, for we really were much fatigued by the campaign. We take away with us a gold cross from the top of the Kremlin, and every soldier had a little fortune. But on the way back the winter came down on us a month earlier than usual, a matter which the learned (like a set of fools) have never sufficiently explained; and we are nipped with the cold. We were no longer an army after that, do you understand? There was an end of generals and even of the sergeants; hunger and misery took the command instead, and all of us were absolutely equal under their reign. All we thought of was how to get back to France; no one stooped to pick up his gun or his money; everyone walked straight before him, and armed himself as he thought fit, and no one cared about glory.

'The emperor saw nothing of his star all the time, for the weather was so bad. There was some misunderstanding between him and heaven. Poor man! how bad he felt when he saw his Eagles flying with their backs turned on victory! That was really too rough! Well, the next thing is the Beresina. And here and now, my friends, anyone can assure you on his honour, and by all that is sacred, that *never*, no, never since there have been men on earth, never in this world has there been seen such a fricassee of an army, caissons, transports, artillery and all, in such snow as that and under such a pitiless sky. It was so cold that you burned your hand on the barrel of your gun if you happened to touch it. There it was that the pontooners saved the army, for the pontooners stood firm at their posts; it was there that Gondrin behaved like a hero, and he is the sole survivor of all the men who were dogged enough to stand in the river so as to build the bridges on which the army crossed over, and so escaped the Russians, who still respected the Grand Army on account of its past victories. And Gondrin is an accomplished soldier,' he went on, pointing to his friend, who was gazing at him with the rapt attention peculiar to deaf people, 'a distinguished soldier who deserves to have your very highest esteem.

'I saw the emperor standing by the bridge,' he went on, 'and never feeling the cold at all. Was that, again, a natural thing? He was looking on at the loss of his treasures, of his friends, and those who had fought with him in Egypt. Bah! there was an end of everything.

Women and wagons and guns were all engulfed and swallowed up, everything went to rack and ruin. A few of the bravest among us saved the Eagles, for the Eagles, look you, meant France, and all the rest of you; it was the civil and military honour of France that was in our keeping, there must be no spot on the honour of France, and the cold should never make her bow her head. There was no getting warm except in the neighbourhood of the emperor; for whenever he was in danger we hurried up, all frozen as we were—we who would not stop to hold out a hand to a fallen friend.

'They say, too, that he shed tears of a night over his poor family of soldiers. Only he and Frenchmen could have pulled themselves out of such a plight; but we did pull ourselves out, though, as I am telling you, it was with loss, ay, and heavy loss. The Allies had eaten up all our provisions; everybody began to betray him, just as the Red Man had foretold. The rattle-pates in Paris, who had kept quiet ever since the Imperial Guard had been established, think that *he* is dead, and hatch a conspiracy. They set to work in the Home Office to overturn the emperor. These things come to his knowledge and worry him; he says to us at parting: "Good-bye, children; keep to your posts, I will come back again."

'Bah! Those generals of his lose their heads at once; for when he was away, it was not like the same thing. The marshals fall out among themselves, and make blunders, as was only natural, for Napoleon in his kindness had fed them on gold till they had grown as fat as butter, and they had no mind to march. Troubles came of this, for many of them stayed inactive in garrison towns in the rear, without attempting to tickle up the backs of the enemy behind us, and we were being driven back on France. But Napoleon comes back among us with fresh troops; conscripts they were, and famous conscripts too; he had put some thorough notions of discipline into them—the whelps were good to set their teeth in anybody. He had a bourgeois guard of honour too, and fine troops they were! They melted away like butter on a gridiron. We may put a bold front on it, but everything is against us, although the army still performs prodigies of valour. Whole nations fought against nations in tremendous battles, at Dresden, Lützen, and Bautzen, and then it was that France showed extraordinary heroism, for you must all of you bear in mind that in those times a stout grenadier only lasted six months.

'We always won the day, but the English were always on our track, putting nonsense into other nations' heads, and stirring them up to revolt. In short, we cleared a way through all these mobs of nations; for wherever the emperor appeared, we made a passage for him; for on the land as on the sea, whenever he said, "I wish to go forward," we made the way.

'There comes a final end to it at last. We are back in France; and in spite of the bitter weather, it did one's heart good to breathe one's native air again, it set up many a poor fellow; and as for me, it put new life into me, I can tell you. But it was a question all at once of defending France, our fair land of France. All Europe was up in arms against us; they took it in bad part that we had tried to keep the Russians in order by driving them back within their own borders, so that they should not gobble us up, for those northern folk have a strong liking for eating up the men of the south, it is a habit they have; I have heard the same thing of them from several generals.

'So the emperor finds his own father-in-law, his friends whom he had made crowned kings, and the rabble of princes to whom he had given back their thrones, were all against him. Even Frenchmen and allies in our own ranks turned against us, by orders from high quarters, at Leipsic. Common soldiers would hardly be capable

of such abominations; yet these princes, as they called
themselves, broke their words three times a day! The
next thing they do is to invade France. Wherever our
emperor shows his lion's face, the enemy beats a retreat;
he worked more miracles for the defence of France than
he had ever wrought in the conquest of Italy, the East,
Spain, Europe, and Russia; he had a mind to bury every
foreigner in French soil, to give them a respect for France,
so he lets them come close up to Paris, so as to do for
them at a single blow, and to rise to the highest height
of genius in the biggest battle that ever was fought, a
mother of battles! But the Parisians, wanting to save
their trumpery skins, and afraid for their twopenny
shops, open their gates, and there is a beginning of the
ragusades, and an end of all joy and happiness; they make
a fool of the empress, and fly the white flag out at the
windows. The emperor's closest friends among his
generals forsake him at last and go over to the Bourbons,
of whom no one had ever heard tell. Then he bids us
farewell at Fontainebleau:

'"Soldiers!" . . . (I can hear him yet, we were all crying
just like children; the Eagles and the flags had been
lowered as if for a funeral. Ah! and it was a funeral, I
can tell you; it was the funeral of the Empire; those smart
armies of his were nothing but skeletons now.) So
he stood there on the flight of steps before his château,
and he said:

'"Children, we have been overcome by treachery, but
we shall meet again up above in the country of the brave.
Protect my child, I leave him in your care. *Long live
Napoleon II!*"

'He had thought of killing himself, so that no one
should behold Napoleon after his defeat; like Jesus Christ
before the Crucifixion, he thought himself forsaken by
God and by his talisman, and so he took enough poison
to kill a regiment, but it had no effect whatever upon him.

Another marvel! he discovered that he was immortal;
and feeling sure of his case, and knowing that he should
be emperor for ever, he went to an island for a little while,
so as to study the dispositions of those folk who did not
fail to make blunder upon blunder. Whilst he was
biding his time, the Chinese and the brutes out in Africa,
the Moors and what not, awkward customers all of them,
were so convinced that he was something more than
mortal, that they respected his flag, saying that God would
be displeased if anyone meddled with it. So he reigned
over all the rest of the world, although the doors of his own
France had been closed upon him.

'Then he goes on board the same nutshell of a skiff
that he sailed in from Egypt, passed under the noses of
the English vessels, and sets foot in France. France
recognizes her emperor, the cuckoo flits from steeple to
steeple; France cries with one voice: "Long live the
emperor!" The enthusiasm for that Wonder of the Ages
was thoroughly genuine in these parts. Dauphiné behaved handsomely; and I was uncommonly pleased to
learn that people here shed tears of joy on seeing his grey
overcoat once more.

'It was on 1st March that Napoleon set out with two
hundred men to conquer the kingdom of France and
Navarre, which by 20th March had become the French
Empire again. On that day he found himself in Paris,
and a clean sweep had been made of everything; he had
won back his beloved France, and had called all his soldiers
about him again, and three words of his had done it all:
"Here am I!" 'Twas the greatest miracle God ever
worked! Was it ever known in the world before that a
man should do nothing but show his hat, and a whole
Empire became his? They fancied that France was
crushed, did they? Never a bit of it. A National Army
springs up again at the sight of the Eagle, and we all march
to Waterloo. There the Guard fall all as one man.

Napoleon in his despair heads the rest, and flings himself three times on the enemy's guns without finding the death he sought; we all saw him do it, we soldiers, and the day was lost! That night the emperor calls all his old soldiers about him, and there on the battle-field, which was soaked with our blood, he burns his flags and Eagles—the poor Eagles that had never been defeated, that had cried: "Forward!" in battle after battle, and had flown above us all over Europe. That was the end of the Eagles—all the wealth of England could not purchase for her one tail-feather. The rest is sufficiently known.

'The Red Man went over to the Bourbons like the low scoundrel he is. France is prostrate, the soldier counts for nothing, they rob him of his due, send him about his business, and fill his place with nobles who could not walk, they were so old, so that it made you sorry to see them. They seize Napoleon by treachery, the English shut him up on a desert island in the ocean, on a rock ten thousand feet above the rest of the world. That is the final end of it; there he has to stop till the Red Man gives him back his power again, for the happiness of France. A lot of them say that he is dead! Dead? Oh! yes, very likely. They do not know him, that is plain! They go on telling that fib to deceive the people, and to keep things quiet for their tumbledown government. Listen; this is the whole truth of the matter. His friends have left him alone in the desert to fulfil a prophecy that was made about him, for I forgot to tell you that his name Napoleon really means the *Lion of the Desert*. And that is gospel truth. You will hear plenty of other things said about the emperor, but they are all monstrous nonsense. Because, look you, to no man of woman born would God have given the power to write his name in red, as he did, across the earth, where he will be remembered for ever! . . . Long live "Napoleon, the father of the soldier, the father of the people!"'

'Long live General Eblé!' cried the pontooner.

'How did you manage not to die in the gorge of the redoubts at Borodino?' asked a peasant woman.

'Do I know? We were a whole regiment when we went down into it, and only a hundred foot were left standing; only infantry could have carried it; for the infantry, look you, is everything in an army——'

'But how about the cavalry?' cried Genestas, slipping down out of the hay in a sudden fashion that drew a startled cry from the boldest.

'*Hé*, old boy, you are forgetting Poniatowski's Red Lancers, the Cuirassiers, the Dragoons, and the whole boiling. Whenever Napoleon grew tired of seeing his battalions gain no ground towards the end of a victory, he would say to Murat: "Here, you! cut them in two for me!" and we set out first at a trot, and then at a gallop, *one, two!* and cut a way clean through the ranks of the enemy; it was like slicing an apple in two with a knife. Why, a charge of cavalry is nothing more nor less than a column of cannon balls.'

'And how about the pontooners?' cried the deaf veteran.

'There, there! my children,' Genestas went on, repenting in his confusion of the sally he had made, when he found himself in the middle of a silent and bewildered group, 'there are no agents of police spying here! Here, drink to the Little Corporal with this!'

'Long live the emperor!' all cried with one voice.

'Hush! children,' said the officer, concealing his own deep sorrow with an effort. 'Hush! *He is dead*. He died saying, "*Glory, France, and battle*." So it had to be, children, he must die; but his memory—never!'

Goguelat made an incredulous gesture; then he whispered to those about him: 'The officer is still in the service, and orders have been issued that they are to tell the people that the emperor is dead. You must not think any harm of him, because, after all, a soldier must obey orders.'

As Genestas went out of the barn, he heard La Fosseuse say: 'That officer, you know, is M. Benassis's friend, and a friend of the emperor's.'

Every soul in the barn rushed to the door to see the commandant again; they saw him in the moonlight, as he took the doctor's arm.

'It was a stupid thing to do,' said Genestas. 'Quick! let us go into the house. Those Eagles, cannon, and campaigns! . . . I had quite forgotten where I was.'

'Well, what do you think of our Goguelat?' asked Benassis.

'So long as such stories are told in France, sir, she will always find the fourteen armies of the Republic within her, at need; and her cannon will be perfectly able to keep up a conversation with the rest of Europe. That is what I think.'

A few moments later they reached Benassis's dwelling, and soon were sitting on either side of the hearth in the *salon*; the dying fire in the grate still sent up a few sparks now and then. Each was absorbed in thought. Genestas was hesitating to ask one last question. In spite of the marks of confidence that he had received, he feared lest the doctor should regard his inquiry as indiscreet. He looked searchingly at Benassis more than once; and an answering smile, full of a kindly cordiality, such as lights up the faces of men of real strength of character, seemed to give him in advance the favourable reply for which he sought. So he spoke:

'Your life, sir, is so different from the lives of ordinary men, that you will not be surprised to hear me ask you the reason of your retired existence. My curiosity may seem to you to be unmannerly, but you will admit that it is very natural. Listen a moment: I have had comrades with whom I have never been on intimate terms, even though I have made many campaigns with them; but there have been others to whom I would say: "Go to the paymaster and draw our money," three days after we had got drunk together, a thing that will happen, for the quietest folk must have a frolic fit at times. Well, then, you are one of those people whom I take for a friend without waiting to ask leave, nay, without so much as knowing wherefore.

'Captain Bluteau——'

Whenever the doctor had called his guest by his assumed name, the latter had been unable for some time past to suppress a slight grimace. Benassis, happening to look up just then, caught this expression of repugnance; he sought to discover the reason of it, and looked full into the soldier's face, but the real enigma was wellnigh insoluble for him, so he set down these symptoms to physical suffering, and went on:

'Captain, I am about to speak of myself. I have had to force myself to do so already several times since yesterday, while telling you about the improvements that I have managed to introduce here; but it was a question of the interests of the people and the commune, with which mine are necessarily bound up. But now, if I tell you my story, I should have to speak wholly of myself, and mine has not been a very interesting life.'

'If it were as uneventful as La Fosseuse's life,' answered Genestas, 'I should still be glad to know about it; I should like to know the untoward events that could bring a man of your calibre into this canton.'

'Captain, for these twelve years I have lived in silence; and now, as I wait at the brink of the grave for the stroke that shall cast me into it, I will candidly own to you that this silence is beginning to weigh heavily upon me. I have borne my sorrows alone for twelve years; I have had none of the comfort that friendship gives in such full measure to a heart in pain. My poor sick folk and my peasants certainly set me an example of unmurmuring resignation; but they know that I at least understand

them and their troubles, while there is not a soul here who
knows of the tears that I have shed, no one to give me the
hand-clasp of a comrade, the noblest reward of all, a
reward that falls to the lot of every other, even Gondrin
has not missed that.'

Genestas held out his hand, a sudden impulsive movement by which Benassis was deeply touched.

'There is La Fosseuse,' he went on in a different voice;
'she perhaps would have understood as the angels might;
but then, too, she might possibly have loved me, and
that would have been a misfortune. Listen, captain,
my confession could only be made to an old soldier who
looks as leniently as you do on the failings of others, or
to some young man who has not lost the illusions of
youth; for only a man who knows life well, or a lad to
whom it is all unknown, could understand my story.
The captains of past times who fell upon the field of
battle used to make their last confession to the cross
on the hilt of their sword; if there was no priest at hand,
it was the sword that received and kept the last confidences between a human soul and God. And will you
hear and understand me, for you are one of Napoleon's
finest sword-blades, as thoroughly tempered and as strong
as steel? Some parts of my story can only be understood by a delicate tenderness, and through a sympathy
with the beliefs that dwell in simple hearts; beliefs which
would seem absurd to the sophisticated people who make
use in their own lives of the prudential maxims of worldly
wisdom that only apply to the government of states.
To you I shall speak openly and without reserve, as a
man who does not seek to apologize for his life with the
good and evil done in the course of it; as one who will
hide nothing from you, because he lives so far from the
world of to-day, careless of the judgments of man, and
full of hope in God.'

Benassis stopped, rose to his feet, and said: 'Before I

begin my story, I will order tea. Jacquotte has never missed asking me if I will take it for these twelve years past, and she will certainly interrupt us. Do you care about it, captain?'

'No, thank you.'

In another moment Benassis returned.

IV

THE COUNTRY DOCTOR'S CONFESSION

'I WAS born in a little town in Languedoc,' the doctor resumed. 'My father had been settled there for many years, and there my early childhood was spent. When I was eight years old I was sent to the school of the Oratorians at Sorrèze, and only left it to finish my studies in Paris. My father had squandered his patrimony in the course of an exceedingly wild and extravagant youth. He had retrieved his position partly by a fortunate marriage, partly by the slow persistent thrift characteristic of provincial life; for in the provinces people pride themselves on accumulating rather than on spending, and all the ambition in a man's nature is either extinguished or directed to money-getting, for want of any nobler end. So he had grown rich at last, and thought to transmit to his only son all the cut-and-dried experience which he himself had purchased at the price of his lost illusions; a noble last illusion of age which fondly seeks to bequeath its virtues and its wary prudence to heedless youth, intent only on the enjoyment of the enchanted life that lies before it.

'This foresight on my father's part led him to make plans for my education for which I had to suffer. He sedulously concealed my expectations of wealth from me, and during the fairest years of my youth compelled me, for my own good, to endure the burden of anxiety and hardship that presses upon a young man who has his own way to make in the world. His idea in so doing was to instil the virtues of poverty into me—patience, a thirst for learning, and a love of work for its own sake.

He hoped to teach me to set a proper value on my inheritance, by letting me learn, in this way, all that it costs to make a fortune; wherefore, as soon as I was old enough to understand his advice, he urged me to choose a profession and to work steadily at it. My tastes inclined me to the study of medicine.

'So I left Sorrèze, after ten years of the almost monastic discipline of the Oratorians; and, fresh from the quiet life of a remote provincial school, I was taken straight to the capital. My father went with me in order to introduce me to the notice of a friend of his; and (all unknown to me) my two elders took the most elaborate precautions against any ebullitions of youth on my part, innocent lad though I was. My allowance was rigidly computed on a scale based upon the absolute necessaries of life, and I was obliged to produce my certificate of attendance at the École de Médecine before I was allowed to draw my quarter's income. The excuse for this sufficiently humiliating distrust was the necessity of my acquiring methodical and business-like habits. My father, however, was not sparing of money for all the necessary expenses of my education and for the amusements of Parisian life.

'His old friend was delighted to have a young man to guide through the labyrinth into which I had entered. He was one of those men whose natures lead them to docket their thoughts, feelings, and opinions every whit as carefully as their papers. He would turn up last year's memorandum book, and could tell in a moment what he had been doing a twelvemonth since in this very month, day, and hour of the present year. Life, for him, was a business enterprise, and he kept the books after the most approved business methods. There was real worth in him though he might be punctilious, shrewd, and suspicious, and though he never lacked specious excuses for the precautionary measures that he took with regard to me. He used to buy all my books; he paid for my lessons;

and once, when the fancy took me to learn to ride, the good soul himself found me out a riding-school, went thither with me, and anticipated my wishes by putting a horse at my disposal whenever I had a holiday. In spite of all this cautious strategy, which I managed to defeat as soon as I had any temptation to do so, the kind old man was a second father to me.

'"My friend," he said, as soon as he surmised that I should break away altogether from my leading-strings, unless he relaxed them, "young folk are apt to commit follies which draw down the wrath of their elders upon their heads, and you may happen to want money at some time or other, if so, come to me. Your father helped me nobly once upon a time, and I shall always have a few crowns to spare for you; but never tell me any lies, and do not be ashamed to own to your faults. I myself was young once; we shall always get on well together, like two good comrades."

'My father found lodgings for me with some quiet, middle-class people in the Latin Quarter, and my room was furnished nicely enough; but this first taste of independence, my father's kindness, and the self-denial which he seemed to be exercising for me, brought me but little happiness. Perhaps the value of liberty cannot be known until it has been experienced; and the memories of the freedom of my childhood had been almost effaced by the irksome and dreary life at school, from which my spirits had scarcely recovered. In addition to this, my father had urged new tasks upon me, so that altogether Paris was an enigma. You must acquire some knowledge of its pleasures before you can amuse yourself in Paris.

'My real position, therefore, was quite unchanged, save that my new *lycée* was a much larger building, and was called the École de Médecine. Nevertheless, I studied away bravely at first; I attended lectures diligently; I worked desperately hard and without relaxation, so strongly was my imagination affected by the abundant treasures of knowledge to be gained in the capital. But very soon I heedlessly made acquaintances; danger lurks hidden beneath the rash confiding friendships that have so strong a charm for youth, and gradually I was drawn into the dissipated life of the capital. I became an enthusiastic lover of the theatre; and with my craze for actors and the play, the work of my demoralization began. The stage, in a great metropolis, exerts a very deadly influence over the young; they never quit the theatre save in a state of emotional excitement almost always beyond their power to control; society and the law seem to me to be accessories to the irregularities brought about in this way. Our legislation has shut its eyes, so to speak, to the passions that torment a young man between twenty and five-and-twenty years of age. In Paris he is assailed by temptations of every kind. Religion may preach and Law may demand that he should walk uprightly, but all his surroundings and the tone of those about him are so many incitements to evil. Do not the best of men and the most devout women there look upon continence as ridiculous? The great city, in fact, seems to have set herself to give encouragement to vice and to this alone; for a young man finds that the entrance to every honourable career in which he might look for success is barred by hindrances even more numerous than the snares that are continually set for him, so that through his weaknesses he may be robbed of his money.

'For a long while I went every evening to some theatre, and little by little I fell into idle ways. I grew more and more slack over my work; even my most pressing tasks were apt to be put off till the morrow, and before very long there was an end of my search after knowledge for its own sake; I did nothing more than the work which was absolutely required to enable me to get through the examinations that must be passed before I could become a doctor. I attended the public lectures, but I no longer paid any attention to the professors, who, in my opinion, were a set of dotards. I had already broken my idols—I became a Parisian.

'To be brief, I led the aimless drifting life of a young provincial thrown into the heart of a great city; still retaining some good and true feeling, still clinging more or less to the observance of certain rules of conduct, still fighting in vain against the debasing influence of evil examples, though I offered but a feeble, half-hearted resistance, for the enemy had accomplices within me. Yes, sir, my face is not misleading; past storms have plainly left their traces there. Yet, since I had drunk so deeply of the pure fountain of religion in my early youth, I was haunted in the depths of my soul, through all my wanderings, by an ideal of moral perfection which could not fail one day to bring me back to God by the paths of weariness and remorse. Is not he who feels the pleasures of earth most keenly, sure to be attracted, soon or late, by the fruits of heaven?

'At first I went through the experience, more or less vivid, that always comes with youth—the countless moments of exultation, the unnumbered transports of despair. Sometimes I took my vehement energy of feeling for a resolute will, and overestimated my powers; sometimes, at the mere sight of some trifling obstacle with which I was about to come into collision, I was far more cast down than I ought to have been. Then I would devise vast plans, would dream of glory, and betake myself to work; but a pleasure party would divert me from the noble projects based on so infirm a purpose. Vague recollections of these great abortive schemes of mine left a deceptive glow in my soul and fostered my belief in myself, without giving me the energy to produce. In my indolent self-sufficiency I was in a very fair way to become a fool, for what is a fool but a man who fails to justify the excellent opinion which he has formed of himself? My energy was directed towards no definite aims; I wished for the flowers of life without the toil of cultivating them. I had no idea of the obstacles, so I imagined that everything was easy; luck, I thought, accounted for success in science and in business, and genius was charlatanism. I took it for granted that I should be a great man, because there was the power of becoming one within me; so I discounted all my future glory, without giving a thought to the patience required for the conception of a great work, nor of the execution, in the course of which all the difficulties of the task appear.

'The sources of my amusements were soon exhausted. The charm of the theatre does not last for very long; and, for a poor student, Paris shortly became an empty wilderness. They were dull and uninteresting people that I met with in the circle of the family with whom I lived; but these, and an old man who had now lost touch with the world, were all the society that I had.

'So, like every young man who takes a dislike to the career marked out for him, I rambled about the streets for whole days together; I strolled along the quays, through the museums and public gardens, making no attempt to arrive at a clear understanding of my position and without a single definite idea in my head. The burden of unemployed energies is more felt at that age than at any other; there is such an abundance of vitality running to waste, so much activity without result. I had no idea of the power that a resolute will puts into the hands of a man in his youth; for when he has ideas and puts his whole heart and soul into the work of carrying them out, his strength is yet further increased by the undaunted courage of youthful convictions.

'Childhood in its simplicity knows nothing of the perils of life; youth sees both its vastness and its difficulties, and at the prospect the courage of youth sometimes flags. We are still serving our apprenticeship to life; we are new to the business, a kind of faint-heartedness overpowers us, and leaves us in an almost dazed condition of mind. We feel that we are helpless aliens in a strange country. At all ages we shrink back involuntarily from the unknown. And a young man is very much like the soldier who will walk up to the cannon's mouth, and is put to flight by a ghost. He hesitates among the maxims of the world. The rules of attack and of self-defence are alike unknown to him; he can neither give nor take; he is attracted by women, and stands in awe of them; his very good qualities tell against him, he is all generosity and modesty, and completely innocent of mercenary designs. Pleasure and not interest is his object when he tells a lie; and among many dubious courses, the conscience, with which as yet he has not juggled, points out to him the right way, which he is slow to take.

'There are men whose lives are destined to be shaped by the impulses of their hearts, rather than by any reasoning process that takes place in their heads, and such natures as these will remain for a long while in the position that I have described. This was my own case. I became the plaything of two contending impulses; the desires of youth were always held in check by a faint-hearted sentimentality. Life in Paris is a cruel ordeal for impressionable natures, the great inequalities of fortune or of position inflame their souls and stir up bitter feelings. In that world of magnificence and pettiness envy is more apt to be a dagger than a spur. You are bound either to fall a victim or to become a partisan in this incessant strife of ambitions, desires, and hatreds, in the midst of which you are placed; and by slow degrees the picture of vice triumphant and virtue made ridiculous produces its effect on a young man, and he wavers; life in Paris soon rubs the bloom from conscience, the infernal work of demoralization has begun, and is soon accomplished. The first of pleasures, that which at the outset comprehends all the others, is set about with such perils that it is impossible not to reflect upon the least actions which it provokes, impossible not to calculate all its consequences. These calculations lead to selfishness. If some poor student, carried away by an impassioned enthusiasm, is fain to rise above selfish considerations, the suspicious attitude of those about him makes him pause and doubt; it is so hard not to share their mistrust, so difficult not to be on his guard against his own generous thoughts. His heart is seared and contracted by this struggle, the current of life sets towards the brain, and the callousness of the Parisian is the result—the condition of things in which schemes for power and wealth are concealed by the most charming frivolity, and lurk beneath the sentimental transports that take the place of enthusiasm. The simplest-natured woman in Paris always keeps a clear head even in the intoxication of happiness.

'This atmosphere was bound to affect my opinions and my conduct. The errors that have poisoned my life would have lain lightly on many a conscience, but we in the South have a religious faith that leads us to believe in a future life, and in the truths set forth by the Catholic Church. These beliefs give depth and gravity to every feeling, and to remorse a terrible and lasting power.

'The army were the masters of society at the time when I was studying medicine. In order to shine in women's eyes, one had to be a colonel at the very least. A poor student counted for absolutely nothing. Goaded by the strength of my desires, and finding no outlet for them; hampered at every step and in every wish by the want of money; looking on study and fame as too slow a means of arriving at the pleasures that tempted me; drawn one way by my inward scruples, and another by evil examples; meeting with every facility for low dissipation, and finding nothing but hindrances barring the way to good society, I passed my days in wretchedness, overwhelmed by a surging tumult of desires, and by indolence of the most deadly kind, utterly cast down at times, only to be as suddenly elated.

'The catastrophe which at length put an end to this crisis was commonplace enough. The thought of troubling the peace of a household has always been repugnant to me; and not only so, I could not dissemble my feelings, the instinct of sincerity was too strong in me; I should have found it a physical impossibility to lead a life of glaring falsity. There is for me but little attraction in pleasures that must be snatched. I wish for full consciousness of my happiness. I led a life of solitude, for which there seemed to be no remedy; for I shrank from openly vicious courses, and the many efforts that I made to enter society were all in vain. There I might have met with some woman who would have undertaken the task of teaching me the perils of every path, who would have formed my manners, counselled me without wounding my vanity, and introduced me everywhere where I was likely to make friends who would be useful to me in my future career. In my despair, an intrigue of the most dangerous kind would perhaps have had its attractions for me; but even peril was out of my reach. My inexperience sent me back again to my solitude, where I dwelt face to face with my thwarted desires.

'At last I formed a connection, at first a secret one, with a girl, whom I persuaded, half against her will, to share my life. Her people were worthy folk, who had but small means. It was not very long before she left her simple sheltered life, and fearlessly entrusted me with a future that virtue would have made happy and fair; thinking, no doubt, that my narrow income was the surest guarantee of my faithfulness to her. From that moment the tempest that had raged within me ceased, and happiness lulled my wild desires and ambitions to sleep. Such happiness is only possible for a young man who is ignorant of the world, who knows nothing as yet of its accepted codes nor of the strength of prejudice; but while it lasts, his happiness is as all-absorbing as a child's. Is not first love like a return of childhood across the intervening years of anxiety and toil?

'There are men who learn life at a glance, who see it for what it is at once, who learn experience from the mistakes of others, who apply the current maxims of worldly wisdom to their own case with signal success, and make unerring forecasts at all times. Wise in their generation are such cool heads as these! But there is also a luckless race endowed with the impressionable, keenly sensitive temperament of the poet; these are the natures that fall into error, and to this latter class I belonged. There was no great depth in the feeling that first drew me towards this poor girl; I followed my instinct rather than my heart when I sacrificed her to myself, and I found no lack of excellent reasons wherewith to persuade myself that there was no harm whatever in what I had done. And as for her—she was devotion itself, a noble soul with a clear, keen intelligence and a heart of gold. She never counselled me other than wisely. Her love put fresh heart into me from the first; she foretold a splendid future of success and fortune for me, and gently constrained me to take up my studies again by her belief in me. In these days there is scarcely a branch of science that has no bearing upon medicine; it is a difficult task to achieve distinction, but the reward is great, for in Paris fame always means fortune. The unselfish girl devoted herself to me, shared in every interest, even the slightest, of my life, and managed so carefully and wisely that we lived in comfort on my narrow income. I had more money to spare, now that there were two of us, than I had ever had while I lived by myself. Those were

THE COUNTRY DOCTOR'S CONFESSION 217

my happiest days. I worked with enthusiasm, I had a definite aim before me, I had found the encouragement I needed. Everything I did or thought I carried to her, who had not only found the way to gain my love, but above and beyond this had filled me with sincere respect for her by the modest discretion which she displayed in a position where discretion and modesty seemed wellnigh impossible. But one day was like another, sir; and it is only after our hearts have passed through all the storms appointed for us that we know the value of a monotonous happiness, and learn that life holds nothing more sweet for us than this; a calm happiness in which the fatigue of existence is felt no longer, and the inmost thoughts of either find response in the other's soul.

'My former dreams assailed me again. They were my own vehement longings for the pleasures of wealth that awoke, though it was in love's name that I now asked for them. In the evenings I grew abstracted and moody, rapt in imaginings of the pleasures I could enjoy if I were rich, and thoughtlessly gave expression to my desires in answer to a tender questioning voice. I must have drawn a painful sigh from her who had devoted herself to my happiness; for she, sweet soul, felt nothing more cruelly than the thought that I wished for something that she could not give me immediately. Oh! sir, a woman's devotion is sublime!'

There was a sharp distress in the doctor's exclamation which seemed prompted by some recollection of his own; he paused for a brief while, and Genestas respected his musings.

'Well, sir,' Benassis resumed, 'something happened which should have concluded the marriage thus begun; but instead of that it put an end to it, and was the cause of all my misfortunes. My father died and left me a large fortune. The necessary business arrangements demanded my presence in Languedoc for several months, and I went thither alone. At last I had regained my freedom! Even the mildest yoke is galling to youth; we do not see its necessity any more than we see the need to work, until we have had some experience of life. I came and went without giving an account of my actions to anyone; there was no need to do so now unless I wished, and I relished liberty with all the keen capacity for enjoyment that we have in Languedoc. I did not absolutely forget the ties that bound me; but I was so absorbed in other matters of interest, that my mind was distracted from them, and little by little the recollection of them faded away. Letters full of heartfelt tenderness reached me; but at two-and-twenty a young man imagines that all women are alike tender; he does not know love from a passing infatuation; all things are confused in the sensations of pleasure which seem at first to comprise everything. It was only later, when I came to a clearer knowledge of men and of things as they are, that I could estimate those noble letters at their just worth. No trace of selfishness was mingled with the feeling expressed in them; there was nothing but gladness on my account for my change of fortune, and regret on her own; it never occurred to her that I could change towards her, for she felt that she herself was incapable of change. But even then I had given myself up to ambitious dreams; I thought of drinking deeply of all the delights that wealth could give, of becoming a person of consequence, of making a brilliant marriage. So I read the letters, and contented myself with saying: "She is very fond of me," with the indifference of a coxcomb. Even then I was perplexed as to how to extricate myself from this entanglement; I was ashamed of it, and this fact as well as my perplexity led me to be cruel. We begin by wounding the victim, and then we kill it, that the sight of our cruelty may no longer put us to the blush. Later reflections upon those days of error have unveiled for me many a dark depth in the human heart. Yes, believe me, those who best have fathomed the good and evil in human nature have honestly examined themselves in the first instance. Conscience is the starting-point of our investigations; we proceed from ourselves to others, never from others to ourselves.

'When I returned to Paris I took up my abode in a large house which, in pursuance of my orders, had been taken for me, and the one person interested in my return and change of address was not informed of it. I wished to cut a figure among young men of fashion. I waited a few days to taste the first delights of wealth; and when, flushed with the excitement of my new position, I felt that I could trust myself to do so, I went to see the poor girl whom I meant to cast off. With a woman's quickness she saw what was passing in my mind, and hid her tears from me. She could not but have despised me; but it was her nature to be gentle and kindly, and she never showed her scorn. Her forbearance was a cruel punishment. An unresisting victim is not a pleasant thing; whether the murder is done decorously in the drawing-room, or brutally on the highway, there should be a struggle to give some plausible excuse for taking a life. I renewed my visits very affectionately at first, making efforts to be gracious, if not tender; by slow degrees I became politely civil; and one day, by a sort of tacit agreement between us, she allowed me to treat her as a stranger, and I thought that I had done all that could be expected of me. Nevertheless I abandoned myself to my new life with almost frenzied eagerness, and sought to drown in gaiety any vague lingering remorse that I felt. A man who has lost his self-respect cannot endure his own society, so I led the dissipated life that wealthy young men lead in Paris. Owing to a good education and an excellent memory, I seemed cleverer than I really was; forthwith I looked down upon other people, and those who, for their own purposes, wished to prove to me that I was possessed of extraordinary abilities, found me quite convinced on that head. Praise is the most insidious of all methods of treachery known to the world; and this is nowhere better understood than in Paris, where intriguing schemers know how to stifle every kind of talent at its birth by heaping laurels on its cradle. So I did nothing worthy of my reputation; I reaped no advantages from the golden opinions entertained of me, and made no acquaintances likely to be useful in my future career. I wasted my energies in numberless frivolous pursuits, and in the short-lived love intrigues that are the disgrace of *salons* in Paris, where everyone seeks for love, grows blasé in the pursuit, falls into the libertinism sanctioned by polite society, and ends by feeling as much astonished at real passion as the world is over a heroic action. I did as others did. Often I dealt to generous and candid souls the deadly wound from which I myself was slowly perishing. Yet though deceptive appearances might lead others to misjudge me, I could never overcome my scrupulous delicacy. Many times I had been duped, and should have blushed for myself had it been otherwise; I secretly prided myself on acting in good faith, although this lowered me in the eyes of others. As a matter of fact, the world has a considerable respect for cleverness, whatever form it takes, and success justifies everything. So the world was pleased to attribute to me all the good qualities and evil propensities, all the victories and defeats which had never been mine; credited me with conquests of which I knew nothing, and sat in judgment upon actions of which I had never been guilty. I scorned to contradict the slanders, and self-love led me to regard the more flattering rumours with a certain complacence. Outwardly my existence was pleasant enough, but in reality I was miserable. If it had not been for the tempest of misfortunes that very soon burst over my head, all good impulses must have perished, and evil would have triumphed in the struggle that went on within me; enervating self-indulgence would have destroyed the body, as the detestable habits of egotism exhausted the springs of the soul. But I was ruined financially. This was how it came about.

'No matter how large his fortune may be, a man is sure to find someone else in Paris possessed of yet greater wealth, whom he must needs aim at surpassing. In this unequal contest I was vanquished at the end of four years; and, like many another harebrained youngster, I was obliged to sell part of my property and to mortgage the remainder to satisfy my creditors. Then a terrible blow suddenly struck me down.

'Two years had passed since I had last seen the woman whom I had deserted. The turn that my affairs were taking would no doubt have brought me back to her once more; but one evening, in the midst of a gay circle of acquaintances, I received a note written in a trembling hand. It only contained these few words:

'"I have only a very little while to live, and I should like to see you, my friend, so that I may know what will become of my child—whether henceforward he will be yours; and also to soften the regret that some day you might perhaps feel for my death."

'The letter made me shudder. It was a revelation of secret anguish in the past, while it contained a whole unknown future. I set out on foot, I would not wait for my carriage, I went across Paris, goaded by remorse, and gnawed by a dreadful fear that was confirmed by the first sight of my victim. In the extreme neatness and cleanliness beneath which she had striven to hide her poverty I read all the terrible sufferings of her life; she was nobly reticent about them in her effort to spare my feelings, and only alluded to them after I had solemnly promised to adopt our child. She died, sir, in spite of all the care lavished upon her, and all that science could suggest was done for her in vain. The care and devotion that had come too late only served to render her last moments less bitter.

'To support her little one she had worked incessantly with her needle.   Love for her child had given her strength to endure her life of hardship; but it had not enabled her to bear my desertion, the keenest of all her griefs.   Many times she had thought of trying to see me, but her woman's pride had always prevented this.   While I squandered floods of gold upon my caprices, no memory of the past had ever bidden a single drop to fall in her home to help mother and child to live; but she had been content to weep, and had not cursed me; she had looked upon her evil fortune as the natural punishment of her error.   With the aid of a good priest of Saint Sulpice, whose kindly voice had restored peace to her soul, she had sought for hope in the shadow of the altar, whither she had gone to dry her tears.   The bitter flood that I had poured into her heart gradually abated; and one day, when she heard her child say "Father," a word that she had not taught him, she forgave my crime.   But sorrow and weeping and days and nights of ceaseless toil injured her health.   Religion had brought its consolations and the courage to bear the ills of life, but all too late.   She fell ill of a heart complaint brought on by grief and by the strain of expectation, for she always thought that I should return, and her hopes always sprang up afresh after every disappointment.   Her health grew worse; and at last, as she was lying on her deathbed, she wrote those few lines, containing no word of reproach, prompted by religion, and by a belief in the goodness in my nature.   She knew, she said, that I was blinded rather than bent on doing wrong.   She even accused herself of carrying her womanly pride too far.   "If I had only written sooner," she said, "perhaps there might have been time for a marriage which would have legitimated our child."

'It was only on her child's account that she wished for

the solemnization of the ties that bound us, nor would she have sought for this if she had not felt that death was at hand to unloose them. But it was too late; even then she had only a few hours to live. By her bedside, where I learned to know the worth of a devoted heart, my nature underwent a final change. I was still at an age when tears are shed. During those last days, while the precious life yet lingered, my tears, my words, and everything I did bore witness to my heartstricken repentance. The meanness and pettiness of the society in which I had moved, the emptiness and selfishness of women of fashion, had taught me to wish for and to seek an elect soul, and now I had found it—too late. I was weary of lying words and of masked faces; counterfeit passion had set me dreaming; I had called on love; and now I beheld love lying before me, slain by my own hands, and had no power to keep it beside me, no power to keep what was so wholly mine.

'The experience of four years had taught me to know my own real character. My temperament, the nature of my imagination, my religious principles, which had not been eradicated, but had rather lain dormant; my turn of mind, my heart that only now began to make itself felt— everything within me led me to resolve to fill my life with the pleasures of affection, to replace a lawless love by family happiness—the truest happiness on earth. Visions of close and dear companionship appealed to me but the more strongly for my wanderings in the wilderness, my grasping at pleasures unennobled by thought or feeling. So though the revolution within me was rapidly effected, it was permanent. With my southern temperament, warped by the life I led in Paris, I should certainly have come to look without pity on an unhappy girl betrayed by her lover; I should have laughed at the story if it had been told me by some wag in merry company (for with us in France a clever epigram dispels all feeling of horror at a crime), but all sophistries were silenced in the presence of this angelic creature, against whom I could bring no least word of reproach. There stood her coffin, and my child, who did not know that I had murdered his mother, smiled at me.

'She died. She died happy when she saw that I loved her, and that this new love was due neither to pity nor to the ties that bound us together. Never shall I forget her last hours. Love had been won back, her mind was at rest about her child, and happiness triumphed over suffering. The comfort and luxury about her, the merriment of her child, who looked prettier still in the dainty garb that had replaced his baby-clothes, were pledges of a happy future for the little one, in whom she saw her own life renewed.

'The curé of Saint Sulpice witnessed my terrible distress. His words wellnigh made me despair. He did not attempt to offer conventional consolation, and put the gravity of my responsibilities unsparingly before me, but I had no need of a spur. The conscience within me spoke loudly enough already. A woman had placed a generous confidence in me. I had lied to her from the first; I had told her that I loved her, and then I had cast her off; I had brought all this sorrow upon an unhappy girl who had braved the opinion of the world for me, and who therefore should have been sacred in my eyes. She had died forgiving me. Her implicit trust in the word of a man who had once before broken his promise to her effaced the memory of all her pain and grief, and she slept in peace. Agatha, who had given me her girlish faith, had found in her heart another faith to give me—the faith of a mother. Oh! sir, the child, *her* child! God alone can know all that he was to me! The dear little one was like his mother; he had her winning grace in his little ways, his talk and ideas; but for me, my child was not only a child, but something more; was he not the token of my forgiveness, my honour?

'He should have more than a father's affection. He should be loved as his mother would have loved him. My remorse might change to happiness if I could only make him feel that his mother's arms were still about him. I clung to him with all the force of human love and the hope of heaven, with all the tenderness in my heart that God has given to mothers. The sound of the child's voice made me tremble. I used to watch him while he slept with a sense of gladness that was always new, albeit a tear sometimes fell on his forehead; I taught him to come to say his prayer upon my bed as soon as he awoke. How sweet and touching were the simple words of the *Paternoster* in the innocent childish mouth! Ah! and at times how terrible! *"Our Father who art in heaven,"* he began one morning; then he paused—"Why is it not *our mother*?" he asked, and my heart sank at his words.

'From the very first I had sown the seed of future misfortune in the life of the son whom I idolized. Although the law has almost countenanced errors of youth by conceding to tardy regret a legal status to natural children, the insurmountable prejudices of society bring a strong force to the support of the reluctance of the law. All serious reflection on my part as to the foundations and mechanism of society, on the duties of man, and vital questions of morality date from this period of my life. Genius comprehends at first sight the connection between a man's principles and the fate of the society of which he forms a part; devout souls are inspired by religion with the sentiments necessary for their happiness; but vehement and impulsive natures can only be schooled by repentance. With repentance came new light for me; and I, who only lived for my child, came through that child to think over great social questions.

'I determined from the first that he should have all possible means of success within himself, and that he should be thoroughly prepared to take the high position for which I destined him. He learned English, German, Italian, and Spanish in succession; and, that he might speak these languages correctly, tutors belonging to each of these various nationalities were successively placed about him from his earliest childhood. His aptitude delighted me. I took advantage of it to give him lessons in the guise of play. I wished to keep his mind free from fallacies, and strove before all things to accustom him from childhood to exert his intellectual powers, to make a rapid and accurate general survey of a matter, and then, by a careful study of every least particular, to master his subject in detail. Lastly, I taught him to submit to discipline without murmuring. I never allowed an impure or improper word to be spoken in his hearing. I was careful that all his surroundings, and the men with whom he came in contact, should conduce to one end—to ennoble his nature, to set lofty ideals before him, to give him a love of truth and a horror of lies, to make him simple and natural in manner, as in word and deed. His natural aptitude had made his other studies easy to him, and his imagination made him quick to grasp these lessons that lay outside the province of the schoolroom. What a fair flower to tend! How great are the joys that mothers know! In those days I began to understand how his own mother had been able to live and to bear her sorrow. This, sir, was the great event of my life; and now I am coming to the tragedy which drove me hither.

'It is the most ordinary commonplace story imaginable; but to me it meant the most terrible pain. For some years I had thought of nothing but my child, and how to make a man of him; then when my son was growing up and about to leave me, I grew afraid of my loneliness. Love was a necessity of my existence; this need for affection had never been satisfied, and only grew stronger with years. I was in every way capable of a real attachment; I had been tried and proved. I knew all that a steadfast love means, the love that delights to find a pleasure in self-sacrifice; in everything I did my first thought would always be for the woman I loved. In imagination I was fain to dwell on the serene heights far above doubt and uncertainty, where love so fills two beings that happiness flows quietly and evenly into their life, their looks, and words. Such love is to a life what religion is to the soul; a vital force, a power that enlightens and upholds. I understood the love of husband and wife in no wise as most people do; for me its full beauty and magnificence began precisely at the point where love perishes in many a household. I deeply felt the moral grandeur of a life so closely shared by two souls that the trivialities of everyday existence should be powerless against such lasting love as theirs. But where will the hearts be found whose beats are so nearly *isochronous* (let the scientific term pass) that they may attain to this beatific union? If they exist, nature and chance have set them far apart, so that they cannot come together; they find each other too late, or death comes too soon to separate them. There must be some good reasons for these dispensations of fate, but I have never sought to discover them. I cannot make a study of my wound, because I suffer too much from it. Perhaps perfect happiness is a monster which our species should not perpetuate. There were other causes for my fervent desire for such a marriage as this. I had no friends, the world for me was a desert. There is something in me that repels friendship. More than one person has sought me out, but, in spite of efforts on my part, it came to nothing. With many men I have been careful to show no sign of something that is called "superiority"; I have adapted my mind to theirs; I have placed myself at their point of view, joined in their laughter, and overlooked their defects; any fame I might have gained, I would have bartered for a little kindly affection. They parted from me without regret. If you seek for real

feeling in Paris, snares await you everywhere, and the end
is sorrow. Wherever I set my foot, the ground round
about me seemed to burn. My readiness to acquiesce
was considered weakness; though if I unsheathed my
talons, like a man conscious that he may some day wield
the thunderbolts of power, I was thought ill-natured; to
others, the delightful laughter that ceases with youth,
and in which in later years we are almost ashamed to
indulge, seemed absurd, and they amused themselves at
my expense. People may be bored nowadays, but none
the less they expect you to treat every trivial topic with
befitting seriousness.

'A hateful era! You must bow down before mediocrity, frigidly polite mediocrity which you despise—and
obey. On more mature reflection, I have discovered
the reasons of these glaring inconsistencies. Mediocrity
is never out of fashion, it is the daily wear of society;
genius and eccentricity are ornaments that are locked
away and only brought out on certain days. Everything that ventures forth beyond the protection of the
grateful shadow of mediocrity has something startling
about it.

'So, in the midst of Paris, I led a solitary life. I had
given up everything to society, but it had given me nothing in return; and my child was not enough to satisfy my
heart, because I was not a woman. My life seemed to
be growing cold within me; I was bending under a load of
secret misery when I met the woman who was to make me
know the might of love, the reverence of an acknowledged
love, love with its teeming hopes of happiness—in one
word—love.

'I had renewed my acquaintance with that old friend
of my father's who had once taken charge of my affairs.
It was in his house that I first met her whom I must love
as long as life shall last. The longer we live, sir, the
more clearly we see the enormous influence of ideas upon

the events of life. Prejudices, worthy of all respect, and bred by noble religious ideas, occasioned my misfortunes. This young girl belonged to an exceeding devout family, whose views of Catholicism were due to the spirit of a sect improperly styled Jansenists, which, in former times, caused troubles in France. You know why?'

'No,' said Genestas.

'Jansenius, Bishop of Ypres, once wrote a book which was believed to contain propositions at variance with the doctrines of the Holy See. When examined at a later date, there appeared to be nothing heretical in the wording of the text, some authors even went so far as to deny that the heretical propositions had any real existence. However it was, these insignificant disputes gave rise to two parties in the Gallican Church—the Jansenists and the Jesuits. Great men were found in either camp, and a struggle began between two powerful bodies. The Jansenists affected an excessive purity of morals and of doctrine, and accused the Jesuits of preaching a relaxed morality. The Jansenists, in fact, were Catholic Puritans, if two contradictory terms can be combined. During the Revolution, the Concordat occasioned an unimportant schism, a little segregation of ultra-Catholics who refused to recognize the bishops appointed by the authorities with the consent of the Pope. This little body of the faithful was called the Little Church; and those within its fold, like the Jansenists, led the strictly ordered lives that appear to be a first necessity of existence in all proscribed and persecuted sects. Many Jansenist families had joined the Little Church. The family to which this young girl belonged had embraced the equally rigid doctrines of both these Puritanisms, tenets which impart a stern dignity to the character and mien of those who hold them. It is the nature of positive doctrine to exaggerate the importance of the most ordinary actions of life by connecting them with ideas of a future existence. This is the source of a splendid and delicate purity of heart, a respect for others and for self, of an indescribably keen sense of right and wrong, a wide charity, together with a justice so stern that it might well be called inexorable, and lastly, a perfect hatred of lies and of all the vices comprised by falsehood.

'I can recall no more delightful moments than those of our first meeting at my old friend's house. · I beheld for the first time this shy young girl with her sincere nature, her habits of ready obedience. All the virtues peculiar to the sect to which she belonged shone in her, but she seemed to be unconscious of her merit. There was a grace, which no austerity could diminish, about every movement of her lissom, slender form; her quiet brow, the delicate grave outlines of her face, and her clearly cut features indicated noble birth; her expression was gentle and proud; her thick hair had been simply braided, the coronet of plaits about her head served, all unknown to her, as an adornment. Captain, she was for me the ideal type that is always made real for us in the woman with whom we fall in love; for when we love, is it not because we recognize beauty that we have dreamed of, the beauty that has existed in idea for us is realized? When I spoke to her, she answered simply, without shyness or eagerness; she did not know what a pleasure it was to me to see her, to hear the musical sounds of her voice. All these angels are revealed to our hearts by the same signs; by the sweetness of their tones, the tenderness in their eyes, by their fair, pale faces and their gracious ways. All these things are so blended and mingled that we feel that charm of their presence, yet cannot tell in what that charm consists, and every movement is an expression of a divine soul within. I loved passionately. This newly awakened love satisfied all my restless longings, all my ambitious dreams. She was beautiful, wealthy, and nobly born; she had been carefully brought up; she had all the qualifications which the world positively demands of a woman placed in the high position which I desired to reach; she had been well educated, she expressed herself with a sprightly facility at once rare and common in France; where the most prettily worded phrases of many women are emptiness itself, while her bright talk was full of sense. Above all, she had a deep consciousness of her own dignity which made others respect her; I know of no more excellent thing in a wife. I must stop, captain; no one can describe the woman he loves save very imperfectly, pre-existent mysteries which defy analysis lie between them.

'I very soon took my old friend into my confidence. He introduced me to her family, and gave me the countenance of his honourable character. I was received at first with the frigid politeness characteristic of those exclusive people who never forsake those whom they have once admitted to their friendship. As time went on they welcomed me almost as one of the family; this mark of their esteem was won by my behaviour in the matter. In spite of my passionate love, I did nothing that could lower me in my own eyes; I did not cringe, I paid no court to those upon whom my fate depended, before all things I showed myself a man, and not other than I really was. When I was well known to them, my old friend, who was as desirous as I myself that my life of melancholy loneliness should come to an end, spoke of my hopes and met with a favourable reception; but with the diplomatic shrewdness which is almost a second nature with men of the world, he was silent with regard to an error of my youth, as he termed it. He was anxious to bring about a "satisfactory marriage" for me, an expression that makes of so solemn an act a business transaction in which husband and wife endeavour to cheat each other. In his opinion, the existence of my child would excite a moral repugnance, in comparison with which the question of money would be as naught, and the whole affair would be broken off at once, and he was right.

"'It is a matter which will be very easily settled between you and your wife; it will be easy to obtain her full and free forgiveness," he said.

'In short, he tried to silence my scruples, and all the insidious arguments that worldly wisdom could suggest were brought to bear upon me to this end. I will confess to you, sir, that in spite of my promise, my first impulse was to act straightforwardly and to make everything known to the head of the family, but the thought of his uncompromising sternness made me pause, and the probable consequences of the confession appalled me; my courage failed, I temporized with my conscience, I determined to wait until I was sufficiently sure of the affection of the girl I hoped to win, before hazarding my happiness by the terrible confession. My resolution to acknowledge everything openly, at a convenient season, vindicated the sophistries of worldly wisdom and the sagacity of my old friend. So the young girl's parents received me as their future son-in-law without, as yet, taking their friends into their confidence.

'An infinite discretion is the distinguishing quality of pious families; they are reticent about everything, even about matters of no importance. You would not believe, sir, how this sedate gravity and reserve, pervading every least action, deepens the current of feeling and thought. Everything in that house was done with some useful end in view; the women spent their leisure time in making garments for the poor; their conversation was never frivolous; laughter was not banished, but there was a kindly simplicity about their merriment. Their talk had none of the piquancy which scandal and ill-natured gossip give to the conversation of society; only the father and uncle read the newspapers, even the most harmless journal contains references to crimes or to public evils, and she whom I hoped to win had never cast her eyes over their sheets. How strange it was, at first, to listen to these orthodox people! But in a little while, the pure atmosphere left the same impression upon the soul that subdued colours give to the eyes, a sense of serene repose and of tranquil peace.

'To a superficial observer, their life would have seemed terribly monotonous. There was something chilling about the appearance of the interior of the house. Day after day I used to see everything, even the furniture in constant use, always standing in the same place, and this uniform tidiness pervaded the smallest details. Yet there was something very attractive about their household ways. I had been used to the pleasures of variety, to the luxury and stir of life in Paris; it was only when I had overcome my first repugnance that I saw the advantages of this existence; how it lent itself to continuity of thought and to involuntary meditation; how a life in which the heart has undisturbed sway seems to widen and grow vast as the sea. It is like the life of the cloister, where the outward surroundings never vary, and thought is thus compelled to detach itself from outward things and to turn to the infinite that lies within the soul!

'For a man as sincerely in love as I was, the silence and simplicity of the life, the almost conventual regularity with which the same things were done daily at the same hours, only deepened and strengthened love. In that profound calm the interest attaching to the least action, word, or gesture became immense. I learned to know that, in the interchange of glances and in answering smiles, there lies an eloquence and a variety of language far beyond the possibilities of the most magnificent of spoken phrases; that when the expression of the feelings is spontaneous and unforced, there is no idea, no joy nor sorrow that cannot thus be communicated by hearts that understand each other. How many times I have tried to set forth my soul in my eyes or on my lips, compelled at once to speak and to be silent concerning my passion; for the young girl who, in my presence, was always serene and unconscious had not been informed of the reason of my constant visits; her parents were determined that the most important decision of her life should rest entirely with her. But does not the presence of our beloved satisfy the utmost desire of passionate love? In that presence do we not know the happiness of the Christian who stands before God? If for me more than for any other it was torture to have no right to give expression to the impulses of my heart, to force back into its depths the burning words that treacherously wrong the yet more ardent emotions which strive to find an utterance in speech; I found, nevertheless, in the merest trifles a channel through which my passionate love poured itself forth but the more vehemently for this constraint, till every least occurrence came to have an excessive importance.

'I beheld her, not for brief moments, but for whole hours. There were pauses between my question and her answer, and long musings, when, with the tones of her voice lingering in my ears, I sought to divine from them the secret of her inmost thoughts; perhaps her fingers would tremble as I gave her some object of which she had been in search, or I would devise pretexts to lightly touch her dress or her hair, to take her hand in mine, to compel her to speak more than she wished; all these nothings were great events for me. Eyes and voice and gestures were freighted with mysterious messages of love in hours of ecstasy like these, and this was the only language permitted me by the quiet maidenly reserve of the young girl before me. Her manner towards me underwent no change; with me she was always as a sister with a brother; yet, as my passion grew, and the contrast between her glances and mine, her words and my utterance, became more striking, I felt at last that this timid silence was the only means by which she could express her feelings. Was she not always in the *salon*, whenever I came? Did she not stay there until my visit, expected and perhaps foreseen, was over? Did not this mute tryst betray the secret of her innocent soul? Nay, whilst I spoke, did she not listen with a pleasure which she could not hide?

'At last, no doubt, her parents grew impatient with this artless behaviour and sober love-making. I was almost as timid as their daughter, and perhaps on this account found favour in their eyes. They regarded me as a man worthy of their esteem. My old friend was taken into their confidence; both father and mother spoke of me in the most flattering terms; I had become their adopted son, and more especially they singled out my moral principles for praise. In truth, I had found my youth again; among these pure and religious surroundings early beliefs and early faith came back to the man of thirty-two.

'The summer was drawing to a close. Affairs of some importance had detained the family in Paris longer than their wont; but when September came, and they were able to leave town at last for an estate in Auvergne, her father entreated me to spend a couple of months with them in an old château hidden away among the mountains of the Cantal. I paused before accepting this friendly invitation. My hesitation brought me the sweetest and most delightful unconscious confession, a revelation of the mysteries of a girlish heart. Evelina . . . Lord!' exclaimed Benassis; and he said no more for a time, wrapped in his own thoughts.

'Pardon me, Captain Bluteau,' he resumed, after a long pause. 'For twelve years I have not uttered the name that is always hovering in my thoughts, that a voice calls in my hearing even when I sleep. Evelina (since I have named her) raised her head with a strange quickness and abruptness, for about all her movements there was an instinctive grace and gentleness, and looked at me. There was no pride in her face, but rather a wistful anxiety. Then her colour rose, and her eyelids fell; it gave me an indescribable pleasure never felt before that they should fall so slowly; I could only stammer out my reply in a faltering voice. The emotion of my own heart made swift answer to hers. She thanked me by a happy look, and I almost thought that there were tears in her eyes. In that moment we had told each other everything. So I went into the country with her family. Since the day when our hearts had understood each other, nothing seemed to be as it had been before; everything about us had acquired a fresh significance.

'Love, indeed, is always the same, though our imagination determines the shape that love must assume; like and unlike, therefore, is love in every soul in which he dwells, and passion becomes a unique work in which the soul expresses its sympathies. In the old trite saying that love is a projection of self—an *égoïsme à deux*—lies a profound meaning known only to philosopher and poet; for it is ourself in truth that we love in that other. Yet, though love manifests itself in such different ways that no pair of lovers since the world began is like any other pair before or since, they all express themselves after the same fashion, and the same words are on the lips of every girl, even of the most innocent, convent-bred maiden—the only difference lies in the degree of imaginative charm in their ideas. But between Evelina and other girls there was this difference, that where another would have poured out her feelings quite naturally, Evelina regarded these innocent confidences as a concession made to the stormy emotions which had invaded the quiet sanctuary of her girlish soul. The constant struggle between her heart and her principles gave to the least event of her life, so peaceful in appearance, in reality so profoundly agitated, a character of force very superior to the exaggerations of young girls whose manners are early rendered false by the world about them. All through the journey Evelina discovered beauty in the scenery through which we passed, and spoke of it with admiration. When we think that we may not give expression of the happiness which is given to us by the presence of one we love, we pour out the secret gladness that overflows our hearts upon inanimate things, investing them with beauty in our happiness. The charm of the scenery which passed before our eyes became in this way an interpreter between us, for in our praises of the landscape we revealed to each other the secrets of our love. Evelina's mother sometimes took a mischievous pleasure in disconcerting her daughter.

"'My dear child, you have been through this valley a score of times without seeming to admire it!" she remarked after a somewhat too enthusiastic phrase from Evelina.

"'No doubt it was because I was not old enough to understand beauty of this kind, mother."

'Forgive me for dwelling on this trifle, which can have no charm for you, captain; but the simple words brought me an indescribable joy, which had its source in the glance directed towards me as she spoke. So some village lighted by the sunrise, some ivy-covered ruin which we had seen together, memories of outward and visible things, served to deepen and strengthen the impressions of our happiness; they seemed to be landmarks on the way through which we were passing towards a bright future that lay before us.

'We reached the château belonging to her family, where I spent about six weeks, the only time in my life during which Heaven has vouchsafed complete happiness to me. I enjoyed pleasures unknown to town-dwellers— all the happiness which two lovers find in living beneath the same roof, an anticipation of the life they will spend together. To stroll through the fields, to be alone together at times, if we wished it, to look over an old water-mill, to sit beneath a tree in some lovely glen among the hills, the lovers' talks, the sweet confidences drawn forth by which each made some progress day by day in the other's heart—ah! sir, the out-of-door life, the beauty of earth and heaven, is a perfect accompaniment to the perfect happiness of the soul! To mingle our careless talk with the song of the birds among the dewy leaves, to smile at each other as we gazed on the sky, to turn our steps slowly homewards at the sound of the bell that always rings too soon, to admire together some little detail in the landscape, to watch the fitful movements of an insect, to look closely at a gleaming demoiselle fly— the delicate creature that resembles an innocent and loving girl; in such ways as these are not one's thoughts drawn daily a little higher? The memories of my forty days of happiness have in a manner coloured all the rest of my life, memories that are all the fairer and fill the greater space in my thoughts, because since then it has been my fate never to be understood. To this day there are scenes of no special interest for a casual observer, but full of bitter significance for a broken heart, which recall those vanished days, and the love that is not forgotten yet.

'I do not know whether you noticed the effect of the sunset light on the cottage where little Jacques lives? Everything shone so brightly in the fiery rays of the sun, and then all at once the whole landscape grew dark and dreary. That sudden change was like the change in my own life at this time. I received from her the first, the sole and sublime token of love that an innocent girl may give; the more secretly it is given, the closer is the bond it forms, the sweet promise of love, a fragment of the language spoken in a fairer world than this. Sure, there-fore, of being beloved, I vowed that I would confess everything at once, that I would have no secrets from her; I felt ashamed that I had so long delayed to tell her about the sorrows that I had brought upon myself.

'Unluckily, with the morrow of this happy day a letter came from my son's tutor, the life of the child so dear to me was in danger. I went away without confiding my secret to Evelina, merely telling her family that I was urgently required in Paris. Her parents took alarm during my absence. They feared that there I was entangled in some way, and wrote to Paris to make inquiries about me. It was scarcely consistent with their religious principles; but they suspected me, and did not even give me an opportunity of clearing myself.

'One of their friends, without my knowledge, gave them the whole history of my youth, blackening my errors, laying stress upon the existence of my child, which (said they) I intended to conceal. I wrote to my future parents, but I received no answers to my letters; and when they came back to Paris, and I called at their house, I was not admitted. Much alarmed, I sent to my old friend to learn the reason of this conduct on their part, which I did not in the least understand. As soon as the good soul knew the real cause of it all, he sacrificed himself generously, took upon himself all the blame of my reserve, and tried to exculpate me, but all to no purpose. Questions of interest and morality were regarded so seriously by the family, their prejudices were so firmly and deeply rooted, that they never swerved from their resolution. My despair was overwhelming. At first I tried to deprecate their wrath, but my letters were sent back to me unopened. When every possible means had been tried in vain; when her father and mother had plainly told my old friend (the cause of my misfortune) that they would never consent to their daughter's marriage with a man who had upon his conscience the death of a woman and the life of a natural son, even though Evelina herself should implore them upon her knees; then, sir, there only remained to me one last hope, a hope as slender and fragile as the willow-branch at which a drowning wretch catches to save himself.

'I ventured to think that Evelina's love would be stronger than her father's scruples, that her inflexible parents might yield to her entreaties. Perhaps, who knows, her father had kept from her the reasons of the refusal, which was so fatal to our love. I determined to acquaint her with all the circumstances, and to make a final appeal to her; and in fear and trembling, in grief and tears, my first and last love-letter was written. To-day I can only dimly remember the words dictated to me by my despair; but I must have told Evelina that if she had dealt sincerely with me she could not and ought not to love another, or how could her whole life be anything but a lie? She must be false either to her future husband or to me. Could she refuse to the lover, who had been so misjudged and hardly entreated, the devotion which she would have shown to him as her husband, if the marriage which had already taken place in our hearts had been outwardly solemnized? Was not this to fall from the ideal of womanly virtue? What woman would not love to feel that the promises of the heart were more sacred and binding than the chains forged by the law? I defended my errors; and in my appeal to the purity of innocence, I left nothing unsaid that could touch a noble and generous nature. But as I am telling you everything, I will look for her answer and my farewell letter,' said Benassis, and he went up to his room in search of it.

He returned in a few moments with a worn pocket-book; his hands trembled with emotion as he drew from it some loose sheets.

'Here is the fatal letter,' he said. 'The girl who wrote those lines little knew the value that I should set upon the scrap of paper that holds her thoughts. This is the last cry that pain wrung from me,' he added, taking up a second letter; 'I will lay it before you directly. My old friend was the bearer of my letter of entreaty; he gave it to her without her parents' knowledge, humbling his white hair to implore Evelina to read and to reply to my appeal. This was her answer:

"'Sir . . .' But lately I had been her "beloved," the innocent name she had found by which to express her innocent love, and now she called me Sir. That one word told me everything. But listen to the rest of the letter:

"'Treachery on the part of one to whom her life was to be entrusted is a bitter thing for a girl to discover; and yet I could not but excuse you, we are so weak! Your letter touched me, but you must not write to me again, the sight of your handwriting gives me such unbearable pain. We are parted for ever. I was carried away by your reasoning; it extinguished all the harsh feelings that had risen up against you in my soul. I had been so proud of your truth! But both of us have found my father's reasoning irresistible. Yes, indeed, Sir I ventured to plead for you. I did for you what I have never done before, I overcame the greatest fears that I have ever known, and acted almost against my nature. Even now I am yielding to your entreaties, and doing wrong for your sake, in writing to you without my father's knowledge. My mother knows that I am writing to you; her indulgence in leaving me at liberty to be alone with you for a moment has taught me the depth of her love for me, and strengthened my determination to bow to the decree of my family, against which I had almost rebelled. I am therefore writing to you, sir, for the first and last time. You have my full and entire forgiveness for the troubles that you have brought into my life. Yes, you are right; a first love can never be forgotten. I am no longer an innocent girl; and, as an honest woman,

I can never marry another. What my future will be, I know not therefore. Only you see, sir, that the echoes of this year that you have filled will never die away in my life. But I am in no way accusing you. . . . 'I shall always be beloved!' Why did you write those words? Can they bring peace to the troubled soul of a lonely and unhappy girl? Have you not already laid waste my future, giving me memories which will never cease to revisit me? Henceforth I can only give myself to God, but will He accept a broken heart? He has had some purpose to fulfil in sending these afflictions to me; doubtless it was His will that I should turn to Him, my only refuge here below. Nothing remains to me here upon this earth. You have all a man's ambition wherewith to beguile your sorrows. I do not say this as a reproach; it is a sort of religious consolation. If we both bear a grievous burden at this moment, I think that my share of it is the heavier. He in whom I have put my trust, and of whom you can feel no jealousy, has joined our lives together, and He puts them asunder according to His will. I have seen that your religious beliefs were not founded upon the pure and living faith which alone enables us to bear our woes here below. Sir, if God will vouchsafe to hear my fervent and ceaseless prayers, He will cause His light to shine in your soul. Farewell, you who should have been my guide, you whom once I had the right to call 'my beloved,' no one can reproach me if I pray for you still. God orders our days as it pleases Him. Perhaps you may be the first whom He will call to Himself; but if I am left alone in the world, then, sir, entrust the care of the child to me."

'This letter, so full of generous sentiments, disappointed my hopes,' Benassis resumed, 'so that at first I could think of nothing but my misery; afterwards I welcomed the balm which, in her forgetfulness of self, she had tried to pour into my wounds, but in my first despair I wrote to her somewhat bitterly:

"'Madam—that single word alone will tell you that at your bidding I renounce you. There is something indescribably sweet in obeying one we love, who puts us to the torture. You are right, I acquiesce in my condemnation. Once I slighted a girl's devotion; it is fitting, therefore, that my love should be rejected to-day. But I little thought that my punishment was to be dealt to me by the woman at whose feet I had laid my life. I never expected that such harshness, perhaps I should say, such rigid virtue, lurked in a heart that seemed to be so loving and so tender. At this moment the full strength of my love is revealed to me; it has survived the most terrible of all trials, the scorn you have shown for me by severing without regret the ties that bound us. Farewell for ever. There still remains to me the proud humility of repentance; I will find some sphere of life where I can expiate the errors to which you, the mediator between heaven and me, have shown no mercy. Perhaps God may be less inexorable. My sufferings, sufferings full of the thought of you, shall be the penance of a heart which will never be healed, which will bleed in solitude. For a wounded heart—shadow and silence.

"'No other image of love shall be engraven on my heart. Though I am not a woman, I feel as you felt that when I said 'I love you,' it was a vow for life. Yes, the words then spoken in the ear of 'my beloved' were not a lie; you would have a right to scorn me if I could change. I shall never cease to worship you in my solitude. In spite of the gulf set between us, you will still be the mainspring of all my actions, and all the virtues are inspired by penitence and love. Though you have filled my heart with bitterness, I shall never have bitter thoughts of you; would it not be an ill beginning of the new tasks that I have set myself if I did not purge out all the evil leaven from my soul? Farewell, then, to the one heart that I love in the world, a heart from which I am cast out. Never has more feeling and more tenderness been expressed in a farewell, for is it not fraught with the life and soul of one who can never hope again, and must be henceforth as one dead? . . . Farewell. May peace be with you, and may all the sorrow of our lot fall to me!'

Benassis and Genestas looked at each other for a moment after reading the two letters, each full of sad thoughts, of which neither spoke.

'As you see, this is only a rough copy of my last letter,' said Benassis; 'it is all that remains to me to-day of my blighted hopes. When I had sent the letter, I fell into an indescribable state of depression. All the ties that hold one to life were bound together in the hope of wedded happiness, which was henceforth lost to me for ever. I had to bid farewell to the joys of a permitted and acknowledged love, to all the generous ideas that had thronged up from the depths of my heart. The prayers of a penitent soul that thirsted for righteousness and for all things lovely and of good report, had been rejected by these religious people. At first, the wildest resolutions and most frantic thoughts surged through my mind, but happily for me the sight of my son brought self-control. I felt all the more strongly drawn towards him for the misfortunes of which he was the innocent cause, and for which I had in reality only myself to blame. In him I found all my consolation.

'At the age of thirty-four I might still hope to do my country noble service. I determined to make a name for myself, a name so illustrious that no one should remember the stain on the birth of my son. How many noble thoughts I owe to him! How full a life I led in those days while I was absorbed in planning out his future! I feel stifled,' cried Benassis. 'All this happened eleven years ago, and yet to this day I cannot bear to think of that fatal year. . . . My child died, sir; I lost him!'

The doctor was silent, and hid his face in his hands; when he was somewhat calmer he raised his head again, and Genestas saw that his eyes were full of tears.

'At first it seemed as if this thunderbolt had uprooted me,' Benassis resumed. 'It was a blow from which I could only expect to recover after I had been transplanted into a different soil from that of the social world in which I lived. It was not till some time afterwards that I saw the finger of God in my misfortunes, and later still that I learned to submit to His will and to hearken to His voice. It was impossible that resignation should come to me all at once. My impetuous and fiery nature broke out in a final storm of rebellion.

'It was long before I brought myself to take the only step befitting a Catholic, indeed my thoughts ran on suicide. This succession of misfortunes had contributed to develop melancholy feelings in me, and I deliberately determined to take my own life. It seemed to me that it was permissible to take leave of life when life was ebbing fast. There was nothing unnatural, I thought, about suicide. The ravages of mental distress affected the soul of man in the same way that acute physical anguish affected the body; and an intelligent being, suffering from a moral malady, had surely a right to destroy himself, a right he shares with the sheep, that, fallen a victim to the "staggers," beats its head against a tree. Were the soul's diseases in truth more readily cured than those of the body? I scarcely think so, to this day. Nor do I know which is the more craven soul, he who hopes even when hope is no longer possible, or he who despairs. Death is the natural termination of a physical malady, and it seemed to me that suicide was the final crisis in the sufferings of a mind diseased, for it was in the power of the will to end them when reason showed that death was preferable to life.

So it is not the pistol, but a thought that puts an end to our existence. Again, when fate may suddenly lay us low in the midst of a happy life, can we be blamed for ourselves refusing to bear a life of misery?

'But my reflections during that time of mourning turned on loftier themes. The grandeur of pagan philosophy attracted me, and for a while I became a convert. In my efforts to discover new rights for man, I thought that with the aid of modern thought I could penetrate further into the questions to which those old-world systems of philosophy had furnished solutions.

'Epicurus permitted suicide. Was it not the natural outcome of his system of ethics? The gratification of the senses was to be obtained at any cost; and when this became impossible, the easiest and best course was for the animate being to return to the repose of inanimate nature. Happiness, or the hope of happiness, was the one end for which man existed, for one who suffered, and who suffered without hope, death ceased to be an evil, and became a good, and suicide became a final act of wisdom. This act Epicurus neither blamed nor praised; he was content to say as he poured a libation to Bacchus: "*As for death, there is nothing in death to move our laughter or our tears.*"

'With a loftier morality than that of the Epicureans, and a sterner sense of man's duties, Zeno and the Stoic philosophers prescribed suicide in certain cases to their followers. They reasoned thus: Man differs from the brute in that he has the sovereign right to dispose of his person; take away this power of life and death over himself, and he becomes the plaything of fate, the slave of other men. Rightly understood, this power of life and death is a sufficient counterpoise for all the ills of life; the same power when conferred upon another, upon his fellow man, leads to tyranny of every kind. Man has no power whatever unless he has unlimited freedom of action. Suppose that he had been guilty of some irreparable error, from the shameful consequences of which there is no escape; a sordid nature swallows down the disgrace and survives it, the wise man drinks the hemlock and dies. Suppose that the remainder of life is to be one constant struggle with the gout which racks our bones, or with a gnawing and disfiguring cancer, the wise man dismisses quacks, and at the proper moment bids a last farewell to the friends whom he only saddens by his presence. Or another perhaps has fallen alive into the hands of the tyrant against whom he fought. What shall he do? The oath of allegiance is tendered to him; he must either subscribe or stretch out his neck to the executioner; the fool takes the latter course, the coward subscribes, the wise man strikes a last blow for liberty—in his own heart. "You who are free," the Stoic was wont to say, "know then how to preserve your freedom! Find freedom from your own passions by sacrificing them to duty, freedom from the tyranny of mankind by pointing to the sword or the poison which will put you beyond their reach, freedom from the bondage of fate by determining the point beyond which you will endure it no longer, freedom of mind by shaking off the trammels of prejudice, and freedom from physical fear by learning how to subdue the gross instinct which causes so many wretches to cling to life."

'After I had unearthed this reasoning from among a heap of ancient philosophical writings, I sought to reconcile it with Christian teaching. God has bestowed free will upon us in order to require of us an account hereafter before the Throne of Judgment. "I will plead my cause there!" I said to myself. But such thoughts as these led me to think of a life after death, and my old shaken beliefs rose up before me. Human life grows solemn when all eternity hangs upon the slightest of our decisions. When the full meaning of this thought is realized, the soul becomes conscious of something vast and mysterious within itself, by which it is drawn towards the Infinite; the aspect of all things alters strangely. From this point of view life is something infinitely great and infinitely little. The consciousness of my sins had never made me think of heaven so long as hope remained to me on earth, so long as I could find a relief for my woes in work and in the society of other men. I had meant to make the happiness of a woman's life, to love, to be the head of a family, and in this way my need of expiation would have been satisfied to the full. This design had been thwarted, but yet another way had remained to me —I would devote myself henceforward to my child. But after these two efforts had failed, and scorn and death had darkened my soul for ever, when all my feelings had been wounded and nothing was left to me here on earth, I raised my eyes to heaven, and beheld God.

'Yet still I tried to obtain the sanction of religion for my death. I went carefully through the Gospels, and found no passage in which suicide was forbidden; but during the reading, the divine thought of Christ, the Saviour of men, dawned in me. Certainly He had said nothing about the immortality of the soul, but He had spoken of the glorious kingdom of His Father; He had nowhere forbidden parricide, but He condemned all that was evil. The glory of His evangelists, and the proof of their divine mission, is not so much that they made laws for the world, but that they spread a new spirit abroad, and the new laws were filled with this new spirit. The very courage which a man displays in taking his own life seemed to me to be his condemnation; so long as he felt that he had within himself sufficient strength to die by his own hands, he ought to have had strength enough to continue the struggle. To refuse to suffer is a sign of weakness rather than of courage, and, moreover, was it not a sort of recusance to take leave of life in despondency, an abjuration of the Christian faith which is based upon the sublime words of Jesus Christ: "Blessed are they that mourn"?

'So, in any case, suicide seemed to me to be an unpardonable error, even in the man who, through a false conception of greatness of soul, takes his life a few moments before the executioner's axe falls. In humbling Himself to the death of the cross, did not Jesus Christ set for us an example of obedience to all human laws, even when carried out unjustly? The word *resignation* engraved upon the cross, so clear to the eyes of those who can read the sacred characters in which it is traced, shone for me with divine brightness.

'I still had eighty thousand francs in my possession, and at first I meant to live a remote and solitary life, to vegetate in some country district for the rest of my days; but misanthropy is no Catholic virtue, and there is a certain vanity lurking beneath the hedgehog's skin of the misanthrope. His heart does not bleed, it shrivels, and my heart bled from every vein. I thought of the discipline of the Church, the refuge that she affords to sorrowing souls, understood at last the beauty of a life of prayer in solitude, and was fully determined to "enter religion," in the grand old phrase. So far my intentions were firmly fixed, but I had not yet decided on the best means of carrying them out. I realized the remains of my fortune, and set forth on my journey with an almost tranquil mind. *Peace in God* was a hope that could never fail me.

'I felt drawn to the rule of Saint Bruno, and made the journey to the Grande Chartreuse on foot, absorbed in solemn thoughts. That was a memorable day. I was not prepared for the grandeur of the scenery; the workings of an unknown Power greater than that of man were visible at every step; the overhanging crags, the precipices on either hand, the stillness only broken by the voices of the mountain streams, the sternness and wildness of the landscape, relieved here and there by Nature's fairest creations, pine-trees that have stood for centuries and delicate rock plants at their feet, all combine to produce sober musings. There seemed to be no end to this waste solitude, shut in by its lofty mountain barriers. The idle curiosity of man could scarcely penetrate there. It would be difficult to cross this melancholy desert of Saint Bruno's with a light heart.

'I saw the Grande Chartreuse. I walked beneath the vaulted roofs of the ancient cloisters, and heard in the silence the sound of the water from the spring, falling drop by drop. I entered a cell that I might the better realize my own utter nothingness; something of the peace that my predecessor had found there seemed to pass into my soul. An inscription, which in accordance with the custom of the monastery he had written above his door, impressed and touched me; all the precepts of the life that I meant to lead were there, summed up in three Latin words—*Fuge, late, tace.*'

Genestas bent his head as if he understood.

'My decision was made,' Benassis resumed. 'The cell with its deal wainscot, the hard bed, the solitude, all appealed to my soul. The Carthusians were in the chapel, I went thither to join in their prayers, and there my resolutions vanished. I do not wish to criticize the Catholic Church, I am perfectly orthodox, I believe in its laws and in the works it prescribes. But when I heard the chanting and the prayers of those old men, dead to the world and forgotten by the world, I discerned an undercurrent of sublime egoism in the life of the cloister. This withdrawal from the world could only benefit the individual soul, and after all what was it but a protracted suicide? I do not condemn it. The Church has opened these tombs in which life is buried; no doubt they are needful for those few Christians who are absolutely useless to the world; but for me, it would be better, I thought, to live among my fellows, to devote my life of expiation to their service.

'As I returned I thought long and carefully over the various ways in which I could carry out my vow of renunciation. Already I began, in fancy, to lead the life of a common sailor, condemning myself to serve our country in the lowest ranks, and giving up all my intellectual ambitions; but though it was a life of toil and of self-abnegation, it seemed to me that I ought to do more than this. Should I not thwart the designs of God by leading such a life? If He had given me intellectual ability, was it not my duty to employ it for the good of my fellow men? Then, besides, if I am to speak frankly, I felt within me a need of my fellow men, an indescribable wish to help them. The round of mechanical duties and the routine tasks of the sailor afforded no scope for this desire, which is as much an outcome of my nature as the characteristic scent that a flower breathes forth.

'I was obliged to spend the night here, as I have already told you. The wretched condition of the countryside had filled me with pity, and during the night it seemed as if these thoughts had been sent to me by God, and that thus He had revealed His will to me. I had known something of the joys that pierce the heart, the happiness and the sorrow of motherhood; I determined that henceforth my life should be filled with these, but that mine should be a wider sphere than a mother's. I would expend her care and kindness on a whole district; I would be a sister of charity, and bind the wounds of all the suffering poor in a countryside. It seemed to me that the finger of God unmistakably pointed out my destiny; and when I remembered that my first serious thoughts in youth had inclined me to the study of medicine, I resolved to settle here as a doctor. Besides, I had another reason.

For a wounded heart—shadow and silence; so I had written
in my letter; and I meant to fulfil the vow which I had made
to myself.

'So I have entered into the paths of silence and submission. The *fuge, late, tace* of the Carthusian brother
is my motto here, my death to the world is the life of this
canton, my prayer takes the form of the active work to
which I have set my hand, and which I love—the work
of sowing the seeds of happiness and joy, of giving to
others what I myself have not.

'I have grown so used to this life, completely out of
the world and among the peasants, that I am thoroughly
transformed. Even my face is altered; it has been so
continually exposed to the sun, that it has grown wrinkled
and weather-beaten. I have fallen into the habits of the
peasants; I have assumed their dress, their ways of talking,
their gait, their easy-going negligence, their utter indifference to appearances. My old acquaintances in
Paris, or the she-coxcombs on whom I used to dance
attendance, would be puzzled to recognize in me the man
who had a certain vogue in his day, the sybarite accustomed
to all the splendour, luxury, and finery of Paris. I have
come to be absolutely indifferent to my surroundings,
like all those who are possessed by one thought, and have
only one object in view; for I have but one aim in life—
to take leave of it as soon as possible. I do not want to
hasten my end in any way; but some day, when illness
comes, I shall lie down to die without regret.

'There, sir, you have the whole story of my life until
I came here—told in all sincerity. I have not attempted
to conceal any of my errors; they have been great, though
others have erred as I have erred. I have suffered greatly,
and I am suffering still, but I look beyond this life to a
happy future which can only be reached through sorrow.
And yet—for all my resignation, there are moments
when my courage fails me. This very day I was almost

overcome in your presence by inward anguish; you did not notice it, but——'

Genestas started in his chair.

'Yes, Captain Bluteau, you were with me at the time, Do you remember how, while we were putting little Jacques to bed, you pointed to the mattress on which Mother Colas sleeps? Well, you can imagine how painful it all was; I can never see any child without thinking of the dear child I have lost, and this little one was doomed to die! I can never see a child with indifferent eyes——'

Genestas turned pale.

'Yes, the sight of the little golden heads, the innocent beauty of children's faces always awakens memories of my sorrows, and the old anguish returns afresh. Now and then, too, there comes the intolerable thought that so many people here should thank me for what little I can do for them, when all that I have done has been prompted by remorse. You alone, captain, know the secret of my life. If I had drawn my will to serve them from some purer source than the memory of my errors, I should be happy indeed! But then, too, there would have been nothing to tell you, and no story about myself.'

V

ELEGIES

As Benassis finished his story, he was struck by the troubled expression of the officer's face. It touched him to have been so well understood. He was almost ready to reproach himself for having distressed his visitor. He spoke:

'But these troubles of mine, Captain Bluteau——'

'Do not call me Captain Bluteau,' cried Genestas, breaking in upon the doctor, and springing to his feet with sudden energy, a change of position that seemed to be prompted by inward dissatisfaction of some kind. 'There is no such person as Captain Bluteau. . . . I am a scoundrel!'

With no little astonishment, Benassis beheld Genestas pacing to and fro in the *salon*, like a bumble-bee in quest of an exit from the room which he has incautiously entered.

'Then who are you, sir?' inquired Benassis.

'Ah! there now!' the officer answered, as he turned and took his stand before the doctor, though he lacked courage to look at his friend. 'I have deceived you!' he went on (and there was a change in his voice). 'I have acted a lie for the first time in my life, and I am well punished for it; for after this I cannot explain why I came here to play the spy upon you, confound it! Ever since I have had a glimpse of your soul, so to speak, I would far sooner have taken a box on the ear whenever I heard you call me Captain Bluteau! Perhaps you may forgive me for this subterfuge, but I shall never forgive myself; I, Pierre Joseph Genestas, who would not lie to save my life before a court-martial!'

'Are you Commandant Genestas?' cried Benassis, rising to his feet. He grasped the officer's hand warmly, and added: 'As you said but a short time ago, sir, we were friends before we knew each other. I have been very anxious to make your acquaintance, for I have often heard M. Gravier speak of you. He used to call you "one of Plutarch's men."'

'Plutarch? Nothing of the sort!' answered Genestas. 'I am not worthy of you; I could thrash myself. I ought to have told you my secret in a straightforward way at the first. Yet no! It is quite as well that I wore a mask, and came here myself in search of information concerning you, for now I know that I must hold my tongue. If I had set about this business in the right fashion it would have been painful to you, and God forbid that I should give you the slightest annoyance.'

'But I do not understand you, commandant.'

'Let the matter drop. I am not ill; I have spent a pleasant day, and I will go back to-morrow. Whenever you come to Grenoble, you will find that you have one more friend there, who will be your friend through thick and thin. Pierre-Joseph Genestas's sword and purse are at your disposal, and I am yours to the last drop of my blood. Well, after all, your words have fallen on good soil. When I am pensioned off, I will look for some out-of-the-way little place, and be mayor of it, and try to follow your example. I have not your knowledge, but I will study at any rate.'

'You are right, sir; the landowner who spends his time in convincing a commune of the folly of some mistaken notion of agriculture, confers upon his country a benefit quite as great as any that the most skilful physician can bestow. The latter lessens the sufferings of some few individuals, and the former heals the wounds of his country. But you have excited my curiosity to no common degree. Is there really something in which I can be of use to you?'

'Of use?' repeated the commandant in an altered voice. 'Good God! I was about to ask you to do me a service which is all but impossible, M. Benassis. Just listen a moment! I have killed a good many Christians in my time, it is true; but you may kill people and keep a good heart for all that; so there are some things that I can feel and understand, rough as I look.'

'But go on!'

'No, I do not want to give you any pain if I can help it.'

'Oh! commandant, I can bear a great deal.'

'It is a question of a child's life, sir,' said the officer, nervously.

Benassis suddenly knitted his brows, but by a gesture he entreated Genestas to continue.

'A child,' repeated the commandant, 'whose life may yet be saved by constant watchfulness and incessant care. Where could I expect to find a doctor capable of devoting himself to a single patient? Not in a town, that much was certain. I had heard you spoken of as an excellent man, but I wished to be quite sure that this reputation was well founded. So before putting my little charge into the hand of this M. Benassis of whom people spoke so highly, I wanted to study him myself. But now——'

'Enough,' said the doctor; 'so this child is yours?'

'No, no, M. Benassis. To clear up the mystery, I should have to tell you a long story, in which I do not exactly play the part of a hero; but you have given me your confidence, and I can readily give you mine.'

'One moment, commandant,' said the doctor. In answer to his summons, Jacquotte appeared at once, and her master ordered tea. 'You see, commandant, at night when everyone is sleeping, I do not sleep. . . . The thought of my troubles lies heavily on me, and then I try to forget them by taking tea. It produces a sort of nervous inebriation—a kind of slumber, without which I could not live. Do you still decline to take it?'

'For my own part,' said Genestas, 'I prefer your Hermitage.'

'By all means. Jacquotte,' said Benassis, turning to his housekeeper, 'bring in some wine and biscuits. We will both of us have our night-cap after our separate fashions.'

'That tea must be very bad for you!' Genestas remarked.

'It brings on horrid attacks of gout, but I cannot break myself of the habit, it is too soothing; it procures for me a brief respite every night, a few moments during which life becomes less of a burden. . . . Come. I am listening; perhaps your story will efface the painful impressions left by the memories that I have just recalled.'

Genestas set down his empty glass upon the chimneypiece. 'After the Retreat from Moscow,' he said, 'my regiment was stationed to recruit for a while in a little town in Poland. We were quartered there, in fact, till the emperor returned, and we bought up horses at long prices. So far so good. I ought to say that I had a friend in those days. More than once during the Retreat I had owed my life to him. He was a quartermaster, Renard by name; we could not but be like brothers (military discipline apart) after what he had done for me. They billeted us on the same house, a sort of shanty, a rat-hole of a place where a whole family lived, though you would not have thought there was room to stable a horse. This particular hovel belonged to some Jews who carried on their six-and-thirty trades in it. The frost had not so stiffened the old father Jew's fingers but that he could count gold fast enough; he had thriven uncommonly during our reverses. That sort of gentry lives in squalor and dies in gold.

'There were cellars underneath (lined with wood of

course, the whole house was built of wood); they had
stowed their children away down there, and one more
particularly, a girl of seventeen, as handsome as a Jewess
can be when she keeps herself tidy and has not fair hair.
She was as white as snow, she had eyes like velvet, and
dark lashes to them like rats' tails; her hair was so thick
and glossy that it made you long to stroke it. She was
perfection, and nothing less! I was the first to discover
this curious arrangement. I was walking up and down
outside one evening, smoking my pipe, after they thought
I had gone to bed. The children came in helter-skelter,
tumbling over one another like so many puppies. It was
fun to watch them. Then they had supper with their
father and mother. I strained my eyes to see the young
Jewess through the clouds of smoke that her father blew
from his pipe; she looked like a new gold piece among a
lot of copper coins.

'I had never reflected about love, my dear Benassis,
I had never had time; but now at the sight of this young
girl I lost my heart and head and everything else at once,
and then it was plain to me that I had never been in love
before. I was hard hit, and over head and ears in love.
There I stayed smoking my pipe, absorbed in watching
the Jewess until she blew out the candle and went to bed.
I could not close my eyes. The whole night long I walked
up and down the street smoking my pipe and refilling it
from time to time. I had never felt like that before,
and for the first and last time in my life I thought of
marrying.

'At daybreak I saddled my horse and rode out into the
country, to clear my head. I kept him at a trot for two
mortal hours, and all but foundered the animal before I
noticed it——'

Genestas stopped short, looked at his new friend un-
easily, and said: 'You must excuse me, Benassis, I am
no orator; things come out just as they turn up in my

mind. In a room full of fine folk I should feel awkward,
but here in the country with you——'

'Go on,' said the doctor.

'When I came back to my room I found Renard finely
flustered. He thought I had fallen in a duel. He was
cleaning his pistols, his head full of schemes for fastening
a quarrel on anyone who should have turned me off
into the dark. . . . Oh! that was just the fellow's way!
I confided my story to Renard, showed him the kennel
where the children were; and, as my comrade understood the jargon that those heathens talked, I begged him
to help me to lay my proposals before her father and
mother, and to try to arrange some kind of communication
between me and Judith. Judith they called her. In
short, sir, for a fortnight the Jew and his wife so arranged
matters that we supped every night with Judith, and for a
fortnight I was the happiest of men. You understand
and you know how it was, so I shall not wear out your
patience; still, if you do not smoke, you cannot imagine
how pleasant it was to smoke a pipe at one's ease with
Renard and the girl's father and one's princess there before
one's eyes. Oh! yes, it was very pleasant!

'But I ought to tell you that Renard was a Parisian,
and dependent on his father, a wholesale grocer, who had
educated his son with a view to making a notary of him;
so Renard had come by a certain amount of book learning before he had been drawn by the conscription and
had to bid his desk good-bye. Add to this that he was
the kind of man who looks well in a uniform, with a
face like a girl's, and a thorough knowledge of the art
of wheedling people. It was *he* whom Judith loved; she
cared about as much for me as a horse cares for roast
fowls. Whilst I was in the seventh heaven, soaring
above the clouds at the bare sight of Judith, my friend
Renard (who, as you see, fairly deserved his name) was
making a way for himself underground. The traitor

arrived at an understanding with the girl, and to such good purpose, that they were married forthwith after the custom of her country, without waiting for permission, which would have been too long in coming. He promised her, however, that if it should happen that the validity of this marriage was afterwards called in question, they were to be married again according to French law. As a matter of fact, as soon as she reached France, Mme Renard became Mlle Judith once more.

'If I had known all this, I would have killed Renard then and there, without giving him time to draw another breath; but the father, the mother, the girl herself, and the quartermaster were all in the plot like thieves in a fair. While I was smoking my pipe, and worshipping Judith as if she had been one of the saints above, the worthy Renard was arranging to meet her, and managing this piece of business very cleverly under my very eyes.

'You are the only person to whom I have told this story. A disgraceful thing, I call it. I have always asked myself how it is that a man who would die of shame if he took a gold coin that did not belong to him, does not scruple to rob a friend of happiness and life and the woman he loves. My birds, in fact, were married and happy; and there was I, every evening at supper, moonstruck, gazing at Judith, responding like some fellow in a farce to the looks she threw at me in order to throw dust in my eyes. They had paid uncommonly dear for all this deceit, as you will certainly think. On my conscience, God pays more attention to what goes on in this world than some of us imagine.

'Down come the Russians upon us, the country is overrun, and the campaign of 1813 begins in earnest. One fine morning comes an order; we are to be on the battle-field of Lützen by a stated hour. The emperor knew quite well what he was about when he ordered us to start at once. The Russians had turned our flank.

Our colonel must needs get himself into a scrape, by
choosing that moment to take leave of a Polish lady who
lived outside the town, a quarter of a mile away; the
Cossack advanced guard just caught him nicely, him
and his picket. There was scarcely time to spring into
our saddles and draw up before the town so as to engage
in a cavalry skirmish. We must check the Russian
advance if we meant to draw off during the night. Again
and again we charged, and for three hours we did wonders.
Under cover of the fighting the baggage and artillery
set out. We had a park of artillery and great stores of
powder, of which the emperor stood in desperate need;
they must reach him at all costs.

'Our resistance deceived the Russians, who thought
at first that we were supported by an army corps; but
before very long they learned their error from their scouts,
and knew that they had only a single regiment of cavalry
to deal with and the invalided foot-soldiers in the depot.
On finding it out, sir, they made a murderous onslaught
on us towards evening; the action was so hot that a good
few of us were left on the field. We were completely
surrounded. I was by Renard's side in the front rank,
and I saw how my friend fought and charged like a demon;
he was thinking of his wife. Thanks to him, we managed
to regain the town, which our invalids had put more or
less in a state of defence, but it was pitiful to see it. We
were the last to return—he and I. A body of Cossacks
appeared in our way, and on this we rode in hot haste.
One of the savages was about to run me through with a
lance, when Renard, catching a sight of his manœuvre,
thrust his horse between us to turn aside the blow; his
poor brute, a fine animal it was upon my word, received
the lance thrust and fell, bringing down both Renard
and the Cossack with him. I killed the Cossack, seized
Renard by the arm, and laid him crosswise before me on my
horse like a sack of wheat.

'"Good-bye, captain," Renard said; "it is all over with me."

'"Not yet," I answered; "I must have a look at you." We had reached the town by that time; I dismounted, and propped him up on a little straw by the corner of a house. A wound in the head had laid open the brain, and yet he spoke! . . . Oh! he was a brave man.

'"We are quits," he said. "I have given you my life, and I had taken Judith from you. Take care of her and of her child, if she has one. And not only so— you must marry her."

'I left him then and there, sir, like a dog; when the first fury of anger left me, and I went back again, he was dead. The Cossacks had set fire to the town, and the thought of Judith then came to my mind. I went in search of her, took her up behind me in the saddle, and, thanks to my swift horse, caught up the regiment which was effecting its retreat. As for the Jew and his family, there was not one of them left, they had all disappeared like rats; there was no one but Judith in the house, waiting alone there for Renard. At first, as you can understand, I told her not a word of all that had happened.

'So it befell that all through the disastrous campaign of 1813 I had a woman to look after, to find quarters for her, and to see that she was comfortable. She scarcely knew, I think, the straits to which we were reduced. I was always careful to keep her ten leagues ahead of us as we drew back towards France. Her boy was born while we were fighting at Hanau. I was wounded in the engagement, and only rejoined Judith at Strasburg; then I returned to Paris, for, unluckily, I was laid up all through the campaign in France. If it had not been for that wretched mishap, I should have entered the Grenadier Guards, and then the emperor would have promoted me. As it was, sir, I had three broken ribs and another man's wife and child to support! My pay, as you can imagine, was not exactly the wealth of the Indies. Renard's father, the toothless old shark, would have nothing to say to his daughter-in-law; and the old father Jew had made off. Judith was fretting herself to death. She cried one morning while she was dressing my wound.

'"Judith," I said, "your child has nothing in this world——"

'"Neither have I!" she said.

'"Pshaw!" I answered, "we will send for all the necessary papers, I will marry you; and as for his child, I will look on him as mine——" I could not say any more.

'Ah, my dear sir, what would not one do for the look by which Judith thanked me—a look of thanks from dying eyes; I saw clearly that I had loved, and should love her always, and from that day her child found a place in my heart. She died, poor woman, while the father and mother Jews and the papers were on the way. The day before she died, she found strength enough to rise and dress herself for her wedding, to go through all the usual performance, and set her name to their pack of papers; then, when her child had a name and a father, she went back to her bed again; I kissed her hands and her forehead, and she died.

'That was my wedding. Two days later, when I had bought the few feet of earth in which the poor girl is laid, I found myself the father of an orphan child. I put him out to nurse during the campaign of 1815. Ever since that time, without letting anyone know my story, which did not sound very well, I have looked after the little rogue as if he were my own child. I don't know what became of his grandfather; he is wandering about, a ruined man, somewhere or other between Russia and Persia. The chances are that he may make a fortune some day, for he seemed to understand the trade in precious stones.

'I sent the child to school. I wanted him to take a good place at the École Polytechnique and to see him graduate there with credit, so of late I have had him drilled in mathematics to such good purpose that the poor little soul has been knocked up by it. He has a delicate chest. By all I can make out from the doctors in Paris, there would be some hope for him still if he were allowed to run wild among the hills, if he was properly cared for, and constantly looked after by somebody who was willing to undertake the task. So I thought of you, and I came here to take stock of your ideas and your ways of life. After what you have told me, I could not possibly cause you pain in this way, for we are good friends already.'

'Commandant,' said Benassis after a moment's pause, 'bring Judith's child here to me. It is doubtless God's will to submit me to this final trial, and I will endure it. I will offer up these sufferings to God, whose Son died upon the cross. Besides, your story has awakened tender feelings; does not that augur well for me?'

Genestas took both of Benassis's hands and pressed them warmly, unable to check the tears that filled his eyes and coursed down his sunburnt face.

'Let us keep silence with regard to all this,' he said.

'Yes, commandant. You are not drinking?'

'I am not thirsty,' Genestas answered. 'I am a perfect fool!'

'Well, when will you bring him to me?'

'Why, to-morrow, if you will let me. He has been at Grenoble these two days.'

'Good! Set out to-morrow morning and come back again. I shall wait for you in La Fosseuse's cottage, and we will all four of us breakfast there together.'

'Agreed,' said Genestas, and the two friends as they went upstairs bade each other good night. When they reached the landing that lay between their rooms, Genestas set down his candle on the window ledge and turned towards Benassis.

'Thunder and lightning!' he said, with outspoken enthusiasm; 'I cannot let you go without telling you that you are the third among christened men to make me understand that there is Something up there,' and he pointed to the sky.

The doctor's answer was a smile full of sadness and a cordial grasp of the hand that Genestas held out to him.

Before daybreak next morning Commandant Genestas was on his way. On his return, it was noon before he reached the spot on the high road between Grenoble and the little town, where the pathway turned that led to La Fosseuse's cottage. He was seated in one of the light open cars with four wheels, drawn by one horse, that are in use everywhere on the roads in these hilly districts. Genestas's companion was a thin, delicate-looking lad, apparently about twelve years of age, though in reality he was in his sixteenth year. Before alighting, the officer looked round about him in several directions in search of a peasant who would take the carriage back to Benassis's house. It was impossible to drive to La Fosseuse's cottage, the pathway was too narrow. The park-keeper happened to appear upon the scene, and helped Genestas out of his difficulty, so that the officer and his adopted son were at liberty to follow the mountain footpath that led to the trysting-place.

'Would you not enjoy spending a year in running about in this lovely country, Adrien? Learning to hunt and to ride a horse, instead of growing pale over your books? Stay! look there!'

Adrien obediently glanced over the valley with languid indifference; like all lads of his age, he cared nothing for the beauty of natural scenery; so he only said: 'You are very kind, father,' without checking his walk.

The invalid listlessness of this answer went to Genestas's heart; he said no more to his son, and they reached La Fosseuse's house in silence.

'You are punctual, commandant!' cried Benassis, rising from the wooden bench where he was sitting.

But at the sight of Adrien he sat down again, and seemed for a while to be lost in thought. In a leisurely fashion he scanned the lad's sallow, weary face, not without admiring its delicate oval outlines, one of the most noticeable characteristics of a noble head. The lad was the living image of his mother. He had her olive complexion, beautiful black eyes with a sad and thoughtful expression in them, long hair, a head too energetic for the fragile body; all the peculiar beauty of the Polish Jewess had been transmitted to her son.

'Do you sleep soundly, my little man?' Benassis asked him.

'Yes, sir.'

'Let me see your knees; turn back your trousers.'

Adrien reddened, unfastened his garters, and showed his knee to the doctor, who felt it carefully over.

'Good. Now speak; shout, shout as loud as you can.'

Adrien obeyed.

'That will do. Now give me your hands.'

The lad held them out; white, soft, and blue-veined hands, like those of a woman.

'Where were you at school in Paris?'

'At Saint Louis.'

'Did your master read his breviary during the night?'

'Yes, sir.'

'So you did not go straight off to sleep?'

As Adrien made no answer to this, Genestas spoke. 'The master is a worthy priest; he advised me to take my little rascal away on the score of his health,' he told the doctor.

'Well,' answered Benassis, with a clear, penetrating

gaze into Adrien's frightened eyes, 'there is a good chance.
Oh, we shall make a man of him yet. We will live together like a pair of comrades, my boy! We will keep
early hours. I mean to show this boy of yours how to
ride a horse, commandant. He shall be put on a milk
diet for a month or two, so as to get his digestion into
order again, and then I will take out a shooting licence
for him, and put him in Butifer's hands, and the two of
them shall have some chamois-hunting. Give your son
four or five months of outdoor life, and you will not
know him again, commandant! How delighted Butifer
will be! I know the fellow; he will take you over into
Switzerland, my young friend; haul you over the Alpine
passes and up the mountain peaks, and add six inches
to your height in six months; he will put some colour
into your cheeks and brace your nerves, and make you
forget all these bad ways that you have fallen into at
school. And after that you can go back to your work;
and you will be a man some of these days. Butifer is an
honest young fellow. We can trust him with the money
necessary for travelling expenses and your hunting ex-
peditions. The responsibility will keep him steady for
six months, and that will be a very good thing for him.'

Genestas's face brightened more and more at every
word the doctor spoke.

'Now, let us go in to breakfast. La Fosseuse is very
anxious to see you,' said Benassis, giving Adrien a gentle
tap on the cheek.

Genestas took the doctor's arm and drew him a little
aside. 'Then he is not consumptive after all?' he asked.

'No more than you or I.'

'Then what is the matter with him?'

'Pshaw!' answered Benassis; 'he is a little run down,
that is all.'

La Fosseuse appeared on the threshold of the door;
and Genestas noticed, not without surprise, her simple

but coquettish costume. This was not the peasant girl of yesterday evening, but a graceful and well-dressed Parisian woman, against whose glances he felt that he was not proof. The soldier turned his eyes on the table, which was made of walnut wood. There was no table-cloth, but the surface might have been varnished, it was so well rubbed and polished. Eggs, butter, a rice pudding, and fragrant wild strawberries had been set out, and the poor child had put flowers everywhere about the room; evidently it was a great day for her. At the sight of all this, the commandant could not help looking en-viously at the little house and the green sward about it, and watched the peasant girl with an air that expressed both his doubts and his hopes. Then his eyes fell on Adrien, with whom La Fosseuse was deliberately busying herself, and handing him the eggs.

'Now, commandant,' said Benassis, 'you know the terms on which you are receiving hospitality. You must tell La Fosseuse "something about the army."'

'But let the gentleman first have his breakfast in peace, and then, after he has taken a cup of coffee——'

'By all means, I shall be very glad,' answered the commandant; 'but it must be upon one condition, you will tell us the story of some adventure in your past life, will you not, mademoiselle?'

'Why, nothing worth telling has ever happened to me, sir,' she answered, as her colour rose. 'Will you take a little more rice pudding?' she added, as she saw that Adrien's plate was empty.

'If you please, miss.'

'The pudding is delicious,' said Genestas.

'Then what will you say to her coffee and cream?' cried Benassis.

'I would rather hear our pretty hostess talk.'

'You did not put that nicely, Genestas,' said Benassis. He took La Fosseuse's hand in his and pressed it as he went on: 'Listen, my child; there is a kind heart hidden away beneath that officer's stern exterior, and you can talk freely before him. We do not want to press you to talk, do not tell us anything unless you like; but if ever you can be listened to and understood, poor little one, it will be by the three who are with you now at this moment. Tell us all about your love affairs in the old days, that will not admit us into any of the real secrets of your heart.'

'Here is Mariette with the coffee,' she answered, 'and as soon as you are all served, I will tell about my "love affairs" very willingly. But the commandant will not forget his promise?' she added, challenging the officer with a shy glance.

'That would be impossible, miss,' Genestas answered respectfully.

'When I was sixteen years old,' La Fosseuse began, 'I had to beg my bread on the roadside in Savoy, though my health was very bad. I used to sleep at Échelles, in a manger full of straw. The innkeeper who gave me shelter was kind, but his wife could not abide me, and was always saying hard things. I used to feel very miserable; for though I was a beggar, I was not a naughty child; I used to say my prayers every night and morning, I never stole anything, and I did as Heaven bade me in begging for my living, for there was nothing that I could turn my hands to, and I was really unfit for work—quite unable to handle a hoe or to wind spools of cotton.

'Well, they drove me away from the inn at last; a dog was the cause of it all. I had neither father nor mother nor friends. I had met with no one, ever since I was born, whose eyes had any kindness in them for me. Morin, the old woman who had brought me up, was dead. She had been very good to me, but I cannot remember that she ever petted me much; besides, she worked out in the fields like a man, poor thing; and if she fondled me at times, she also used to rap my fingers with the spoon if I ate the soup too fast out of the porringer we had between us. Poor old woman, never a day passes but I remember her in my prayers! If it might please God to let her live a happier life up there than she did here below! And, above all things, if she might only lie a little softer there, for she was always grumbling about the pallet-bed that we both used to sleep upon. You could not possibly imagine how it hurts one's soul to be repulsed by everyone, to receive nothing but hard words and looks that cut you to the heart, just as if they were so many stabs of a knife. I have known poor old people who were so used to these things that they did not mind them a bit, but I was not born for that sort of life. A "No" always made me cry. Every evening I came back again more unhappy than ever, and only felt comforted when I had said my prayers. In all God's world, in fact, there was not a soul to care for me, no one to whom I could pour out my heart. My only friend was the blue sky. I have always been happy when there was a cloudless sky above my head. I used to lie and watch the weather from some nook among the crags when the wind had swept the clouds away. At such times I used to dream that I was a great lady. I used to gaze into the sky till I felt myself bathed in the blue; I lived up there in thought, rising higher and higher yet, till my troubles weighed on me no more, and there was nothing but gladness left.

'But to return to my "love affairs." I must tell you that the innkeeper's spaniel had a dear little puppy, just as sensible as a human being; he was quite white, with black spots on his paws, a cherub of a puppy! I can see him yet. Poor little fellow, he was the only creature who ever gave me a friendly look in those days; I kept all my tit-bits for him. He knew me, and came to look for me every evening. How he used to spring up at me! And he would bite my feet, he was not ashamed of my poverty; there was something so grateful and so kind in his eyes that it brought tears into mine to see it. "That is the one living creature that really cares for me!" I used to say. He slept at my feet that winter. It hurt me so much to see him beaten, that I broke him of the habit of going into houses to steal bones, and he was quite contented with my crusts. When I was unhappy, he used to come and stand in front of me, and look into my eyes; it was just as if he said: "So you are sad, my poor Fosseuse?"

'If a traveller threw me some halfpence, he would pick them up out of the dust and bring them to me, clever little spaniel that he was! I was less miserable so long as I had that friend. Every day I put away a few halfpence, for I wanted to get fifteen francs together, so that I might buy him of Père Manseau. One day his wife saw that the dog was fond of me, so she herself took a sudden violent fancy to him. The dog, mind you, could not bear her. Oh, animals know people by instinct! If you really care for them, they find it out in a moment. I had a gold coin, a twenty-franc piece, sewed into the band of my skirt; so I spoke to M. Manseau: "Dear sir, I meant to offer you my year's savings for your dog; but now your wife has a mind to keep him, although she cares very little about him, and rather than that, will you sell him to me for twenty francs? Look, I have the money here."

'"No, no, little woman," he said; "put up your twenty francs. Heaven forbid that I should take their money from the poor! Keep the dog; and if my wife makes a fuss about it, you must go away."

'His wife made a terrible to-do about the dog. Ah! good God! any one might have thought the house was on fire! You never would guess the notion that next came into her head. She saw that the little fellow looked on me as his mistress, and that she could only have him against his will, so she had him poisoned; and my poor spaniel died in my arms. . . . I cried over him as if he had been my child, and buried him under a pine-tree. You do not know all that I laid in that grave. As I sat there beside it, I told myself that henceforward I should always be alone in the world; that I had nothing left to hope for; that I should be again as I had been before, a poor lonely girl, that I should never more see a friendly light in any eyes. I stayed out there all through the night, praying God to have pity on me. When I went back to the high road I saw a poor little child, about ten years old, who had no hands.

'"God has heard me," I thought. I had prayed that night as I had never prayed before. "I will take care of the poor little one; we will beg together, and I will be a mother to him. Two of us ought to do better than one; perhaps I shall have more courage for him than I have for myself."

'At first the little boy seemed to be quite happy, and, indeed, he would have been hard to please if he had not been content. I did everything that he wanted, and gave him the best of all that I had; I was his slave in fact, and he tyrannized over me, but that was nicer than being alone, I used to think! Pshaw! no sooner did the little good-for-nothing know that I carried a twenty-franc piece sewed into my skirt-band than he cut the stitches, and stole my gold coin, the price of my poor spaniel! I had meant to have masses said with it. . . . A child without hands, too! Oh, it makes one shudder! Somehow that theft took all the heart out of me. It seemed as if I was to love nothing but it should come to some wretched end.

'One day at Échelles, I watched a fine carriage coming slowly up the hill-side. There was a young lady, as beauti-ful as the Virgin Mary, in the carriage, and a young man, who looked like the young lady. "Just look," he said; "there is a pretty girl!" and he flung a silver coin to me.

'No one but you, M. Benassis, could understand how

pleased I was with the compliment, the first that I had ever had; but, indeed, the gentleman ought not to have thrown the money to me. I was all in a flutter; I knew of a short cut, a footpath among the rocks, and started at once to run, so that I reached the summit of the Échelles long before the carriage, which was coming up very slowly. I saw the young man again; he was quite surprised to find me there; and as for me, I was so pleased that my heart seemed to be throbbing in my throat. Some kind of instinct drew me towards him. After he had recognized me, I went on my way again; I felt quite sure that he and the young lady with him would leave the carriage to see the waterfall at Couz, and so they did. When they had alighted, they saw me once more, under the walnut-trees by the wayside. They asked me many questions, and seemed to take an interest in what I told them about myself. In all my life I had never heard such pleasant voices as they had, that handsome young man and his sister, for she was his sister I am sure. I thought about them for a whole year afterwards, and kept on hoping that they would come back. I would have given two years of my life only to see that traveller again, he looked so nice. Until I knew M. Benassis these were the greatest events of my life. Although my mistress turned me away for trying on that horrid ball-dress of hers, I was sorry for her, and I have forgiven her; for, candidly, if you will give me leave to say so, I thought myself the better woman of the two, countess though she was.'

'Well,' said Genestas, after a moment's pause, 'you see that Providence has kept a friendly eye on you, you are in clover here.'

At these words La Fosseuse looked at Benassis with eyes full of gratitude.

'Would that I were rich!' came from Genestas. The officer's exclamation was followed by profound silence.

'You owe me a story,' said La Fosseuse at last, in coaxing tones.

'I will tell it at once,' answered Genestas. 'On the evening before the battle of Friedland,' he went on, after a moment, 'I had been sent with a dispatch to General Davoust's quarters, and I was on the way back to my own, when at a turn in the road I found myself face to face with the emperor. Napoleon gave me a look.

'"You are Captain Genestas, are you not?" he said.

'"Yes, your Majesty."

'"You were out in Egypt?"

'"Yes, your Majesty."

'"You had better not keep to the road you are on," he said; "turn to the left, you will reach your division sooner that way."

'That was what the emperor said, but you would never imagine how kindly he said it; and he had so many irons in the fire just then, for he was riding about surveying the position of the field. I am telling you this story to show you what a memory he had, and so that you may know that he knew my face. I took my oath in 1815. But for that mistake, perhaps I might have been a colonel to-day; I never meant to betray the Bourbons, France must be defended, and that was all I thought about. I was a major in the Grenadiers of the Imperial Guard; and although my wound still gave me trouble, I swung a sabre in the battle of Waterloo. When it was all over, and Napoleon returned to Paris, I went too; then when he reached Rochefort, I followed him against his orders; it was some sort of comfort to watch over him and to see that no mishap befell him on the way. So when he was walking along the beach he turned and saw me on duty ten paces from him.

'"Well, Genestas," he said, as he came towards me, "so we are not yet dead, either of us?"

'It cut me to the heart to hear him say that. If you

had heard him, you would have shuddered from head to foot, as I did. He pointed to the villainous English vessel that was keeping the entrance to the harbour. "When I see *that*," he said, "and think of my Guard, I wish that I had perished in that torrent of blood."

'Yes,' said Genestas, looking at the doctor and at La Fosseuse, 'those were his very words.'

"'The generals who counselled you to not charge with the Guard, and who hurried you into your travelling carriage, were no true friends of yours," I said.

"'Come with me," he cried eagerly, "the game is not ended yet."

"'I would gladly go with your Majesty, but I am not free; I have a motherless child on my hands just now."

'And so it happened that Adrien over there prevented me from going to St Helena.

"'Stay," he said, "I have never given you anything. You are not one of those who fill one hand and then hold out the other. Here is the snuff-box that I have used through this last campaign. And stay on in France; after all, brave men are wanted there! Remain in the service, and keep me in remembrance. Of all my army in Egypt, you are the last that I have seen still on his legs in France." And he gave me a little snuff-box.

"'Have '*Honneur et patrie*' engraved on it," he said; "the history of our two last campaigns is summed up in those three words."

'Then those who were going out with him came up, and I spent the rest of the morning with them. The emperor walked to and fro along the beach; there was not a sign of agitation about him, though he frowned from time to time. At noon, it was considered hopeless for him to attempt to escape by sea. The English had found out that he was at Rochefort; he must either give himself up to them, or cross the breadth of France again.

We were wretchedly anxious; the minutes seemed like hours! On the one hand there were the Bourbons, who would have shot Napoleon if he had fallen into their clutches; and on the other, the English, a dishonoured race, they covered themselves with shame by flinging a foe who asked for hospitality away on a desert rock, that is a stain which they will never wash away. Whilst we were anxiously debating, someone or other among his suite presented a sailor to him, a Lieutenant Doret, who had a scheme for reaching America to lay before him. As a matter of fact, a brig from the States and a merchant vessel were lying in the harbour.

'"But how could you set about it, captain?" the emperor asked him.

'"You will be on board the merchant vessel, sire," the man answered. "I will run up the white flag and man the brig with a few devoted followers. We will tackle the English vessel, set fire to her, and board her, and you will get clear away."

'"We will go with you!" I cried to the captain. But Napoleon looked at us and said: "Captain Doret, keep yourself for France."

'It was the only time I ever saw Napoleon show any emotion. With a wave of his hand to us he went in again. I watched him go on board the English vessel, and then I went away. It was all over with him, and he knew it. There was a traitor in the harbour, who by means of signals gave warning to the emperor's enemies of his presence. Then Napoleon fell back on a last resource; he did as he had been wont to do on the battle-field, he went to his foes instead of letting them come to him. Talk of troubles! No words could ever make you understand the misery of those who loved him for his own sake.'

'But where is his snuff-box?' asked La Fosseuse.

'It is in a box at Grenoble,' the commandant replied.

'I will go over to see it, if you will let me. To think
that you have something in your possession that his
fingers have touched! . . . Had he a well-shaped hand?'

'Very.'

'Can it be true that he is dead? Come, tell me the
real truth?'

'Yes, my dear child, he is dead; there is no doubt
about it.'

'I was such a little girl in 1815. I was not tall enough
to see anything but his hat, and even so I was nearly
crushed to death in the crowd at Grenoble.'

'Your coffee and cream is very nice indeed,' said Genestas. 'Well, Adrien, how do you like this country? Will
you come here to see mademoiselle?'

The boy made no answer; he seemed afraid to look at
La Fosseuse. Benassis never took his eyes off Adrien;
he appeared to be reading the lad's very soul.

'Of course he will come to see her,' said Benassis.
'But let us go home again, I have a pretty long round to
make, and I shall want a horse. I dare say you and
Jacquotte will manage to get on together whilst I am
away.'

'Will you not come with us?' said Genestas to La
Fosseuse.

'Willingly,' she answered; 'I have a lot of things to
take over for Mme Jacquotte.'

They started out for the doctor's house. Her visitors
had raised La Fosseuse's spirits; she led the way along
narrow tracks, through the loneliest parts of the hills.

'You have told us nothing about yourself, Monsieur
l'Officier,' she said. 'I should have liked to hear you tell
us about some adventure in the wars. I liked what you
told us about Napoleon very much, but it made me feel
sad. . . . If you would be so very kind——'

'Quite right!' Benassis exclaimed. 'You ought to
tell us about some thrilling adventure during our walk.

Come, now, something really interesting like that business
of the beam in the Beresina!'

'So few of my recollections are worth telling,' said
Genestas. 'Some people come in for all kinds of adventures, but I have never managed to be the hero of any
story. Oh! stop a bit though, a funny thing did once
happen to me. I was with the Grand Army in 1805,
and so, of course, I was at Austerlitz. There was a
good deal of skirmishing just before Ulm surrendered,
which kept the cavalry pretty fully occupied. Moreover, we were under the command of Murat, who never
let the grass grow under his feet.

'I was still only a sub-lieutenant in those days. It
was just at the opening of the campaign, and after one of
these affairs, that we took possession of a district in which
there were a good many fine estates; so it fell out that
one evening my regiment bivouacked in a park belonging
to a handsome château where a countess lived, a young
and pretty woman she was. Of course, I meant to lodge
in the house, and I hurried there to put a stop to pillage
of any sort. I came into the *salon* just as my quartermaster was pointing his carbine at the countess, his
brutal way of asking for what she certainly could not
give the ugly scoundrel. I struck up his carbine with
my sword, the bullet went through a looking-glass on
the wall, then I dealt my gentleman a back-handed blow
that stretched him on the floor. The sound of the shot
and the cries of the countess fetched all her people on
the scene, and it was my turn to be in danger.

'"Stop!" she cried in German (for they were going to
run me through the body), "this officer has saved my
life!"

'They drew back at that. The lady gave me her handkerchief (a fine embroidered handkerchief, which I have
yet), telling me that her house would always be open to
me, and that I should always find a sister and a devoted

friend in her, if at any time I should be in any sort of
trouble. In short, she did not know how to make enough
of me. She was as fair as a wedding morning and as
charming as a kitten. We had dinner together. Next
day I was distractedly in love, but next day I had to be in
my place at Güntzburg, or wherever it was. There was
no help for it, I had to turn out, and started off with my
handkerchief.

'Well, we gave them battle, and all the time I kept on
saying to myself: "I wish a bullet would come my way!
Good God! they are flying thick enough!"

'I had no wish for a ball in the thigh, for I should
have had to stop where I was in that case, and there would
have been no going back to the château, but I was not
particular; a nice wound in the arm I should have liked
best, so that I might be nursed and made much of by
the countess. I flung myself on the enemy, like mad;
but I had no sort of luck, and came out of the action quite
safe and sound. We must march, and there was an end
of it; I never saw the countess again, and there is the whole
story.'

By this time they had reached Benassis's house; the
doctor mounted his horse at once and disappeared.
Genestas recommended his son to Jacquotte's care, so
the doctor on his return found that she had taken Adrien
completely under her wing, and had installed him in
M. Gravier's celebrated room. With no small astonishment, she heard her master's order to put up a simple
camp-bed in his own room, for that the lad was to sleep
there, and this in such an authoritative tone, that for
once in her life Jacquotte found not a single word to say.

After dinner the commandant went back to Grenoble.
Benassis's reiterated assurances that the lad would soon
be restored to health had taken a weight off his mind.

Eight months later, in the earliest days of the following

December, Genestas was appointed to be lieutenant-colonel of a regiment stationed at Poitiers. He was just thinking of writing to Benassis to tell him of the journey he was about to take, when a letter came from the doctor. His friend told him that Adrien was once more in sound health.

'The boy has grown strong and tall,' he said; 'and he is wonderfully well. He has profited by Butifer's instruction since you saw him last, and is now as good a shot as our smuggler himself. He has grown brisk and active too; he is a good walker, and rides well; he is not in the least like the lad of sixteen who looked like a boy of twelve eight months ago; anyone might think he was twenty years old. There is an air of self-reliance and independence about him. In fact, he is a man now, and you must begin to think about his future at once.'

'I shall go over to Benassis to-morrow, of course,' said Genestas to himself, 'and I will see what he says before I make up my mind what to do with that fellow,' and with that he went to a farewell dinner given to him by his brother officers. He would be leaving Grenoble now in a very few days.

As the lieutenant-colonel returned after the dinner, his servant handed him a letter. It had been brought by a messenger, he said, who had waited a long while for an answer.

Genestas recognized Adrien's handwriting although his head was swimming after the toasts that had been drunk in his honour; probably, he thought, the letter merely contained a request to gratify some boyish whim, so he left it unopened on the table. The next morning, when the fumes of champagne had passed off, he took it up and began to read.

'My dear father——'

'Oh! you young rogue,' was his comment, 'you know how to coax whenever you want something.'

'Our dear M. Benassis is dead——'

The letter dropped from Genestas's hands; it was some time before he could read any more.

'Everyone is in consternation. The trouble is all the greater because it came as a sudden shock. It was so unexpected. M. Benassis seemed perfectly well the day before; there was not a sign of ill health about him. Only the day before yesterday he went to see all his patients, even those who lived farthest away; it was as if he had known what was going to happen; and he spoke to every-one whom he met, saying: "Good-bye, my friends," each time. Towards five o'clock he came back just as usual to have dinner with me. He was tired; Jacquotte noticed the purple flush on his face, but the weather was so very cold that she would not get ready a warm foot-bath for him, as she usually did when she saw that the blood had gone to his head. So she has been wailing, poor thing, through her tears for these two days past: "If I had *only* given him a foot-bath, he would be living now!"

'M. Benassis was hungry; he made a good dinner. I thought he was in higher spirits than usual; we both of us laughed a great deal, I had never seen him laugh so much before. After dinner, towards seven o'clock, a man came with a message from Saint Laurent du Pont; it was a serious case, and M. Benassis was urgently needed. He said to me: "I shall have to go, though I never care to set out on horseback when I have hardly digested my dinner, more especially when it is as cold as this. It is enough to kill a man!"

'For all that, he went. After nine o'clock the post-man, Goguelat, brought a letter for M. Benassis. Jac-quotte was tired out, for it was her washing-day. She gave me the letter and went off to bed. She begged me to keep a good fire in our bedroom, and to have some tea ready for M. Benassis when he came in, for I am still sleeping in the little cot-bed in his room. I raked out the fire in the *salon*, and went upstairs to wait for my good friend. I looked at the letter, out of curiosity, before I laid it on the chimney-piece, and noticed the handwriting and the postmark. It came from Paris, and I think it was a lady's hand. I am telling you about it because of things that happened afterwards.

'About ten o'clock, I heard the horse returning, and M. Benassis's voice. He said to Nicolle: "It is cold enough to-night to bring the wolves out. I do not feel at all well." Nicolle said: "Shall I go up and wake Jacquotte?" And M. Benassis answered: "Oh! no, no," and came upstairs.

'I said: "I have your tea here, all ready for you," and he smiled at me in the way that you know, and said: "Thank you, Adrien." That was his last smile. In a moment he began to take off his cravat, as though he could not breathe. "How hot it is in here!" he said, and flung himself down in an arm-chair. "A letter has come for you, my good friend," I said; "here it is"; and I gave him the letter. He took it up and glanced at the handwriting. "Ah! God help me!" he exclaimed, "perhaps she is free at last!" Then his head sank back, and his hands shook. After a little while he set the lamp on the table and opened the letter. There was something so alarming in the cry he had given that I watched him while he read, and saw that his face was flushed, and there were tears in his eyes. Then quite suddenly he fell, head forwards. I tried to raise him, and saw how purple his face was.

'"It is all over with me," he said, stammering; it was terrible to see how he struggled to rise. "I must be bled; bleed me!" he cried, clutching my hand. . . .

"Adrien," he said again, "burn this letter!" He gave
it to me, and I threw it on the fire. I called for Jacquotte and Nicolle. Jacquotte did not hear me, but
Nicolle did, and came hurrying upstairs; he helped me
to lay M. Benassis on my little bed. Our dear friend
could not hear us any longer when we spoke to him, and
although his eyes were open, he did not see anything.
Nicolle galloped off at once to fetch the surgeon, M.
Bordier, and in this way spread alarm through the town.
It was all astir in a moment. M. Janvier, M. Dufau,
and all the rest of your acquaintance were the first to
come to us. But all hope was at an end, M. Benassis
was dying fast. He gave no sign of consciousness, not
even when M. Bordier cauterized the soles of his feet.
It was an attack of gout, combined with an apoplectic
stroke.

'I am giving you all these details, dear father, because
I know how much you cared for him. As for me, I am
very sad and full of grief, for I can say to you that I cared
more for him than for anyone else except you. I learned
more from M. Benassis's talk in the evenings than I ever
could have learned at school.

'You cannot imagine the scene next morning when
the news of his death was known in the place. The
garden and the yard here were filled with people. How
they sobbed and wailed! Nobody did any work that
day. Everyone recalled the last time that they had seen
M. Benassis, and what he had said, or they talked of all
that he had done for them; and those who were least
overcome with grief spoke for the others. Everyone
wanted to see him once more, and the crowd grew larger
every moment. The sad news travelled so fast that men
and women and children came from ten leagues round;
all the people in the district, and even beyond it, had
that one thought in their minds.

'It was arranged that four of the oldest men of the

commune should carry the coffin. It was a very difficult task for them, for the crowd was so dense between the church and M. Benassis's house. There must have been nearly five thousand people there, and almost everyone knelt as if the Host were passing. There was not nearly room for them in the church. In spite of their grief, the crowd was so silent that you could hear the sound of the bell during mass and the chanting as far as the end of the High Street; but when the procession started again for the new cemetery, which M. Benassis had given to the town, little thinking, poor man, that he himself would be the first to be buried there, a great cry went up. M. Janvier wept as he said the prayers; there were no dry eyes among the crowd. And so we buried him.

'As night came on the people dispersed, carrying sorrow and mourning everywhere with them. The next day Gondrin and Goguelat, and Butifer, with some others, set to work to raise a sort of pyramid of earth, twenty feet high, above the spot where M. Benassis lies; it is being covered now with green sods, and every one is helping them. These things, dear father, have all happened in three days.

'M. Dufau found M. Benassis's will lying open on the table where he used to write. When it was known how his property had been left, affection for him and regret for his loss became even deeper if possible. And now, dear father, I am waiting for Butifer (who is taking this letter to you) to come back with your answer. You must tell me what I am to do. Will you come to fetch me, or shall I go to you at Grenoble? Tell me what you wish me to do, and be sure that I shall obey you in everything.

'Farewell, dear father, I send my love, and I am your affectionate son,

'ADRIEN GENESTAS.'

'Ah! well, I must go over,' the soldier exclaimed.

He ordered his horse and started out. It was one of those still December mornings when the sky is covered with grey clouds. The wind was too light to disperse the thick fog, through which the bare trees and damp house fronts seemed strangely unfamiliar. The very silence was gloomy. There is such a thing as a silence full of light and gladness; on a bright day there is a certain joyousness about the slightest sound, but in such dreary weather Nature is not silent, she is dumb. All sounds seemed to die away, stifled by the heavy air.

There was something in the gloom without him that harmonized with Colonel Genestas's mood; his heart was oppressed with grief, and thoughts of death filled his mind. Involuntarily he began to think of the cloudless sky on that lovely spring morning, and remembered how bright the valley had looked when he passed through it for the first time; and now, in strong contrast with that day, the heavy sky above him was a leaden grey, there was no greenness about the hills, which were still waiting for the cloak of winter snow that invests them with a certain beauty of its own. There was something painful in all this bleak and bare desolation for a man who was travelling to find a grave at his journey's end; the thought of that grave haunted him. The lines of dark pine-trees here and there along the mountain ridges against the sky seized on his imagination; they were in keeping with the officer's mournful musings. Every time that he looked over the valley that lay before him, he could not help thinking of the trouble that had befallen the canton, of the man who had died so lately, and of the blank left by his death.

Before long, Genestas reached the cottage where he had asked for a cup of milk on his first journey. The sight of the smoke rising above the hovel where the charity-children were being brought up recalled vivid memories

of Benassis and of his kindness of heart. The officer
made up his mind to call there. He would give some alms
to the poor woman for his dead friend's sake. He tied
his horse to a tree, and opened the door of the hut without
knocking.

'Good-day, mother,' he said, addressing the old woman,
who was sitting by the fire with the little ones crouching
at her side. 'Do you remember me?'

'Oh! quite well, sir! You came here one fine morning
last spring and gave us two crowns.'

'There, mother! that is for you and the children.'

'Thank you kindly, sir. May Heaven bless you!'

'You must not thank me, mother,' said the officer; 'it
is all through M. Benassis that the money has come to
you.'

The old woman raised her eyes and gazed at Genestas.

'Ah! sir,' she said, 'he has left his property to our poor
countryside, and made all of us his heirs; but we have
lost him who was worth more than all, for it was he who
made everything turn out well for us.'

'Good-bye, mother! Pray for him,' said Genestas,
making a few playful cuts at the children with his riding
whip.

The old woman and her little charges went out with
him; they watched him mount his horse and ride away.

He followed the road along the valley until he reached
the bridle-path that led to La Fosseuse's cottage. From
the slope above the house he saw that the door was fastened
and the shutters closed. In some anxiety he returned to
the highway, and rode on under the poplars, now bare and
leafless. Before long he overtook the old labourer, who
was dressed in his Sunday best, and creeping slowly
along the road. There was no bag of tools on his shoulder.

'Good day, old Moreau!'

'Ah! good day, sir. . . . I mind who you are now,'
the old fellow exclaimed after a moment. 'You are a

friend of monsieur, our late mayor! Ah! sir, would it not have been far better if God had only taken a poor rheumatic old creature like me instead? It would not have mattered if He had taken me, but *he* was the light of our eyes.'

'Do you know how it is that there is no one at home up there at La Fosseuse's cottage?'

The old man gave a look at the sky.

'What time is it, sir? The sun has not shone all day,' he said.

'It is ten o'clock.'

'Oh! well, then, she will have gone to mass or else to the cemetery. She goes there every day. He has left her five hundred livres a year and her house for as long as she lives, but his death has fairly turned her brain, as you may say——'

'And where are you going, old Moreau?'

'Little Jacques is to be buried to-day, and I am going to the funeral. He was my nephew, poor little chap; he had been ailing a long while, and he died yesterday morning. It really looked as though it was M. Benassis who kept him alive. That is the way! All these younger ones die!' Moreau added, half jestingly, half sadly.

Genestas reined in his horse as he entered the town, for he met Gondrin and Goguelat, each carrying a pick-axe and shovel. He called to them: 'Well, old comrades, we have had the misfortune to lose him——'

'There, there, that is enough, sir!' interrupted Goguelat, 'we know that well enough. We have just been cutting turf to cover his grave.'

'His life will make a grand story to tell, eh?'

'Yes,' answered Goguelat, 'he was the Napoleon of our valley, barring the battles.'

As they reached the parsonage, Genestas saw a little group about the door; Butifer and Adrien were talking with M. Janvier, who, no doubt, had just returned from

saying mass. Seeing that the officer made as though he
were about to dismount, Butifer promptly went to hold
the horse, while Adrien sprang forward and flung his
arms about his father's neck. Genestas was deeply
touched by the boy's affection, though no sign of this
appeared in the soldier's words or manner.

'Why, Adrien,' he said, 'you certainly are set up again.
My goodness! Thanks to our poor friend, you have
almost grown into a man. I shall not forget your tutor
here, Master Butifer.'

'Oh! colonel,' entreated Butifer, 'take me away from
here and put me into your regiment. I cannot trust myself now that M. le Maire is gone. *He* wanted me to
go for a soldier, didn't he? Well, then, I will do what he
wished. He told you all about me, and you will not
be hard on me, will you, M. Genestas?'

'Right, my fine fellow,' said Genestas, as he struck
his hand in the other's. 'I will find something to suit
you, set your mind at rest—— And how is it with you,
M. le Curé?'

'Well, like everyone else in the canton, colonel, I feel
sorrow for his loss, but no one knows as I do how irreparable it is. He was like an angel of God among us.
Fortunately, he did not suffer at all; it was a painless
death. The hand of God gently loosed the bonds of a
life that was one continual blessing to us all.'

'Will it be intrusive if I ask you to accompany me to
the cemetery? I should like to bid him farewell, as it
were.'

Genestas and the curé, still in conversation, walked on
together. Butifer and Adrien followed them at a few
paces' distance. They went in the direction of the little
lake, and as soon as they were clear of the town, the
lieutenant-colonel saw on the mountain-side a large piece
of waste land enclosed by walls.

'That is the cemetery,' the curé told him. 'He is the

first to be buried in it. Only three months before he
was brought here, it struck him that it was a very bad
arrangement to have the churchyard round the church;
so, in order to carry out the law, which prescribes that
burial grounds should be removed to a stated distance
from human dwellings, he himself gave this piece of land
to the commune. We are burying a child, poor little
thing, in the new cemetery to-day, so we shall have begun
by laying innocence and virtue there. Can it be that
death is after all a reward? Did God mean it as a lesson
for us when He took these two perfect natures to Himself? When we have been tried and disciplined in youth
by pain, in later life by mental suffering, are we so much
the nearer to Him? Look! there is the rustic monument
which has been erected to his memory.'

Genestas saw a mound of earth about twenty feet high.
It was bare as yet, but dwellers in the district were already
busily covering the sloping sides with green turf. La
Fosseuse, her face buried in her hands, was sobbing
bitterly; she was sitting on the pile of stones in which
they had planted a great wooden cross, made from the
trunk of a pine-tree, from which the bark had not been
removed. The officer read the inscription; the letters
were large, and had been deeply cut in the wood.

D. O. M.

HERE LIES

THE GOOD MONSIEUR BENASSIS

THE FATHER OF US ALL

PRAY FOR HIM

'Was it you, sir,' asked Genestas, 'who——?'
'No,' answered the curé; 'it is simply what is said

everywhere from the heights up there above us down to Grenoble, so the words have been carved here.'

Genestas remained silent for a few moments. Then he moved from where he stood and came nearer to La Fosseuse, who did not hear him, and spoke again to the curé.

'As soon as I have my pension,' he said, 'I will come to finish my days here among you.'